Storm Constantine's Wraeththu Mythos

Para Mort

Wraeththu Tales of Love and Death

Para Mort

Wraeththu Tales of Love and Death

Edited by Storm Constantine
and Wendy Darling

IMMANION
PRESS
Stafford, England

Contents

The Wraeththu

A Brief Definition of Their Origin

Humanity is in decline, ravaged by insanity, natural disasters, conflict, disease and infertility. A mysterious new race has risen from the ghettos and ruins of the decaying, dying cities. The young are evolving into a new species, which is stronger, sharper and more beautiful than their forerunners. Androgynous beings, they transcend gender and race. They possess keen psychic abilities and the means, through a process called inception, to transform humans into creatures like themselves. But they are wild in their rebirth and must strive to overcome all that is human within them in order to create society anew. They are the Wraeththu...

A Word on Pronouns

Within the Wraeththu Mythos, hara are referred to as 'he', since back in the early 1980s when I first started writing within the mythos, this pronoun seemed to me less gender specific than 'she'. A lot has changed in both culture and language since then, (which necessitates the inclusion of this clarification), but to glue a new pronoun over all the stories would feel at best clunky and contrived. I ask readers to look beyond the loaded meaning of the male pronoun, and to read it as non-gender specific.

Storm Constantine

Introduction

Storm Constantine

While some people out there revel in schmaltzy, romantic love stories, there are those of us – who are into the darker side of literature – who prefer their love tales spicier, not with erotica particularly, although that can certainly play a part, but in theme. Love and death are often married in fiction. The strongest and most affecting romantic works involve unrequited love, maddened jealousy, vengeance, murder and even spurned or slaughtered lovers reaching from the grave. Or else a mysterious and captivating lover might be something other than human to start with.

For this sixth Para anthology, I asked the Wraeththu Mythos writers to ponder the darker aspects of love and desire, to confront the ghosts and monsters that might lurk behind beauty or apparent innocence. I induced them to explore the morbid gardens of doomed love, where the lovers never really have a chance. *Do your sweetest worst*, I wished them. I wasn't disappointed.

For those who might not have read any Wraeththu books before, this volume in your hands is a shared world project, based upon my novels in the three science fantasy trilogies 'The Wraeththu Chronicles', 'The Wraeththu Histories' and 'The Alba Sulh Sequence'. The first volume of these, (*The Enchantments of Flesh and Spirit*), was published in the late 1980s – Immanion Press has recently released the fourth edition of the trilogy, with lavish new covers by official Wraeththu artist, Ruby.

The world of Wraeththu had been my constant companion – and continues to be – since long before my first book was published. Although I write across genres, and have created other worlds with rich histories, Wraeththu remains my first love. These characters originally made themselves known to my imagination way back when I was a young teenager – they were androgynous beings with heightened physical, mental and spiritual powers, who rose from the ashes of a shattered human civilisation to create a new and hopefully better world. Conflict arose from the fact they struggled to live up to their potential, and in most cases were so traumatised by their transformation from human to har they were – at least initially – incapable of healthy evolution.

I've included a brief explanation of the Wraeththu and their world before this introduction, and you'll also find a glossary of terms at the end of the book.

Previous anthologies in the series have covered the origins of Wraeththu, then stories set in their far future, followed by musings on how strange mutations might have evolved in various hara, and also a collection on their spiritual relationship with animals. Mythos writers also explored the ghostly and supernatural in the volume previous to this. *Para Mort* delves deep into the heart of love between Wraeththu, the darkest aspects of it. But at the same time, I didn't want to book to be entirely doom and gloom. Love brings joy as well as misery, salvation as well as damnation. My story *Give Them Darkness* is an adaptation of an old Sheridan Le Fanu piece *The Fortunes of Sir Robert Ardagh*. I simply remoulded some of the supernatural elements of that piece for my tale; plotwise it is entirely different.

The poems in this book are written by an old friend of mine, Ben Fouracre, who I met through my dealings with the music scene in the 80s and 90s. The poems are actually song lyrics, but their melancholy tone fit the ambience of this collection perfectly, so I asked him if I could include some of them.

As usual, I'm delighted that another Para anthology includes authors from around the world – Scotland, England, America, Germany, Czech Republic, Japan and South Africa – expanding upon the Wraeththu Mythos. So now, sit back, snuggle up by a fire in the winter gloom, and discover the dark secrets of the hearts of Wraeththu.

Storm Constantine,
November 2020

The Pictish Beast

Amanda Kear

"Well, what do you think?"

Blair watched slightly apprehensively as Aunt Muriel surveyed his handiwork. The old woman paced round the carved stone, examining it from all angles and occasionally lifting her glasses to peer more closely at some detail, or standing on tiptoe to examine the portion above her head. Spring sunshine spilled in the barn door to compliment the lights set up inside. The play of light and shadow illuminated the relief images perfectly.

Blair had always been entranced by the imagery of the ancient Picts, carved on symbol stones scattered across the north-east of Scotland. The mysterious paired pictograms. The animals which obviously held great meaning to that ancient people. The mythological creatures they revered: centaur, water-horse and the enigmatic Pictish Beast.

For the face of this stone he had chosen a pair of abstract symbols – crescent-and-V-rod paired with double-disc and Z-rod –then added figures of horsemen and warriors beneath. The rear of the slab was carved with horses and cattle, in deference to the farmland where he proposed to erect it. His stone contained no Christian iconography. He wanted this to be about the original Pictish symbols; enigmatic, elegant. Their meaning lost to time.

He shuffled his feet, impatient for her verdict. "What do you *think?*"

Muriel glanced at him. "As a retired archaeologist, as a very amateur art critic, or as your doting auntie?"

He made an exasperated noise. "All of the above."

A mischievous smile. "Och, you are *far* too easy to tease, Blair Marshall."

She ran a hand over the Celtic knotwork on the edge of the stele. "It's grand. Undeniably Pictish, but also very *you*. I've seen some dire imitations of Pictish art in my day, all stiff and formal. Your lines curve an' flow beautifully."

He grinned, only now admitting to himself how much the approval of his only living relative meant to him.

Muriel continued to circle the stone. "It's intriguin' to see the symbols an' animals fresh and crisp, not weathered by the ages. They'll look grand for centuries to come."

"So, I have your permission?"

"Laddie, you had my permission, even if you intended to erect giant stone willies all over my land, with pretentious inscriptions about the effect of the stock exchange on modern masculinity."

"Muriel, you have a very strange view of contemporary art."

"You've dragged enough very strange contemporary artists home with you to colour my perceptions forever."

Heat rose in Blair's cheeks at the reminder of some of the more, ah, idiosyncratic, individuals he'd brought to Muriel's door. Her ramshackle farmhouse had been part holiday home, part sanctuary in a parochial society, which distrusted artists in general and male artists suspected of sleeping with other men in particular.

Which brought him, in a roundabout way, to the other matter. "And you don't mind me moving my studio here? Working here?"

"Why would I mind? I'd be glad of the company. Make a nice change from Elaine Ritchie droppin' by to bemoan the cost of red diesel an' the antics of her feckless offspring."

"Only, it's getting… difficult… in the city. And I don't want to drag trouble to your door."

Gang violence and curfews. Shortages and power cuts. Suspicion and blame.

Formerly genteel or bohemian neighbourhoods were now gated communities, bristling with CCTV and scowling sentries. The guardians of public morality were baring their teeth at anyone who didn't fit with their own, very narrow definition of acceptable human behaviour.

He'd gone to Edinburgh to escape narrow-minded and backwards country life. Now the staid farming communities seemed like safe havens. These days, the peasants with pitchforks and flaming torches lived in the suburbs and the inner cities.

Muriel tutted and crossed to link her arm with his. "You're family, Blair. Unless you've joined one of these death-cult gangs the tabloids are all in a tizzy about, then you'll always be welcome here. Besides..." She paused and steered him out into the sunshine. Gestured dramatically at their surroundings: ramshackle house, tumbledown outbuildings and rusting farm machinery which rightfully belonged in a scrapyard. "When I die, a' this will be yours," she pronounced in a portentous manner.

Blair grinned and gave her a theatrical bow. "M'lady, I shall endeavour to keep your kingdom as immaculate and regal as it is now."

They talked details over several cups of tea: the progress on selling his Edinburgh flat, how much he could expect to raise, how it would be apportioned. Muriel only wanted a peppercorn rent from him, saying it would cost him more than enough to convert her barn into a proper sculptor's studio and to buy the huge slabs of Old Red Sandstone he needed. Blair was insistent some of his money went towards things the farmhouse urgently needed, such as repairs to the roof or replacing window frames which let in every draught in winter.

Their debate was interrupted by the sound of a vehicle engine in the yard outside. Muriel cocked an ear. "That'll be Elaine, come to sniff out any gossip."

His aunt worked very little of her land herself. Instead she rented the bulk of it out to neighbouring farmers. Elaine Ritchie grazed her beef cattle on Muriel's pastures, and had some acreage for growing winter fodder. Other tenants grew barley, vegetables and soft fruits. Muriel's own produce were an eclectic mixture of ancient grains and rare breed sheep, raised more as archaeological experiment than commercial farming venture.

The visitor was indeed Mrs Ritchie, accompanied by a venerable Labrador and a blond youth with Vitruvian proportions and a t-shirt so tight, it sent Blair's libido into hysterics. He wrenched his gaze away from the young man, and kept it fixed on Mrs Ritchie, mumbling polite inanities to her questions about his presence.

"An' you'll ken my eldest, Donal."

Ye gods, the blond Adonis was Donal Ritchie? Donal the snotty nosed brat, Donal the gangly stick insect? Blair's fleeting encounters with Mrs Ritchie's brood on visits to the area had always been from the perspective of someone a decade older than the aforementioned Donal, and therefore very dismissive of hanging out with 'little kids'. The youth must be what, eighteen, nineteen, now?

Blair looked over at the young man and gave what he hoped was an urbane smile, and not slack jawed amazement or drooling lust. Donal returned his gaze appraisingly, speculatively... and Blair's gaydar pinged. Surely not?

"So you're, uh, working your Mum's farm now?" he asked.

Donal shrugged. "For the time bein'. Mum thinks I should go to agricultural college."

This sparked a rambling debate between Donal, his mother and Aunt Muriel on modern farming practices, what falling population levels and rising fuel prices meant for food production, and whether the local foresters switching to horses to haul timber was a conservation triumph, economic necessity or passing fad. Blair was peripheral to these discussions, contributing mostly to provide refills of tea and biscuits.

Eventually Muriel suggested Blair took Donal to see his symbol stone, whilst she and Mrs Ritchie discussed next season's rent.

"So you're gay, right?" Donal was standing with hands shoved in pockets, regarding the symbol stone. He didn't look at Blair as he said this.

"Uh... yeah," he answered cautiously. This was the moment where new paths would open up... or everything would go pear-shaped. "You?"

A shrug. "I like both. Women an' men."

Donal drifted round the stone. Blair couldn't tell if he liked it or was just being polite.

"You're makin' more standing stones?" Donal asked.

The topic of sexual preferences appeared to have been dropped. Blair pulled himself back to the safer topic of his art. "I, uh, yeah. Yes. Eight in all. Want to see the designs?"

"Okay."

Blair retrieved the portfolio with sketches and printouts from where it was propped against the wall. "There's more on my laptop, but this will give you an outline. How much do you know about Pictish art?"

"Seen it, don' know much about it. Celtic patterns, crosses, animals. An' thon weird one." Donal reached to tap the sheet which had variants of the Pictish Beast sketched all over it.

The Pictish Beast: a mythological creature which adorned many of the symbol stones. A long snout tucked into its chest; limbs more like flippers than paws or hooves; some sort of horn, crest or mane sweeping back from its forehead. The Pictish Beast was an enigma. Human scholars had argued whether it was purely mythological or might have its origins in a real animal. They had never quite agreed what the animal might be: suggested creatures were as diverse as a dolphin, a seahorse, or even an elephant as imagined by a people who had never seen one in the flesh. Those favouring a supernatural affinity described it as a kelpie, a sea serpent or even the Loch Ness Monster.

To him the Beast looked embryonic. Something partly formed and awaiting birth. Or re-birth.

Blair realised he'd been prattling about the Beast for several minutes, caught up in his own enthusiasm. He made a sideways glance, hoping he hadn't bored Donal to tears.

But the young man had a smile on his face, leaning in to study the design for the stone which would bear the Pictish Beast. "Rebirth? I like that. You're helpin' a new world to be born."

Blair's ego couldn't help but swell, for all he realised a few sculptures would not alleviate falling birth rates, pollution or hate crimes. A new world, born from ancient imagery. The idea tickled him.

Donal had moved on to the sketch of symbol pairs chosen for each of the eight stones. He frowned.

"They're a' male – bull, boar, stag, stallion…"

"Hmm. I don't think we can say what sex the adder, eagle or the salmon are. But yes, most of the others are male. I guess it was a fertility or virility thing."

"If they wanted fertility, then they needed female symbols too. Cow, sow, hind, mare."

"Uh, I suppose so."

"You should dae it – put both on. Male and female."

"But I want to recreate the authentic symbol pairs."

"Thought the pairs were only on one side. Can't you put what you like on the other?"

He could. He fully intended to. He'd just never considered variants of the authentic symbols as an option. Male-female symbolism, one face of the stone for each? It wasn't startlingly original, but it was intriguing. A nice touch his non-binary friends would appreciate.

Thoughts of which of the designs could best be adapted for the purpose were pushed aside as Donal slipped an arm around his waist, then slid a hand down to caress Blair's arse.

"Wanna fuck?"

He had never wanted anything so much in his life.

Blair had to admit to himself that he was seriously in lust. Donal drifted in and out of his bed on a whim, or to some erratic pattern Blair could not discern. Some of it was to do with keeping Mrs Ritchie ignorant of her son's sexual preferences. Some of it was the demands of farm work not coinciding with the hours Blair preferred to labour on converting Muriel's outbuilding to a fully functional studio. And some – the portion that Blair could not help but feel twinges of jealously and resentment towards – was Donal spending his free time with friends more akin to his own age. That the latter included a few new friends whom Mrs Ritchie heartily disapproved of only heightened Blair's envy of the time Donal chose to spend with others.

So he was in lust. Definitely one hundred percent not in love. Moping about when Donal hadn't been around for a few days; doodling sketches of him in his design notebook; pouncing on his every suggestion for alterations to the stones... that was lust wasn't it? Definitely not love. No, not love.

Donal was... his muse. Yes, that was it. A likeminded person, a sounding board. Someone happy to accompany him to see symbol stones in local museums, and who shared his opinion such stones belonged in the open air, not locked away and bathed in artificial light. Part of the landscape. Part of the community.

His muse. A lover, but not *in* love.

Definitely one hundred percent not in love.

The first stone was to be erected on the grass verge of the rutted farm road which led to Muriel's house. A stone sentinel to watch over the entrance to her land. Muriel had recruited a whole slew of local farmers and labourers to assist in the transport and placement of the stone, pointing out they would all likely turn up to gawk anyway, so idle hands may as well be put to good use.

The carved slab weighed a smidgen under five hundred kilos. Phase one was supposed to be loading and transport, but actually devolved into everyone chipping in with their own tuppence worth on the logistics while drinking mugs of tea. Blair was trying to be in a dozen places at once, supervising the loading, answering questions about his art project, and trying to make sure scampering children and wandering dogs did not end up crushed by the stone or run over by the hoist machinery.

Running parallel to this was a disappointment Donal was not present. He had to bite his tongue to stop himself asking Mrs Ritchie where her son was.

Eventually the whole dog and pony show got on the move, and the slab was conveyed to its destination. Blair felt his heart skip as he spotted the object of his lust as part of the team tasked with digging the socket hole for the stone's base. Donal had stripped to the waist, displaying his outdoorsman's tan; chatting amiably with a group of young men and… women? A couple of individuals were androgynous in a way Blair didn't normally associate with strait-laced farmer folk. He felt a twinge of jealousy when Donal laughed at a comment by one of the androgynous youths.

Concentrate, Blair! Today is about Art, not soap opera emotions.

He threw himself into organising, trying to project an image of an alpha male as the stone was unloaded and moved into position.

A cheer as the stone was lowered into the waiting hole. Blair removed the protective wrappings from the lowest portion of the stele. He personally placed the packing stones around the base, shedding his own shirt as he worked, sweating in the warm spring sunshine. Finally he stood back to observe as layers of soil were trickled in and tamped down. Hoping no-one was noticing he was as absorbed by Donal's muscles as he was with monitoring the filling of the hole.

When he was satisfied the stone was stable, Blair unfastened the straps which attached it to the hoist, and carefully unwrapped it, to a smattering of applause and a few whoops. He stepped back to admire the play of sunshine and shadow across the carvings.

Surprisingly, the pair of androgynous youths pushed forward to lay the cut turves back over the bare soil around the stone. One sprinkled the contents of his water bottle over the turf, then took a handful and flicked it at the stone, for all the world like a priest blessing an object with holy water.

"Nae worries." Donal was suddenly at his side. "Thon's just Stuart wantin' the grass to grow. He's into re-growth, re-wilding, rebirth – thon kind of things. You should talk to him about your Pictish beast."

From the supercilious, almost hostile look Stuart shot their way, Blair wasn't sure he wanted to discuss his personal take on the Beast with this arrogant stranger. Stuart managed to project an aura of spiky danger, like a cat which might claw at you without warning. Blair turned instead to the older generation of farmer folk, basking in their compliments about his carvings and answering queries about future stones.

Things evolved into a party from then on, as Muriel produced cans of beer and bottles of her raspberry wine from the back of her battered Land Rover.

Blair sipped at his mug of raspberry wine, and pretended to listen to Mr Robertson and Mrs Ritchie bewailing whatever horror story they'd heard on the news that morning: areas of Aberdeen declared off-limits after a spate of arson attacks, the Army called in to deal with looters and rioters. His real focus of attention was where Stuart and the other androgynous youth were holding court. A fair portion of the local teens, Donal included, had flocked to the pair.

But no, that wasn't quite true. The *boys* were drawn to Stuart's orbit. The teenaged girls were noticeably excluded. He spotted a trio of young women glaring daggers Stuart's way. On the pretext of getting more wine, Blair ambled their way.

"Afternoon, ladies." He raised his mug in a toast. They swapped anecdotes for a while; the girls keen to hear tales of an artist's lifestyle, and Blair picking their brains on the local social scene.

"So," he eventually asked. "Who's that Stuart guy? I don't remember him from my visits here."

Brows furrowed, nostrils tightened.

"Stuart Geddes," said the oldest girl coldly. She nodded at one of her companions. "Heather's cousin."

Heather looked mortified. The third girl abruptly muttered something about having to get back to work and strode away with set jaw and clenched fists.

Blair felt like he'd stepped into a minefield. "Sorry, was it something I said?"

Heather replied: "Marian and Stuart were engaged. Then he went off on some laddish trip to the Highlands and now he won't have anything to do with her. Now he's like *that*." The final word was delivered with icy venom, and a glower at where the aforementioned Stuart was sprawled languidly on the trailer which had carried the stone, toying with his long hair.

"Ah." Blair suspected he also might be classified as 'like that', and decided discretion was the better part of valour. He steered the conversation onto safer ground.

The party began to break up, as people headed back to late afternoon chores. Stuart's coterie was one of the last groups to disperse. Donal ambled over to where Blair and Muriel were packing mugs and beer cans back into the Land Rover. Stuart and the other androgynous youth watched Donal depart from their orbit. Blair had the uncomfortable feeling Stuart was giving permission for – or possibly even ordering – Donal to spend time with him.

"Need a hand?" Donal asked.

"Sure."

"Y'know, we were thinkin'…" said Donal as they collected up the various debris from the stone raising and drinking. "Maybe for the next stone you could ask the foresters to haul it. Use horses, save on diesel, y'know."

From the tone and the quick glance Donal sent to the group of youths, Blair suspected 'we' meant Stuart. However, the idea had merit. The Forestry team used a team of Clydesdales for hauling felled timber.

He nodded. "Yeah, good idea. I'll have a word with them, see what they say. Maybe we could do the second stone as a trial run and go from there?"

Donal flashed him a smile which set his blood to racing.

His studio was finished, the seven remaining slabs of sandstone had been delivered, and now he could get down to the serious work of carving the stones.

Donal continued to drop in and out of his life, and in and out of his bed. Blair felt full of light and joy and life on the days when Donal was there, all thoughts of work subsumed by the need to cram as much conversation and physical contact as possible into each hour. On days without Donal's presence, he would mope for a while, then bury his frustration in a surge of creative energy. The second stone – the wolf stone – was finished in record time.

Moving back here, Blair decided, was the best decision of his life.

"But if we put it *there* no-one will be able to see it from the main road!" Blair protested.

Donal was full of ideas about what he should and shouldn't do with the stones. Sometimes it was endearing, sometimes inspiring, and occasionally it was infuriating, like when Donal nagged him to some action which made no concession to the practicalities or timescale of carving each stone.

Last week's suggestion had been he should only erect the stones on Celtic feast days – solstices, equinoxes and the mid points between them. Blair had looked them up in the calendar and ruled it impractical: he'd never get the third stone completed in time for Beltane, and Midsummer coincided with the local agricultural show, so the resident farmers and foresters would have far too much else to occupy their time. Donal had reluctantly conceded.

Today's suggestion was about the sites chosen for the stones.

"Yes, that's the point. This is the final stone, the central stone. The heartstone. Folk should go to some effort to view it, not just glance at it as they drive by. This one should be *special*." Donal laid his hand reverently on the image of the Pictish Beast carved into the sandstone.

"Go on a pilgrimage to see it?" He said it in jest, but as he uttered the words, ideas were stirring and sparking.

He strode to where his laminated map of Aunt Muriel's land was mounted on the wall and gazed at the annotations showing where he had intended to erect each of his stones. "Yes, yes, yes!" The first few could go where intended, but after that if he placed them not in a circle but a spiral, then there would be a path – a progression – ending at the location Donal had suggested.

"You are a genius!" He grabbed Donal into a hug and twirled round, lifting the lad's feet off the ground and threatening to send tools and paperwork flying.

Donal gave a quirk of a smile, less flattered than Blair expected him to be.

"I was thinking circles and boundaries. But this fits the contours of the land. Look." Blair grabbed a marker and feverishly scribbled on the map, marking new positions for the stones. "We'll have to make sure Davy Robertson is okay with his stone in the middle of his pasture rather than at the edge, and the fifth one will be in woodland..."

Donal shrugged. "It's your Aunt's land. Surely her word is law?"

"Hmm." Blair's mind had raced off down another track. "If I swap those two over, the salmon and goose stone will be by the burn, with a view of the winter wheat fields, where the migratory geese feed. That's very resonant. And the horse and adder stone will be near the bridle path. Oh this is marvellous!"

Muriel was amenable to the change, and a few phone calls assured Blair that none of her tenants objected to which stone they got or exactly where it was erected, so long as it didn't interfere with the operation of farm machinery.

Conversation settled down to logistics and practicalities.

"We might need to build some sort of plank bridge, over the burn. So visitors don't get their feet wet crossing to see it."

Another of Donal's casual shrugs. "Easily done. Me, Nechtan an' Talorcan can knock it up for you in no time."

"Nechtan and Talorcan?" More new friends? Blair tried — and failed — to quash his jealousy of Donal spending his limited free time with others.

"Stuart and Murray. They changed their names."

His resentment calmed a little as he realised Nechtan and Taloran were just the regular, local, alpha males in a new guise. But changing their names to those of Pictish Kings? Now that was just plain weird. "They picked Pictish kings? Why?"

"It's complicated. You wouldn't understand."

That stung. Blair scowled. "Yeah, because I don't know anything about the Picts, do I?"

Donal chewed at his lip, fretting a moment. He sighed. "It's about belongin'. This place — the land. The Kingdom of Circinn. Connectin' with old ways. Forgotten ways."

"Pictish ways?" he asked cynically.

"Pagan ways."

"You do know the Picts converted to Christianity, don't you?"

Donal cocked his head to one side. "Maybe they shouldn't have. Maybe the world would be a better place if they hadn't."

The world was most decidedly not a better place this morning. Muriel had the radio on as they ate breakfast together, and the news was a litany of violence, civil unrest and shrill media pundits demanding the government Do Something. The bogeyman *de jour* was apparently someone or something called Raythoo.

"Why do you listen to that?" Blair asked. "It's all so depressing."

Muriel gave him a stern look. "You can't just bury your heid in the sand, Blair."

He was going to do his damnedest to try. His world had contracted nicely since he'd returned here — Donal, sculpture, Muriel's farming chit chat, village gossip. If they could become a little Brigadoon, completely cut off from the outside world, it would suit him down to the ground.

The trouble was, Brigadoon was not self-sufficient. They might have farms aplenty, so they were never going to starve, but the whole interconnectedness of the world these days made itself felt. There were shortages of the oddest things. One month you wouldn't be able to find shaving foam, shampoo or washing up liquid for love nor money. The next the village pub would be complaining the brewery had failed to deliver any beer.

The power was erratic too. Blair had more than a few days of enforced idleness, unable to use his cutting tools, because the electricity had cut off. Some things he could do by hand, of course. But it was much more time consuming, and even with the barn-come-studio doors thrown wide open, sometimes the light was inadequate. Plus, it was so much more annoying when the power cuts were unscheduled ones.

The one upside was if Donal was present when the power went out, there were other, more entertaining and energetic ways of keeping themselves occupied in dimly lit buildings. Blair smiled into his mug of tea at the memory.

The trial run moving the second stone by horse-drawn transport was a success. It had a smaller crowd than the first stone – the novelty having worn off a little – but more than enough warm bodies to make the endeavour a swift and efficient one. Donal's friends, the re-named Nechtan and Talorcan among them, again commandeered the task of preparing the hole for the stone, and again did their weird thing with the water.

They seemed almost possessive about the stone, which made Blair's hackles rise. The stones were his, and the stones were the community's. He tried to push down the feeling. The youths were local, and part of the community, after all. It was just... He couldn't help but feel Nechtan and Talorcan were somehow *dangerous*. An eerie prickling at the back of the neck when they were around; one of those 'someone just walked on my grave' feelings.

He rationalised this as just a subliminal manifestation of his jealousy toward anyone whom Donal enjoyed spending time with. A pair of fey teenagers with delusions of grandeur couldn't actually be dangerous, after all. Could they?

"He's cute, isn't he? Donal."

The aforementioned Nechtan had slinked over while Blair's

attention was elsewhere. He'd shed his shirt and work boots; bare feet accentuating his cat-like saunter. He swigged from a water bottle in a way which made Blair believe the clear liquid inside was not water.

"In an old-fashioned, masculine way, of course," Nechtan-who-was-Stuart continued.

The words may have been different, but the meaning was clear: *He's mine if I want him. I can take him from you, any time I like.*

Blair countered with his own hidden message: "Do you like the stones, Stuart? Are you an artist yourself?" *Donal likes me because I'm more than a young farmer who's a big fish in a small pond.*

A delighted laugh was not the response he expected. "Oh, they are perfect. Exactly what we need." If there was subtext to that, Blair could not decode it.

Nechtan pivoted gracefully to head back to his devotees. As he did so his long hair swung out to reveal a tattoo on his shoulder blade.

The Pictish Beast.

Weeks passed and summer gripped the land, shimmering with August heat. Two more stones were finished and erected. Each time there was an unsettling encounter with Nechtan, and the feeling that he was being toyed with.

It didn't help that he'd accidentally overheard part of a conversation which involved him. The pair were apart from their courtiers for once, withdrawn to the shelter of a copse of trees to smoke. Blair was bundling up the wrappings he used for a stone, so they wouldn't flap about in the breeze and alarm the horses. Then the wind shifted, bringing with it the scent of cannabis and a snatch of conversation.

"What about the sculptor?" That voice was Talorcan/Murray.

"No. Too old. Althaia would kill him."

"Pity. He's useful."

"Perhaps more than you think, if we resort to more, ah, *traditional* methods of keeping the Sulh and Caledii out."

Then the fickle breeze shifted again, sending their words elsewhere. What would kill him? Althaia? Was that another young man who had changed his name? Or had Blair misheard? Whatever the word, it sent a mixture of unease and indignation running through him. Entitled teenage brats, thinking him past it at twenty-nine!

He returned to the gathering and made sure Donal witnessed him being the life and soul of the party.

A handful of days later, he was cycling to the village shop when he spotted the collection of pale objects at the base of the first stone. Blair halted to get a closer look. A circle of seashells and quartz cobbles, worn smooth by the waves. At their centre was a piece of blue sea glass, with the burnt-out stub of a birthday cake candle on it. How odd.

It niggled at the back of his mind as he went on his errand. Who had left them? Some local child with a pocket of seaside treasures? A tourist who thought the stone was genuinely old? Tourists were few and far between these days, as fuel prices rose higher and higher. So, a local artist, maybe?

Back from the shop, he found he couldn't settle to his work. With a sigh, Blair admitted to himself he wasn't going to be content until he'd looked at the other stones. He laid aside his tools, popped into the house to tell Muriel to eat lunch without him, and set off.

It started out well enough and had him tending more towards the view this was some practical joke of Donal's. The second stone was festooned with daisy chains, and bunches of wildflowers at its base. The third had a collection of feathers and a faint smell of incense.

As he approached the fourth, however, several crows and a magpie flapped into the air and wheeled off to perch in a nearby tree. A herring gull stood its ground for a moment or two longer, ripping at something on the ground and departing with an unidentifiable chunk in its beak and… blood on its feathers.

It was one of Muriel's sheep – a part grown lamb. The birds had made quite a mess of it. His first thought it was a fox or dog kill was dashed when he got close enough to see a wreath of barley heads around its neck, and the sprayed pattern of what looked horribly like blood over the lower portion of the stone. Blair felt a sudden chill.

This was no practical joke.

Police constable Fiona MacIntosh came to investigate, bringing the local vet, Alice, with her. Alice confirmed the sheep's throat had been cut. Things didn't progress much further from there.

"Look, I'm really sorry about your sheep, Muriel, but we're kind of snowed under. We've got three missin' persons to deal with. And I shouldn't really be tellin' you this, but..." Constable MacIntosh looked around furtively, as if her superiors might be hiding in the hedge or behind the stone. "There's two bodies turned up on the Law Hill. Might be foul play."

"Good lord," exclaimed Muriel. "Who?"

"Oh, we're pretty sure they aren't anyone local," the policewoman said hurriedly. "Some city nutter decided to dump bodies out in the sticks, is my bet. But we've got a CID murder squad from Edinburgh throwin' their weight around, bangin' on about gangs, cults and revenge killings. Plus the Coull twins and Duncan MacLeish have run away from home. Probably on some ridiculous teenage bender, but their parents are convinced they've been kidnapped or axe murdered. So I can't put in much time on anything less, um..."

"Serious?" said Blair.

"Newsworthy?" suggested Muriel.

"Aye, that's about the size of it," said MacIntosh. "So, take some photos, put in for the insurance, and I'll give you a crime number for it."

Muriel frowned. "Someone sacrificin' a lamb at the foot of a standin' stone doesn't count as cult activity?"

Constable MacIntosh gave an apologetic smile. "I'll run it by the senior investigating officer, but..."

"He thinks we're country bumpkins tryin' to fake an insurance claim?"

"Pretty much."

"And if the bastards who did this come back?" Blair demanded.

"Muriel, is your shotgun licence up to date?" asked MacIntosh.

"Yes, of course."

"Then if you see a stranger near your sheep, pepper their arse with buckshot and ask questions later!"

He'd tried phoning Donal to tell him about the sheep, but his messages went unanswered. Days passed. A week. No returned calls, no texts, nothing. It was like Donal had dropped off the face of the Earth.

Blair was in a tizzy, not knowing what to do. Was this some inept way of dumping him? Or was there some sort of crisis at the Ritchie farm? Donal wasn't the type to have run off with the missing sixteen-year olds. Maybe he was helping with the search? But surely he would have told Blair about that? Mobile coverage was spotty these days, and the internet was about as reliable as a chocolate teapot, but it had been over a week. Surely he'd have heard *something* from Donal by now?

He tried to think of excuses to turn up on the Ritchie family's doorstep, but couldn't come up with one which didn't degenerate into *Hi Mrs Ritchie, I've been shagging your son and I want to know if he still loves me?*

Assuming Donal had ever loved him in the first place. The pair of them had been very cagey in that respect, never mentioning the L word to each other.

He continued to fret and stress, until one day he spotted Donal's mother outside the village shop. He plucked up his courage to speak to her, saying a cordial good afternoon, then launching into his real question: "Is Donal around, Mrs Ritchie? Or has he left for college?"

Mrs Ritchie's face went from politely neutral to a petulant glower. "No. He's off on some damn fool gap year thing."

Blair blinked. "Gap year?" he repeated inanely. He felt cold wash over him as his heart sank. Donal had *left*? Left the area. Left *him*!

She harrumphed. "Those ne'er do-well friends of his put the notion into his head. He's off spiritually finding himself or some such nonsense. Perfectly good kirk a few miles away, if he wanted spirituality. Nae need to go harin' off to god knows where."

"He's abroad?"

"Not as yet, though they were talkin' about some place in France with standin' stones. They're at some retreat in the Highlands, then apparently doing a tour of 'sacred spaces', whatever that means."

Blair made sympathetic noises, attempting to keep control of his emotions and not reveal how devastated he was. Why had Donal left without *telling* him?

He locked himself away for a week, barely eating, obsessively sketching Donal's image over and over again. Muriel tried to tempt him out of his room now and then, and eventually gave up and just brought up snacks and cups of tea or sat and watched as he drew.

Eventually Blair broke down and let her take him in to her arms; bawled his heartbreak into her shoulder. How he would never love like that again. How the world was empty and pointless. Muriel hushed and there-thered and told him if she ever caught up with Donal Ritchie she'd skelp his arse for him.

She badgered Blair for his contacts list and called all of his Edinburgh friends, telling them he needed visitors to cheer him up. A couple came – Izzy and Malcolm – and tried to brighten his mood with artsy chatter and funny stories from his student days. It was only when he found Izzy crying in the kitchen, he realised all was not right in their lives either.

"What's going on?"

"Oh, the world's just horrible now, Blair. Edinburgh's becoming a police state and Dundee's not much better. Check points, rationing, police raids in the middle of the night. Not to mention old biddies tutting at me because I don't have a pack of squalling brats in tow. Apparently, I'm a selfish cow because I'm not single-handedly trying to reverse falling birth rates!"

Blair tried to lighten the mood, empathy for Izzy's distress pulling him little out of his own gloom. "I'm pretty sure you can't do that *single*-handedly," he said.

Izzy gave a tearful, hiccupping laugh. "There's just no room for art and beauty in the world anymore," she said. "I'm thinking of moving back to Mull."

"But you hate Mull. You said it made the middle of nowhere look bustling and cosmopolitan."

A sniffle. "Yes. But the middle of nowhere feels safe now. I need some safe and boring in my life."

"This is the middle of nowhere, right here," Blair offered.

Izzy shook her head. "It's not. You might think it is but believe me it's not."

Izzy and Malcolm stayed for a fortnight, insisting they pay their way by scrubbing the house from top to toe and by painting huge murals on the corrugated iron walls of some of the outbuildings. Their choice of colours was a bit eclectic, paint being in short supply. The subject matter was famous landmarks of the region, old and new: Victoria & Albert Dundee, Arbroath Abbey, Glamis Castle. A celebration of mankind's millennia long history. An unspoken plea it continue for centuries more.

After they departed, Blair threw himself into work, spending long hours each day assisting Muriel on the farm or working on his sculptures.

He didn't want to be remembered as some clingy or needy ex. So he restricted himself to only emailing Donal a picture of each stone as it was completed. The images never evoked a response.

Sometimes he woke in the night, thinking he'd heard Donal's voice. Sometimes he'd go to his studio in the morning and could swear his tools had been moved or design sketches rearranged. Sometimes, he thought he caught a glimpse of a familiar blond figure in the trees or disappearing around the corner of an outbuilding. It was like he was being haunted by the ghost of their relationship.

November arrived, and Blair began to carve the final stone. His work on it was sporadic. Partially because there were labour shortages on the surrounding farms: with half Europe in turmoil and fuel prices soaring, virtually none of the professional crews of pickers came over to harvest fruit and veg, and those who did departed when city violence spilled out into the countryside, or they got news of deepening crises back home. There was also a crippling shortage of young locals to provide the labour. Gossip in the Village shop and pub was less the usual tutting that young people today were work shy layabouts, and more fretful worrying about yet another youth who had 'fallen in with the wrong sorts' and run off to the city for a life of drug-fuelled violence.

Blair had no experience driving farm machinery or looking after animals, but he could lend his back to vegetable picking and packing. He laid down his sculptor's tools for the time being and pitched in. As compensation, he set himself the goal of getting the final stone finished before Christmas.

He didn't know if it was the hard outdoors work he was unused to, or subliminal frustration about less time dedicated to sculpting, but he began to dream about messing up the final stone. Picking the wrong symbols or carving them incorrectly. The Pictish Beast flowed and rippled through his sleep, wanting to be reborn.

Awake, he would pore over his design sketches, trying to figure out what was bothering him. One side of the slab would be emblazoned with an eagle and the Pictish Beast. The reverse would bear another, bigger eagle on the reverse, to be the female counterpart to the male eagle on the facing side and would be paired with one of the abstract symbols. Each day he flicked through his reference sheets of other symbols, trying out other combinations.

Nothing seemed quite right.

Blair was once more spending the evening poring over his research on symbol combinations, when a shadow fell across him. He glanced round expecting to see Muriel.

Donal.

But at the same time not Donal. Taller, more slender, with hair tumbling down to his waist. An artist's impression of Donal, rendered in flesh and bone.

"You're back!" His impulse to play it cool lasted about a microsecond. Blair was on his feet and gripping Donal in a fierce and oh-God-am-I-really-that-needy hug. A bitchy part of him inside wanted to scream *You left me!* at the top of his lungs. Instead he broke the embrace and stood back. "You lost weight. Looks good on you."

It did. Donal was gorgeous. It was just... he was now more androgynous, less masculine. It would take a bit of getting used to.

"How was the trip? Visit anywhere cool? You back for good, or just to see family? How're Stuart and the others? Nechtan and the others, I mean." Blair stopped, realising he was prattling inanely. *Move on, Blair, move on. He hasn't been in contact for months – he's hardly likely to want to jump instantly back into your bed, is he?*

"The others are fine." Donal smiled at him, but it was a strange, sad smile. Somehow wistful or tinged with pity.

"Are they back too?" he asked. *Who are my rivals?* he meant. *Which of them should I be hating the most for luring you away?*

"Kinda. Got business in the area," said Donal, then nodded towards the final stone under its dust sheet. "How are thon stones comin' along?"

"Last one. Just started it."

"But...?"

Blair looked at him sharply, surprised Donal could hear the unspoken 'but'. "I'm having second thoughts about the last few symbols. What to pair with the female eagle."

Donal was suddenly alert, cocking his head to listen to something outside. Blair could hear nothing.

"Got to go," the young man said, and was out the studio door and gone with startling speed. When Blair reached the door and stared out into the farmyard, there was no sign he had ever been there.

Blair was useless for the rest of the evening. Running over the encounter again and again, looking for nuances and subtext which probably weren't even there. When he mentioned to Muriel that Donal was back, she remarked that Mrs Ritchie had mentioned no such thing. Which was worrying and gratifying at the same time. Blair's romantic hopes took a boost that Donal had chosen to speak to him before his family; but couldn't help but wonder if there was some ulterior motive there.

Of course, his aching heart hoped fervently the ulterior motive was Donal about to dump whoever his current lover was and forge his way back to Blair's arms.

The next few weeks were... odd. Donal came by again and again. Always at night. Always vanishing abruptly; sometimes after a few minutes, sometimes after an hour or so. Always wanting to talk about the symbol stone. Coaxing and cajoling Blair to work faster, to dedicate more time to sculpting it.

He combined flirting with the cajoling. But no sex. A cuddle, or perhaps a kiss. A caress now and then. But in all other ways Donal had become weirdly prudish; not wanting Blair to touch anywhere near his groin, and never shedding a cubic inch of clothing.

Blair became a maelstrom of sexual frustration and heartbreak.

"Maybe this stone isn't male or female. Maybe it's something else. Something new."

Donal had been absent three days now. His parting words kept bouncing around Blair's mind. Could he represent something new with ancient images?

He became more and more drawn to the symbol of two entwined snakes, each gripping the other's fish-like tail in its mouth. The symbol had always intrigued him: fish-serpents, neither one thing nor the other. He'd wanted all his symbol pairs to be authentic ones, but he found himself doodling alternative combinations, with one of them always the entwined fish-serpents. Eventually he realised his notebook was filled with a symbol trio, repeated over and over again: the 'cauldron', the mirror-with-comb and the fish-serpents.

He had found his final carving.

He was done. The last stone finished.

Blair checked it over once more, filled with the familiar twin feelings of achievement and sadness for the end of a project. Christmas was still a week away. He'd made his target date for completion with time to spare. He'd contact the foresters in the New Year and arrange a date to erect it.

After that… he might have to put art on hold for a while. Around the farms there was talk of battening down the hatches; of concentrating on crops to feed themselves and the local area, rather than trying to prop up an increasingly unreliable national food distribution network. The older generation shaking their heads over the lack of a flour mill or slaughterhouse locally. The younger generation already slipping into an economy of barter and favours owed, as cash became of less and less value.

Contemporary art, he suspected, was about to become a bit of a luxury for a while. A few years, maybe, until everything settled down and went back to normal.

Until then, he'd see if his skill as a sculptor could be put to use locally as a stonemason. And he'd help Muriel with the sheep, and to get some vegetable plots going. Join the harvesting crews when needed.

At least Donal was back. He could forego his art for a while if he could have Donal in his life again.

Muriel popped her head into his studio. "Blair? The police are here. They need to talk to us."

Police?

Constable MacIntosh and a plain clothes colleague sat in the kitchen, both looking haggard and stressed. Blair muttered polite greetings and sat down, a feeling of dread prickling at him.

The plain clothes woman introduced herself as Detective Constable Patel and launched in without preamble: "There have been some deaths at the Geddes farm. We need you to tell us where you were yesterday evening, and any vehicles you saw on the roads during that time. Any strangers about in the village."

"Deaths? Who? How?"

DC Patel shook her head. "We can't tell you anything until we've informed the relatives."

Muriel asked the obvious question: "When you say deaths, do you mean... gang stuff?"

"I really can't say until we've informed the family," said DC Patel.

Constable MacIntosh piped up. "So if you've seen Stuart Geddes – Nechtan Geddes – whatever he's callin' himself these days... We need to contact him."

Blair shook his head. "Sorry, no. I haven't seen Stuart for months. Donal might know where he is. Donal Ritchie."

He and Muriel reported their movements, and he racked his brains trying to think of anyone he might have seen. A potato lorry lumbering through the dark winter evening. Alice the vet walking her dogs.

Constable MacIntosh's radio blurted into life, and she retreated into the hallway to answer it. She reappeared before Blair had time to answer Patel's next question. "Boss? Big fire up at the church. We're needed."

And with that they were gone, the wail of sirens disappearing into the distance.

Christmas was going to be a sombre affair. The village was in shock at the brutal murder of the Geddes family, and then the death of the local minister in the still unexplained blaze at the kirk. Muriel was trying to organise a replacement Christmas service at the pub, but no-one was really in the mood for celebrating.

The oddest thing was that the outside world didn't seem to care. In the summer, when unidentified corpses had been found nearby, the place was awash in detectives and reporters, flooding in from the nearby cities. Now a few murders was just background noise as the world went to hell in a handbasket. Only the local coppers cared.

Stuart/Nechtan and his followers were prime suspects, for the simple reason they'd all vanished. Donal had vanished with them.

Blair refused to believe his Donal would be involved in anything as heinous as murder.

He awoke near midnight, convinced he'd heard people and horses in the yard outside. Stumbled from bed and peered out into the darkness. Nothing. Just a dream. Sleep eluded him for a while, the notion there was someone outside refusing to settle for quite some time.

When morning came, he was groggy from the disrupted slumber. He stumbled through household chores on autopilot, until Muriel despaired and sent him to haul a sack of turnips out to the sheep, hoping exercise and the biting cold of the Winter Solstice afternoon would perk him up.

He was wending his way back when he heard two shotgun reports and a piercing scream.

"Muriel?" Blair hurtled back towards the farmhouse.

She was lying half in and half out of the doorway, a feral figure standing over her. A knife glistened wetly. The figure roared something triumphal – incomprehensible – and raced off with inhuman speed.

"No!" he staggered to a halt, dropped to his knees by Muriel. Blood everywhere. Eyes staring sightlessly. "No, no, no!"

He clutched her to him and rocked, wailing out grief and shock until he was near numb with the cold, and Muriel was stiff and inert.

"Shh. It's okay." Arms encircled him, pulled him gently away from her body.

Donal.

Muriel was gone but Donal was here. Bright, shining, glorious Donal, bare chested despite the winter chill, with the symbols of the Picts inscribed on his skin. Grief shrivelled his very soul at the same time as joy sought to expand it.

"Here, drink this." Donal held a flask to his lips and fiery liquor burned its way down his throat. "Keep you warm while we raise the stone, eh?"

"The stone?" What did the stone have to do with this? Muriel was dead. Muriel was *murdered*. "I—I have to call the police." Describe the killer, help them catch him, *do something*.

Donal smiled a sad smile and offered the flask again. Blair grabbed and gulped, knowing he shouldn't – that he should be sober when the cops came – but desperately wanting alcohol to kill the pain.

All the time Donal spoke. Melodically, soothingly.

In her honour. It's what she would have wanted. A memorial. The words tumbled over him, like water. He was numb, like a stone on a riverbed. The water caressing, swirling... eroding him from boulder to cobble to pebble.

"Yes," he said. "Yes, in her honour. The stone will be a memorial. On her land."

"Your land now," said Donal. There was a strange edge to his voice.

Yes, if Muriel was dead, the farmhouse and all her land fell to him. His inheritance. Blair looked at the dried blood on his hands. He had never wanted anything less than he wanted this. He let himself be guided away from the house, bathed in orange light as the sun dipped towards the horizon. Two of Donal's friends were there; slim, wild-haired figures merging with the shadows.

"The stone. We need to transport the stone..."

"All sorted." Donal's voice was coaxing, reassuring. "Talorcan and Deocilunon arranged everythin'. The stone is waitin' for you."

A momentary prickle of annoyance surfaced that someone had moved his stele without permission, then it sank again into the numbness of shock and grief. Donal's arm steered him away from the farmhouse and outbuildings. Blair plodded on in a near stupor. After a while landmarks and his surroundings began to register.

"Wait. We're going the wrong way. The east field is that way."

Donal twisted to face him, cupped a hand around his cheek, leaned in for a long, lingering kiss. Blair eagerly accepted; irrationally hoping something as normal as a kiss would wash away all the confusion and horror.

Donal broke contact. "We're goin' to do this properly, eh?"

For a moment Blair thought he was referring to the kiss.

"Walk the stones. Start to finish, spiral to centre. Old to new."

"Properly?" What was proper about tonight? Muriel was dead. Her blood was on his skin, his clothing.

One of Donal's friends spoke. "Yes. We walk the stones to fix things. Set them on their proper path."

Blair failed to grasp what they meant. But fixing things sounded good. And Donal – after directing an annoyed glance at the one who had spoken – patted Blair's shoulder reassuringly and shepherded him onwards.

They paused at each stone. Donal and the others ran their hands over the carvings reverently, whispering to them. Poured a trickle of something into the soil at the base of each. They were *his* stones, *his* carvings, yet Blair felt like an outsider. Felt there was some subtext or hidden meaning he was failing to grasp.

"The light's fading. We should go back for a torch."

Twilight was rapidly fading into full dark. The moon loomed large as it rose.

"Don' worry. We can see fine in this light."

Blair had a sense the 'we' did not include him.

There was a glimmer of firelight through the tall hawthorn hedge, which marked the final field boundary. Blair caught the murmur of voices and scent of smoke as the wind gusted his way. Donal made a satisfied sound and picked up the pace, forging toward the gate. Stumbling a little on the rutted ground, Blair glanced back at the two silent, hard-faced angels who followed them, and halted in shock.

Their eyes gleamed in the firelight like cats' eyes.

"What...? That's not..."

Donal's grip on him tightened, jerked him onwards insistently, in contrast to the serene tone of his voice. "C'mon, nearly there."

The stone was already standing. Illuminated by twin bonfires and surrounded by a ring of youths.

He stared at it, not understanding. Who had...?

Stuart – Nechtan – stood in front of the stone, arms and face smeared with blood. *Muriel's* blood? His voice boomed out: "The Sulh and the Caledii want this territory."

The onlookers chanted a reply: "We are Circinn, and this land is *ours!*"

"We claim it as our birthright."

"We are Circinn, and this land is *ours!*"

"We bind our spirits to the land."

"We are Circinn, and this land is *ours!*"

Blair looked to Donal in confusion as his friend added his voice to the chant, and saw… An alien being. Human yet not human. Neither male nor female. Something else. Something new.

Something which could never love him.

The two hard-faced angels who had accompanied him took him from Donal's side, pulled him to the stone. Held him upright in front of it, when his legs dragged woodenly and threatened collapse.

"Who is this human?" Nechtan asked in a ritual singsong way.

"The last of his line. The last to hold title to this land." Donal's voice, from somewhere close behind him.

Blair tried to twist round and look Donal in the eyes, but his movements were sluggish, as if he was a fly trapped in resin, solidifying into amber.

"Why is he here?"

"Rebirth. The old world dies. The new arises."

Donal leaned forward, pressing against Blair. The warmth from his body slicing through the winter cold, his words a whisper: "I'm sorry. But we need this. My tribe has to survive. *I* have to survive."

Blair felt his hair gripped, his head pulled back, and then the fiery sharp slash of a blade across his neck. Blood sprayed on the stone in front of him. And sprayed, and sprayed…

"I am Alpin har Circinn, and I claim this land for my tribe!" Donal howled it, exultant. A cheer went up, feral and triumphant. A drum began to beat.

They let him fall, then. Let gravity and shock suck him down to crumple at the foot of his stone. Voiceless, bleeding out into the fresh packed soil. The carved stone eyes of the Pictish Beast watched him, his blood dripping from its face.

Blair's last vision was of the tribe of youths twirling and stamping in some savage dance. He could not tell which of them was Donal.

Three Miles Down

Ben Fouracre

Three miles down
Cold light leaks out
Through windows and wires
Doorways and dead eyes

Lost in the crowd
And my heart is so open
Open to the blows
Crushed and I'm broken
Face down
Learning how to breathe

I know where to find you
In your favourite room
With the memories you crave
The chances you take

Take what you want I'm leaving
There's nothing to believe in
I can see no hope
But I'll take what you've got
I'll take what you've got

The Scream of Memory

Wendy Darling

As usual, it was the scream that woke me.

Deva!

For months, the same dream had jolted me from sleep: a replay of a scene from my past, climaxing in a scream.

Six or seven years earlier, I'd been a Varr on horseback fighting a rogue tribe over territory. That day, there had been killing, both horses and hara, close combat, and I'd been nicked by a thrown dagger myself. Two killings in particular appeared before my sleeping mind over and over.

A tall har in a long black cloak turned around, appearing startled by my approach. Had he thought the fight was over? Despite being taken unawares, the har swiftly moved to attack. Taking up what looked like an old sword of human make, he began to charge through the soggy battle ground, strewn with fallen bodies. Before the har had made it more than ten feet, I let fly an arrow into his neck. Artery neatly severed, the har crumpled to the ground. I had no doubt he'd bled out in under a minute.

Although I hadn't felt much of a reaction at the time – one act of violence among hundreds – in the dream I questioned myself: Did I need to shoot? Couldn't I have just turned my horse around and gone? Was it fair, my excellent shooting versus a har charging from across a field with a sword? In that actual moment, such questions hadn't merited any consideration. We Varrs were bent on eliminating all opponents and with rare exceptions – war prizes of flesh – after a battle, we left no har standing.

The second killing was another matter. It followed shortly after the first, with an unarmed har rushing toward the fallen har's body, shrieking that name: *Deva*. Even as I felled the weeping har with another swift arrow, the name elongated into a scream that woke me over and over.

In real time, the entire sequence had played out over only a couple of minutes. Although I hadn't quite forgotten it, even amongst all the old memories of killing, death, and loss, it wasn't until recent weeks that the memory had resurfaced, clear as if it were yesterday.

"Bran, what is it?"

Kirik, my chesnari, was squeezing my shoulder and looking at me worriedly.

I didn't answer, but rather rubbed my hands over my face.

"The same? The one you won't tell me about?"

I drew the thick comforter up to my chin and nodded. The air was chill: we'd fallen asleep after aruna and had forgotten to tend the fire.

The bed creaked as Kirik rose to his knees and straddled me, both hands on my shoulders. "I want you to tell me."

I took a slow breath through my nose, attempting to subdue my irritation. I didn't want to talk about it. The past was the past. The dreams would end on their own. Eventually. "I know you mean well..."

"Yes. I do. And I'm sick of you waking up in a panic and not telling me why."

"It doesn't matter," I deflected. "It's just something that happened years ago."

This conversation was a repeat of numerous others, and as such Kir supplied the next line: "If it doesn't matter, tell me." The look on his face, outlined by moonlight from the windows, was beseeching.

Our eyes locked, and though I'd said no a dozen times before, in this instance I felt myself caving.

"Alright," I began. "But remember, this was years ago."

I went on to describe the dream, giving a bit of context about where and when, along with an account that took longer than the actual encounter.

"I didn't even go up to them after they fell," I said.

"You killed the other har, too?"

"I assume so. He fell." I took Kir's hands. "Another arrow. He went down beside... *Deva*. I left them like that and moved on to something else."

My partner had a look on his face I couldn't place.

"Are you angry with me?" I asked quietly.

Kirik crawled off me to stand on the floor beside the bed. "No, I'm not."

Clearly, he was in fact angry. I knew my partner too well to be fooled.

He stared at the floor. "Do you remember anything else about these hara? Beside the cloak and the one name?"

I saw the scene in my mind's eye. "Yes. They were both darker skinned. Like...." I hesitated. "Like you. From Asia, I suppose."

From the steely look Kiri was giving me, I knew that I would have been better off keeping that detail to myself.

Nonetheless I continued. "The first one had dark hair, longer than was popular among warriors then. The second had short hair, dyed bright red, with red painted on his cheeks as well."

"Why do you think you remember this?"

I shook my head. "I don't know."

The love Kir and I shared had nothing to do with those dark days of destruction and war. And yet it had everything to do with it.

We had met only a year prior in busy but peaceful Galhea, where we'd both come to live, after lives both of us kept deliberately shrouded. In the new life I'd created for myself, I worked in a brewery, charming hops and wheat into happiness, and had my own small apartment above a tavern that happened to be our brewery's best customer. It was at the bar that we two had met, he having just arrived, looking for work and lodging. After some chatting with me, he had a job as a cook and a bed with me. It was never complicated, and for that we both felt fortunate.

Early on, we'd bumped up against the past in conversation and whenever we did – speaking of a town, a friend, a way of life now gone – we seemed to arrive at a silent agreement: *We are not going back there.* Once, unusually drunk after indulging in a brew a co-worker had sent home with me to 'try', I did blurt out something or other, talking about my bow and arrows, how many men and hara I had killed with them.

I didn't get very far, for Kir took the drink from my hand and said to me seriously: "Bran. I don't want to know."

I let him take the drink and set it on the bedside table. "Fine," I'd said. "Let's let the past be the past."

Despite the lack of intimacy in this one area, I grew closer to Kirik that I ever had to anyhar. We shared a similar disposition – hardworking but not entirely serious, cynical when it came to government announcements news, but able to be cheerful when good things did indeed come out of government plans.

Neither of us had any substantial caste training, nor were we particularly spiritual. Our form of worship, of communion, was aruna, the perfection of which to us proved the existence of a deity. How could anything so elevated, so perfect, simply spring from nothing? The burden of the past and the uncertainty of the future left me during our union, leaving me to focus on the harmony and freedom I had found in the present.

It was a year – to the day – since we'd me that the dreams began. The one dream, of bow, arrow, death, and *Deva*.

We'd spent the evening at the home of the brewery owner, not because the har had planned an anniversary celebration for us but because it was his harling's feybraiha celebration. We'd had fine food and drink, and meanwhile I'd been able to introduce most of my co-workers to my chesnari, of whom they'd heard me speak. Kirik, though I have not mentioned it, was born beautiful, even before he became har, and it was a pleasure for me to see the want in the eyes of others. I was a lucky har.

It was getting late, when Kir pulled me aside and spoke into my ear. "I think I'm going to go home. Don't know what it is, but I have a terrible headache and anyway, I have an early shift tomorrow."

I shrugged and made to grab my things and leave, only for him to tell me to stay on. This was my boss's party and an early departure might be noticed. The harling and his first aruna partner were stll in the hall. Better stay for politeness sake at the very least.

"And you might slip some of those leftover desserts into your purse, if no one is looking," he suggested, giggling. I told him I'd purloin a few of the pastries he liked best.

Arriving home well after midnight, I found Kir dozing in bed, a candle burning low. The air smelled of incense as I undressed and settled down beside him. He roused and opened his eyes halfway. "Did you bring dessert?" he asked. I nodded. "Good. I'll have them for breakfast." And back to sleep he went.

A few hours later, dead of night, I woke from the dream, feeling horrified by what I'd seen. It was only the truth, but those days were nothing I dwelled on, and it was a shock to face them without meaning to.

Kirik, awakened, put his hand on my shoulder. "Bran, what is it?"

And just as I did ever time for weeks after, I lied and told him it was nothing.

The morning after I'd told Kir the truth, I found myself alone in our apartment. While he prepped lunch in the tavern kitchen, I scraped together a breakfast of bread and butter and an herbal cigarette I hoped would dull my headache. As the smoke curled toward the ceiling, I considered how I'd broken our nearly unspoken rule about bringing up the past. I had apparently been trying to follow it, but faced with Kir's pleading and a sleepy head, I'd given in. No more of that.

I had the first half of the day to myself, thanks to my employer's extending leave to all party-goers, and when I got home from a short shift later, I found Kir had set the table with a meal of tavern leftovers and a carafe of a wine he normally saved for special occasions.

"Thanks for this," I told him, sitting down opposite. "I think I forgot lunch."

Kir filled my glass. "That sounds like you."

We tucked into our food and for some moments didn't talk, until: "I'm sorry I brought that up."

Kir looked at me as though he didn't understand.

"You know what I mean. The dream. I'm sorry. I won't talk about it again."

He set down his glass of wine. "I did ask you."

"Let's not belabour this."

"Fair enough."

And that was all that was said. The bandage was once again firmly wrapped around the wound.

Still the dreams came.

Within a couple of weeks, the usual rhythms of life had resumed and we two were our typically happy, past-avoiding selves. The two or three times the dream had woken me, I'd managed to keep quiet and thus no dead-of-night conversations had ensued. I buried the memories away and slept on towards morning.

It was the end of a long week that I returned home to find Kirik home, again having set a table of tasty leftovers.

"Weren't you going to be working tonight?" I asked him, stepping into the kitchen.

He turned to me and huffed. "How's that for a thank you!"

After freshening up, I returned to the table and sat. As Kir looked up from lighting a candle, the glow caught his cheek, eyes and hair in a way that brought his beauty to the fore.

I was a few moments into appreciating my fortune when Kir set his hands flat on the table and spoke. "I begged off work today so I could go somewhere."

"Oh? Where?" I took up my spoon and tucked into the stew.

"Well, you know my friend Enid?"

Mouth full, I nodded.

"Well, you know what he does for a living, right?"

I was swallowing when I understood his meaning. "You're... Are you with pearl?" I choked.

"Mmm hmm."

We paid a terrible disservice to that stew by wolfing it down far too quickly so we could move to our bed and partake in a different meal.

From that night, the dreams stopped. Or, if they continued, they no longer woke me. After a few days of solid sleep, I felt rested in a way I hadn't in weeks. The disruptions had been affecting me more than I'd realised.

Now that they were gone, there was nothing to do but focus on Kirik and our forthcoming harling. We were fortunate to have a spare room, which could be easily converted to a nursery. With our employers the way they were, flexible and understanding, we would both be able to come up with schedules for harling care. Still, there were matters we needed to get in order, like clothes, emptying the spare room and relocating our junk, and going over names. Mainly, however, I focused on making sure Kir was happy and comfortable.

I doted on him, for example finding out where my boss had bought the party pastries from and buying a box to mark a month since Kir told me the news. I recall he subsisted on those sweets for an entire weekend, ignoring all other food. And I didn't complain, because I certainly was grateful it wasn't me with pearl.

I saw myself from across a soggy field, littered with bodies. A tattoo ran from neck to shoulder to wrist. My arm muscles flexed as I drew my arrow back into the bow, aiming squarely at – me. Suddenly I was hit, falling down beside my lover, who'd also been pierced and now lay dead. Searing pain bloomed in my shoulder, close to my heart. I didn't want to die. This couldn't be the end. I screamed.

Deva!

I woke up with the name still ringing my ears. My throat was dry, eyes gummy, head heavy as if with drink. Normally the nightmare ejected me into full awareness, but not that night.

It was only when I went to rub my eyes that I realised my position. My limbs were tied to the four posts of the bed. What was happening? I flexed and found the bindings taut, nearly immovable. Perhaps if I could just free one arm, use all my strength...

But then Kirik dropped down over my hips, straddling me, and it was not in the way of a delighted lover playing a game. His left hand clamped onto my right shoulder like a talon while his right hand brought a knife to my throat.

I flexed my hands against the bindings, but not because I hoped to escape. I was afraid.

Kirik glared at me viciously, murderously. "Now you finally know how I felt!" he snarled.

My brain was still battling grogginess. "You... were trussed?"

The point of the knife dug harder into the skin just below my jaw. "You killed him."

I killed... who?

Kir pulled the knife away only to smack me hard across the face. And then twice more. Had he broken my nose?

Think fast, I told myself.

I had killed many hara, some men. So had Kir, I imagined. But we didn't talk about that. Except...

"The dream."

The knife was back at my throat. "The dream. *Yes.*"

"I killed two hara."

Suddenly Kir's black eyes were inches away from mine. "You killed one. You only *almost* killed me."

Minutes before, I'd dreamed of being hit by my own arrow. Had I been dreaming of Kir?

"How?" I demanded.

The pressure of the knife point reminded me I needed to refrain from shouting, lest I impale myself.

"I recognised you almost as soon as we met," he remarked conversationally. "I never forget a face. Especially not when the face is attached to the har who killed my chesnari."

I was still catching up. "Your chesnari."

"His name was Deva. That name you keep hearing me scream, the name you screamed yourself over and over tonight."

A swell of panic overtook me. "Having that dream was no coincidence..."

Kir pulled back, knife hand steady, left hand gesticulating. "You must've wondered why you were suddenly dreaming of an incident from years ago. A very *specific* incident? And over and over for weeks?"

I narrowed my eyes. "Of course I did. You know I did. But..." I saw it now. For weeks I had been blind. "You were putting the dreams there."

I didn't know how to carry out the type of magic that would send another har mad, but perhaps Kirik did. There was much I didn't know about him. By silent agreement.

"When I met you, I decided there were advantages in getting together."

"Like... having the opportunity to have your vengeance?"

He ran the knife point back and forth across delicate skin.

"That… and a job. And free rent."

Though I remained tied to the bed, I felt as though the ground had disappeared below me. I was floating, about to fall. ·

"Was it all a lie? A plot?" Surely not. We'd made a pearl!

"Oh, yes. And it worked out so well. We wouldn't talk about our pasts? Perfect. Keep things shallow? Perfect."

I denied this possibility. "Kir. I love you."

His left hand clamped onto one side of my neck, pushing it toward the knife. "You love what I showed you. You don't even know me."

"I think I do, Kir. Nohar is that good an actor."

Suddenly he was off me, standing at the side of the bed where I could see him. "I've waited years for this, you murdering Varr. I vowed that day that I would kill you on sight if our paths ever crossed. I changed my mind on how quickly, and I decided to get with pearl as part of the bargain, but I've reached the moment and I *will* kill you."

Limbs burning against the tight ropes, I studied him, and as happened every so often, but not in a long, long time, I used more than my eyes. I *felt* him.

I felt the lie.

"You don't want this, Kir. You…" I jerked my head, in lieu of waving him off. "Don't interrupt. You don't want this. You want to want it, you made a vow, but you don't."

For years he'd dreamed of meeting the har who killed his chesnari. Finally, he'd found him, set a plan in motion. But there was a complication: he didn't hate me.

Once somehar has made a decision, it's difficult to talk them out of it. Too much pride is involved. You'll lie and exaggerate to avoid giving in. But this was life or death. I had to convince him.

Kir hadn't spoken since I'd made my accusation. I decided to go on, but not out loud.

Let us admit the past. My past. Your past. But we can't live *in it. We need to live* now, *where we fit together perfectly. And where we have a pearl soon to be born.*

This was by far the longest communication I'd ever achieved through mind-speech.

I could see Kir trying to push himself, reignite his anger. But the embers were cooling, turning grey and ashen.

You don't want to kill me. You feel you must, but you don't want to. Untie me.

Kir turned and hurled the knife across the room.

Then, quickly and methodically, he went around the bed, untying me.

"I must be going soft. It's this pearl. A flaw in my plan."

I didn't dare smile, despite the relief I felt.

From that night onward, we spoke of the past. It was like vomiting up everything I'd held inside for years. And yet with every day, I felt lighter. Kir told me he felt the same.

"Were we really any worse than any other hara in those days?" he asked.

"We weren't angels. And for that we must forgive ourselves."

As he pushed out our pearl, Kir screamed. He screamed my name.

Give Them Darkness

Storm Constantine

On Shadetide eve, the dehar Prosperiel took off his lively, grinning mask and became Lachrymide, a dehar of soulful aspect, who gathered lost souls to him on this night of bonefires and feasting. Leaves burned on the festival fires, smoke hugging the ground like mist, and the smell of damp autumn hanging like perfume in the air, as if Lachrymide himself had just walked by, leaving his scent behind him. This was the night when tolling bells were heard deep within the forest, where once, in centuries past, long perished human towns and villages had thrived. You should not look upon the bellringers if you found one, but merely throw them a gift and hurry away. And if you came across Lachrymide at a crossroads, telling his beads of tiny skulls, run away too in case he had a mind to add more shrunken skulls to his rope.

On this day, Halvise har Jarice came down the Orchard Road that cut a stamped brown ribbon of dirt through the fields and led to the Anchemant estate ahead. He rode a nervous black mare with a long, crimped mane. Smoke swirled about the horse's knees and apples fell from the trees as she passed. Some said this was a sign of fruitfulness to come, others said it warned of approaching blight. The black mare was an aspect of Lachrymide, perhaps no coincidence. Halvise rode alone, contrary to common gossip about him having a constant companion, said to be both mysterious and treacherous. Some suggested that this individual was responsible for the revival of the Jarice fortune, the family's luck. Or he was merely part of a fairy tale planted to make the newcomer, or rather the prodigal, seem more intriguing, more of an attractive prospect to a har who liked mystery, who wanted other hara to think he courted danger.

Whether Halvise had invented the stories himself or not, Jansin har

Anchemant was hungry for such things. He was in the Mere Field, which wasn't a field exactly but a vast orchard, its trees of pear, greengage and apple now crowded by high panniers filled with freshly picked fruit, the last of the season, some tampered with to produce a fruit quite different from its original form. Anchemant produce was hardy, lasted long in storage and tasted so dulcet it could bring a har to tears as bittersweet memories poured over his tongue, down his throat to his heart along with the juice. Now, as guests began to appear on the four roads that led to the Anchemant domain, hara sang traditional harvest chants as a welcome, which melded with the scent of succulent fruit and wet, smouldering leaves.

Jansin saw movement on the road from the corner of his eye and turned. He would not have been surprised to see a dark, smoky shape gliding across the path, but instead he saw Halvise har Jarice riding down, wearing an enveloping cloak and a wide-brimmed dark peacock green hat, decorated with a long green feather. Jansin would remember the moment for the rest of his life, mainly because it shaped the path of it.

Jansin was the eldest son of the phylarchs, Scythe and Rillmist. The Anchemant phyle of the Erini tribe occupied the ancient Maske Abbey, which had been reconstructed – and to some degree reimagined – from ruins, a practice common among many Wraeththu sub-tribes. Communities grew up around the old human estates, perhaps because to some degree they had been built in a sense of tribalism – self-sufficient communities that worked the land. Now, Jansin worked alongside the estate staff, his sleeves rolled up, his arms tingling with scratches from brittle twigs, his head dizzy with the intoxicating aroma of the ripest of the fruit, his heart light and free of all cares. He was twenty-three years old and not yet sure what he wanted from life. This day would perhaps have something to do with that. The smell of the season embraced him, that familiar eternal enchantment of the earth. In the late afternoon, many hara would arrive from nearby settlements and outlying farms to participate in the generosity of the Anchemant phylarchy. A huge feast would be laid out on dozens of large trestle tables, which were now being erected around the perimeter of the Home Lea field. Hara in the costume of autumn field spirits would serve those who came to them, and occasionally might utter a personal prophecy.

Normally, Shadetide at Anchemant was something of a minor festival, a precursor to the lavish celebrations of Natalia at the Winter Solstice. It was customary for a small Shadetide feast to be laid out in the barn yard, or within one of the barns if the weather was bad, but generally it was only a staff and family affair. The occasion this year, however, was different. You could feel it – a kind of strained anticipation. And this was because of a guest who nohar had met before: Halvise har Jarice, a guest who had become a neighbour, and must therefore be examined, fed, flattered, assessed. There were reasons for this.

So what was so special about this newcomer? There were rumours concerning him and his wealth, of course. To Jansin, who liked good stories but not when they were presented as fact, they sounded like tarradiddle to entertain harlings on the lengthening evenings. The old domains around Maske Abbey were old, very old, and had had stories sewn to them long before there were hara in the world, and in most cases long before human families had abandoned the traditional mouldering piles, or else had been driven out, slaughtered by the early Erini tribes, who hadn't much cared who they killed – human or har. Ghosts haunted the area in abundance, of course, and hara told gruesome tales of what might still lie chained in deep oubliettes, moaning for eternity. Halvise must have come home to unearth the past, to seek riches and secure a lucrative blood bond. Or he might simply be curious about the legends associated with his family and its domain and had come to see for himself. The stories, if he did not find them distasteful or embarrassing, could provide amusement over dessert, when hara wanted entertainment.

Perhaps Jansin, the adored scion of the house, didn't realise that he too was entertainment – a story for a story, a deal for a lucrative friendship. But surely Jansin was too sharp for that. He *knew*. It was said that har Jarice planned to renovate his family's lands, draw new hara to his phyle, make his mark, and for that he would need a strong, respected local family behind him, who liked him enough to present their treasure to him – in this case, Jansin. He could soon be the joint phylarch of a new phyle of the Erini. Jansin was not to be given away like an animal, as in some ancient myth of humankind when the daughters – and to some extent the lesser sons – of rich families were rarely anything other than commodities. No, Halvise must look upon this bond – if indeed it should occur – as a great privilege. There would be stipulations, such as the fact that Jansin's parents did not want Halvise to take their family name. He must give Jansin a new name, make it worthy of him. Did Halvise know this? There were many who wondered. A treasure may easily be taken back. Jansin would have to consider the arrangement worthwhile. It was to be hoped Halvise didn't plan to follow in the unreliable footsteps of certain ancestors, who'd reputedly had little sense and no idea how to manage land or provide sound, fair leadership for their tenants and staff. As co-phylarch of Halvise's domain, Jansin would bring it instant respectability. He would rule it with a fair yet iron hand.

The beautiful black horse minced past the mere, lashing her luxurious tail, shaking her cascading mane. She was adorned with ribbons and a smattering of small violet flowers, some of which now fell wilting to the road. Halvise har Jarice appeared to notice for the first time the tall graceful har standing among the fruit trees. He took off his hat, swept it extravagantly through the air in greeting. No, not the first time he'd noticed, not at all.

As for Jansin har Anchemant, he simply smiled and raised a hand. Nothing more. There would be time later for such things – if he'd a mind for them.

The dance of life, smoke on the autumn air. An old smell of burning.

The sumptuous evening feast, for family, close friends and valued colleagues, would be held separately from the less formal revels in yard and field. The diners would gather around the long table in the old Refectory of the abbey, where once monks had dined frugally. The vaulted chamber was heavy with traditional seasonal decorations – swags of brilliant foliage shining gold and bronze, as if carved from precious metals, yet they were real. Candles as thick as a har's wrist dripped their scented wax down the convolutions of elaborate candlesticks, fashioned of bone or wood or buck antlers bound with leather and gut. The feasters were draped in autumnal shades, their hair bound with leaves, their jewellery of copper and tigers' eyes.

Brilliance, beauty and light, yet a festival of the dead. Lachrymide waited languidly in the shadows for his turn of the wheel, which would commence at midnight.

Halvise was seated between Jansin and his younger sibling, Sheen, just down the table from the parents, who appeared to take little notice of their esteemed guest, giving Jansin space to navigate this new friendship, learn its pathways. The remains of the main course had been taken away. The air smelled now of vanilla and spice, in anticipation of the traditional Shadetide dessert called Spirit's Pudding.

So far, the conversation had been trivial, mainly Halvise asking questions about the working of the estate, joking that he needed the advice for he was new to such practices.

"There'll be plenty of time for boring things like that tomorrow, Tiahaar har Jarice," Sheen said silkily, his eyes seemingly flecked with gold in the candlelight. "We've had enough of it for now. Bring out the spicy pudding! Now is the time for more… *interesting* topics. Tell us stories, Tiahaar. We *love* stories."

The diners nearest to Halvise and the brothers went quiet, most eyes fixed expectantly on Jansin, but Jansin said nothing. Instead, he smiled slightly, sipped from his wine, aware of all who watched him. A feather touch crossed his mind: his hostling bestowing a wordless warning that meant 'behave'.

Halvise har Jarice laughed, but not loudly, far from it. He rippled with what seemed to Jansin a dubious humour. "Of my travels?" he asked coquettishly. He withdrew from his pocket a tin containing smoking materials, and a beautifully fashioned clay pipe, its bowl a deer's head.

"Of your *domain*, Tiahaar," Sheen pleaded. "It sounds fascinating, and there are so many legends about it in these parts. Won't you tell us more? Are any of the stories true?" Sheen rested his chin on his hands – a winsome, charming creature, but he was only the aperitif.

"It *is* an unusual property," Halvise conceded, "not least because you cannot enter by its main door."

"Really?" Sheen exclaimed. "I've not heard this. Why *can't* you enter through that door?"

Halvise lit his pipe, leaned back in his seat. He gestured gracefully.

"The common entrance is in the east – that's three hours as the raven flies from Anchemant. From the south, my domain is approached by a tight, treacherous path, hardly more than a steep narrow ledge, which leads to the keep, the oldest part of the building. I'm told many sheep from our flock, as well as more than a few harish and human inhabitants, have fallen to their deaths there over the centuries."

"It seems stupid for the main entrance have been placed there," Sheen said. "Somewhat inconvenient for residents and wanted visitors alike.

"No," Jansin interrupted before Halvise could speak. "It was a symbol to warn uninvited visitors not to approach. They could be hit by missiles from the top of the Keep."

"That's true," Halvise said, a little warily. "To make the path worse, some centuries ago a deep gulf opened up and some of it collapsed. Bridges were fashioned over the years, but they always crumbled. There's a legend that a monstrous serpent lives in the thrashing river below, which rears up to take a bite out of any bridges hara try to build!"

"How tiresome," Sheen said.

"Er... Yes," Halvise agreed uncertainly, perhaps suspicious of being mocked. "Anyway, even should you manage to cross these boundaries, the great doors are two feet thick, hewn of great oaks, special trees harvested just for this purpose. They were brought from the sacred heart of the forest, which is a terrifying place, believe me. The timbers that bind the doors from the inside are immovable."

"Perhaps it is the age of the place that has worn the path and sealed the doors," one of the diners said.

Halvise gave this har a slight flick of attention. "Perhaps so." He turned to the har sitting, but leaning away, from his right side. "What do you think, Jansin?"

Jansin shrugged his perfect shoulders, smiled in a distinctly formal fashion. "I have not seen the place, so I have no opinion," he said.

Halvise smiled sweetly. "Oh, come now. You try to deceive me. You've already smashed some of the Keep's mystery. I'm sure you have *opinions*." And other words hid within the smiles and the light tone: *I would not be here now if you did not, and very informed opinions at that.*

Jansin smiled thinly. "Makes a good tale," he said. He drew in his breath, threw back his head to stare at the vaulted heights above him. "Let's see… I assume one stormy night a furious knocking was heard… no, it was a pounding… *desperate*. The mighty doors flew open… revealing nothing. Leaves blew in, a great cloud of them, and when they drifted to the old, blackened floor, the astonished inhabitants found a shivering har soaked through, and almost senseless, upon the step. They took him in, for he was lovely, but no good came of it, of course…" He paused. "How am I doing? Is my story better or worse than the one you had waiting for us?" Jansin showed his teeth in a smile.

"You certainly know how to ruin a har's attempt to entertain his hosts," Halvise observed dryly.

"It's Jan's way to get attention," Sheen remarked, softening the rebuke with a smile.

"You are a better audience by far," Halvise said to Sheen.

"Isn't that the gist of your story, though?" Jansin said. "If there's a huge eerie storm, somehar has to stagger through it. If somehar – or something – knocks on the great sealed door, then it must be opened." Jansin gestured with both hands. "Storm, har, door… What else could happen?"

"Perhaps you should come and find out," said Halvise.

Jansin smiled his enigmatic smile, said nothing, brushed away his hostling's second warning, as if batting at an etheric fly.

"We will show you our estate tomorrow," Sheen said, "won't we Jansin? We have our own interesting stories, you know."

"Yes, of course," Jansin said. "Ah, here is the dessert. I hope you like it, Tiahaar Halvise. Our cook informs us that a Spirit Pudding cannot be hurried. It has been simmering thoughtfully all day, no doubt absorbing spirits."

"Isn't it a bit early in the year for such things?" Halvise said. "A spiced pudding is surely more of a Natalia custom."

"Why would you think that?" Jansin said. "A Spirit Pudding is surely part of the Feast of the Dead. Unless, of course, your own customs are very different."

Halvise shook his head. "Tiahaar, it's fair to say my family, such as it is – only me – has no customs yet. If they had any in the past, they are forgotten. I intend to make some."

"A worthy aim," said Jansin. "Fun, too, I expect. Perhaps I could join in, offer ideas. I too like making things up…"

At that moment, the pudding, in a gigantic bowl, was rolled in on a trolley. It appeared to be a simple custard embellished by berries and autumn flower petals that released a potent scent of cinnamon, cloves and nutmeg. Portions were delivered to the diners in beautifully decorated, deep dishes, which bore images of fruit trees and doves, but there were tricksy faces hiding among the branches.

"Record your dreams tonight, Tiahaar," Jansin said.

Halvise sampled the pudding, enjoying the fierce and unexpected alcoholic punch it delivered. He nodded. "Very good," he said. "I'm sure to dream well after this."

"Who said anything about 'well'?" Sheen said, grinning.

Halvise har Jarice remained at the Anchemant estate for two days. Most of the time he was with the two brothers, exploring the fields and forests, riding over the yawning heathland. Many tales were swapped, much food and wine consumed. During this time, Jansin had to make up his mind about whether Halvise and his property was a prospect he wished to pursue. He had no real objections. If no horrible accident befell his parents, they could be custodians of Anchemant for centuries to come, but here was a chance for him to have his own domain. Halvise was an entertaining, attractive har, and his faults, which he was sure to have, had so far not manifested. Was this a good sign or not? Jansin knew his own faults. He was haughty, disdainful of most hara, sarcastic, sometimes cold, easily bored… yet he was witty, hard-working, imaginative and creative, and was well-liked despite his negative aspects. He knew he had the capacity to love. He just hadn't used it yet. Was there some way simply to turn it on? Maybe that wouldn't matter. If he was to be co-phylarch of the Jarice domain, it was important to be a fair custodian for it, and Halvise was part of that – to be cared for. If this took some strategic acting, then so be it. He would, though, have to examine the Jarice domain first. If it was truly hopeless and run down, beyond reasonable restoration, he'd probably have to pass on the offer, and if his refusal discouraged other local families, maybe Sheen would like it.

On the last day of Halvise's visit, he and Jansin rode out across the fields, where bonfires smoked, consuming seasonal debris. "So," Jansin said, after a comfortable silence, as the horses ambled lazily through the remains of the corn stalks, "do you plan to visit any more families with land before returning home? I can't be the only decent prospect."

"Don't!" Halvise replied. "You make it sound so cold-hearted. I might just as well ask - am I decent enough for you?"

Jansin tore a corn stalk to chew on, grinned seductively. "Is that a proposal already, Tiahaar?"

Halvise laughed, another of his rather spluttering expressions of embarrassed humour. "Let's not stray into that particular field. How did your family come to occupy Maske Abbey and make it so… flourishing?"

Jansin shrugged. "In a dull way, unfortunately. Forget all the spooky tales Sheen has been feeding you. We have no scandals here. Anchemant is the result of a melding of families, two young harlings, chosen in the usual manner to become phylarchs, and a suitable ruin to be lovingly restored to provide a home for a whole community. Once the estate was established and suitably populated, the older hara went back to their homes. Our parents were left to work out for themselves how to bring abundance to these fields and forests. As you can see, they succeeded."

"Good blood, then."

"There's no guarantee…" Jansin shrugged. "What about you? Why go to a ruin that's been neglected for nearly a century? You have harder work ahead of you than my parents ever did."

"Because the old place deserves some love. It's not a pretty domain like Maske but dramatic and wildly beautiful in its own way. You want to hear the story of how it developed before its fall?"

"Of course I do!"

Halvise grinned, falling into storyteller mode, clearly a favourite of his. "A small, vicious phyle originally occupied Ardarra – much like all the other crumbling demesnes in this land. They didn't last long and their riches, if their *acquisitions* can be called that, came primarily from robbery and raiding. It's said Ardarra executions littered the byways of the land for fifty years, until they eventually rotted from their nooses and cages and fell to earth.

"For a while after that, the place was home only to ghosts. The sole survivor of the family, a har named Sabril, had escaped local justice by fleeing across the sea to Thaine, and was there for many years. Nohar back home heard from him, and low-level hara, who lacked all caste training, had gradually slunk in to live in the ruins of Ardarra. There were rumours, of course, of beautiful spirits and horrific monsters that prowled the stairways and ramparts of the Keep. Then, one day, the har who was, for all intents and purposes, phylarch of Ardarra came home. He was not alone, but curiously his companion was not a chesnari. There was no romantic bond between them. But something... something united them. Sabril had become immensely rich and this appeared to derive from... well, *gambling*."

"How traditionally human," Jansin couldn't help interjecting. "Weren't most of the old estates lost through that absurd vice?"

Halvise laughed. "It was a common failing, yes, but for some it was a desperate last hope. Anyway, Sabril wouldn't, or couldn't, be parted from his new friend, who never revealed his name to outsiders. He spoke to nohar but Sabril, and the hara of the estate disliked and mistrusted him, instinctively avoided him. Animals were the same. He was said to be of medium height, with hair like greasy soot and dark skin – but not from any natural colouring. He was... they called it *stained*."

"Dirt or some kind of decoration?"

"It was more than skin deep, He injured himself quite badly in the forest once, and they said that the meat of his body was of no normal colour either. Dark-skinned hara were asked about him but they wanted no kinship with him, made it clear there was no affinity. Hara called him Wicked Jack, at first as a joke, but it stuck.

"After Jack's accident in the forest, things changed. Sabril had been a fair yet distant overseer, but now he withdrew even further from public life. He allowed no visitors and would speak about the running of the estate only to Dovonni, the highest ranking of his staff, who was reputed to once have been a fierce warrior in the early days of conflict. He is mostly irrelevant to this tale, though. As time passed, Sabril appeared to fall out with his mysterious friend. They no longer saw each other at home, meeting only at competitive events of horses and dogs. Sabril's racing dog was reputed to be a type of wolf but he denied that. Eventually the disquieting companion disappeared completely. Everyhar was relieved, believing that now things might return to normal. Sabril did not take up socialising with local hara again, but he did emerge into the light somewhat, like an invalid after a long illness…"

"Is there such a thing among hara?"

Halvise shrugged. "That is merely how hara described it. This was a long time ago."

"And did things remain as they were?"

Halvise laughed. "This is, I think, where myth-making takes over completely – the story you so adeptly intuited. It's said that one night, a great and unnatural storm passed over Ardarra. Dovonni was making his final rounds of the Keep, checking the security of windows and doors, and crossed the Great Hall, where the barred doors stood, before an imposing staircase of ancient wood. Here, Dovonni paused, as he heard the sound of weeping and lamenting through the wailing of the storm. These sounds appeared to emanate from higher in the house. Dovonni realised with horror these sounds must derive from Sabril, as his chamber lay on the first floor beside the stairs, and the phylarch was prone to nightmares during his spasms of depression. Dovonni couldn't think who else it could be. He was about to run up to see what was wrong when a great pounding came at the doors to the Hall. The househar had no wish to discover who or what might be seeking entrance at this late hour, and at a door that was effectively sealed shut, but before he could make a move of any kind, the candles went out, plunging the Hall into wild darkness. The doors flew open with a resounding crash."

Halvise clapped his hands loudly once for effect, leaning over to Jansin's horse to clap right in his face.

Jansin couldn't help but jump in surprise. "Dear gods," he said, somewhat inadequately.

Halvise was clearly in his proper element now. His eyes shone. His arms wove on the air to illustrate his words. "Dovonni felt somehar or something come rushing past him down the stairs, uttering a ragged cry of pure terror," Halvise continued, uttering his own blood chilling scream. Even the horses were getting uneasy now.

"Dovonni stood frozen upon the stairs. There was a sense of violent movement from below, along with the sound of crashing, howls of agony and a foul, *wet*-sounding growling. Whatever occurred below seemed to persist for ever but then, in a second, all fell silent. All was still. Dovonni fell to his knees, dazed."

Halvise lowered his arms gently. "The storm had passed, apparently taking with it whatever had assaulted the house. Or perhaps the attacker had finished its business and had taken the storm away. Other members of staff began to creep into the eerily still Hall, bringing light with them. Dovonni managed to join them at the threshold to peer outside. They found that the doors were indeed ripped open, their debris hanging from what remained of ancient rusty hinges. There was no sign of Sabril or anyhar else and, when hara went to investigate, the phylarch's chamber was empty and yet in proper order. Everyhar decided to wait till morning to investigate outside. Beyond the threshold, the night wind was still too tempestuous to weather on that narrow excuse for a path."

Halvise paused here. He looked pale.

"Why not use another exit?" Jansin asked.

"I don't know," Halvise replied irritably. "It's just a story."

Jansin laughed. "Fine. What did they find in daylight?"

"As I said, this part is clearly a myth, perhaps taken from some older tale. But the story goes that they did find something, namely Sabril's mangled, unrecognisable body, clutching in its left hand, which was remarkably untouched and still wearing its rings, a hank of sooty hair – weirdly damp and greasy like an old sea rope, dripping tar. It left a foul deposit on whoever touched it."

"An astounding tale," Jansin said, realising he felt a little sick and dizzy. Halvise's report of this event was morbidly matter of fact, as if Sabril's identifiers had found only something meaningless, like a spotless piece of cloth. His apparent lack of feeling was somehow abhorrent. "Was that all?" Jansin asked.

Halvise smiled weakly. "That's all. Can I now persuade you to visit or have I put you off entirely?"

"Not at all… I think I *do* have to see this horrifying and wondrous place for myself."

"I'm glad," Halvise responded. "I'm sure you'll send any hostile presences running."

"I'll do my best," Jansin said. He paused, having recovered his equilibrium, then said, "There's a story that, like Sabril, you too have a mysterious companion who is somewhat... *distant* from other hara."

"You must mean my secretary," Halvise said at once. "He's a type who likes to keep to himself."

Jansin nodded, arching his brows meaningfully. "I *see*."

Halvise's mouth dropped open in alarm. "You can't believe that he's in any way connected with Sabril's companion...?"

Jansin laughed. "Your face! No, I believe nothing. After all, if that story was true, and Sabril was the last of your line only to end up no more than a dismembered hand, how could you possibly exist? Unless he had an heir you've not mentioned."

Halvise shook his head. "No... I have relatives in Thaine, a lot of them, but we have never been close."

"And none of them wanted to lay claim to that huge old domain with an immense amount of land?"

"No. They have their own place, which is much more convivial and bounteous."

"Fortunate for you."

"That remains to be seen," Halvise said.

"But what of his parents?" Sheen asked, rolling luxuriously on his brother's bed after Jansin had come in from his ride with Halvise to prepare for dinner. "Weren't they interested in Ardarra either?"

Jansin had related all he could recall of Halvise's tale. "He didn't talk of them. They seem no longer to exist."

"Could he possibly be incepted?" Sheen laughed mischievously. "Maybe he's Sabril, Jan! They only ever found his hand, didn't they?"

Jansin shook his head, grinning, pulling on his evening costume. "He looks too young. You can feel the difference between the incepted and the pureborn."

"Of course, but... why has he come to claim Ardarra now?"

"He said he felt it was time to make a home, do something with the old land. The hara there are what's left of the original warrior troupe and their descendants. But they lack the expertise to tend the fields and develop the property. Halvise wants to assist in their education, develop their skills."

"Sweet Aru, you make it sound so dull."

"Remember, those same hara might have a lot to reveal about their benefactor, should you encounter them outside their phylarch's presence."

Sheen sighed. "Very true. Let's hope he hasn't yet earned their utter loyalty. You must admit there's good reason for you to have suspicions, brother."

"My thoughts too. How intriguing. You'll come with me to Ardarra, of course?"

"Try and stop me."

Jansin was surprised to discover that the Keep of Ardarra was in fact relatively small – a dour black box of stone, comprising five floors, most of which were devoid of furniture. The roof was in disrepair and the home of an angry tribe of unusual black pigeons, who resented harish intrusion.

The rest of the domain swept to west and east in two wings, of a different architecture that was much more elegant and welcoming than that of the dour black Keep. There were dozens of empty rooms in the extensions, but instead of concentrating on them, Halvise had ordered renovations to begin on the staff quarters in the house and the abundance of ramshackle cottages within the domain's walls. It was still well fortified.

Halvise clearly loved the place and Jansin found this endearing. He admired also Halvise's choice of priorities for the work. The staff would remember that. Halvise was already kindling loyalty. Whether an obstacle to his plans were unsafe foundations or a rabble of violent pigeons, they would be handled with equal fairness, being an essential part of the spirit of Ardarra.

During his visit, Jansin decided also to visit Halvise's chamber one night. He did this secretly, so as not to give Halvise any prior warning, seeking to surprise him with his mysterious friend. But when Jansin came in, dressed only in a diaphanous robe and carrying a tall, narrow candle, he found Halvise alone. At first, he seemed almost frightened then melted into the role of thoughtful lover, always mindful of what Jansin might find pleasing.

There was only one other thing to attend to before Jansin made up his mind for sure. There had been no sign of the companion, and Halvise brushed off enquiries about him as if they were unimportant. Jansin was not content with this, but neither did he want to raise suspicion or cause argument.

It required careful wrangling to persuade Halvise to show Sheen his horses and dogs without Jansin being present, and even more wrangling to charm the Domain Manager, Wozren, into taking Jansin for a ride around Ardarra's boundaries, but the brothers managed this without too much trouble. They were adept at getting their own way.

Wozren was a somewhat stern har, who was clearly not a type fond of gossip, but he was all Jansin had to work with. Jansin made some fuss over choosing which horse to ride, suggesting first one, then another and another, until the well-stocked stable had been almost exhausted with his suggestions. Then he hit upon the horse he'd been looking for – a beast that would provide an opening for questions. He expected it must be one of Halvise's favourites, a rich chestnut mare with a hint of fire in her eye, but a generally amiable temperament. "This one," Jansin began his routine again.

Wozren glanced at him sharply, paused in what he was about to say for a moment. "Perhaps not that one, Tiahaar. I don't have the authority to give you permission to ride her."

Jansin fussed the mare's neck, scratched her mane. "Oh, is Halvise that possessive of his prize mares?" he said suggestively.

Wozren's eyes became slits. "Of that, I can't say. But she's not Halvise's mare, in any case. That's Vorsey's mount."

"Vorsey?"

"He's a close friend of Tiahaar Jarice. He lives… among us."

"Oh, I see…" Jansin had noted Wozren's choice of words, the acid that had dripped into his tone.

"I've not met this har," Jansin said.

"Have you not?" Wozren said. He shook his head. "I doubt you will, either."

"Oh, is he leaving?"

"Never that," said Wozren. "He's just not a har who cares for the company of others."

Wozren went quickly into the tack room, clearly to end the conversation, He returned carrying a saddle and bridle. "Let me suggest a mount for you, Tiahaar." He placed the tack on the door of an empty stall. "I'll fetch Cloudstar for you. I can see you like fire in a horse and she's not long broken. Tiahaar Halvise expects great things from her."

"Thank you." Jansin said.

If Wozren gave Jansin Cloudstar to ride in order to keep him quiet and occupied, he succeeded. Cloudstar was in fact far *livelier* than the animals Jansin was used to riding. Neither was this mare a comfortable seat. Realising his chances would be slim, Jansin made use of a break, while Wozren unpacked a lunch he'd brought with him, perhaps now wishing he hadn't.

Jansin took a moment to bask in the landscape. They had stopped on a hilltop overlooking a wide tarn that was teeming with water birds. Around the lake, a forest spread out across softly-undulating hills that displayed every possible shade of bronze, orange and gold in their autumn finery. To the west, the seashore was just about visible. Jansin looked forward to exploring. Ardarra was indeed rich in natural beauty, easy to fall in love with.

Wozren hummed softly to himself as he arranged the lunch on a tablecloth he'd spread on the ground.

They sat down and began to eat, making small talk, but eventually, Jansin said, "Please excuse me, Tiahaar, but I need to be blunt with you."

These words caused Wozren to start at once in surprise, or perhaps dread. He began to stand up, but Jansin gestured for him to remain seated. Wozren sat back down, like an obedient but unhappy dog.

"Forgive me, please, but listen," Jansin said. "I'll not waste words. It's clear hara aren't happy to talk about Halvise's friend, Vorsey. And the... circumstances concerning him are *odd*. You know my position. Please tell me if there's something I should know."

Wozren stared at Jansin for a few moments, then began to nod his head slowly, clearly to communicate with himself rather than Jansin.

"Tiahaar Halvise is a good har," he said. "He has great plans for this old place. Those of us with eyes to see can tell you'd be a good fit, both as phylarch and companion to him. It's the wish of the staff here for you to accept Halvise's proposal. The only objection you'll find is from the *other* one. But we reckon he's no match for you."

"Thank you for your compliments, Tiahaar," Jansin said, realising some intense discussion must've taken place among the staff. "I must ask you something... Given what you've said to me, is Halvise... *weak?*"

Wozren stared at Jansin. "Not that, no. I'm sorry, I've said enough. Be strong. Be true. Be in love, if you can find it within you. Halvise doesn't give a lot out, I know that. But I promise the other one will not best you."

Wozren packed away the remains of the lunch. There were no more words between them, but once all was stored in the saddle bags, Wozren mounted his horse. "I hope I've put your mind at rest somewhat, Tiahaar," he said. "But I trust you're aware of my position too. Now, we must get back." He managed a strained smile. "I have work waiting,"

Jansin remounted also. "Of course... Thank you, Tiahaar."

Wozren allowed a smile. "If you're to come to us, best call me Wozren."

"I will. Thank you again."

Wozren set off at a canter along the forest path.

The bonding ceremony took place at Natalia, as nohar could see any reason to delay. The ritual was held at Ardarra and attended well by hara of the local area who were extremely curious about Halvise and his domain. Vorsey was not present. There was some mumbled nonsense from Halvise that his assistant had urgent business to attend to concerning livestock. Jansin did not argue. This was to be their day, not Vorsey's and in Jansin's opinion would be more enjoyable if Halvise's weird companion wasn't there.

Once Jansin's family had returned home after the ceremony, the weeks passed without any unusual incidents. There was so much work to be done it took up everyhar's time. Exhausted, they'd fall into bed at night almost as soon as they'd eaten their evening meal.

There was still no sign of Vorsey, and Halvise continued to

sidestep enquiries about him.

One evening after dinner, Jansin confronted Halvise about it. "If Vorsey is to remain part of our household, I must meet him," he said, his fraying patience having now fallen to pieces completely.

"I'm sorry," Halvise said. "It's complicated."

"In what way *complicated*?" Jansin's tone was now icy.

Halvise paused, covered his mouth with the fingers of one hand for a moment. "There are things I've not yet told you."

"Then you'll tell me now."

They locked gazes for some seconds, and Jansin felt a wave of deep sorrow pass through him. He sensed that Halvise would not tell him everything and even what he did reveal might not be the truth. Jansin also realised, with even deeper sorrow, that he was beginning to care for this har and might therefore make mistakes over the forthcoming minutes. He must remain strong and impartial. Yet instinctively, he reached out and hugged Halvise, feeling a frailty in the har's bones. Halvise did not respond other than to squirm uncomfortably.

Jansin let him go. "Tell me."

"Vorsey is more than a secretary, but he did not want you to know this yet."

"In what way 'more'?"

"Not what you're thinking. Vorsey lost his family and my parents took him in. We grew up together, as brothers."

So, Halvise did have parents, and they sounded to be decent hara to take in an orphan. Still…

"Why does he not want me to know about him and for how long did he think such a deceit could last?"

Halvise sighed deeply. Perhaps he'd had this conversation before, with somehar else, and knew how it could end. "Please don't take his behaviour personally. He won't meet anyhar new."

Jansin uttered an angry sound. "I don't care. He clearly thinks I'm an idiot therefore implying you're an idiot too. This is not flattering. If he's at Ardarra I will meet him later this evening. It's not up for negotiation. Do you understand?"

"Yes, but *you* don't. Vorsey is damaged and shy. Even if he was here, he wouldn't meet you."

Jansin snorted in derision. "What a grubby situation. So, we have a dilemma. Him or me. How cheap. Abhorrent. Still, make up your mind. I outrank him here."

Halvise's eyes flared with more emotion than Jansin had ever seen in him. "This has nothing to do with rank! How can you be so cold and spiteful?"

"I bonded with you, not your adopted brother. This is now my home. He can no longer just do as he pleases. If his desires come before mine with you, remember I gave up my beloved home to come here – *and* my beloved family. If this is the way things must be, with this weird har creeping around unseen in my house, then please have transport ready to go to Anchemant in an hour. Clearly I made a mistake with you."

Jansin swept away. He noticed now where they were, where they'd wandered as they'd sniped at one another. The Great Hall. The sweeping staircase. He began to walk up it, heard Halvise expel a muffled sound of anguish behind him. He paused.

"You think I want this?" Halvise said in a ragged voice. "I've been gifted with the most wonderful things – being your chesnari, finding another family, revitalising this sorrowful old place. And I'm risking it all because my brother is sick and has nohar else but me."

Jansin turned. "Then send him back to your *other* family."

"That's... that's impossible."

"Are they dead?"

"No but they've suffered enough to know their charity was misplaced."

Jansin was silent for a moment. "You've lost them too, haven't you?" he said softly.

Halvise met Jansin's eyes, nodded. "They think I was... No, I can't speak of it, not yet. Please don't leave me, Jan, but give me time."

"Very well. But I want some of your story later today. By the end of this week, you will introduce me to Vorsey. I shall be understanding, within reason. I won't tolerate tantrums or sullen silence. We shall behave like reasonable adults, custodians of a renowned domain. Is this acceptable to you?"

"Yes."

"Until later, then."

Jansin carried on up the stairs, feeling he was not the first har to have done so under these circumstances. Ardarra was indeed haunted.

Vorsey looked older than Jansin had anticipated. He was not that attractive a har, although his face was sculpted well upon his bones, and he possessed some fairer features in the deep lustre of his eyes and the shape of his lips and jaw. However, his posture was stooped, his wrists stuck bonily from his jacket sleeves, and his hair did indeed look greasy and sooty, as if some hideous concoction was rubbed into it. His skin was dark and of a peculiar shade that Jansin couldn't quite identify. It was neither green nor blue, but certainly not a colour he'd seen before. It also seemed to change in hue as Vorsey's mercurial moods were displayed in his face. From the moment he laid eyes on Vorsey, Jansin could not help but think how much he resembled Sabril's strange companion from the story Halvise had told him.

Some days after the argument, Halvise introduced this individual to Jansin in the empty library. Jansin had made a point of not visiting Halvise's bedroom during the intervening nights, and had made it clear he didn't want a visitor to his room either. This was not punishment exactly, but a warning to indicate Jansin would not allow things to slip back to how they'd been. There must be changes, and if he had to use emotional blackmail to achieve this, so be it. Vorsey must get over his prejudices very quickly or suffer the consequences.

Jansin wondered why Halvise had chosen the library for this interview. It wasn't yet a friendly room. Apart from small oases of decorating materials amid a desert of plaster dust and rubble, there were a few unmatched, upholstered chairs within it, ragged and with stuffing leaking from them, dwarfed by the size of the chamber. Most of the bookshelves were empty. The fire was lit, though, and a mellow winter sunlight streamed in through the tall windows, bringing a sense of what the room could be, one day.

Vorsey was slumped in a chair, his legs stretched out. His chair was placed so his back was to the door. He did not stand up when Jansin came into the room.

Jansin had made an effort with his appearance, aware he'd done so to intimidate this apparent enemy. He held out his hand, spoke in a low sultry tone, "I'm so glad to meet you at last."

Vorsey cast a glance at his brother and stood up. After some moments, he took the offered hand. His own was dry and scaly, which was preferable to damp, Jansin supposed. There was certainly something reptilian about Vorsey.

"Halvise tells me you're responsible for much of his good fortune," Jansin said. He sat down in the nearest empty chair to Vorsey. "It must be such a boon to predict the outcome of a race. Considering all hara are supposed to possess psychic abilities to some degree, you'd think the practice of betting on the relative stamina of animals would have abated, really."

"It is more of an art than that," Halvise said.

Jansin put his head to one side. "Is that so, Vorsey?"

"Yes," Vorsey mumbled.

"Well, in that case, it must be very helpful in respect of restoring this magnificent old house." He turned to Halvise. "We must, of course, invite other members of your family over when more renovations have taken place. It's time for all rifts to be healed."

"No," Vorsey said dully.

"Yes," Jansin said in an airy tone. "I will see to it."

"We'll speak of it," Halvise said. He looked agonised. "Perhaps both families can meet here at one of the festivals later this year."

Jansin decided to release his chesnari from this vile encounter, although he was certain Vorsey would find a way to worm out of the proposed get together. Halvise must have sensed this too but at least had made a reasonable suggestion. "Yes, good idea, Hal." He stood up. "Well, let's keep this brief. Thank you for meeting with me, Vorsey. I appreciate you feel uncomfortable around new faces. I'll be mindful of that and avoid treading on your toes in the house. When you feel ready, perhaps we can go for a ride together, and you can tell me your ideas for the restoration of the estate." He smiled encouragingly at Vorsey.

"Can I go now?" Vorsey asked Halvise.

"Yes," Halvise said, his expression dark.

Vorsey fled the room.

There was a moment's silence, during which Halvise appeared to be recovering from a physical assault. He was unsteady on his feet, dazed.

"I'm sorry I put you through that," Jansin said. "You're right. I know nothing. Vorsey's in a worse mental state than I thought. This meeting must have made him very anxious also. It was selfish of me to demand it."

Halvise nodded slowly. "Well, it had to happen sooner or later."

Jansin went to embrace Halvise, who remained unyielding in his hold. "I think we know there will be difficulties ahead, but we must be united over this. And honest. Vorsey is clearly a very damaged creature, and I'm prepared to put up with that, but there will have to be limits. Perhaps there is somehar who can help him."

"No," Halvise said. "You misunderstand, Jan. Vorsey isn't sick in the way you think. He's different to other hara, not least because his hostling was murdered while Vorsey was still a pearl within him. You can imagine the detrimental effects of that."

Jansin grimaced. "I'd rather not!" he exclaimed in revulsion. "You really should have told me all this sooner, Hal."

"I'm sorry about that. It's not something I find easy to talk about."

"I still think there might be hara out there somewhere who could help. Healers of the Gelaming, for example."

Halvise shook his head. "There's no point even trying. Vorsey would never comply. He'd just vanish. Not even the Gelaming could keep him confined."

Jansin exhaled impatiently through his nose. *We'll see about that,* he thought. "Well, think what you like, Hal, But I can't just leave it. At the very least you must agree to me speaking to my family about it."

"Of course you can. But it will do no good."

"Then at least I will have tried."

Halvise nodded glumly. "You won't believe me until you have evidence for yourself, I can see that."

"Quite."

That night, Jansin went to Halvise and, with the curtains wide open, they took aruna together in the light of the full moon. The fire burned fiercely in the grate and the room was cozy and homely. This was bliss, Jansin thought. Worth fighting for. He ignored any suggestion of shadows across the window, or shapes that seemed to slither across the floor. This was his imagination working too hard. He must learn to look on Vorsey rationally – a mentally ill har, who disliked change of any kind, and wanted his life to remain as it was. But Halvise had a life too. He was not obliged to sacrifice it completely for his brother. Vorsey must learn enough about being a normal har to allow Halvise to live a normal life.

The next night, after a very busy day of physical work, Jansin went to sleep alone in his room. He drifted off almost immediately as he was exhausted, but presently was awoken. It sounded as if somehar was running around the house, up and down the corridor beyond his door. This could only be one har. Sighing, Jansin put on a dressing robe and opened his bedroom door. At once there was silence.

"You need cleverer tricks than that," Jansin said coldly and shut his door.

Once he was back in bed, all was quiet for a while, then the noise started up again. This time, it sounded as if somehar was within the walls of the house itself, scampering behind the panelling. Such a cliché! Jansin resolved to ignore it. If Vorsey should come bursting through the panels wielding a weapon, he'd have to take action but for now he simply put a pillow over his head and presently fell asleep.

The next morning, Jansin checked the walls and found easily a door that opened onto walkways behind the wooden panels of the room. Today, he would see to it that his room was boarded up from potential intrusion. He'd do this himself.

Downstairs, Halvise was just leaving the breakfast room as Jansin entered it. "Sorry to rush off," he said. "There are some deliveries…"

"It's fine," Jansin said. "Once I've eaten, I'll join you."

The staff had left breakfast out for them – other than those whose work required them to remain in the house, everyhar else was already out working on the new cheesery and dairy, which were being housed in buildings attached to the Home Farm – as the large farm built closest to the main house was known. This work had been initiated by the arrival of Ardarra's first herd of cows.

Jansin began to fill a plate with eggs, bacon and toast. "Did you hear the ruckus last night?" he asked in a casual tone.

"Ruckus? What do you mean?" Halvise put on his jacket, began sidling towards the door.

"Somehar – and of course we have to assume it's Vorsey – was galloping up and down the corridors as well as in what appeared to be walkways within the panelling."

Halvise laughed nervously. "Really? Are you sure?"

"Well, you can come and see for yourself. I'd assumed you'd know about these passageways. They must be fairly common in a property like this."

"No, I didn't know about them."

"Doesn't matter. I'll board my room against them today. You might mention to Vorsey I'd prefer him not to behave like a harling, though. I'm sure it's great fun running about trying to scare hara but…"

"Jan, really!" Halvise exclaimed. "Vorsey would do no such thing. I know his failings more than anyhar, but he'd never sink to doing anything like that. You must have imagined it, been half asleep, or it was a bird or some animal…"

Jansin shook his head. He mustn't get angry. His accusation did sound preposterous, after all. "Well, maybe Vorsey can help me look for whatever intruded."

"I'll ask him to look."

"Can't I ask him? Oh wait, no… We have to protect his delicate feelings from the oppression of me asking him to do something. Yes, of course, *you* do it."

"Jan, we mustn't fight…"

Jansin sat down with his breakfast. "You're right. I'm sorry. I'll see to my bedroom walls before joining you."

"Would you like me to help you?"

"No, it won't take long."

"See you later, then."

"Hal…"

Halvise paused at the door. "Yes?"

"Where is Vorsey's private room? He's like a wraith in this house."

Halvise answered at once. "He has a few rooms on the second floor, in the west wing. He prefers the space and and calm away from the bustle of the main house."

Jansin nodded. "Far from our rooms, then."

Halvise risked a smile. "I expect you're happy about that." He came back from the threshold and kissed Jansin on the mouth. "Please call me if you should need help. Gods know what lurks behind all that ancient panelling. And by that, I mean dangers such as loose boarding and rusty nails, not lumbering ghouls."

Jansin laughed. "Don't worry. If I need you, I'll yell. But I doubt anything hiding in there will scare me. We have enough ghouls in the house itself."

Halvise grinned. "Ouch! That's harsh."

Halvise didn't appear angry at this obvious dig at Vorsey. Jansin was reassured by that.

When Jansin went upstairs he placed protections of both physical and magical types around his personal space. If anyhar tried to sneak into his room that way again, they'd get burned, quite painfully. Nothing would satisfy Jansin more than hearing the scamper of feet, followed by an agonised howl. He hoped Vorsey did try to scare him again.

The argument started at around 6 pm that evening. At first, it was merely a mumble of low voices that occasionally rose in cadence. Jansin, sitting in the living room reading a local newspaper, wasn't sure what he was hearing at first. Were there birds in the house? Presently, the voices became louder, yet less understandable. Still, now Jansin could tell for sure that the sounds were harish. He went to the Great Hall and crept halfway up the stairs, straining to listen, to make out what was being said. The sounds were coming from Halvise's room. The room that allegedly had once been Sabril's.

No matter how hard he tried, Jansin could not make out what was being said, other than that Halvise and Vorsey were sniping at each other. Slowly, drawn by the sounds, the staff had begun to gather in the Great Hall, some of them venturing onto the stairs. They stood behind Jansin, staring at him in enquiry. He shook his head, put a finger to his lips to ask for silence.

The argument went on for around ten minutes, but still the words could not be understood. Then, there was a sound of glass or porcelain being broken. After that, a short, stunned silence, then it seemed as if the darkest halls of the underworld had opened. If a poltergeist was at work, it could not have made more noise or caused greater terror. When heavy items hit the door, it bulged outwards unnaturally, in a way wood should not be able to do. There was a sound also that made Jansin think of something running around the picture rail, high up in the room. Scampering, slipping, scratching. The sound was somehow in his head, rather than outside of him.

"What in Aru's name…?" somehar asked in a bewildered voice.

"Have you tried the door, Tiahaar?" Wozren yelled at Jansin, having pushed his way to the front of the crowd.

"Not yet," Jansin said, "although I think we'll have to. Only the dehara know what's going on in there."

"I'll try," Wozren said. He gestured at those behind him. "Keep back, and don't clog our escape route."

Hara shuffled aside to leave a space down the centre of the stairs.

Boldly, Wozren walked up to the door, knocked upon it. This had no effect, no doubt because it couldn't be heard above the row.

"Open it," Jansin said.

Wozren nodded. "Might be difficult," he said. "This door's almost as thick at those to the gorge down there." He jerked his head in the direction of the Hall below.

"Just try."

Shrugging, he opted to attempt the obvious and reached to turn the door handle. To everyhar's utter shock, the door slipped open at once.

Beyond, all was quiet. Utterly still.

When hara ventured into the room, they found Halvise slumped at his desk next to the bed, his head upon his hands, while Vorsey was stretched out in a padded armchair by the fireplace. From the shudder of Halvise's body, he appeared to be weeping, but trying to control himself. Vorsey looked extremely comfortable, purely at ease.

Jansin put a hand briefly upon Halvise's shoulder, squeezed it. "What is going on?" he demanded, speaking to Vorsey, who was smirking.

Halvise merely raised his head then lowered it back into his hands. He expelled a miserable sound, part sob, part growl.

"Wozren, prepare a carriage for me," Vorsey said, his smirk widening into a smug grin. Whatever he'd done or said, he regarded it as a victory. "Now, where shall I go?" He pondered; head thrown back. "Anchemant, perhaps? It's three hours' by the crow's wing, or so I've heard."

"Just get out, you foul beast!" Jansin said in a low, deadly voice. "Get out and never return."

Vorsey leapt from his chair to land right in front of Jansin. He snarled, but Jansin did not even flinch. "You want a physical fight?" Jansin said. "You don't scare me. You're pathetic. Strike me. See where it gets you."

Vorsey spat at the floor. "Are you sure? It might mess up your hair, break a nail."

"Oh, is that what you think? You're stupid as well as insane, then."

Vorsey raised a fist to strike, but the next moment he was glaring up at Jansin from the floor, his lip cut. He didn't retaliate.

"Thought as much," Jansin said. "Escort Tiahaar Vorsey out, Wozren, Take two hara with you."

"I'll drive the carriage, get him far away."

"Don't go alone," Jansin said. "I mean that, Wozren."

"I understand."

"I'll stay here to watch over Halvise. Two of you remain with me."

Vorsey followed Wozren from the room, muttering low insults.

Jansin addressed the rest of the staff. "Carry on with your duties as normal. Make dinner, enjoy your meal. But..." and here he lightened his tone, "...I insist Lician uses his secret cook's keys and breaks out the best cider brandy. Give everyhar a robust measure, Lician. Those of you staying here with me, let's get this room straightened."

"Is he gone for good, Tiahaar?" somehar asked.

"If I have anything to do with it, then yes," Jansin replied.

There was a sense of great triumph and self-congratulation as the hara of Ardarra began to put to rights the damage Vorsey had caused. Some priceless, beautiful items had been smashed, but if their sacrifice helped ensure the removal of Vorsey, it was worth it. The Ardarrans, (as they had begun to refer to themselves), seemed to believe their new phylarchs were invincible. Halvise was kind and fair, but Jansin was strong and fearless: in all, a good combination.

While the tidying continued, Jansin led Halvise from the room, took him to his own chamber. Here, he offered wine. "Tell me what happened," he said.

Halvise sat down on a chair next to the hearth. He appeared stiff, as if his body pained him. "I tried..." He shook his head. "Is it worth *me* trying to do anything? He has power over me. I can't prevent it."

"You can," Jansin said. "You just need to learn how and practice. I'll help you. Everyhar will."

"They'll think I'm weak, useless."

"No, they'll think you're under subtle attack, which is the truth."

Halvise sighed deeply. "All I want is for us to be happy here, have a domain like Anchemant. I want to cut the canker from its heart."

"Then that's exactly what we'll do. Tell me, how much does your income from the races bring to the coffers nowadays? Can you manage without it?"

"Yes. I've been quietly aiming at that for a while, salting money away."

"That's good. So, we don't need to embark upon any endeavours that might arouse suspicions."

Halvise nodded. "What with your family's help and the opening of our own industries, we'll soon be self-sufficient," he said, his voice sounding stronger now. "I don't want to be in debt to Vorsey ever again."

"Have you told him this?" Jansin asked.

Halvise nodded. "Yes, just now. He thought it was hilarious."

Jansin grimaced. "Let him do so for now. He's high on the drama of it all. We must remain calm, act in a measured fashion..." Jansin refilled Halvise's glass.

Halvise nodded once more. "Just tell us all what to do."

"No, Hal," Jansin said. "This trouble belongs to both of us, and to the household in general. We are in this together. We *all* think what to do."

"Vorsey's fury is terrifying. He hardly ever shows it but..." Halvise raised his head. "I think he wants you dead, Jan. I was a fool to think I could simply bring you here and everything would turn out all right. I don't know how to protect you. I've seen his viciousness before..."

"He's gone," Jansin said sharply, "and I'm more than capable of looking after myself."

"He'll *not* be gone... ever."

Jansin shook his head emphatically. "He's made you think that. You must tell yourself – over and over – that this is a lie designed to influence your mind. Now, you must tell me more of the history. I need ammunition, Hal. I need facts. Tell me everything, especially why your parents cast you off. You're obviously keen to repair the relationship, because of the suggestion you made about them coming here."

Halvise sighed. "There was a har..." He rubbed his hands over his face, groaned. "Please bear with me, this won't be easy..."

"In your own time," Jansin said quietly.

"His name was Landry. We'd always been close, but I went away with Vorsey for a year or so, travelling through Thaine, Almagabra, even parts of Jaddayoth, visiting relatives I hardly knew. It was interesting to meet them, but of course the opportunity to pursue such friendships is long gone now."

Halvise winced beneath Jansin's stern raising of a brow.

"All right, it's not lost, but I'll have to work on it. During my travels, and without intending to, I lost touch with my friend back home. It didn't bother me too much, as I'd always felt that when I returned we'd become chesna. My hostling had already found an old property he thought would be good for us. Not too big, but a homestead where I could indulge my love of horses and raise unusual breeds. The future seemed certain. Then the time came for this dream to be realised. Vorsey suggested we go home. I agreed at once...

"The first thing I did when we got back was go to see Landry. This caused a stupendous row between Vorsey and me. To my utter horror, when I left Landry's house, Vorsey was waiting for me within the grounds. He almost leapt on me and yelled so that everyhar could hear. He said Landry wasn't worthy of me, and that the domain my parents had found was for us – him and me – no others. I realised I didn't want that at all. I can't describe what a shock it was to hear him say these things, as there had been no mention of it during our absence from home, never any hint of him wanting to make our friendship an intimate kind. True, he'd become an ever-increasing oppressive presence as our trip went on. I was glad to be home so I could have respite from him, but this... it was totally unexpected. He'd hidden his plans all along."

Halvise left the chair by the hearth and went to lie on the bed on his back, his arms behind his head. "Now the worse part," he said. "I can't bear to say the words but..."

Jansin went to lie beside him, stroked his back. "Speak," he said softly.

"All right..." He took a deep breath. "They said... they said it was an accident. But nohar believed it. There's so much I could tell you, and I will one day, but things turned very bad between Landry and me. Vorsey is adept at manipulating hara, making them doubt themselves and others. I thought he simply sought to drive Landry away, but it was worse than that..."

Halvise paused, rubbed his hands over his face. Jansin remained quiet, sensing Halvise needed him to be. The skin on his chesnari's back felt cold.

"I don't know how he did it. I suppose there was some Garridan narcotic involved... I don't know. All I do know is that one evening Landry and I had a vicious argument. It was over Vorsey, and how I was blinded by him. By that time, I wasn't sure what was real. I was half convinced Vorsey was meant to be my chesnari, and Landry was just a jealous lover who had been rejected. I don't know what happened..."

Halvise swallowed as if his breath burned him on the inside.

"The following morning, I woke up and Landry was dead in my bed. He lay beside me, his limbs twisted, his head turned to the side, so his lifeless eyes stared right at me. He'd been stabbed multiple times and the knife was in my hand..." Halvise swallowed again. The skin around his mouth appeared sallow. Perhaps he would vomit.

"Do you need a bowl?" Jansin asked gently. "You look sick."

"No," Halvise replied. "I'll be fine. It's just..."

"I understand. Start again when you're ready."

For a minute, both hara were silent, then Halvise said, "Nohar had heard a thing. There'd been no cries, no sounds of violence. Yet the moment I saw that horror, I was convinced I'd been responsible. Vorsey's ways must have infected me, made me like him.

"I went downstairs at once, a ghastly sight to present to my household at breakfast. You don't need to hear about what happened in that room, the accusations, the denials, the blame, the confusion. My parents didn't want to believe I'd hurt Landry. Others weren't convinced. I'd changed since I'd been away with Vorsey. I was his now.

"To cut the story short – at least for now – I spent some time in custody with the local judiciary, until eventually it was decided I'd be exiled, along with Vorsey. My family's name was to be protected, as the hara under their protection cared for them passionately. There were many who refused to believe I had anything to do with Landry's death, but the evidence was conclusive. Vorsey had witnesses who had seen him in *The Dark Horse Inn* and could verify he'd been there for the entire night. He'd sat up until nearly dawn, then had gone to bed with a young har who worked at the inn. He was present at breakfast there."

"Hara can be such fools," Jansin said bitterly, but... we were destined to find each other, Hal. Together we can free you."

Halvise nodded glumly. "I want to believe so... Vorsey did it, Jansin. I grew to realise that. He wielded the knife. But there was no proof. If I tried very hard, wracking my brains to remember, it was like trying to look through a keyhole that was a mile long with a faint scene at the end of it, a scene of Vorsey attacking Landry, or me lying senseless next to them. He put the knife into my hand...

"After the murder, Vorsey changed his tactics. He became almost clinging, desperate to hold me close, keep me safe. He did all he could to care for me, to protect me, swore he loved me. He made sure everyhar saw this – how caring he was, how he was sacrificing his life to look after me. Lies! All lies! I knew who really needed looking after. We travelled a lot, made much money with our animals, and eventually Vorsey decided he wanted to develop Ardarra. This seemed a chance for me, however slim. I thought I could manage it – have you as my chesnari and Vorsey as my brother. We'd not been physically close for a long time." Halvise sat up. "Oh, there is no excuse for my stupidity. Now he will destroy all we have." He fixed Jansin with a firm gaze. "You must return to Anchemant, Jan. It's the only sensible course. I won't risk your safety."

"That's not going to happen," Jansin said.

"It must, at least for now."

"No, if he gets me out of here tonight, that's his victory. It mustn't happen. If he won't let go and we need to fight, then we'll fight. I'll not let him win." He smiled reassuringly. "Besides, the staff believe I can best him."

Halvise smiled weakly. "I want to believe that too."

"Then do. It's that simple."

They talked long into the night, Halvise revealing a lot about his childhood and his relationship with Vorsey, much of which was painful to hear.

They fell asleep around 2 a.m. and were awoken around an hour later by the sound of something pounding through the walkways in the walls. The protections Jansin had placed had not held.

Mere seconds later, as Halvise and Jansin emerged from sleep, somehar knocked at the door to announce that Wozren had returned and wanted to speak with them immediately.

Wozren awaited them in the kitchen, perhaps the friendliest room in the house, which clearly was needed at present. He looked wild, shocked.

"What happened?" Jansin demanded.

Wozren shook his head. "I'm not sure you'll believe me."

"Oh, trust me, I will."

"Well, I took the western road towards Darryway, as that was in the opposite direction to Anchemant. Didn't want to take chances about that. Vorsey was in the carriage with Merniot, while Pirrig sat up top with me. We felt on edge, worried Vorsey might go berserk, although I've dealt with that type before.

"Halfway across the heath, we could see the crossroads ahead and somehar – or something – was standing by it. I was in two minds whether to whip the horses and go faster or draw to a halt and see who this individual was.

"'Go faster,' Pirrig said to me.

At that moment, I decided to halt and pulled the carriage up alongside the crossroads. It was Vorsey who waited for us there.

"I was dumbfounded and yelled at Pirrig, 'Check the carriage!'. He leapt down to do so.

Vorsey said to me, 'Slow, aren't you? I can get there faster without you. Go home, Wozren. You'll no doubt see me again soon'.

And with that he turned and ran away up the sloping heath towards the horizon, his coat flapping about him like wings. He ran faster and faster and seemed to disappear before he should have done.

At that moment, Pirrig called to me, 'He's gone, and Merniot's out cold.'

"Thank the gods Merniot was alive. Crossroads are Lachrymide's territory. I know it's not his time of year, but perhaps he was watching out for us. I've no doubt Merniot was supposed to be dead."

"Vorsey's back here already," Halvise said miserably. "We heard him in the walls."

There was a moment's silence, then Jansin said, "Wait for me here. I'll not be long."

"Where are you going?" Halvise asked.

Jansin smiled sweetly, bent to kiss Halvise's head. "To restore my wards upstairs."

"I should come with you.... Don't go alone..."

"Hush. I'll be fine. Back before you know it."

Jansin glided from the room.

In the Great Hall, Jansin lit thick candles. "Come out, cuckoo," he sang softly. "You're there, aren't you? I want to make a deal with you." He stood in silence waiting.

"Cuckoo, cuckoo," he chanted, "feathered in a stolen nest..."

The walls of the Hall shuddered, made a cracking sound.

"Oh, this old place knows you well, doesn't it? Will you not come out, cuckoo?"

Again, the hall shuddered. "You want Halvise?" Jansin asked. He put his head to one side. "You're not answering. What if I told you I want the estate, not the weak fool who inherited it? You're his family's curse, aren't you? I don't care."

There was movement amid a bundle of thick winter coats that

hung upon the wall next to the passageway that led to the domestic quarters. Why hara stored their coats here was something of a mystery since they couldn't leave the Keep except by the kitchen door, or the new main entrance to the east. But perhaps they provided a home... for something.

"Come out," Jansin said, in hardly more than a whisper.

The coats writhed and one from the twisted pile of cloth fell to the floor. Presently, this began to rise, twisting around, until it resolved into a form very like Vorsey, although not completely like him. It was a misshapen shamble of fabric.

"Come here," Jansin said. "I'm sure we have much in common. Let's have this business over with. Does Halvise live or die? If you want him, take him in whatever form you want. I just ask that we share this domain. If you think about it, it will be an arrangement useful for both of us."

The entity, which surely could only be formed of damp filthy fabric, limped its way across the hall. There was the suggestion of a face – shining eyes, a pale jaw.

"He is not *yours*," Vorsey said in a croaking, offended tone.

Jansin shrugged. "I don't care what you think. All I want is a quiet life, to be at one with the land here. I can smooth over any problems for you, but you must come to me first, make the pledge."

Vorsey was no fool. He was an ancient entity with great knowledge and without any trust. "I could simply kill you now," he said. "You know that I can."

"Of course, that's why we're having this conversation."

"Then desist from guarding your thoughts, as that makes me suspicious. I cannot make a pledge with a har of whom I am suspicious."

"Of course not," Jansin said. "I'm afraid it's just habit. I'm sure you're the same. You guard yourself at all times."

"Then drop your guard."

"It is done."

Vorsey sidled closer. "You're a slippery one," he said, edging round the tall har before him. "I wondered what you saw in him. Clearly beneath you. Your family must think Ardarra worth it, and they're right."

"How come? What's so special about this old wreck?"

"Where it's built," Vorsey said. "Ardarra's land is extraordinarily strong, but it's a jealous creature. Needs treating right."

"That much is clear."

"It likes blood."

"And its genius occupies the torrent below," Jansin said.

Vorsey didn't answer this, so Jansin knew he was right.

"There were sacrifices over the years," Jansin said, "until it became too much. An increasing power in the water. Ardarra became dangerous, twisted its occupants. But perhaps it welcomes change now. It's a tired old spirit."

"It does not welcome change…"

"You made yourself part of Ardarra, but you are not the one who dwells in the foam beneath. You are its mite, foraging in its leavings."

"Then what does that make you?"

"This," Jansin said. Moving swiftly, he picked up the can of oil that he'd left earlier at the foot of the stairs. He tipped the contents swiftly over the heaving shape of Vorsey. Then he used a match to light the oil-soaked cloth. It burned swiftly, its voice of flame sounding greedy, but not because the meal was flavoursome. It was merely a way to rid Ardarra of a long-standing internal parasite. The entity itself uttered a high-pitched squeaking of distress

"Spirit of Ardarra, I pledge you my loyalty," Jansin said. "I don't know where that thing came from or how it attached itself to you and the family who are custodians for this site. Perhaps we can talk about that in the future. But for now… we have other business to conclude…"

The remains of the burning cloth lumbered around the hall, shedding sparks and fragments of charred fabric, now emanating a low moaning sound. It was very nearly dead in its present form, and that perhaps was all it ever would be. But never again in control.

"He must pay for all he did," Jansin said, "to all of us. Heal Halvise, your kinshar, good spirit. Make him shed the bad memories of the past. We have new ones to make between us."

The last fragments of Vorsey's earthly vehicle went out in a flatulent puff of smoke.

A whiff of winter roses wafted across the hall. Jansin returned to the kitchen.

"I couldn't tell any of you what I intended to do," Jansin said, having related most of his tale before crossing the threshold, "because then there would be a risk *he* would know. We are free now, and we have freed the true spirit of Ardarra, our friend and protector. Soon, it will tell us its names, its preferences, its history. For now, be aware of its presence as we sit to eat our evening meal." Jansin bowed to the room. "You are ever welcome at our table, kind spirit."

"Jansin..." Halvise breathed.

Jansin smiled upon him. He knew he could never be a hundred percent sure of how much he'd said to Vorsey was true. Did a part of him despise Halvise's weakness? Would it become a problem in the future?

Hara are not made to know these things.

Give them darkness, said the spirit. *Let them make their own light.*

But some light is private and reserved for one alone. There were astounding days ahead, Jansin knew. He and the hara of Ardarra had worked for them. Jansin took Halvise's hand. They would welcome these days as one har.

Fragile Destiny

Daniela Ritter

Eyalah. Your name spills from my lips like an icy brook of pure silver. I picture the brilliant, glittering blueish crystals you had for eyes, which saw so much more than the average har would ever be able to perceive. Your tender, almost fragile body of milky, nearly translucent skin hovered above the ground, or so it seemed, as your steps were as light as newly fallen snowflakes, soundlessly piling up in the crisp winter air.

You looked so beautiful, lying contently in the cold snow, body bare, kept warm only by the powerful magic you wielded. When we took aruna right there, between the summits of the mountains, watched only by ice and rock, it was a most holy communion. We were isolated from the world and all of its inhabitants and formations. A gentle act of true love turning into a roaring grissecon all by itself.

This was the kind of magic we had. We were meant for each other. Each of my vibes enhancing and accelerating yours, and the other way around. You just needed to look at me, and as soon as I could sense a slight part of your energy reaching out for mine, I could heal the most deadly wounds. My touch on your shoulder and you could change the weather itself with a wave of your hand.

We were Nahir Nuri, exceptional hienamas. Each one of us was very talented, but combined we felt as if we could one day equal the Aghama himself.

Tarien and Eyalah. Born on opposite sides of the world, yet inevitably drawn to each other. Rarely anyhar advanced in caste training as quickly as those two had, and more than once their teachers had told them they were meant to fulfil a great destiny one day.

At first they did not know about each other. Yet each one adapted the same nomadic lifestyle, staying with hara just as long as they felt they could learn something from them, and then moving on. They learnt the basics of sewing, carpentry, agriculture and such to support the hara who were kind enough to take them in. While their caste training progressed, they also offered magic as exchange.

Their lives were simple. They did not care for luxury or deep friendships. Their innermost drive to move on made them feel like these were not the things they needed.

The first thing Tarien knew about Eyalah, was a tickling feeling, that came to him whenever he meditated or used mind touch. At first he waved it off as lack of practice, or some unspecific disturbing arcane torrent interfering with his own magic. But the tingling feeling became a steady companion. It occupied his thoughts, his dreams.

Then, after a while, he noticed that whenever he wandered off as usual, going wherever his feet carried him, he unwittingly followed a certain direction. As soon as he had noticed, the tingling became stronger. And when one night he meditated on it, concentrating on it, he noticed that it was *somehar*, not *something*, that occupied his mind.

Interested, he let the sensation wash over him, bathed in it. It was nearly like sharing breath. He experienced the faint idea of somehar's soul, somehar's being. Blue, polished gems falling from an hourglass, producing the most clear, exquisite sound while piling up. White light reflected from and went through them. Although the crystals were blue, they created fractions of shiny rainbows.

Tarien was excited. He instantly knew that he was to meet this har someday. This person was the end of his solitary journey, and maybe the beginning of a journey together.

He was not impatient, for he knew that time was working in his favour and that he would meet the stranger when he was ready. And when the day came, when he had also perfected his ability to travel the otherlanes, he found himself at the shore of the sea. The Girdle of Tiamat glittered blue and clearly in front of him, like the crystals he had come to watch frequently in his meditations. This was the day.

Tarien lifted his arms and shut his eyes, allowing himself to slip into the current of the unseen ways. When he fully came to after his journey on the ethereal paths, he found himself standing opposite another har, waiting at the shore and facing the sea, just like he had done only some moments ago.

In this har's eyes he found the crystals from his dreams, and he knew instantly who he was. The other showed him a shy smile, which told him that he recognized Tarien, too, in quite the same way. In the blink of an eye Tarien, could taste the crystals from the other's lips. They synced with each other, and lay down right where they were standing.

Later Tarien reported, laughing, that he could not even remember if he had been ouana or soume in that moment because the urge to unite with the other had overwhelmed all of his conscious thoughts. The other har had just smiled at him.

Eyalah. This was the name Tarien had kissed from his skin, smelled in his hair and heard in the friction of their uniting bodies.

The solitude had ended.

Both Tarien and Eyalah were amazed how well they fit together. It took no longer than half a day and they could finish each other's sentences. What Tarien lacked in skills of cooking, Eyalah made up, and the other way around when it came to sewing. Even personal visualisations each of them used in meditations were strangely similar.

After discovering this, they were impatient to try out how well they could work together when practicing magic. It nearly ended in a disaster. Thrilled, both of them let go and went with the magical current as they were used to, careless with pure excitement. But with powers fused to one, mended and wielded so easily by each of them, they went way past their limit. Cracks appeared loudly mid-air, threatening and piercing, as if the world around them was a mirror about to shatter. Quick thinking made the hara power down carefully, and the cracks slowly faded.

Shocked and shivering, they hugged each other closely and swore to take time for magical practice. It was the kind of mistake a har only made once. They were damn lucky to survive and knew it.

Promises for keeping an eye on each other for the rest of their lives followed, and when they finally relaxed, they knew that they were chesna now. It did not even feel like a choice. There was just nohar anywhere who would ever share this special connection they had. It was natural.

Smiling, they took aruna once more, carefully this time, maybe like the first-time hara did.

Tarien and Eyalah continued their former lifestyle together. They went where they felt they were needed, and indeed they could always help with tasks which the local hara could not fulfil on their own, both in magic and craftsmanship. And they kept studying and practising.

They became the travelling hienamas quite a lot of hara heard about, never bragging with their abilities, but doing and learning what they needed and then disappearing again. It was impossible to find them, especially when they started travelling the otherlanes regularly on their journeys. Tarien and Eyalah would never meddle with harish affairs for too long, anyway. They were happy hermits, each other being the most important thing in their lives.

When they needed an even longer break from other hara, they retreated to the mountains. Any mountains. They loved the cold and the isolation they provided. Thermokinesis kept them from freezing and left only the pleasant aspects of walks in the snow.

On one of these walks they found a lost cabin by a neglected track in central Almagabra. They instantly fell in love with it and since then put a lot of work into getting it back in shape. They knew that sooner or later they would need to spend a lot of time in solitude to meditate and further concentrate on their magical practice. Not that they needed any excuse for some time alone, but this time they intended to work especially hard.

The higher the caste, the more difficult it is to find and break one's own limits. Still, each of them knew that if it was even possible to grow in power, each of them had the perfect words, thoughts and magical tools to help the other. Even if they didn't know – yet – what exactly that would take.

"And done!" Eyalah smiled.

Tarien shook his head. "Tell me again, why did you insist on putting up drapes in front of the windows? It's not that anyhar ever comes here and watches us from the outside!"

Eyalah crossed his arms. "We might need to get it dark in here in the middle of the day for a meditation. You never know. And since when do you question my impulses?"

Tarien laughed. "I love your impulses, and you know that. It just occurred to me for a moment that you look so satisfied with building a long-time home. I never took you for the type."

Blinking, Eyalah glanced at the curtains and then at his chesnari. "I see. But I guess this is not settling down. Something very important is to happen here, and I don't want to be distracted just because something isn't perfect."

"You are perfect. And that is the only thing that counts," Tarien insisted and shared breath. "Let's have a drink, shall we?"

Smiling, he fetched the teapot he had prepared from the little stove and filled two cups. While his eyes were focused on the cups, his thoughts began to wander and stumbled over a question. "Do you ever wonder why we do this?" he asked quietly.

"Do what?" Eyalah replied, confused.

Tarien made a careful sweep with his arm, trying not to spill tea, before handing the cup to his chesnari. "All of this. Our whole lives long we did nothing but study and become stronger. What for?"

"Destiny?" Eyalah offered.

Tarien snorted. "That's a little weak for an answer. I mean, if we keep on thinking we're destined to do something great one day – are we really led by the dehara to become an important tool, or are we just being arrogant?"

On this, Eyalah pondered for a while, sipping carefully from the cup. "We help a lot of hara, though."

"Yes, we do," Tarien sighed. "Still, we keep on practicing and practicing like we want to reach a level at which we could have destroyed Fulminir by clapping our hands. Do we really need to be that powerful?"

Eyalah shrugged. "What would you rather do with your life?"

Grudgingly Tarien looked down into his cup. "I have no answer to that. And that bothers me."

They sat in silence for a while.

"You know," Eyalah finally spoke. "It is said that when you advance spiritually, you become less and less attached to your body. I like to think of it as a new plane of existence we can access. Imagine how would feel if we took aruna and our souls mingled, but longer and more intense than we know it. We would be one, more than ever before." He smiled slightly. "I would like that very much."

Seeing that smile, Tarien could not do anything but return it. "I would like that very much, too."

Having finished their tea, they went out for a walk. The crisp, fresh air made the dark thoughts in Tarien's head fade at once. Smiling, he watched as Eyalah pranced down the track in front of him, spirits lifted by the snow.

He was very lucky, Tarien thought. He had found his one true soul mate, and nothing could come between them. Was this not good enough a reason to appreciate life? He felt silly, worrying about a deeper meaning of their lives. Life was good, here and now.

BAM!

A snowball hit Tarien right on the nose. Apparently, he made a face so dumb that Eyalah couldn't stop laughing.

And a moment later, Tarien laughed, too. "Oh, just you wait!" he threatened playfully, picking up snow himself.

"Come get me!" Eyalah beckoned, hurrying some steps backwards.

And then, suddenly, Eleyah's foot wouldn't move the way he had expected it to. He fell, just like the snowball from Tarien's hand had done. When it hit his own foot, the cold, white sphere burst into a thousand pieces.

I could do nothing but watch you fall. From the look on your face, you were just as surprised. You had never been the clumsy type, but then, you could not possibly have seen the rock beneath the snow. There were a lot of rocks there. We had not known, since we had never seen the landscape in warmer seasons.

Many thoughts rushed through my head – some of them awfully trivial – in these split seconds, which seemed like hours to me. I would not be able to be with you in time to catch you, not even travelling the otherlanes. Why did you have to hurry backwards, when every harling learns, that this is dangerous? Was there a hidden crevasse behind you? If there was, was it the reason, why nohar ever came here, because so many had fallen in deep to meet death? Or would you just be welcomed by soft snow, making a snow angel afterwards? Would you hit your head?

I had barely noticed my hands moving, but I felt the warm tingling between my fingers. My subconsciousness was ready, eager to do something.

My elbows pulled back, gaining momentum. I had no straight thought about what I was going to do.

You hit the ground. Too late to make a magical attempt to catch you. But it was even worse: Your neck hit another damn, pointy rock. I heard a harrowing crack, making me panic.

My hands slashed forward, all my thoughts poured into one intention: Don't you dare leave your body, yet!

I felt magic discharge from my fingertips and froze in that very pose. My whole body shook — not from the cold, but from the horror. Despite my desperate attempt to keep you, you did not move.

Not daring to think about any consequences from the former incident, Tarien carefully ventured forward to pick up Eyalah's limp body — his chesnari showed no reaction at all. Tarien had to force himself not to think. The pain lingering at the back of his mind was just unbearable. Absent-mindedness was better than horror.

Sternly, he carried Eyalah back into the cabin, put him down on the nest of blankets they used as a bed and carefully locked the door. Then he sat down beside him, hands folded in his lap, just staring.

Eyalah lay still, his eyes empty. What was even worse, was that his head lay in a most unnatural angle to his body, as he now realised. Tarien shivered again.

"Oh, come on," he whispered. "That was not enough to ki... kind of... make you too uncomfortable." Determined not to accept it, he strictly banned the possibility of his lover's death from his mind. Instead, he took Eyalah's head carefully into his hands and placed it in a more natural position. Like one would do with an unconscious person, he stretched the neck in a way that would avoid the loose tongue blocking the air ways. He felt slight vibrations in his fingertips doing so, but not of the magical kind. In the silence of the cabin Tarien imagined, that he could hear lose bones grinding on each other.

No denial in that, Eyalah's neck was broken. Tarien giggled nervously, ignoring the blood that had stained his fingers now, coming from the wound. "Well, if that's all what is wrong... Would be ridiculous if I couldn't fix that, wouldn't it?"

Of course, there was no answer. As desperate anger overwhelmed him, Tarien slapped his hand onto Eyalah's chest. "Oh, come on! Breathe now, will you? Breathe! Breathe!"

Concentrated on this one thought, he let a powerful surge of agmara flow down his arm. And indeed, there suddenly was a faint hissing between Eyalah's lips.

Tarien sighed in relief. "Thank you, Devourer and Creator, for not taking him, yet!" he exclaimed, turning his face upwards for the moment, as to speak to the dehar Aruhani directly. Satisfied, he watched Eyalah's chest softly tilting up and down for a while. Still, when he checked his face, his chesnari's eyes were as empty as before.

Grudgingly, Tarien felt for his pulse. Nothing. "Silly me," he chuckled hoarsely and placed his hand on Eyalah's chest again, extending his higher senses. "Where are you..? There. Beat, heart... beat!" He let lose another wave of agmara, which was answered by an almost unnoticeable pounding.

Tarien nodded, but then looked up and down Eyalah's body. "This means, I have to re-activate every single function, right...? Phew... Agave, stand by me... I better get going!"

When he turned from his Chesnari to gather his notebook, his pen and some snacks in order to work out a plan, he did not realise that the vital functions he had forced upon Eyalah's body had already seized.

During the next few hours Tarien focused on creating a plan, in which order he would have to work on Eyalah's organs to get his body to function normally. He scribbled frantically into his notebook, combining all the knowledge about simple biology and metaphysical energies he ever heard about.

Whenever he was stuck, he would vanish into the otherlanes and show up someplace else, where it was currently night. He quickly "borrowed" books without the owner's knowledge and piled them up on his table in the mountain cabin.

Sometimes, when he was pondering on something, he would tend to Eyalah's body mechanically, cleaning him up or rearranging his pose into something more lively, while ignoring the red and violet stains which meanwhile covered his chesnari's back. His determination kept him from seeing what the signs strongly suggested.

Poor Eyalah. I'm sorry. The blanket was too thin, right? You are all cold and stiff. Come here, I will take a break and warm you.

Tarien lay in the dark, staring up the ceiling, holding his chesnari's dead body close. "Don't worry... I will fix you, dear. I will fix you. Just you wait." The whispered words were unnaturally loud, echoing strangely from the wooden walls of the cabin. Anxiously, Tarien shivered. "You are still in there, aren't you?"

He closed his eyes for a moment and felt for Eyalah's aura, looking for the slightest sign of life.

Satisfied, his lips curled into a smile. "There you are..."

It was faint, but there definitely was the echo of blue crystals clicking against each other. Tarien was convinced: Eyalah was not gone yet.

A little while later, when he decided, that Eyalah was warm enough for now, the first thing Tarien did was administer a treatment with healing agmara. The usual response, like the feeling that the energy offered was absorbed by the body, was missing. But Tarien dismissed the fact, convinced that the cells had simply soaked up an almost unnoticeable amount which he could not make out this time. He also tried to get the heart beating and the lungs breathing again, but this time it did not work.

"Wrong sequence, silly," he moaned. "Better work on the correct one and form it into a ritual." So he took up his scribbling again.

Once in a while, impulses forced him to pause writing and get different paraphernalia instead. That was something to hang on to. Solid things, promising success of his ambitious mission. Progress visible for the mundane eye. Signs that he was actually working towards his goal.

One of the first things he gathered was strong incense, which spread its enticing smell from a corner near Eyalah. The smell was to please his chesnari, of course. Solely for that purpose.

After Tarien had gathered everything he felt he needed to get, he compared his equipment with the list he had made and finally nodded, confirming his own actions.

Then the real preparations began. He started chanting, lit the first candle in his hand and called out for the energy from the centre of creation, eager to finally revive Eyalah.

There, my love. I got it. See? All the candles around here? The signs and sigils I drew around you with white chalk? Do you smell the special incense? I will

91

*call upon the dehara now, beg for their guidance and assistance. I know it's
hard, but... help me, okay? Give me whatever you can. I need your energy,
every tiny bit. We can do this, together! As always!*

*Ah, there you go. Your muscles are not stiff any more. You want to live.
That's what it means. Relax. I will perform the most powerful majhahn
Wraeththukind knows. I know you couldn't say "no" right now, but... it's me.
You know me. Technically, it's not pelki. This is an act of love. I love you.
And I know you love me.*

Relax now. Relax and follow my voice, my body.

The discharge of energy, both magical and corporeal, was so intense,
that Tarien was on the verge of unconsciousness. All of his mind had
been focused on faint blue crystals, filling them with colour, making
them hard and solid, making them shine with bright radiance.

Bright greenish light coming from everywhere nearly blinded him,
though he could not tell if his physical or metaphysical eyes saw it.

He felt that the body beneath him was warm, hot even, every last
cell filled to the brim with the energy forced upon it.

Still gasping for air, Tarien excitedly held his breath, so that he
could listen if Eyalah finally responded. He kept own lungs from
working for so long that his vision blackened. Unwillingly, he
collapsed onto his chesnari and drew in air again but took the
opportunity to listen for a heartbeat inside the beloved chest.

None was to be heard.

Tarien angrily clenched his teeth. There must have been a mistake
at some point! Somewhere in all his calculations had been a mistake.
There was no other explanation why it had not worked. Tarien
carefully retracted from his lover, getting up with shaky legs.

Frustrated, he covered Eyalah with the blanket again and got
dressed. Carefully he checked the room. All candles were lit, he had
not forgotten a single one. They were the right colour and size and
put everywhere where he had planned them to be. The symbols on
the floor were complete, no line was blurred. The incense had been
the correct one and was still burning.

He had even felt Eyalah's energy, he was absolutely sure about
that. He had been participating?

So what had been the Aghama-damned mistake?

With a cry of pure desperation Tarien kicked the candle closest to him. Wax splashed everywhere, but at least the movement was enough to smother the flame.

Why, damn, why did bloody death reach out for Eyalah so persistently?

Tarien blinked slowly, as the answer came to him. No! How could he have overlooked?

Disappearing into the otherlanes, Tarien visited hundreds of places, with sickening speed, and checked his assumption. There it was. Calendars and festival preparations, which told him the exact date. The worst possible day for trying to conjure up life.

Shadetide.

Now that his attention was drawn to the fact, he felt the slight undercurrent in the energies. And it was getting stronger, for back in the cabin, the sun was setting.

Out of options, Tarien dropped onto the floor and pulled Eyalah up onto his lap, holding him close. "You are not getting him, Lachrymide. The gate to the spirit world is wide open, and you have plenty of other souls to collect. Don't be so greedy! And if you still want him, you will have to take me, too!"

Tarien growled the words with a low voice. It was the first time he ever had been disrespectful to a dehar. Surely, he could try to take Eyalah with him through the otherlanes, to a place where Shadetide night already was over. But he was not entirely sure his chesnari was stable enough for such a journey. So he could do nothing but hold vigil and fight, if he must.

Hours of dreadful waiting followed. Tarien's mind was blank. It was not the peaceful blankness which facilitated meditation, but the moment when one comes to a certain stillness, chained to the very moment, unable to go back in time and reluctant to face the future. He was faltering, knowing he had to move on eventually, rather sooner than later.

Still he could not let go. He would not. He would never! A future without Eyalah was no option.

Then it suddenly came to him: Maybe he could work out a ritual to rewind time? That would be the most challenging venture he had ever undertaken, but if he could not do it, who else could?

Well, Eyalah would certainly be able to do it. And as his lover was not dead or something like that, he could certainly help on some spiritual plain. Then Tarien could go back in time and prevent him from falling. They would go back to the cabin and have a good, relieved laugh about what a grim future they had evaded together. And then...

As Tarien's eyes were scanning the room for potential threats, they came to a sudden stop. The curtains. The silly curtains Eyalah had put up were moving in a non-existent breeze. A bright light fell through the windows behind them, painting a dark harish silhouette onto the swaying canvas.

Tarien held his breath, chilled to the bone. Never before had a dehar manifested before him. He could well imagine Lachrymide being angry enough to do so, now. Although he was usually a compassionate dehar, surely cursing at him would have changed his mood? Tarien imagined dark red hair behind the veil, which was the curtains, and a round belly heavy with a pearl he himself might never have the chance to create with his chesnari. The whole appearance was mocking him.

"Get lost..." Tarien had meant to sound threatening, but his voice was weak and trembling. He knew he could not fight this, not without Eyalah at his full powers and awake by his side. He would go down now, but at least he would go down fighting.

When he slowly raised his arm, it felt unbelievably heavy, and Tarien realised just how tired he was. There went his last chance for victory. He could not even think straight anymore and had no idea what kind of spell he would throw at Lachrymide once the dehar ventured forward to collect Eyalah's soul.

He did not want to give up, but in the end he secretly hoped that it would at least be over quickly.

Suddenly the curtains were flung apart. Tarien flinched and hugged Eyalah's body hard. He instinctively turned his head away, but nothing happened. When he finally dared looking back to the window, his blood went cold.

It was not Lachrymide. Kissed by the unnaturally bright moonlight and naked in all of his beauty, Eyalah was looking at him. His eyes were incredibly sad, his whole body transparent and ethereal, like a fading memory.

Tarien held his breath. His fingertips pressed against the body in his arms. It was still there, so how could there be two Eyalahs? But even as his heart wanted to play dumb, his mind knew the answer.

"You're... you're dead, aren't you?" he whispered.

To his confusion, the spectral Eyalah shook his head and pointed to the limp body that mirrored him.

At first, Tarien did not know what to make of this, which made Eyalah smile. He seemed to concentrate on something. Tarien did not hear his chesnari's voice, but his own. Words uttered in his mind, at a time which already seemed so long ago.

Don't you dare leave your body, yet!

As the realisation hit him, Tarien dropped the body, staring at the real Eyalah in shock. "I..." he croaked. "I trapped you inside your dead body?"

Eyalah slowly nodded, looking him directly into his eyes. It was clear that he was not pleased with the situation.

Tarien hugged himself, trying to gain some comfort. "And... there's nothing I can do to get you back to life, is there? You want to come back, but you just can't! You can't even move on, because you're stuck. And as much as you wish to be back with me..."

He stopped himself. Eyalah did not seem to agree with what he said, but looked out of the window, longingly. Then Tarien heard Eyalah's voice in his head. Again, it was words he knew from before.

It is said that when you advance spiritually, you become less and less attached to your body. I like to think of it as a new plane of existence we get access to.

It made sense. How could one be any less attached to his own body than when being dead?

"So, no going back for you." Tarien sighed quietly. "You are happy with the situation – if... you are set free, that is."

Eyalah turned his head and gave him a look of disgust, further bringing up sentences spoken before.

Imagine how it would feel if we took aruna and our souls mingled, but longer and more intense than we know it. We would be one, more than ever before. I would like that very much.

Tarien sobbed. "You're not happy without me..." Eyalah smiled, and his whole appearance seemed to glitter with silvery sparkles.

Wondering what to do now, Tarien came up with another option he had not thought about until that moment. "Well, then... Can't you be reborn or something? I'll wait for you to grow up and then..."

Eyalah chuckled, without making a sound.

Tarien did not need words, the answer came to him. He sighed. "Even if you came back, you would become somehar different. It'd be a whole new life, right? We still would not be... us."

Nodding a confirmation, Eyalah tapped the window behind him silently.

This is not settling down. Something is not perfect. Come, get me!

And again:

We would be one, more than ever before.

Tarien took a deep breath, trying to make sense of what Eyalah was telling him. Slowly, an idea took form in his thoughts. "It was not an accident, was it? Not really. It was destiny. You were meant to die. To get rid of your body for good. We always followed our instincts where to go and were led to where hara needed us. And now... We... we are needed elsewhere, where we can't take our bodies with us!"

Eyalah soundlessly clapped his hands and smiled. Tarien noticed that he seemed tired all of a sudden. Also, his colours seemed to fade. Communicating had become very tiresome for him, even on the eve when the door to the spirit realm stood wide open.

Tarien did not think twice. He closed his eyes and adeptly fell into deep meditation. Opening his inner eyes, he visualised himself rising from his body and stepping towards Eyalah. His chesnari's eyes lit up with excitement, only a little confused when Tarien turned his back to him.

"Hold on tight now," Tarien ordered. "I don't want to be separated from you again." Eyalah clasped his arms around his chesnari's waist, hugging him strongly. Tarien could almost feel a *physically* warm chest pressed against his back.

He turned his eyes to where his mundane body still sat meditating. From where the heart was, a silver thread hung in the air, connecting to his spectral form's chest. With Eyalah it was the same, only that his body seemed darker now, dyed in a sick blue. Also the silver thread was rather a thick steel chain, which surely would not be broken easily. The sight of this made Tarien a little nauseous.

Still, whatever he had created, he was sure he could undo. By sheer will he conjured up a silvery pair of scissors in his hand. He took both the chain and the thread in his other hand. Allowing no doubts whether it would work, he determinedly cut the two lines.

At once scissors and lines disappeared, and the weight of worlds seemed to be lifted from his shoulders. He cumbersomely turned around in Eyalah's embrace to face his chesnari and smiled. "Better now?"

"Much better," Eyalah cheered, welcoming Tarien's arms around his shoulders. Communicating was much easier now.

"So... where to? Shall we wait until we are... picked up by somehar or something?" Tarien was at a loss with the situation, for he felt no draft into any special direction at the moment: but felt happier than he had ever been.

"I think we should go there," Eyalah nodded towards the window, which was no window anymore but a huge glowing opening, glittering in a million colours.

Tarien took a look around. The room was much darker now, and he could not see clearly. He mused that the slumped heap he could barely make out were their lifeless bodies, now cast off and unimportant. He did not even care. The only thing he could see well was what seemed to a portal.

"Where does it go?" he asked. He felt Eyalah's spectral body stiffen with excitement.

"I think it leads to Samuntala." Tarien gasped. The Aghama's realm, vast and colourful, where every dehar ever made up had his place.

"And... what do we do there?"

"What we have always been doing, silly," Eyalah laughed. "Learn and serve. I think somewhere in there is a dehar to whom we can offer our services."

"Seeing wonders no mortal eyes, not even harish ones, could ever perceive," Tarien concluded, struck with awe.

"I would like that very much," Eyalah whispered.

"I would like that very much, too," Tarien answered silently.

The cabin was left empty. Nohar ever rediscovered the site, because what happened there never became important for anyhar else. Nohar ever learned the fate of the travelling hienamas.

Four years after the incident, a snow slide claimed the cabin, burying the bones inside forever. Quite a few important books on healing magic were lost.

Living Stories, Living Bones

E. S. Wynn

It was Dalst who taught me how to tease the stories out of bones. Human bones. Human stories, but sometimes the bone-stories of other beasts as well. Cats, cattle, raccoons, but never hara, never our own.

And never the living.

Living stories from living bones– I had to learn that myself. I had to teach myself in an instant under the barrel of a gun in order to save him. I had to break our one unspoken rule to keep the hara holding him at gunpoint from pulling the trigger. I had to learn the stories, the strongest stories of an alien, violent mind, and I had to speak them to save myself, to save Dalst, to save us all.

There is a cavern under the old human city beyond the woods that is full of bones. Dalst was the one who found it, the one who showed it to me. The stories there are rich and varied, lives full of kisses and playful laughter. Shallow flickers of joy rise in pastel hues at the back of my mind whenever I touch those bones, those fragments of lives that were lived when the city was lit up and humming, when the skyscrapers and houses still had their skins of glass and tin. Only the bones remain now, the iron girders, the concrete, the bent edges of rusty rebar, but once, the city was alive. Once, the city was more than just stories and bones.

Every story in every skull in that cave ends in tears. It's addicting, feeling them, feeling the memories pulse through the dead remnants of so many. With control, with practice, you can tease out the colorful images, tease out the joy, but the mind always tends to wander inexorably toward death, toward the ever-present questions of why and how it happened. What made these bones? Fear. Fear made these bones. Fear, greed and a blind hatred of something not fully understood. Every skull in the cave tells an ending story of fear and violence, of execution, disposal. Hundreds of humans suspected of being hara, of being infected by some kind of terrifying virus before it was really understood what the change was, how it happened, how it moved through the blood of the blessed. Men and women, humans rounded up by humans, executed openly, and yet none of them were hara. None of them were incepted. Sifting through the bone stories, it almost seems like an excuse, like those doing the killing only wanted a reason to execute so many and bury them so quickly. None of those who did the killing are among the dead. None of their stories remain, only the mystery, only the speculation.

Every death carries the same patterns. I see the fear in the eyes of parents and children when they die. I see the red and blue lights flashing through the wet night, hear the loud clack of rifles readied for dispensing death. I see the tears in the eyes of lovers as they hold hands for one final time, as they sob into brick walls, knowing nothing will save them. The lucky ones are given blindfolds before they die. Some plead, some beg, offer their belongings, their bodies. Nothing changes. Nothing stops the bullets.

I think about the stories, about the cave, that mass human grave beneath the old human city, when Ghent and his savage hara set fire to our village. The fire moves through the night like the lights of the human animals who slew their own in such unbelievable numbers and so quickly. Hara are seized in doorways, in shadows by snarling, beastly bandits Ghent has stirred into savage action with stories of slaughter and promises of pelki. I grab Dalst when it happens, grab one of our harvesting hand scythes that are sharp, so sharp, and try to shout out a plan in fragments.

It doesn't come, doesn't form, doesn't last past the first of Ghent's hellions bashing through our front door. The raider's rifle barks, chewing holes in walls, screaming wide of the mark. I swing the scythe so desperately that I lose it in his chest. Dalst is blind, stumbling in the fog of shock. I reach for him, seize his wrist. He drops his own hand scythe as I jerk him through the shattered door, drag him into the night, wide-eyed and desperate to escape, to survive. Neither of us look back. The night is chaos. The only sane way is out, out to the woods, to the broken city beyond.

We don't make it. We stray into the rutted road, rush past two ramshackle houses wreathed in searing flame, and then a shadow flies out of the night, hits Dalst so hard I lose my grip on him, lose him in the flickering, the murkiness of the roadside. I shout, something feral stirring in my chest, but suddenly there is a sharp set of teeth before me, brilliant and vicious in the firelight.

I stop. I don't want to, but it happens. The mind behind those teeth is heavy, oppressive, reaches out through the night to wrap itself around me, around my thoughts like a massive, unfeeling fist. In the time it takes me to fight past it, to free myself from that forced stupor, there's a gun in my face. Cold and black, like the guns from the stories in the bones. Icy, bestial, *human*. The muzzle of another gun in another cruel pair of hands, which lifts Dalst by the chin as if sniffing at his neck, hunting the jugular.

"Tepai," Dalst whispers my name. His eyes are yellow in the firelight, swiveling to meet mine. He knows. He knows what I'm thinking. He knows the desperation born out of love, and what it can drive a har to do. I want to throw myself at our captors. I want to bear them both to the ground with a single rush and tear them into ragged dashes of bleeding meat – and love almost convinces me I can do it without being shot, without being spread across the rutted road before my nails can even scratch ragged fabric. Dalst knows, he understands, but he has always had a clearer, calmer head than I.

"You two," one of the hara says, and I can tell from the way the others hunch and cower around him that he is their leader, the one who stirs the whole pack into action. "You're *a thing*, aren't you? Lovers?"

I glare back, say nothing. In the firelight, I see that grin again, that damned sharp grin, and I see the echo of that grin on the face of the har holding Dalst.

"I like breaking lovers," he says, grimy hands seizing my chin, crawling up my face to nest in my hair, dragging trails of mud and blood with them as they go. "They suffer louder and longer. There's more crying, more screaming, more desperation."

"Let us go," Dalst tries, the words so soft, not pleading or angry.

"Never," the leader of the pack says, pushing me over into the mud. "Take them both to the cages. I want these two for my personal entertainment."

I try to shout, try to scream, but a rough-gloved hand shoves my face into the mud until I stop fighting, until I go limp, and just let them drag me by an ankle into the darkness. Dalst disappears into shadow, dragged along a different route, but his eyes stay with me, in my mind. Strangely calm, strangely resigned.

The fires rage all through the night. Dalst and I are locked in separate cages of welded rebar and chicken wire, but no one else comes. There are no other cages, and no one arrives to rescue us or torment us. I can barely keep my eyes open when the dawn comes, and I end up collapsing against the bars of my cage, naked and weeping, cold hand vainly reaching for Dalst.

Only when the cages are lifted on litters like sedan chairs do I wake. All around us, wicked hara grin and pick their teeth. Every one of them is caked in drying blood, in soot and dirt. I try to stand in the short cage, start to rail and howl, but one look from the leader of the pack puts a gun in Dalst's face. I get the message without even the need for words. I stop, unwilling to put my lover's life in danger. Dalst's eyes are watery, and he rests against the bars of the cage like a tired warrior at the end of his final battle, like he's given up hope. Like he's ready to die. I stare at him with a singular intensity, wonder desperately what he is feeling, why he isn't fighting as relentlessly as I am. At some point, he glances at me, and it's all I can do not to throw myself at the wall of the cage again. I wrap my hand around one of the bars and whisper his name. When he looks away again, I snort, almost growl, feel suddenly as bestial as the hara carrying the cages around us. The gun, more than the cage, keeps me contained.

I pick up snatches of conversation as we are carried toward our doom. I learn names, hunt for weaknesses, but the raiders carrying us seem cohesive, trusting of one another, and totally subservient to their leader, to the crimson-maned, tattoo-covered har who calls himself Ghent. Briefly, I wonder how much of their loyalty is mind-play, how much of it is reinforced through trickery and charms like the oppressive fist of muddying thought with which Ghent had stunned me when first I faced him. The whole tribe of raiders might be subtly under his control, willingly or otherwise.

The journey is slow and long. I try to keep my mind busy with memories, with stories I can recall that came from Dalst's cave full of bones. It takes the edge from dire, cruel reality, remembering animal moments, animal lives. The soft touches of cats, their flickering loves, their lazy days spent in furry knots, in colonies beneath the ruins. Happy memories of hunting, of mice they stalked through the shadows of silent concrete. Birds, beautiful to behold, and even more beautiful in the eyes of a hunting feline. Their songs are crisp on the ears, their wings bold and brilliant, so desirable, yet so out of reach.

The remembered longing of lost cats draws my mind back to Dalst, back to my beautiful unreachable love. His hair lies soft on the floor of the cage, cascades down through pale fingers, and his eyes are closed, turned within. The memories of the bones – surely, he must also be indulging in those moments of stolen happiness.

The sun has nearly reached its zenith when a cluster of tents rises before us from the sandy shore of a wide and rippling lake. Crude, and painted with ocher or blood, the hides of the tents look odd, look less like the hides of deer or cattle and more like the hides of hara. The biggest tent is smeared with strange symbols, with bestial images, with snarling bears and gutted bulls. When our group comes to a stop, Ghent goes in among the tents and beats on their sides, barks words I cannot understand, words that sound jagged and hateful. One by one, the tents empty out, and a line of pale, emaciated hara assembles before the great tent, some of them bruised, others scratching, nervous. None of them look directly at Ghent.

"The pots are cold," Ghent snarls. "Not a single fire is lit to welcome our return!" He stalks up and down the line of hara like a lion, his fists clenching and unclenching. There's so much rage within him, so much fire and hate that it distracts me for a moment, and I find myself wondering what his stories are, what his bones might reveal if I had them in my hands.

"We come back from a raid with meat, and the only celebration we find is this cold silence!"

Somehar opens his mouth to speak, but Ghent hits him so hard across the face that the har collapses instantly, as if dead. The other hungry hara scatter a little, but not too far. Guns are drawn. Guns and sharp, angry teeth. Ghent gestures at the fallen har. "Pick him up. Pick him up and truss him or you'll join him in the stewpot tonight."

More barked orders chase the hara as they work quickly to process their moaning friend. Knives are drawn, and I look away, unable to face the barbarity. A single quick scream cuts the air, then dies in a gurgle. Tears break from my eyes, tears born of terror. The hara carrying our cages bring us to the door of the biggest tent, set us in the sand and break away, disappearing into tents and knots of frantically-working hara. Only Ghent stays, his cruel eyes fixed on us, on me and Dalst.

"What is your name?" he asks me, settling on the sand just beyond the bars of the cage, just out of reach. His eyes are stunning, violet, and his hair is as rich as a cascade of torn silk. I hate him, but his charisma is infectious. I hate him, despite his exquisite brilliance.

"I know this one's name is Dalst," he says, gesturing at my lover. "I know how much you care for him. I can see it in your eyes. It's palpable, *tangible*." There's a breathiness in his voice, something like lust, a desire for what Dalst and I have, a desire to seize it and pierce it with a thousand slow-bleeding wounds. When he turns toward my lover, watching as if considering, as if deciding what kind of torment to visit upon him, I speak up, words rushing out of me in an attempt to get his attention back, to keep it off the one I love.

"Tepai," I blurt. "My name is Tepai."

"Tepai." Ghent smiles softly. "I've done this a few times before. I know which one of a couple to kill first. Can you guess which one of you that will be?"

"Me," I blurt, grabbing the bars of the cage.

Ghent only grins wider, doesn't even flinch.

"Please, make it me."

"The more passionate one always says that." There's glee in his eyes that I hate. "It's so much more satisfying to watch the passionate one rail and rage while the one thing they love more than anything else in the world is taken apart, slowly and painfully, right in front of them."

"Why do you do this?" I ask.

"Because it's fun," he says, but there's a darkness creeping in at the edge of his grin. Anger, wariness.

"No," I shake my head, lick my lips. "Ghent, why do you do this? Why do you really do this?"

"You're not like the others." Ghent stands, suddenly disturbed. Staring down at me, he towers over my cage, hands hiding in the pockets of his worn pants. "Perhaps I will kill you first. Perhaps your friend will be more entertaining once we start cutting on you instead."

"We won't give you the satisfaction you desire," I say, keeping the words as level as I can. "We've seen death first-hand so many times that we are unafraid to die."

Ghent hesitates for a long moment, searching my eyes for deceit. When he finally speaks, there is a heaviness to his tone, a fatigue. "It has been weeks since my tribe has had a feast," he says. "Tonight, we will eat well. I think I'll slaughter you both side-by-side with my own blade."

I look away, refuse to answer. In the silence, my eyes find Dalst's, meet for a moment. There's a clarity in his stare now, an unnerving calmness that makes me look away once more, lose myself in the subtle movement of lake against sandy shore. By the time I look up again, Ghent is gone. The sounds, the bustle of his tribe preparing for the coming feast, lingers like a cold weight in my belly.

I wait in my cage. It feels like hours, but the sun hardly moves, only reddens with the thick smoke of the rising fires. Every joint of the rebar cage is welded solidly. Every point I can think to check for a weak spot is hard, unyielding iron and steel. Picking apart the thin chicken wire wrapped around the cage gives me something to do, gives me a sense of hope, hope that maybe, if I can free enough of the soft wire, I can try to pick the lock holding the door shut.

It's a vain hope, and I know it. I've never tried to pick a lock before, have only heard stories about it, but a vain hope is better than none at all.

When Ghent and two strong hara in skull-faced masks come for us, I have a cluster of tiny, semi-rigid wires hidden in my hands. They don't seem to notice the holes I've unravelled in the wire, and for that I am grateful. The locks come free, the gates squeal and squeak,

Ghent watching as his raiders reach for me and Dalst, seize us in rough hands and drag us out into the sand.

I struggle, just enough to distract the har seizing me, then go for his eyes with the wires the instant I'm outside. Thin sticks of metal bend against the bone of his mask, but one length finds its mark, bites deep. He screams, howls, and lets go of me.

Suddenly free, I whirl on Ghent. His gun slides from the holster, rises and barks, but the shot flies wide. There's screaming, but it isn't mine, isn't Ghent's. I hit him hard enough to knock him into the sand, to seize his throat with one desperate hand, pin his frantic arms under me. I'm ready to kill him, ready to end him permanently, but as I look toward Dalst, I see the other har draw his own gun, press it firmly against the side of my lover's head.

"Let him go," the har holding Dalst growls.

My eyes flick from my lover's stare to the stare of the har with the gun. Time seems to slow. Another bark cuts the air, another threat, and I find my eyes locked with Ghent's again, losing myself in the light already fading in those cool pools of violet abyss.

There are stories in his veins, I realise. Stories in the living bones, just beneath his rough and filthy skin. In the space of a breath, I find myself in the midst of them, find myself flying through all the torment that made him the hellion he has become. In the crimson horrors of his mind, I find a child beneath a layer of insulating fog, a human child hollow-eyed with regret, with grief and fear. I see cruelties, I see beatings, screaming teeth, bleeding lips. I see all of his stories and he sees them with me. Knots held in muscles and mind for years start to unknot and, as I pour all of my stories into him, he shudders, soaking up the flow, drowning in beauty, in love, in softness and tenderness. One hand reaches out, and I let it go. One hand reaches, and I see the fingers spread like the petals of a flower.

"Stop," Ghent whispers, voice hoarse, stilted even, as I loosen my grip on his throat. "Stop."

The har holding the gun doesn't move for a long, painfully quiet moment. Reeling from the memories, the pain hiding deep within Ghent's tortured psyche, I twist myself loose and collapse beside him. Instantly, there are hands on me, hara with knives yanking me away from Ghent, carrying me toward the great tent.

"Stop!" Ghent shouts again, and suddenly everyone freezes.

There is a terrible moment of silence. I try to look past the hands, the grimy arms, try to find some flicker of Ghent or Dalst, but there is nothing but the ragged clothing and filthy flesh. Footsteps fall heavy in sand, and then somehar shoves the hara holding me aside, grabs me and forces me to my knees.

"What was that?" Ghent puts one hand on the side of my face, and the gesture is as desperate as it is gentle.

"We all have stories in our bones," I tell him. "I've seen yours. I've seen the child you were. I've seen the hell you've been through."

"I've seen," he stumbles, touching the side of his head, then turning back to me, wild-eyed. "Show me more."

My eyes meet his, and I know there is iron in my stare. "Let Dalst go, and I'll show you whatever you want."

The nod is slow, almost drunken. Turning around, he gestures to the har holding Dalst. "You heard Tepai. Let him go."

"I'm not going anywhere without Tepai," Dalst spits back.

"Dalst, don't waste this," I shout. "Go!"

"Ghent..." Dalst stands, takes a couple of careful steps toward us. "I have stories too. This gift, it's something that can be taught. I taught Tepai. I've seen many more stories than he has."

I open my mouth to respond, but before I can get the words out, Ghent turns, suddenly giving Dalst his full attention. I'm desperate, and the look in Dalst's eyes is worrying me. I reach out, brush my fingers against Ghent's arm, send him just a flash of memory. It isn't much, just the memory of a sweet kiss on a perfect spring day, but it's enough to stop him in his tracks.

It's only a few feet between Ghent and Dalst. We move smoothly, come together evenly, and in the touch we share stories in a way we've never done before. Even with all those days spent among the bones in the dead city, we've never shared our stories this way. Ghent soaks up every memory we share through him, shivers as the stories light him up like live current. The waves wash over and through him, over and through us all, and by the time we come back, the sun is at the horizon again. There is sand in my mouth, and a crowd has gathered, watching us in silent wonder.

"I have done so much that I regret," Ghent pants into the sand, his eyes unfocused. "I see what I have done in a different way now." He swallows. "I should die. I want to die now."

"Death comes for all of us soon enough," I whisper back. "Better to live and try to atone while we still can."

"You've seen my memories," he says. "You know what I've done."

I understand his pain, his readiness to die. The memories of slaughter, of torture, cannibalism and hate lie heavy within me, leave a sour taste in my mouth when I think of them. It's all I can do to force myself over, rise on my elbows and look him right in the eyes. A monster, but still also just a child.

"I know what you've done, but I also know what you are capable of," I tell him. Beside him, Dalst lies sprawled in the sand, eyes closed, breathing coming regular, but ragged. "The horrors you've lived through, the horrors you've created – they're nothing compared to the horrors you could help others overcome. They're nothing compared to the hells you could lift other hara out of."

Ghent's eyes rise to the sky, go unfocused again, as if he's considering. All around us, the hara of his tribe stand waiting, watching.

"Show me how to tease the stories from bones," he finally says, and when he looks at me, I can see the child in his violet eyes again. "Teach me. Teach us all, and we can become the tribe of stories, the memory-keepers of the dead. We can atone by remembering innocents instead of wronging them."

"It's a start." I get to my feet slowly, purposefully. Ghent stares at me for a long moment before I finally offer my hand, help him stand again. Once he's even with me, I reach out, brush one thick frond of crimson hair out of his eyes. "There is more we could do than just gather and remember stories. There are more hara in the world like you, Ghent, or that could be like you, like you've become. In time, we could seek them out and share our stories with them. We could help them see their own stories more clearly. We could help them move beyond their pain, help them grow to become better, wiser, more loving."

"We will guide you, Ghent," Dalst says, putting his hand on the har's shoulder. "We will guide all of you, if you wish it."

"We do," Ghent says, shivering. All around us, other hara start to murmur, shifting uncertainly. In the pause, Ghent looks to one of the shyest hara in the crowd, gestures for him to join us.

"Come," Ghent says, and there's a heartbreaking amount of gentleness in his voice. "Come. I promise I won't hit you. I'll never hit any of you ever again. Come, embrace us. This is a new time for our tribe. A new dawn. We will face our pain and we will overcome it. We will face our pain instead of letting it fester and turn us toward cruelty."

The shy har hesitates a little, but as I watch him, I swear that I can see the slight lines of a smile forming across his face. When I touch him, I feel his stories, move into and through them, and as his eyes meet mine, I fill him with my own memories, watch the way it opens him, unfolds all of his pain, leaves nothing but wonder and understanding in its place.

Surface

Ben Fouracre

I would follow you down
Lead you to water
If I thought you would drown
Without pulling me under

I'm digging my fingers in
Digging a deep hole
Sink ourselves into it
To keep out the cold

I would take it all back
Every last piece of pain
If I thought you'd forget it
It won't happen again

My arms are wrapped around
Our bodies entwined
I sink into your life
You sink into mine

Stop making plans
Just concentrate
On breaking the surface

Shadows in the Royal

Nerine Dorman

If anyhar had told me that I'd one day see myself seated in a plush carriage, rushing like a breath of wind into the arid Heartland, I'd have informed them to check to see which herbs they had been smoking. Our transport was a sleek thing, three gleaming carriages linked to a locomotive powered by the sun, the winds and the Dehara alone knew what sort of magic the driver had invoked. Soundless, but for the faint hissing of its runners, our streamlined conveyance drew us through the coastal forests, slipped its serpentine way up a mountain pass between frowning sandstone buttresses, and brought us into the arid interior where scimitar-horned gemsbok raised curious, black-masked heads to watch us pass.

I kept my face turned to the window, feigning fascination with the scenery that flashed by in a matter of heartbeats, but I was all too aware of Vaer sitting across from me at our table. His presence was a fizz-crackle of agitation tinged with remorse – an emotion I'd never thought he'd ever indulge in. Granted, his sorrow wasn't for me, as much as I'd wished it so in many of my elaborate fantasies during the intervening years since our first, bitter parting. That he'd returned to me with much handwringing and sighs should have provided a surfeit of satisfaction. Except that it didn't.

The years had been kind to him; his golden-brown skin was soft, speaking of an easy life out of the sun. Those same, elegant hands were folded over each other, bearing his ubiquitous collection of silver rings – his only remaining vanity, it seemed. Hands that used to cup my face so that he might lean in to share breath. He had hacked off his glossy black locks, so that the remnants brushed his nape in messy tufts. Haunted brown eyes so shadowed they were almost black occasionally flashed in my direction, brimming over with his darkness. So much hurt. Gone too was the elaborate velvet coat and the extravagant hats. I'd be tempted to say he'd donned sackcloth and ashes, for he was garbed in a simple grey shirt that hung down to mid-thigh over similarly drab trousers – still tailored, but otherwise unremarkable. His boots, much scarred and badly in need of polish, were more patched than whole. So unusual of him.

To give myself some credit, I'd refrained from remarking about his appearance since he'd first shown up at Hope House that past week. I'd been too taken aback by the mere fact that he'd all but materialised unannounced at my chamber of healing. Who was I to judge? Especially in the aftermath of the yawning chasm of seasons that had fallen between us.

At first, I'd feared him an apparition, a visitation of my past impinging itself on my present. But even after I'd blinked, he remained exactly where he was. All too real, too solid. Flesh, not spirit.

"Iqela?" His voice was rough at the edges. He still couldn't manage the click of the 'q', in my name's pronunciation. After what, twenty, nearly thirty years, I couldn't bring myself to correct him either. Not like the old days, where his tongue would fumble over consonants unfamiliar to his city-bred vocabulary, and his attempts would turn into a laughing game we played as he tried and failed to say my name correctly. Back then I'd fooled myself that he'd mispronounced my language on purpose, just to amuse me.

"You." That was all I was able to say that first moment when I stood like a lightning-struck umcheya tree.

All sights and sounds had brightened and rushed about me. The robin-chats in the ximafana thicket that shrouded my chamber had fallen silent, and the usually sharp scent of the blooms turned foetid.

He'd glanced down at his clasped hands, the picture of abject contrition.

How it must've wounded him deeply to come crawling to me for help. He, who would never admit to any wrongdoing.

"I need your help." He all but choked on the words. Would not meet my gaze. Guilty.

I'd had to sit down, my heart colliding against the bony embrace of its home. I'd been rendered speechless. I had not intended to say yes. My lips betrayed my intention to utter the single syllable of 'no'. "What do you need?" I'd whispered instead, hardly daring to believe that I beheld him in truth.

His story of woe had come tumbling out, rainwater flooding a gulley, dragging all manner of detritus to the ocean of his regret. Chesna found, and lost again, under tragic circumstances. I kept my words about the chesna supplanted in his heart to myself. Vaer needed me now, my skill in particular, to lay to rest the unquiet spirit of his beloved. As for why that spirit was unquiet, he didn't say, and I didn't voice my suspicions on that either.

It had taken me years to recover from him, from the way he'd grown like a strangler fig around my heart, squeezing, stealing my strength, my joy. His soul was a black sun, drawing into it all light. Time and distance had allowed me to see this. At the time, it'd felt as if I'd amputated some vital part of me, and many times I'd wondered how things would've turned out had I remained. Perhaps I too would have died.

I could never argue with Vaer about matters of the heart, because there we'd differ until the stars fell from the sky and the very fabric of the universe unravelled. Vaer's damned pride was a slow-acting poison that seeped into those around him, and now it had touched me again. I had no choice but to follow through with this last chapter of our story. For it would be the last. Closure.

For all that we were supposed to be an enlightened race, we were still prone to hearts running astray. Love, and love freely, some said. But this was not possible for all among us. Perhaps that made me selfish, but my heart was not something to be shared with just anyhar. For sure, I'd had liaisons with others since Vaer, but nothing that lasted, nothing that truly satisfied. My heart was brittle, a prickly sea urchin, to be handled with care and most certainly not stepped upon. Vaer had been the wrong one to love. For me, at least. I'd flown too close to that black sun of his, and he had scorched me, and I was the one who'd deemed it best to retreat, for my love was too deep. Hope House had been about as far south as I could go short of booking passage on a sailing ship. If I couldn't heal myself, I could heal others, and perhaps find some measure of comfort. Yet Vaer had found me, after all.

And here we were, in the Heartland. Far, far away from the restless ocean and its shifting shores.

Once upon a time, when hara were but a dream, and mankind still squabbled over the bones of a dying world, this place had another name, given to it by the pale foreigners who'd stolen the land from its first people. But the Wraeththu had washed away the blood and named this tiny village Forgiveness. It was still a tiny green gem in the midst of an arid land, drawing water deep from beneath the earth, because the nearby Reed River only flowed when there'd been rains, and even now, under the custodianship of the Wraeththu, rain was infrequent in the region.

This wasn't a part of the land that spoke to me, even though I had to admit that it was undeniably beautiful – big bold sky arching over the gold-ochre earth, and the settlement itself contained by the gentle ridges of bluish mountain ranges surrounding it. In the distance, vultures circled, their long wings outstretched as they spiralled on the thermals. I knew from past experience that they nested there, on the eastern ridge where the hara of this land brought their dead. We'd hiked up there a few times in the past – for the view but also to see the newly hatched chicks. Such things amused Vaer back then.

Although most of the original human habitation had been demolished, and had been replaced with conical, adobe structures that made me think of mud-daubers' nests, the old, double-storey hotel with its wraparound balcony and ornamental lacework remained – too grand, too eccentric.to be forgotten so that it could return to the earth. The structure nestled among its more contemporary brethren, incongruous with its three crenelated, rectangular turrets and guarded by a half dozen spindly sentinel cypresses. A redbrick paved entrance boasted a burbling fountain, fringed by a wealth of ancient rosebushes boasting bloody red blooms.

While the surrounding newer buildings were finished in an assortment of geometric patterns in warm, earthy tones, whoever maintained the hotel had contrived to paint it a shining, near blinding white that made it gleam in the afternoon glare. I had to shade my eyes against the discomfort as we disembarked on the platform directly opposite the establishment.

This was it: the location where Vaer's great romance had come to such a tragic end. The very love story that had driven me from his side. The har's name was Saffron Bridgewood, a delicate foreigner washed ashore in southern climes. I couldn't compete with his supposedly cultured ways, his claims of ties to the Gelaming and others we only ever heard about in travellers' tales. I had known the relationship would be ephemeral, but Vaer was never one to listen to good advice. It hardly surprised me that Saffron had withered in the harsh landscape, much like his namesake. Out of place; far from home. Ours is not a kind land.

Perhaps it was somehow fitting, too, that Forgiveness was where our own story had begun so many years gone that I no longer wished to count their passing.

"This place hasn't changed at all," I told him, though I knew full well it had. There hadn't been nearly as many new structures back then. And the railway had yet to be rebuilt. There were no trains running back then when we'd ridden with convoys of caravans or even struck off on foot to truly obscure settlements goodness knew where.

Renowned singer that he was, Vaer had been much in demand, back then, though considering him now, I doubted he still enjoyed the same kind of popularity.

Vaer shouldered his bag, his lips pulled into a bloodless line. "Oh, it's changed a lot."

I had nothing to say to that, but merely gestured for him to move forward.

Hara here were short of stature and dark of skin, their hair, for the most, tightly braided against their scalps or shaved in intricate patterns. They regarded us incuriously, for this was a nexus point for travellers, and hara from all over stopped here to refresh themselves before continuing on their journeys.

The proprietor who met us at the door was a southerner, like Vaer. Tall but paler of skin and garbed in a loose-fitting robe of sky blue with wide sleeves that had been finished with a pattern of white beads at the deep V of the neck. I couldn't recall him from my previous visit to the hotel.

He bowed deeply. "Tiahaar Vaer, welcome back to the Royal. I hope you have found some measure of healing during this time." He then glanced at me, a small frown creasing his brow.

I stepped over threshold after Vaer, garbed in my homespun shirt and trousers. A har who sought to slide into the background. Unremarked and unremarkable. It wouldn't surprise me if a har dressed in a peacock feather cloak flounced downstairs demanding a gin and tonic as well as a string quartet. I no longer fit in here.

"This is Tiahaar Iqela," Vaer announced, once again butchering my name. "He is here to assist me."

The proprietor bowed. "Welcome, Tiahaar." He didn't so much as raise a brow at my appearance.

A short interchange followed while I admired the ancient framed prints that decorated the hall. Most depicted birds and wildlife – stilted, disproportionate creatures painted by human hands centuries before. In many cases the paper had turned to yellowed ivory, the ink faded. Here and there, spots of discoloration bloomed.

The air smelt of camphor and the faintest trace of stale smoke, and while the entrance was quiet, an air of watchfulness lingered within the structure. If I glanced at the stairs from the corner of my eye, I might glimpse smudged figures. But I didn't. There'd be enough time for that later. All the small hairs on my nape and arms prickled.

An old cabinet turned out to be a peculiar device in which a large, notched metal disc was mounted behind glass. A symphonium, a helpful placard announced in Old English. I hadn't noticed it here before, but it was undeniably antique. Through double doors to my left, was a large room where ancient billiard tables with scarred felt lurked, as well as the crouched form of a grand piano. Two desultory hara leaned by the bar, their heads bowed in close consultation while one rotated a bottle on the bar top. The old stuffed eland head I recalled from my last stay still hung from the wall there, although it looked as though it was missing an eye, and the tip of one horn had been snapped off. I could only speculate as to what had been the cause of its deterioration. A bar fight? Target practice courtesy of a drunken har?

Somehar touched my upper arm with chill fingers, and I started.

Vaer. He focused his attention on a point about hand or two to my left. "Come. We can go to our room."

Our room.

Like that wouldn't be awkward.

I shouldered my pack and followed him up the stairs, with their threadbare runner that might once have been maroon. Every step creaked or squeaked as we made our way to the first floor.

Vaer had taken a room beneath the main turret, the same one we'd stayed in all those years ago. A familiar four-poster bed with forest green drapes dominated the space, but the unnervingly large, three-panelled mirror that had been positioned directly opposite it was new. I sank gratefully into an overstuffed wingback chair by the balcony door; it still felt as if the floor was moving beneath my feet – an aftereffect of the train journey. I pointedly tried to ignore my multiplied reflection.

My companion moved about like a sleepwalker, unpacking his things into the cupboard, opening the balcony door to let in the hot late afternoon air – the room still held a distinct chill to it. The prickling on my nape hadn't ceased since I stepped over the threshold.

"This is where it happened," I said.

Vaer paused in straightening his coat on a hanger. His lips pulled into a taut line. "Yes." That one word was barely a whisper.

I wanted to be angry with him, but all I felt was a weary resignation at old patterns that were resurfacing. Many years ago, it had also been like this too: Vaer making decisions based on what he felt was best for those hara in his orbit. Only now his dark light was tarnished, and I resented him for making assumptions on my behalf.

"How did he do it?"

Vaer froze. He'd deflected on the method ever since he'd come to me at Hope House, and I'd held back from pushing him on the details because I understood that the discussion of the tragedy would be traumatic for him. But this had gone on too long now. If I was to help him, I had to know more.

I heaved out a sigh. "You have to face this eventually. You do realise that, don't you?"

Wordlessly he went to the en-suite bathroom, where he paused at the door and beckoned me to come.

As much as I wanted to indulge in an eye-roll, I refrained as I rose and followed him.

And I *knew*. Instantly. A warm bath and a sharp blade, blood spilling out in lazy crimson blooms. How dramatic.

How dreadful. That this sickness of the heart and soul should have been allowed to take root and bring forth such toxic fruit. That *a har* should fall prey to a condition that was altogether so *human*.

The certainty of this made me pause, breathe deeply around the nausea that churned in my belly.

Not a single tangible sign of any past suicide lingered in the bathroom, but the spiritual agitation here was so evident it set my teeth on edge. When I viewed the pristine white tiles through narrowed eyes, I glimpsed blurry memories. A limp hand smearing red fingerprints. A whiff of the iron tang of blood, so faint. The walls remembered. The sorrow was a palpable thing, a heavy miasma pressing down on all sides.

"They've been unable to let this room since..." Vaer kept his gaze trained on his feet.

"I'm not surprised," I snapped. "And you expect us to sleep in here tonight? Have you taken leave of your senses?"

His expression hardened, and he turned to me. "I'm doing the best I can, under circumstances."

"What did you do to drive him to do the unthinkable?"

"It wasn't me."

"Of course not! It's never you, is it? Have you ever considered that you might be the one who is toxic? That you become a sickness to those who draw close to you? How many of your chesna have remained by your side for longer than a year? Be honest." Now that I looked at him in the bright light of the bathroom – and by that, I mean *really* observed him on all spectrums available to me – I could detect the shadow within him. Faint, but there. A sucking eddy that gave the appearance of bending energy towards the gaping hole that should be his heart centre. It was beyond my capabilities to help him.

"I should never have agreed to this," I muttered, heading back into the main room. Fool that I was, I'd been flattered that Vaer had come to me, needing me. In truth, if I remained, he'd drain me until I too became a ghost. Thing was, one could never help a har if that har wasn't willing to admit that he had a problem.

And in Vaer's case, he always externalised his problems. They were always somehar else's fault. I had the wisdom to understand this now, but back then I had felt as if I were somehow the defective one for extricating myself from his world.

His black sun might have been poisoning me, but at the same time I'd been nurtured by his darkness. I'd basked in it though it sickened me.

"Please." Vaer breathed the word on my neck, and I jerked in fright. He'd moved so silently I hadn't been aware that he was so close. Cold hands gripped my shoulders, but he kept me at arm's length. I don't know how I would have responded if he'd pulled me into an embrace.

I should've ripped myself away from him, but I couldn't. "You're the one who needs help, Vaer, and I'm not sure I'm the one who can offer you the healing you seek. Unless you're willing to accept it."

"It's not about me," he said. "It's about Saffron."

"And you're just going to keep repeating these same patterns. And more hara will be hurt. Or die, even." But my guilt gnawed at me. I *could* help Saffron. This was part of my training – to ease the souls, not only of the living but of the dead.

"Why do you think I've brought you here? I want closure."

"It's still only about you, isn't it?"

He shoved me away from him so violently I staggered and caught myself against the bed. The last I saw of him was his back, however I allowed myself a wry grin of amusement, for he didn't slam the door.

I sighed and sagged onto the bed. The linen was cool against my skin, camphor and sunshine, and I allowed myself to close my eyes, so I didn't stare into the pressed tin ceiling. I wasn't tired, but I needed to find the calm within me, because my heart was racing and my breath ragged. So many uncomfortable memories rose from the depths of my heart and paraded themselves before me.

I'd loved Vaer, deeply, madly and truly. He had that effect on hara. If ever there had been one who'd been in possession of the command to look, it'd been him, the Vaer of my past, and not this haunted shadow who'd dragged me halfway to the middle of nowhere to cast out the ghosts of his past.

But I needed to know Saffron, beyond the pretty blond waif who'd supplanted me at Vaer's side. That was if I was to help him in any way. Help *both* of them, if I were entirely honest. As much as I liked the idea of causing Vaer discomfort as a form of payback, holding grudges was no good, even if these petty grievances gave me a small measure of power. I was not willing to relinquish the upper hand.

The working I settled upon was simple. I needed to frame an understanding of what had truly occurred that fateful night, especially since it was unlikely I'd have the full story out of Vaer. I locked the door to the room and left the key in the lock – this way even if somehar tried to gain ingress, they'd cause an awful jostling. Then I went to the balcony door and adjusted the louvred blinds. Immediately the mood in the room grew close, brooding, and long fingers of dread squeezed my heart despite me having done exactly what I was about to do many times before.

I'd brought my small oil lamp from Hope House: a carefully wrought thing made in the style of an old-style human lantern from centuries before. A real hermit's guiding light; I considered it an apt choice. Out of all the containers of fragrant oil I'd brought, I chose the pelargonium infused with lavender, a combination of joy and serenity. The blend could be construed to be a little on the nose, but this entire quest was one that was fraught with so much unhappiness, I needed all the comfort I could gather.

While the lantern spread its tiny brave light into the gloom of the main room, I went to the bathroom, where I washed my face then cupped my hand so that I could drink water straight from the tap. The liquid tasted faintly brackish, as I recalled it from my previous stay – the kind of water a har could drink in great quantities but which failed to refresh. When I studied myself in the mirror, watching the tiny drops make runnels down my skin, I glimpsed a second face, pale next to my own. It was only for an instant, and when I turned to get a better look, the apparition was gone.

A trick of the light, that was all, somehar might be tempted to say under better circumstances, but the air was charged, throbbing against my ears like the booming of a large drum impossibly distant yet still audible. When I was younger, such visions would have scared me spitless. Yet try as I might, I couldn't summon my usual serenity in such rites. This was too close to the bone, too deeply entrenched in my own past.

"You will be able to rest soon, Saffron," I said to the not-quite-empty room and felt immediately foolish for having done so.

I sighed and rounded my shoulders. "You should have left him when you had the chance." *Like I did.*

But had I, really? Could I honestly say that Vaer hadn't left behind poisoned barbs?

He'd found me again, after all, when I'd tried my best to put as much distance between myself and him as possible. It was uncanny, really. Like no matter where I went, the physical distance between us meant nothing.

When had this become about me? A healer should be objective, dispassionate even.

I wiped my face on one of the unnaturally white towels, then made my way back to the bedroom. Shadows bent and danced around my lantern. On one hand a har could say it was the slight breeze curling in through the window. On another, it might be that the veil between worlds was growing thin. Both were equally true, depending on how one viewed the situation.

The skin on my arms raised in gooseflesh, and I rubbed them vigorously until the feeling passed. Now was not the time to allow my body to distract me. I stripped down to my leggings then sat cross-legged on the floor with my lantern set on the coffee table before me. The small flame danced and licked, turning and twisting in air that should be still but wasn't. A moth fluttered too close, but thankfully veered off. I tried to grow more present, inhaled and exhaled deeply and evenly to smooth my ragged breathing. My pulse hammered, though, and my mouth grew unaccountably dry. Usually the process of slipping into trance was seamless, but that afternoon it was like clawing my way through clutching vines, each memory hooking into me and jerking me down unpleasant avenues.

Saffron smiling, lifting a wine glass to his lips that evening we met him downstairs.

The duet he and Vaer sang just before closing. I should have known then that the two made a peculiar alchemy together, one I could only aspire to.

Not that Vaer and I weren't good together. Ours was a magic all of its own, a juxtaposition of opposites – rough sandstone curling with mist. Now Vaer and Saffron… Light making prisms through a waterfall. Golden bars of sunlight slicing through verdant foliage of an ancient forest.

I could go on with the comparisons as the memories flooded me: each small betrayal, the secret glances, smiles. The way they'd leaned towards each other when they thought I wasn't looking.

Perhaps if I'd pretended that this gradual drawing away between me and Vaer was of no consequence, things would have played out differently. But for Vaer. He couldn't let me go. Wouldn't. It was a matter of pride, of wanting to be the har who held all the threads and could knot or release them as was his wont.

And why not the three of us together? It was not unheard of among our kind for a patchwork of the heart and body.

I didn't like sharing.

For Vaer it was a game, to see how far he could push our mutual infatuations. The gravity of his black sun inescapable.

Though I was loath to admit it, I had been half sick in love with Saffron myself; he existed as the antithesis of everything that I was. Was I sorry that he was dead? Yes and no.

Who was the har who truly needed healing here?

The admission coated my tongue with bitterness, and I was jerked back into the present, into the hotel room with its unquiet spirit. Blue-grey dusk filtered through the curtains that sighed with the balmy breeze. More time had passed than I'd expected. Outside a dog yipped, and a low murmur of voices from below, in the bar, sounded more like river rapids. Normal, everyday life. Not me, shrouded in thickening shadows. Alone.

Without warning the flame of my oil lamp was snuffed, and the room was plunged in swift darkness so that only the barest outlines of the furnishings were visible. I sucked in my breath, my skin prickling with alarm.

"Saffron?" I hated the quaver in my voice.

Ethereal laughter echoed at the edges of my awareness.

He has his claws sunk into you too, doesn't he?

I wasn't sure if I'd imagined the voice that dripped those hollow words.

"I'm here to help you," I said.

Help? Don't be absurd.

A loud shattering of glass from the bathroom had me leap to my feet, and I rushed to see what had broken. Only when I got there, the bathroom was as pristine as I'd left it. Except the face peering back at me from the mirror was not my own. Skin pale like wax, long flaxen hair clotted with blood. A ghoulish grin that betrayed the skull beneath the skin. Pink tongue licking over colourless, chapped lips.

I blinked, and my familiar dark complexion leered back at me. Same skull beneath a thin veneer of living flesh, however.

"You don't need to do this," I told him.

No response. Just the thrum of my blood rushing through my veins, a think sheen of perspiration cooling on my skin.

This wasn't working, was it?

It wouldn't work, not until I'd faced my own demons.

Which meant I had to have it out with Vaer, and I hated that he might see how rattled I was.

"Damn you," I muttered then went to throw on my jackal skin kaross. I shut the door behind me and descended to the common room. I knew full well where I'd find Vaer.

The har slumped in the corner of the bar, half leaning against the wall and resting an elbow on the polished blackwood countertop. Another har – a northerner, judging by his guttural accent – was regaling him animatedly about a journey he'd undertaken. Snatches of "you should have seen the size of the lion" reached me from across the crowded barroom.

The glimpse I had of Vaer's face showed me a blank mask. I knew that expression well – one of studied indifference that the uninitiated would mistake for mild interest. It meant his thoughts had flown elsewhere, tumbling like a river through a deep ravine.

Music floated above the susurrus of voices, tinny piano played by an older harling. Nohar paid him any attention, and his shoulders were hunched as he picked out the notes with careful fingers. Smoke of assorted herbal blends turned the air soupy, cloying even. The kind of smell that would cling to a har's skin and hair hours later. I didn't want to be there, slipping between the press of bodies of happily drinking and laughing hara. Contact with them in such a place was alien to me now. I didn't even socialise at the common areas at Hope

House, and I wasn't about to start making a habit of it.

Vaer slid his gaze to me almost nonchalantly once I insinuated myself into his space. The storytelling har—a rangy blond who looked to have spent more than his fair share of time in the sun—glanced at me in a way that suggested he believed I was beneath his notice, a small frown marring his forehead as he evaluated then dismissed me.

"Vaer." I hesitated halfway in reaching out to touch his arm.

He lifted his glass to his lips and tongued at the liquor and ice.

"I need you." Those three words almost didn't make it past my lips. How many times had I spoken them to an empty room? "This won't work without you."

Vaer put down his glass so that the ice cubes danced. His companion now studied me with the same intensity a har would reserve for an annoying fly they might flick from their shoulder.

"Fine." Vaer wouldn't look at me. Without greeting his friend, he shoved through the knots of hara and quickly vanished beyond my line of sight.

I shrugged apologetically to the blond har then followed, certain without needing to turn and look, that the har scrutinised me as I departed, most likely wondering what sort of hold I had on his intended liaison for the night. Vaer was waiting for me on the first landing, one hand clutching the banister so hard his knuckles were white against a thin veneer of skin. His jaw worked, and he still wouldn't quite meet my gaze.

"I'm sorry…about earlier," I said, even though I wasn't sorry. Not in the least, for those had been words that had to be said. Now that they were flown, I could continue.

He clenched that hand of his so hard I was sure I heard the railing creak. "I've been behaving abominably." How that admission must gall him.

"No more than usual." I allowed myself a wry smile.

"Well then, let's go." He turned, continued walking, and I followed him.

He flung himself down on the armchair once we arrived back in our room, limbs sprawled awkwardly, like the tendons had been snipped. "How are we to go about this?"

"I'll need you to join me in a working, as you are integral to the banishing."

"I was hoping to avoid this sort of thing," he muttered.

"You've been avoiding 'this sort of thing' your entire life, I'd hazard." I didn't bother trying to hide my waspish tone. "And you're no doubt still going through your years wreaking disaster in the lives of others."

"Last I saw it took two to dance to that tune," he returned.

"But some of us know when to stop."

He flashed me a wry smile. "What, and to go live like some ascetic and make amends by healing every broken-winged har who comes your way?"

"Better than drowning myself in guilt. You're not quite at your former glory yourself."

"Oh, here we start with the melodrama again."

I bared my teeth at him in an expression that wasn't quite wry amusement. "It's not taking us long to get back to where we left off, is it?"

"We were good together."

"While it lasted. Until we became poison to each other. Like you eventually poisoned Saffron."

He blanched.

"Don't deny it," I told him. "We both know this to be true. It may have taken me years, but I healed." I wouldn't admit to him that his absence had gnawed at me the way a missing limb might bother an amputee, and that now, being with him was picking away at the healed tissue of my heart. How much longer until I was bleeding out again?

"He could leave any time he wanted to. Just like you."

"Not all hara are grass, that can bend with the storm winds," I said.

"Always one with the pretty analogies."

"Look," I said, firming my voice. "We can dance around each other as much as we like, but that won't change the fact that we need to work together to lay Saffron to rest."

"I love him," Vaer said in a small voice. "I know you think me a heartless monster, nothing but a sinkhole, but I wouldn't have come all the way to find you if it weren't for the fact that I don't want him to be like this. In some limbo."

"You've got a funny way of showing your enthusiasm to find peace then."

"I know. And I'm sorry. Sorry for everything. For you and me, how it all went sour. I wish I were like one of those hara who can work their way through all the castes and find fulfilment in our more magical natures, but I honestly feel as if I'm the broken one. Like there's some fundamental part of me that's missing."

I went over to him and placed a hand on his shoulder. "It's not too late, you know."

He shook his head with a rueful laugh, his gaze at a point in the middle distance. "Oh, I've tried."

"I could help... Once we put Saffron to rest, that is."

"Too much water under the bridge. That's the problem with you—you always want to help, and in helping you lose yourself in the process. No. This is something I have to figure out for myself. Whatever we have together does not last long before it sickens. We both know this."

I exhaled and tried to mask my relief. For once, he'd made an astute observation, one that I couldn't disagree with, even if it hurt with its stunning realisation. The implications were vast, and I knew then that no matter how things progressed here with our work, I would not return to Hope House. I had known that when I'd closed the door to my cabin behind me, even if I had not admitted it to myself then.

"Very well," I said, and went to my lantern. I lit it then turned the wick so that the tongue of flame licked our shadows on the wall.

"What now?" he asked.

"We will do a meditation, so that I may connect to Saffron through you. I will make a gateway, and we will show him how to reach it."

"It sounds deceptively simple."

"It would be, if I were in the right state of mind. But things have been unsettled, and I've realised I need you for this. You are the hook."

"More like the bait." He laughed.

"Don't jest. Perhaps I should reword and say that you are the focus that I need to reach Saffron. I have very little connection to him."

"C'mon, you met him."

"Regrettably, yes, but I didn't stay long enough to truly get to know him now, did I?"

He gave a small shrug. "Fair enough."

The lantern should have enough oil to burn for as long as we needed it to. Then I dragged the coffee table to the centre of the room so that there was space for us to sit on either side, facing each other across the lantern.

"Rearranging the furniture now?" he asked.

I glanced at the ceiling, exhaled slowly to avoid snarking him, and shook my head. "Nothing like that." I gestured at the side opposite me. "Come, take a seat. Maybe remove your boots."

"That simple?"

"Yes. I'll keep it *that* simple. For you." I didn't tell him that I didn't expect he'd be able to experience the rite fully. I would try, but his being fully immersed wasn't mandatory. So long as I was able to, that was all that we needed.

I shucked my kaross and seated myself cross-legged opposite him. Once again, the small flame twisted, though I could feel no errant breezes in the room. At the corner of my eye the dark pooled and swarmed, moving just outside my field of vision if I tilted my head to get a better look.

"Right. I want you to close your eyes and concentrate on your breathing. Then I want you to remember Saffron. Imagine that each memory is a precious stone that you can pick up and examine. Keep doing that until I tell you to stop."

"Really?" His brows shot up.

"Yes, really. It's not like I'm asking you to open your veins."

He grunted as if I'd punched him in the belly. A low blow, and I winced inwardly at my sharp tongue. I should know better, but I couldn't help myself. Instead of apologising, I closed my eyes, started breathing, all too aware of the heat radiating off of him. He was like a furnace, and it took me longer than I wish to grow accustomed to him being present. But it was that essential element that had been lacking during my previous attempt snapped into place, a rightness and completion to offer me the anchor upon which to hang the rite.

Using the tongue of my ancestors, I called upon Lande, the jackal-headed one. He was of this land and had worn many faces through many ages. Dimly, I was aware of how Vaer stiffened, his sharp, indrawn breath of air. The balmy interior of the room grew cool, and the nayati of my dreamwork superimposed itself over my apprehension of the old hotel room.

When I opened my eyes in this spiritual nayati, Vaer stood opposite me, a simplified version of himself, drawn in clean lines—the Vaer of my memories with his ragged black fall of hair to the small of his back. The Vaer without the defeated slope to his shoulders. His brow was furrowed, his lips working silently as he spoke to himself while sorting through his memories. He had followed me after all.

"You can open your eyes now," I told him.

He blinked, glanced about him, his face slack with admiration. "What is this place?"

Perhaps familiarity with a space caused me to overlook the wonder of it. My nayati I'd formed over the years through acts of meditation and dreamwork, and it resembled a perfect overturned bowl, its inner surface radiant with a nacreous light. It was bare save for the lantern, which through all the many rituals existed in both planes.

"I hadn't realised..." Vaer turned on his feet.

"That I could do this?"

He nodded.

"Not all work requires a physical temple."

"I've never..." Wonder blazed in his eyes.

I allowed myself a brief, tight smile. "Now come. We can't spend all our time being distracted. I need you to keep bringing up those memories of Saffron. Visualise them in the space between us."

His expression grew pained for a moment but then he squared his shoulders and nodded that he was ready.

I began the chant, indicating that he should join me. Our voices echoed, twined about each other like smoke as I led him in the words that would create the right circumstances. Or so I hoped.

"I call upon you, Saffron, whose blood has been spilled, whose sorrow increased until its weight dragged you into darkness. Come to us. Come find your peace."

In many ways, this was a deceptively simple rite. Intent was what grounded us in this aetheric nayati, but we needed to grasp that elusive focus with both hands. Vaer's memories slipped like soap bubbles. I couldn't slacken in my chant to request that he sharpen his focus, and to compound matters, his gaze was distant. Wherever he was, it was miles away.

Usually, the visions would appear as faint wisps in the heart of the nayati, a projection of sorts. But all we had now was an undifferentiated haze, a bleak fog that leeched the colour from its immediate surrounds and created a cold patch within its vicinity. Was I even the right har to try do this? Clammy fingers of doubt closed around my throat, and my voice faltered. Was this to be my last, spectacular failure with Vaer? Would Saffron's spirit continue to mock me?

Aborting this working now would be a final admission to Vaer that I was incapable of facing up to our shared past. Saffron would continue to suffer for that failure, his spirit trapped in grey limbo, incapable of moving on. I would walk away and spend the rest of my life wondering what I could have done differently, and maybe Saffron would haunt me too, gazing back at me with my eyes every time I glanced in a mirror.

Just as I feared I'd have to call for a retreat so we could embark on a recalibration of our intent, a faint pinprick of light formed between us. The space around it shimmered and rippled, the way noonday sunlight played on clear mountain pool. A humming filled the air, underpinned by the distant tinkling of broken glass. Vaer's eyes snapped open, his expression growing fraught as he watched how that glowing mote grew larger.

I redoubled my efforts in maintaining the chant, becoming conscious of the drag on my power—water being siphoned off without being replaced. We didn't have much time. Eventually I'd have to break off.

Out of that mote, a har materialised before us, slim, his pale skin translucent and filled with constellations that twisted and turned before us. He opened his eyes, raised his head and turned to Vaer.

You.

I stopped, drew a deep breath. "Saffron Bridgewood, we have called you here to bid you farewell, to cut your ties to the world of matter so that you can find your wholeness by returning to your ancestors."

The spirit turned its liquid eyes to me, and the ghost of a smile played on his lips. He shook his head.

"You must go. There is nothing left for you here. The Dehara call to you, will guide you, if you allow them."

Vaer's eyes were wide, and he gazed in rapt fascination at the apparition.

"Lande, hear me, open the Black Gate. Take the spirit of Saffron Bridgewood and guide him to the completion of his journey."

I knew the Dehar was present, for the scent of burnt vegetation filled my senses, and familiar shapes danced at the periphery of my vision. Saffron stiffened, his form growing nebulous at the edges, as though at any instant he might dissolve. I couldn't let this happen, and I drew hard upon my own powers, exerting my will on the spirit before it could flicker away.

An opalescent vortex spun into existence above Saffron. This was as it should be. He noticed it too, for he tilted his head so he could get a better look. The spirit frowned then glared at me. "No," he mouthed.

"Go. It is your time," I replied.

Saffron shook his head, turned, and to my consternation, extended his right hand to Vaer. Pinpricks of alarm shot down my spine. All this time, Vaer had stood motionless, his full attention fixed on the apparition. So long as his attention did not waver, I could hold the magic in place.

But then Vaer's expression softened from fascination to hope, and he reached out to Saffron. I fully expected his fingers to pass right through the spirit's, but before I could even shout a warning, Saffron had him firmly in his grasp.

How could this be? The vortex above us stuttered, then renewed its eddies, twisting faster and faster. Somewhat lopsided, it grew bulbous as it descended. This was not right.

A terrible paralysis seized me, and try as I might, I could not break free from it. My lips were sealed, my tongue stilled, and I could only watch as Saffron and Vaer both brightened. Their forms blurred around the edges then became wholly indistinct, a nebula of sparks and motes that danced to the rhythms of the slowly sinking vortex.

Then hands gripped my shoulders, their grasp on me implacable, and scorched vegetable scent grew so strong it dulled all other senses. I still managed to shake my head. *No, no, no, this can't happen—*

I came to sprawled on the zebra hide that lay across the parquet floor, small grains of dirt adhering to my sweat-slicked skin. Above me the pressed tin ceiling revolved in a sickening echo of the vortex that had swallowed up my nayati. For a good few minutes, all I could do was lie there, the sound of crashing waves relentless in my ears. Or maybe it was only my blood, rushing through my veins, arteries, my lungs bellows sucking in great gouts of air. My extremities tingled with painful pins and needles, and my limbs would not obey me.

"Vaer?" I croaked, but no answer came.

Apart from my breathing, our room was terribly, horribly silent.

Shakily I dragged myself onto my knees. My lantern had gone out, and the room was dim, with a little light from the streetlamps from outside making bars through the narrow louvred blinds. Yet the motionless hump of Vaer's body was unmistakable. When I narrowed my eyes, I couldn't detect a scrap of his aura. Whatever essence had animated him, had long since fled.

"No, no, no, no!" I scrambled closer so that I could cradle his cooling corpse. His head flopped as I raised him onto my lap. His eyes stared into eternity.

Naturally the hotel's proprietor was anxious that Vaer's transition cause as little stir as possible. He provided several old sheets as a shroud, as well as a donkey and cart for us to transport Vaer to the burial place.

The hara here venerated a vulture-headed Dehar, Assiya, and practised sky burials. At a loss for anyhar else who'd care what happened with Vaer's mortal remains, I accompanied the hotel's serving-har who drove the cart, and we set out early the next morning to take care of matters. Though the sun was barely peeking over the horizon, the day was already stiflingly warm. I missed the cool sea breezes of the south coast keenly, and the cicadas screeched in the stands of eucalyptus we passed along our way, warning us that the day would only grow hotter.

I was still numb after all that had transpired, turning the events over and over like river-smoothed pebbles in a relentless current. What had I done wrong? Had Vaer engineered this entire encounter, knowing that I would create the opportunity for him to reach out to Saffron one last time? I wasn't certain I could give him enough credit for that much forethought. After all, he'd never been comfortable with matters of the spirit and our kind's more inherent magical natures.

I'd washed my hands and face innumerable times since the botched ritual, bathed three times, but the taint clung to me. Guilt yes, but also a perverse notion that what I'd brought into being was right. For Vaer. For Saffron. What I wasn't prepared for was the slow simmer of anger within me, that I'd allowed myself to be used one last time. That I was the one who wasn't good enough, not the one he'd chosen in the end.

Such ugliness was unworthy of my role as a healer, but I would not, could not deny that I suffered these pangs. Damn you, Vaer.

The iron-rimmed wheels of the donkey cart crushed the stones of the narrow track that zig-zagged up the ridge, the swaddled body behind us on the cart's bed juddering. Below us the broad valley spread out in dusty tones, encapsulated by a fathomless blue sky. A flock of sheep made small white flecks that a harling and his dog were herding out into the veld, from kraal on the outside of the hamlet. Far in the distance, near a lonely farmstead guarded by spindly cypresses, a rooster let loose a rusty crowing. Life went on, even if it felt as if my grief were a heavy, immutable thing that begged time to stand still.

This early in the morning, the vultures sunned themselves on ledges, their wide wings shaken out and their plumage loose to soak up warmth. Our path brought us below their cliffside nests, to an open area littered with bone fragments and the faint, lingering odour of carrion. Or maybe I imagined the latter.

The serving-har drew the donkey cart right up until the end of the track, which terminated in a roughly circular area bare of vegetation—I assumed this was the case as it was just the right size for a cart to turn. The actual burial area had been loosely paved with stones, laid out in concentric circles radiating from a large, flat slab of pale sandstone at odds with the reddish-brown rock around it.

Together, the serving-har and I lifted Vaer's remains and carried the burden between us so that we could lay it out on the plinth. The har then returned to the cart without further explanation, where he busied himself in the preparation of a long-stemmed pipe. The rest of the ritual was up to me, evidently.

Above me, the attention of a score of beady eyes was electric, made the small hairs on my nape shiver with imagined violence. Talons scraped on stone. Birds' heads bobbed, twisted to the side so they could get a better view. I'd presided over three funerals in all my years, and each harish community had their own customs. Some consigned the body to flames, others buried deep in the earth to nourish the roots of a sapling. I'd heard of burials at sea, but sky burials?

I wasn't sure I was prepared for the process.

Next to the plinth, rusted with stain and gore, was an old sledgehammer—for breaking the skull and larger bones so the birds could get to the marrow and take all of the dead with them. My stomach gave a small lurch, and for a good few heartbeats all I could do was stare at the too-still form before me. Was I certain that he was dead? I knew the signs, but it still struck me as absurd that the har, whose breath I'd shared, whose body had been joined with mine in communion, was no more. All that remained was cold, dead flesh. Already the faint whiff of carrion reached me. Meat spoiled quickly in this environment.

I was the only har who cared enough to guide Vaer's remains from this world. If I'd not stepped up to the task, I could only assume that a har as indifferent as the one waiting at the cart would have been obliged. He would not have worked with as much reverence as I did, unwinding the shroud, carefully placing each limb. Saying a few words and sprinkling with scented oil.

Vaer's mouth wouldn't close, and no matter how I tried, his lids remained open, his milky gaze unfocused. The skin beneath his head and at his shoulders was stained dark with the settling blood, while his flesh had taken on the hue of tallow. Whatever familiarity had made this Vaer was fled in that accursed ritual chamber. What I beheld was only a placeholder. And yet... A heaviness dragged at me.

This high above the broad valley the only sounds were the crunching of my boot soles on the loose gravel and the sigh of the wind. And the heavy wingbeats as first one then another vulture unfurled its massive wings and sailed down to the ground. Up close, they provided a somewhat comical sight as they circled us. Like hunchbacked mummers adorned with feathered cloaks, their queer heads turning this way and that as they observed. Curious. Hungry. One bird yawned, its beak snapping shut with an audible click once it was done. They hopped, wings partway unfurled, coming ever closer.

I couldn't watch the grisly feast. Couldn't bring myself to observe the initial onslaught as I turned my back and returned to the cart. But I'd carry the sound of tearing flesh, the grunts, cackling, hissing and shuffling of the vultures at their dismal occupation with me for a long, long time. I'd like to think of our existence in these bodies of ours as somehow being inexhaustible, an improvement on the flesh and bone of our human ancestors, immune to the ravages of time, able to bounce back from damage to carry us forward indefinitely. It is not easy to be faced with our inherent fragility. We are not immovable mountains. Though we are resilient, we cannot always avoid accident. And sometimes an ailment is so profound that it is beyond our arts to heal. Such conditions may not be physical in origin. They can be deep and of the spirit, where we cannot reach despite our best efforts. As with Vaer. While outwardly he might present a face to the world that is beautiful and seemingly flawless, beneath the surface that sickness might lurk, perhaps to drag down other luckless hara before it runs its course.

Wordlessly, the serving-har passed his long-stemmed pipe to me, and I inhaled deeply of the smoke, closed my eyes, and let the herbs wriggle their leafy fingers from my lungs and into my blood. Warmth suffused me, tingling at my extremities. I exhaled, and watched the fine mist dissipate into the bright blue of the sky where swifts dipped and twisted.

"It's a pity," the serving-har said, with the slightest dip of his head towards where the birds crouched and scrabbled over their offering, their cruel beaks hooking and tearing at the meat, separating bone from sinew. A ribcage opened like the petals of a grim flower as birds buried their heads in the viscera. Took all that had been Vaer into themselves.

I flinched back to meet his gaze. "I don't have the right words."

"You don't always need words. Some things are bigger than that, and we can't explain how or why."

I grunted at that slice of uncommon wisdom from a har who gave every appearance of being more concerned with affairs of earth and water rather than the stars and souls. What was the point in living or loving, if it was only going to be taken away from you? Perhaps not through misfortune or bad blood, but eventually all things ran their course along the wheel of the years, to be changed, to begin their cycle anew.

In silence we watched as the cackling birds finished. Sly-eyed jackals slunk around the periphery of the feast, growing bolder when the birds ignored them, and they could dart in and steal scraps. What remained was no longer Vaer. He'd fled with the dawn, going wherever it was that our souls departed to. Perhaps one day I'd meet the gaze of another har and see familiar eyes laughing at me. Transmuted, made whole.

And therein lay the seed of my own healing.

One of my teachers had always told me I'd never become a better healer until I'd learnt to heal myself. I'd scoffed, said I knew perfectly well what was going on in my own head and heart. Except now I could smile secretly to myself that the har had been right after all. Perhaps this whole business of living was inherently meaningless in the grander scheme of things. It could also be argued that our efforts in this world were largely futile, and inevitably ended in some small tragedy, as the one that was playing itself out currently.

But, unlike Vaer, I'd walk away from this place of bones. I'd pack my things and I'd set out from the aptly named hamlet of Forgiveness to wherever my path took me. I was free, and I could be kind to myself. I could find those small moments of bliss each day where I could celebrate the small things that mattered: sunlight on my face, a bright pebble washed up on a beach, cold water on a hot day, seeing another har smile… Wherever Vaer travelled now, I could only wish him peace, as my own peace now took to the clear blue sky on strong, broad-swept wings.

The First Touch

Ben Fouracre

Hand on my head
As I go down
Take my breath
As I go down
Close my eyes
And take a step
It doesn't get
Any easier

I feel nothing
I feel nothing
On the first touch

Just fall back
And let you catch me
Take my comfort
When you lie to me
I don't need you
To come around
When I'll only
Wear you down

I feel nothing
I feel nothing
On the first touch

The Waste Remains

Fiona Lane

Slowly the poison the whole blood stream fills.
It is not the effort nor the failure tires.
The waste remains, the waste remains and kills.

- William Empson, "Missing Dates"

Do not travel east of Almagabra, past the Sea of Shadows. Do not make for the high, rocky mountains rising from the land like broken teeth. Do not carry with you your hopes and dreams and offer them up to an inscrutable har with dark eyes and an even darker soul in the hope of some sort of redemption. Don't say you weren't warned.

If you do decide to take this foolhardy course there will be numerous obstacles to overcome. You will be obliged to pass through Ferike, with its enchanted forests and castles, and with its hara of high learning and poetical disposition. If you have your wits about you there, you might not be sold as a slave.

You will come to Gimrah, where after your headlong flight you will be treated with hospitality, plied with an abundance of food and drink, and where you can buy a fine horse to replace your exhausted steed. Do not stay, as they will slit your throat in the night for having treated your horse badly.

You can go north and travel through Hadassah and Natawni, which is a bad route to take, or you can travel south through Maudrah, which is worse. This is what Amsuhiran har Ta-zii did, and he lived to regret it, which is about the best outcome you can hope for in Maudrah.

Eventually you will come to Garridan, where the mountains start to rise, as if the land itself is trying to escape from what lies below, and if you possess even the vaguest hint of anything resembling self-preservation, at that point you will turn around and retrace your steps back to the benign shores of Almagabra. This is not what Amsuhiran har Ta-zii did, and whether or not he lived to regret it will become clear in due course. Have patience!

They are a handsome tribe, the Garridan. Tall and long-limbed, with pale skin and dark, haunted eyes. It is said that they leave behind them the scent of lilies when they depart. And that their skin glitters in the dark with a cold, pale radiance. Many a har would give his life to know the exquisite joy of taking aruna with one of the Garridan.

Many a har, in fact, has.

It would be unfair to describe the Garridan as dangerous, because the word *dangerous* does not possess the ability to truly convey the nature of the Garridan. Neither do the words *lethal*, *fatal*, *deadly* or *menacing*, but we shall have to use them anyway, and probably in abundance. That is how it is with the Garridan. Don't say you weren't warned.

Another word we shall need to employ with regularity is *poisonous,* and here we come to the heart of the matter. Distracting though their beauty, their perfume, and their remarkable glow-in-the-dark epidermis may be, it is not, alas, what they are famed for all throughout Jaddayoth and beyond, beyond even the shores of distant, balmy Almagabra. The infamy of the Garridan rests upon their skill in the composition, manufacture and deployment of substances of a highly toxic nature.

They are poisoners.

Most tribes of Wraeththu have, in some form or other, opted to specialise in a particular lifestyle. The Kalamah have collectively decided that there is no better life to be lived than that to be found in emulating the feline mind. The Maudrans find that their inner joy can best be expressed in the outer woe of obeying stringently theocratic rules and regulations. The Mojags – well, they are not the first sentient creatures ever to have discovered the delights of combat and conquest, and those optimists among us who hope that they may be the last will probably be used to experiencing the disappointment that is shortly to be theirs.

The Gelaming, for all our sins and graces, have dedicated themselves to peace and enlightenment, and the betterment of all Wraeththu-kind, whether they want to be bettered or not. (Usually not.)

It is difficult for many to comprehend why the Garridan should have chosen to make toxicology their path to fulfilment, but imagine this scenario: The Universal Life Force, in whichever way you chose to define it, has tired of its flawed creation, the human race, and has swept them aside in favour of its new beloved. Wraeththu are everything that humans are not; they are spiritually advanced, and their bodies are perfection; no illness or pathogen can infect them, no drugs or intoxicants can cause them harm.

At least, not the ones currently available.

One thing the Universal Life Force forgot to remove from Wraeththu-kind, along with all the other flaws, was the sin of curiosity. Curiosity is an odd thing; it is a double-edged sword. The desire to learn is a good thing. The desire to learn *that which should probably not be learned*, less so. It was the downfall of Humankind and may yet be the downfall of Wraeththu-kind. We await the outcome with interest.

Be that as it may, the Garridan, confronted with the ineffective nature of the poisons available to them, set about creating new and more deadly ones, a vocation for which, as it turned out, they had a natural talent.

In the beginning, the Garridan created these poisons as defensive weapons to be used in the protection of their tribe and their lands. Although it must be said there were a significant number of incidents in which it appeared that attack had been settled upon as the best form of defence. As peace returned to Jaddayoth under the guiding watch of the Gelaming (may their glorious leadership never fail us), the Garridan, like other tribes, turned to trade with their neighbours as a substitute for murder and thievery, though in the case of the Garridan, the items they were trading usually led to a further outbreak of the former.

Naturally, the fruits of the Garridan's labours were viewed with disapproval by the more upstanding tribes, particularly the Natawni, whose principles were so offended by the nature of the Garridan's product that they insisted upon a complete embargo on dealing with them and the severing of all diplomatic relations. Thus it came about that the import of the customised venom used to coat the *Tiek*, the bone needle used for ritual assassination by that tribe, could only be facilitated by documenting the inbound cargo as "lampshades". Why lampshades we shall never know, but the Natawni are nothing if not a problem-solving tribe.

The har whose skill in formulating this particular export had done so much for inter-tribal relations lived in the mountains of Garridan, far from the other members of his tribe, whose company he did not value. Here, he had constructed for himself a home built from the blackest of obsidian, fashioned into columns and arches and high oriel windows set with glittering glass. From these windows he could look down and spot the approach of anyhar from a distance, and in the event of any appearing, take suitable measures to ensure that his front door was firmly locked and barred, the lights extinguished, and all signs of life absent.

In truth, he was not often to be found in the columned halls of the obsidian palace. He spent the better part of his life down in the cellars beneath, for it was here he had his laboratory, and it was here you might find him at any time of the day or night, engrossed in the distilling of a tincture of unspecified ingredients, oblivious to all else around him.

He took his name from one of the many moods of the weather which stalked the mountainsides on which he had built his home. His name was not Snow – not that pristine whiteness which covered the high peaks in summer and fell silent and sacred in the valleys in winter. It was not Rain – not those soft and steady droplets of liquid water which cause lush green life to flourish wherever they fall. His name was Sleet. You may make of that what you will.

His laboratory was everything you might have hoped for, given what you have learned of him so far. A long flight of stairs led to the entrance, lit by flickering lanterns set into recesses in the wall, whose 4soot had added another layer of deadened blackness to the black obsidian rock. At the bottom, the descent took a leftward curve, whereupon, with a disorientating suddenness, the narrow stairs opened out into a large room with a high vaulted ceiling on which the smoky lanterns cast their flickering shadows.

The walls were lined with shelves containing antique jars the colour of dirty seawater, their ground-glass stoppers held firmly in place by fraying twine. On a few, the name of some powder or reagent was etched into the glass in a long-forgotten language. Others bore no description, but their contents could be seen dimly through the glass sides of the jars – dried fungi, gnarled roots, strange, mummified serpents and sea-creatures preserved in viscous liquid. And other things which it did not pay to examine too closely.

In the centre of the room was a large workbench set out with glass flasks and retorts, and the coiled tubing of distillation columns through which bubbled pungent liquids. Beside these were a number of notebooks, bound in shagreen and containing copious results and observations of experiments, all written in black ink in Sleet's cramped hand.

Some hara hold to the belief that life is governed by chance and serendipity; that great discoveries can be made by throwing the cards of inquisition into the air and allowing them to land where they will. Sleet was not such a har. Sleet was meticulous in everything he did. Sleet experimented carefully, defined his parameters, recorded his results and compared them with previous observations, all in the service of determining the optimum method to achieve his aim.

For example, a problem which had occupied his mind for some days now: What is the best way to bring about a har's death by preventing him from breathing? If you are a Mojag, you would simply separate the har's head from his body with the sharpest sword you can find. It's messy, but it gets the job done. A Kalamah would suffocate him with a silken cushion pressed over his face. Only the *finest* silk would suffice, naturally.

The Gelaming would suck the very oxygen from the air with their tedious lectures on morality.

A Garridan, of course, would use poison, but even then, there are different ways to achieve the desired result. He could, by the mixing together of certain specific liquids, produce a cloud of noxious vapours, which, when inhaled would scald the inner surface of the victim's lungs, causing them to bubble and bleed and fill with fluid instead of air. This was generally considered to be a clumsy method only suitable for beginners, as it produced so much mess in the way of expelled body fluids that you might as well hand the job to a Mojag and be done. Besides, any competent healer might well undo the damage and ruin all the good work, and that would not do.

Then there is our old friend The Poppy, whose bitter juice contains the gift of forgetting. The forgetting of all worries and the forgetting of pain, and eventually, if the dose is judged correctly, the forgetting of the breathing reflex keeping the victim alive. A classic, but sadly unreliable, since many hara are immune to Morpheus' final sting, having cultivated too close a relationship with him for pleasure.

In any case, Sleet considered these methods to be crude and amateurish. To him, there was an artistry in finding the most elegant and precise technique, which in this case required burrowing down deep into the life-sustaining processes of the body, where the complex molecules performed their biochemical dances and completed their predestined cycles, and there to jam a biochemical spanner in the works.

When Sleet did his work, it mattered not that the har had a functioning set of lungs, or a brain capable of sending the signal to breathe; all of these were in vain when the chemical processes were interrupted and the har died from an unseen cause, gasping for air that could not help him, his lips turning that tell-tale shade of blue known as cyan.

For the past two days and nights Sleet had been refining his work on a particular decoction, honing its edge like that of a knife one molecule thick. He had slept little, if at all, and was tired, and that may have been the reason he did not hear the hesitant footsteps on the stairs, the soft scuttling behind him in the dark corner at the back of the laboratory, or the quick intake of breath as he turned around, but he could not help but see the startled face of the intruder, as directly in front of him, eyes wide with surprise or fear or both, stood Amsuhiran har Ta-zii.

(Yes, him. I told you to have patience. And now it is rewarded! Hurrah.)

Sleet's absence from the obsidian palace and its fine oriel windows for the past two days had resulted in him failing to spot the approach of Amsuhiran har Ta-zii, and failing to hear him banging on the locked and barred door with his fists, shouting Sleet's name. In the normal scheme of things, that would not have proved a problem for Sleet, for at that point one of two things ought to have occurred. The first being that the intruder would take the obvious course of action and simply depart, never to be seen again. The second, less likely but still plausible scenario being that the intruder would continue to bang with his fists and shout, until he was unable to do either, and would then perish from hunger, thirst, exposure or spite.

Either of these outcomes would have been acceptable to Sleet. In the event, neither of them came to pass because Amsuhiran har Tazii was not a har given to taking the obvious course of action. And while he was every bit as stubborn as you would expect of a har who had travelled east of Almagabra, though Maudrah, to Garridan, he was not stupid, and at his third attempt to gain entrance by banging on the door and crying the name of the har within, he realised that he was getting nowhere and the wise words of a learned shaman of his acquaintance came to him. Roughly translated from the shamanic tongue, this maxim stated that while doing a stupid thing once was merely stupid, doing it several times was the very definition of imbecility,

At this point, Amsuhiran realised that pursuing a new strategy would benefit his cause, and he had made his way around to the rear of the obsidian palace, to the place where the servants and the serfs and the hara who delivered foodstuffs and all the other banal necessities of life gained their entrance. It was a low, mean, door, devoid of grandeur or pomp, and also, handily for Amsuhiran, devoid of locks and bolts, because although Sleet had no serfs or servants, he did have a healthy appetite. This, coupled with his antipathy towards social interaction, led to him leaving the small back door unlocked so that the har from the village who delivered his food might simply deposit it there and leave without so much as a greeting or farewell. And as you have by now cleverly deduced, led to a small, exhausted har gaining entry into the back reaches of the palace and making his way through its empty, echoing halls, down the twisting staircase and into the very heart of Sleet's laboratory, to stand wide-eyed and frozen in front of the infamous master of the house.

It would have been easy for Sleet to have killed him, there and then. Perhaps with one of the poison darts which he habitually kept about his person. Perhaps by simply snapping his neck, for Sleet was a strong har, tall and sinewy, and Amsuhiran was not. In either case, no court of justice in Garridan would have pronounced a guilty verdict upon Sleet, because his property – his home – had been invaded, and that put him in the right. And they may, indeed, have had other reasons for not wishing to gain the enmity of one of Garridan's foremost practitioners of the poisoner's art. Truly, we can only speculate.

However, the question of Sleet's culpability for the murder of Amsuhiran har Ta-zii did not, thankfully for both Amsuhiran and this tale, arise. As Amsuhiran stood there in front of Sleet, rigid with fear, Sleet found himself intrigued. Normally, he would have been highly displeased to have his work interrupted, but by chance he had experienced an epiphany regarding the direction his endeavours were taking him only moments before Amsuhiran's appearance, and he felt that a small pause in his labours for regrouping his thoughts and – perhaps – a moment of self-congratulation, was in order.

He stretched and untangled limbs cramped from hours spent poring over his work, then poured himself a glass of the bubbling liquid from the retort, inhaling its vapours deeply. With a feral smile, he offered the same to his uninvited guest. Amsuhiran refused it, with a shaky smile. Which, although it was only a herbal tisane, was probably wise.

"And now," Sleet began, in a voice full of cautioning, "perhaps you would be so good as to tell me why you have intruded into my house?"

Amsuhiran looked up at him with obsidian-dark eyes fringed with sooty lashes, in which tears swam and threatened to spill at any moment, and in a trembling voice told a tragic tale of love and loss; of a har whom Amsuhiran had loved more than life itself, a har in whose face the sun rose and set and in whose voice the angels sang; a har who had lived in far-off Almagabra, and, unfortunately, had also died in far-off Almagabra after an unfortunate incident involving arunic auto-asphyxiation.

Amsuhiran's voice trembled all the more as he described to Sleet the pain he had felt on his beloved's death; how he had spent a year and a day prostrate with grief, how he had prayed to the dehar of abandoned lovers, only to be abandoned by that inconstant entity. Until one day he had, by chance, heard a tale of how a har had once descended into the underworld in pursuit of his dead love, and there had reclaimed him and returned him to the land of the living. Upon hearing this tale, Amsuhiran had determined that he, too, would do the very same, and had spent another year and a day attempting to discover how a living har might enter the underworld, the land of the dead, where only those whose bodies had ceased to live might go.

Eventually, in the course of many whispered, furtive conversations in the dimly-lit back rooms of disreputable inns and hostelries, he had learned that in order to visit the land of the dead and be able to return, a har must ingest a certain poison which separates the body from the soul. If the poison is administered in the correct dose, eventually life will return to har's body. But this poison was very rare, and the knowledge of how to utilise its terrible properties even rarer. In those dim, dusty back rooms, one name was spoken, in hushed and fearful tones, over and over again. And that name was Sleet Aphanizomen Flos-Aquae har Garridan.

When Amsuhiran had finished speaking, he gazed pleadingly at Sleet. Sleet poured himself another glass of the herbal tisane and without a word took himself over to a battered old leather couch pushed against one wall. He had spent many a night in the laboratory on this couch, on those occasions when his luxurious bedroom in the high tower did not seem worth the climb. He sat down in its sagging depths and indicated to Amsuhiran to do the same. Amsuhiran perched nervously on the edge of the couch, as if fearing that if he settled himself more comfortably into its lumpy embrace it might swallow him up entirely.

Sleet studied Amsuhiran carefully. In addition to his eyes, which were large and dark, Amsuhiran had long black hair, reaching past the mid-point of his body, straight as rain on a wind-less day, slick as spilled oil. And he had golden skin, blushed with pink and softened with the lightest downy fuzz of hairs, which seemed to form a glowing halo round his face in the lamplight.

Sleet stared at that skin, and a memory formed in his mind. Of a time, some years ago, when he had travelled to the lands of the Kalamah tribe, in search of a rare species of amphibian known for its toxic skin. It had taken many weeks of travel, south through the territory of the Mojag tribe. The Mojag - that fiercest and most war-like of Wraeththu tribes, whose hostility towards strangers was legendary, who would kill any har not of their own tribe without a second thought. And who let a lone, travelling Garridan har by the name of Sleet pass without let or hindrance, because even the Mojag are not *that* stupid.

Eventually he had come to the land of the Kalamah, where he was treated graciously and given food and lodgings with an alluring har of high status. His host had a peach tree in his garden, and from it Sleet had plucked and eaten a ripe fruit, warm from the sun. It had soft, furry skin, like a mole, and when he bit into it the flesh was yielding, like that of a dead animal which had lain rotting for days, but the sweet juice flooded his mouth and ran down his chin and onto his shirt, and filled him with something approaching ecstasy.

Sleet had dreamed of peaches ever since, his nights filled with the remembrance of their scent and taste, but the trees did not grow in Garridan, the cold winds killed them, and those fruits brought from Kalamah were rotten by the time they got there, grey with fungus. But as he gazed at Amsuhiran's golden skin, it was as if he could once again taste the sweetness of the peach and feel its soft-furred texture in his mouth.

Resisting the temptation to bite into Amsuhiran's rose-gold cheek, Sleet returned his attention to the har's story. He stifled a yawn. It was an old tale. Older even, in all probability, than Wraeththu. There were many versions of it, told by many tribes. Sleet suspected that Amsuhiran had heard it from the Ferike. The Ferike were fond of telling tales. Writing down stories in their leather-bound books using those ridiculous quill pens that they affected. Making things up. Lying. Sleet respected any skill expertly executed, even lying, but was all nonsense, of course – nohar ever returned from the dead. Death was final. Irrevocable. The priesthood of the Maudrah tribe, the Niz, endorsed this view theologically and enthusiastically, and Sleet agreed with them, professionally.

No amount of elegant Ferike penmanship could make a lie the truth, but Amsuhiran believed it, and Sleet was not above taking advantage of a har's gullibility.

It is fair to say that Sleet's professional services did not come cheap, but those who want the best must be prepared to pay for it. When Sleet mentioned a figure in excess of what would comfortably keep a har housed and provisioned for a year, Amsuhiran did not flinch, or turn pale, or exhibit any other signs of embarrassment, financial or otherwise. Instead, the tears welled up in his eyes again as he informed Sleet that he had travelled to Garridan from Almagabra through the lands of Maudrah, where his fine Gimranish horse and all his money had been stolen by those righteous purveyors of moral propriety, the Niz.

It was a tale which would have melted a heart made of stone. Sleet's heart was apparently made of some mineral with an even higher melting point, for it remained in a solid state even as Amsuhiran declared that he owned but one thing in this world, and he would grant that to Sleet in return for his fabled poison.

In case Sleet had not deduced what the one thing in this world that he owned was, Amsuhiran untied the leather thong at the neck of his shirt and let it fall open, revealing his body beneath, which was as golden and haloed as his face.

Sleet studied the vision before him for a few moments, and the taste of peaches was in his mouth.

"Your offer is accepted." he said.

Oh, I expect some of you will now be denying that there is anything unwholesome in this transaction, for do not hara regularly give freely of themselves and their bodies in arunic congress? Your dishonesty in failing to account for the power imbalance here, and your avoidance of seeing the unpleasantly mercenary nature of the act is duly noted. If you cannot deal with the reality of this sort of thing you should go back to Almagabra, as it's not going to get any better

So then, having agreed the purchase price for his expertise, Sleet took Amsuhiran by the hand and led him to the other side of his laboratory where a large slab of stone lay supported on a raised dais. This stone was not obsidian, but marble. Cold and white, veined with grey lines, like vessels filled with blood that had turned to dust. Here Sleet removed the rest of Amsuhiran's clothing, and laid him on his back on the cold marble, and Amsuhiran's fingers clutched nervously at the edge of the slab, feeling the channel cut there, and deliberately not dwelling upon what the purpose of it might be.

Then Sleet placed his mouth delicately upon Amsuhiran's, and their breath exchanged and mingled, and became a summer's day in Kalamah, with all the bees buzzing and the soft fuzz of peach skin touching harish skin, and as they became one, Amsuhiran's juices flooded Sleet's mouth and filled him with something approaching ecstasy.

Once the payment had been fulfilled, Amsuhiran sat up, his back now as cold as the marble, although the stone itself seemed not to have gained any warmth from the har.

"Now," he said.

Sleet gave a curt nod of agreement. He did not particularly want to do what he was about to do, but this was business, and his own desires did not come into it. While his moral failings were many, his business reputation was second to none, and he intended to keep it that way.

He walked over to the tall racks of shelves which held the glass-stoppered bottles and selected one without hesitation. It seemed indistinguishable from those around it and bore no identifying marks upon its surface other than the omnipresent dust and cobwebs. From a small drawer, which opened only reluctantly, he took a sharpened quill or spine, possibly from some long-dead creature of the sea or land, its desiccated appearance giving no clue as to its origins.

He took both the jar and the quill over to the marble slab and set them down in front of Amsuhiran.

"What is in this jar is known to no other har," he told him. "It is a poison. It will kill you. It will kill your body, but not your soul. Your body will die, and your soul will be free to roam the underworld where souls abide which have no living body to inhabit. Yet on the third day, your body will live again, and your soul will return. What changes may have been wrought upon it by its severing from your body, I cannot say. Do you agree to have this poison introduced into your body?"

"I do," said Amsuhiran. His voice trembled slightly, but his golden skin seemed to have lost none of its radiance.

"Then write your name upon this agreement," said Sleet,

producing a piece of parchment with standard clauses upon it, for even the Garridan have laws, and self-administered poison is codified within those laws, which should come as a surprise to nohar.

Amsuhiran looked at the quill in Sleet's hand, and Sleet made an impatient sound and handed him the practical pen with its own internal ink reservoir which he used for writing his notes. Amsuhiran signed the document, and Sleet studied it carefully for a few moments. His lips seemed to silently form the syllables of Amsuhiran's name, and then he studied the golden har carefully, as if trying to conjoin the two together, to make what he knew of one fit seamlessly with the other.

When he was satisfied, he opened the glass jar, laying the stopper carefully aside, and introduced the quill into it, blunt end first. At the very bottom there was a smear of a black substance, sticky and almost solid, which may once have been liquid but was now thick and viscous, like tar, or dried blood.

Sleet had collected this substance from a lake in the north of Garridan known for its beauty and its danger. Its azure waters gave no clue to its deadliness, but no animals lived near it, no birds flew, no subterranean creatures crept or crawled within the soil around its shores. Sleet had taken the water from this lake and in his laboratory he had boiled and condensed it, titrated and measured it, added reagents and catalysts, and with all the skills at his command had folded the molecules to his will until they assumed a form that fitted exactly the receptors at the neuromuscular junction of a har's nervous system, as precisely as a key fits a lock. It had taken him many months, and when he had finished he felt himself pleased with his work, for he had created what he considered to be a work of artistry and a thing of beauty, in its own dark way.

With the sharpened end of the quill he pierced the skin of Amsuhiran's upper arm, a swift, sudden prick that caused the har to wince briefly. A drop of blood ran down Amsuhiran's arm, and when it had reached nearly to the elbow, Sleet touched the other end of the quill to it, the end coated with a small amount of the black substance, and immediately it touched the blood, the blood itself turned black at that point. Then the blackness started to rise up the rivulet of blood running down Amsuhiran's arm, quickly and urgently, as if eager to do its lethal business.

The blackness reached the small wound in Amsuhiran's skin from where the blood issued forth, and entered his body. For a moment, nothing happened, and then Amsuhiran's body started to shake and convulse, and he would have fallen to the floor if Sleet had not caught him. He took him and laid him on the marble slab, and held him there as his convulsions threatened to twist his body apart. Soon they grew weaker, and within a mercifully short space of time Amsuhiran lay still and lifeless on the slab. His skin was still golden, but his lips were bluish grey, and his flesh grew cool rapidly on the marble.

Sleet checked that all breathing and heartbeat had ceased, nodded to himself with satisfaction, then took up his practical pen and returned to his workbench to write his notes on a fresh page in his book.

He noted down the date and the time and the name of the poison (which shall not be disclosed here, for reasons of self-preservation) and the dose and the effects and the dimensions of the body of the subject. What he did *not* write down was that what he had told Amsuhiran was a lie.

Oh, he had not lied about the effects of the poison, it brought about the death of the body as promised. And he had not lied that the soul would live on for Sleet knew that the soul could not die. Even *he* could not create a poison that could kill the immortal part of a har. But the tale he had attested to, of the underworld to where Amsuhiran's detached soul might go in order to be reunited with his deceased love – that was pure invention.

Sleet knew that many hara believed in the existence of a post-mortem paradise where they would be reunited with those they had cared for in their earthly existence. Some thought of it as an Elysian Arcadia where rare birds sang in the blossom-filled boughs of shade-giving trees and fountains tinkled like the sound of distant laughter. Others envisaged a darker, more sombre land full of sighing shades and lost spirits. Sleet did not much care one way or the other. Fear of death took many forms, and it was not his job to disillusion hara by informing them that there was nothing after death – no birds, no fountains, no shades, and no lost love waiting to be led by the hand back to the land of the living.

These tales had taken root largely due to the reports of hara who had suffered catastrophic injury or illness to the point of death but had recovered and lived to recount their experience. Sleet could not even be bothered to tell such individuals that the visions they saw were a result of a brain deprived of oxygen creating its own reality. Or in certain cases (which he may or may not have been instrumental in bringing about), hallucinations caused by psychotropic drugs. In fact, Sleet considered it a kindness to allow hara their fantasies. It relieved them of their anxieties, and if, by happy chance, it also resulted in Sleet relieving them of payment for services rendered, then he considered it a victory for all concerned.

He raised his head from his book and closed his eyes, remembering for a moment his payment from Amsuhiran, and, unusually for him, a wistful sigh escaped his lips. He looked over at the body on the slab, cold and still, gilded in the flickering torchlight, like a har cast from solid gold. Stone and metal. Earth elements.

Despite the fact that his notes were still incomplete, he felt drawn to the slab. Closing his book, he walked over and let his gaze rest on the motionless form of Amsuhiran. The chest did not rise and fall, taking in air to the lungs and delivering oxygen to the blood. The heart did not pump, sending that blood around the body to give up its oxygen to the metabolic pathways in the cells. And yet, the body persisted, the flesh remained uncorrupt. Golden and perfect. Peach fuzz covering every inch, save for the pubis where it grew longer and darker and thicker, bringing to mind the pelt of a furred animal.

Sleet was overcome with the desire to touch that fur again, to feel its softness beneath his fingertips and hear the long-dead bees buzzing in his ears. He stripped himself of all his clothing, climbed up onto the slab and lay on top of dead Amsuhiran. The flesh under him was cold, and when he entered into it, he found that it was as cold inside as it was outside.

Oh, don't pretend that you are shocked! You already knew what sort of har Sleet is – a poisoner and a sexual predator – and you were quite willing to accept *that*. Don't look away now. I told you it wasn't going to get any better. You should have stayed in Almagabra if you are such a sensitive soul, but it's too late now. You are complicit.

Accept it.

For three days and nights the body of Amsuhiran lay on the slab watched over by Sleet, for whatever values of "watched" you choose to assign. On the third day the body took one deep, gasping breath into its lungs as the soul returned home, and the body was Amsuhiran again. He pulled himself up into a sitting position and vomited up green bile and stomach acids, then began to weep bitterly and copiously.

Sleet took his second-best cloak of fur and wrapped it around Amsuhiran, disregarding the corrosive body fluids on both the slab and Amsuhiran himself. Between his shivering sobs, Amsuhiran related to Sleet his experiences in the underworld, describing a place full of fire-breathing serpents and winged creatures of light, where although he had roamed for the three days of his death, he had failed to find any trace of his lost beloved.

Sleet added this description to his mental collection of underworlds, for it was one he had not heard before, and he placed his arms around the fur cloak wrapped around Amsuhiran to add warmth and some degree of solace to the weeping har, but Amsuhiran would not be comforted, and he begged Sleet to inject him with the poison a second time, so that he might return to that strange landscape and continue his search.

Sleet found himself torn, which was unusual for him. The poison was dangerous the first time it was administered, doubly so if used on a second occasion. He explained this to Amsuhiran, but Amsuhiran would not be dissuaded, and pleaded so piteously, and offered his body – his warm, golden, living body – with such passionate ardour that Sleet felt his objections dissolve like an ionic compound in water.

So he lifted Amsuhiran, still wrapped in the cloak, from the marble slab and carried him to the battered old couch against the far wall and here he set him down tenderly in the couch's ancient, leathery embrace. Then he removed all of his own clothing and slid naked under the fur next to Amsuhiran, skin against skin, and here he felt summer return. The air was heavy with the scent of sun-baked peaches, and in the moment when noon was at its highest Sleet felt something that was indistinguishable from ecstasy.

When he scraped the poison from the bottom of the jar again, he was careful to take it from the side where it had dried almost fully, because he knew that here it would have lost some of its efficacy. He touched the blade of the quill against the trickle of blood on Amsuhiran's arm only very briefly, and on this occasion the blackness rose lazily, as if it were putting off the inevitable moment, but eventually it reached the wound in Amsuhiran's skin and the convulsions began again, as did Sleet's three day vigil.

This time his notes were brief, ending on an unfinished sentence. He put down his pen, drawn as if by some unseen force to the marble slab. He lay on top of dead Amsuhiran, trying to warm the cold flesh beneath him with his own body heat, and when that failed he sat by the side on a hard chair and lightly ran his fingertips over the soft peach-fuzz on Amsuhiran's skin. He imagined what it would feel like to have somehar do the same to him. He had no peach-fuzz, and he did not like to be touched, but he imagined it nonetheless.

His thoughts also strayed to the har whom Amsuhiran sought so desperately in the underworld. What sort of har had he been, to command such devotion? What spell, or potion, or poison, had given him such power over another? What was it about him that made Amsuhiran risk everything that he might live again?

Sleet also wished that the unknown har was alive, so that he could kill him. And not in a kind, gentle way, employing the Poppy and its seductive sleep, but with a toxin which caused all the muscles in the body to spasm so fiercely that bones and tendons cracked, and the spine twisted and broke, and the victim died in agony. Sleet had watched this particular poison do its work, and even he found it disturbing, yet he felt that he could bear to witness it one more time.

On the third day, Amsuhiran's soul returned to his body with an inrush of air to his lungs, followed immediately by a paroxysm of coughing and an out-rush of frothy blood and serum. Sleet washed away the fluids with the warm water he had prepared, and held Amsuhiran in his arms until the sobbing quietened enough for Amsuhiran to tell him what Sleet already knew – that he had not found his lost love in the underworld, though he had searched through parched lands of fire and flame for what seemed like an eternity.

This gift of premonition, which the dehara had been generous enough to bestow upon Sleet in that moment, also told him what Amsuhiran would ask of him next.

There existed, he knew, the possibility of refusal. In a universe of infinite events, anything could occur. However Sleet knew that his infinite world had been narrowed down by every decision he had taken in his life, diverting him down pathways and corridors, side alleys and dead ends, directing him to where he stood now, in a place where all his life choices came together to make him what he was, and what he would do. And the har that he was would not – *could not* – refuse Amsuhiran's request.

And so having named his price once again, Sleet took Amsuhiran away from the laboratory. Away from the cold marble slab and the lumpen sofa. Up the blackened stairs, through the empty, echoing obsidian halls. Up the spiralling stairs of the high tower to his luxurious bedroom at the top where four great oriel windows looked out in each direction. To the jagged mountains to the north. To the marshlands to the south. To the forests in the east, and toward the dying sun in the west. Sleet gazed out through these windows, as he had done many times before, and noted, without surprise, that the last of the autumn leaves had fallen, and the golden, slanted light which had shone through them was gone. High on the mountain top, the storms of winter were gathering.

In the very centre of the room was a vast bed, stuffed with soft down and feathers, and strewn with silken cushions and the pelts of many rare wild animals. Here, Sleet laid Amsuhiran down, among the musty furs, and here he took him, body and soul, while the wind moaned and shrieked outside the high tower, and threw icy fingers against the leaded windows, which were not liquid enough to be rain and not solid enough to be ice

Inside, there was the scent of summer flowers and the warmth of a long-ago sun. The hum of insect wings. The memory of something once tasted and never forgotten. And as the wind howled his name, and the windows rattled in their leaded frames, and Amsuhiran's fingers clawed his back, Sleet felt something beyond ecstasy.

Afterwards, Sleet took Amsuhiran once again back down to the laboratory. He warned him that the poison was thirty times as dangerous if administered on a third occasion, in the hope that this might dissuade Amsuhiran, but of course it did not. So he took the glass jar again, and scraped the smallest portion from the most dried edge, and diluted it in a solvent, to decrease the number of active molecules still further, before touching it for the briefest of moments against the blood on Amsuhiran's arm. The blackness crawled slowly, so very slowly that Sleet thought that perhaps it would not reach the top of the blood, and he held his breath as it slowed almost to a stop, but with one last exhausted effort it gained the entry point into Amsuhiran's body.

The spasms which followed were almost like unto those generated by the poison that Sleet had wished upon Amsuhiran's dead love. And then Amsuhiran was dead, and his soul no longer resided within his body, and for three days and nights Sleet sat by the marble slab, holding Amsuhiran's dead, cold hand in his.

On the third day, Amsuhiran's soul did not return to his body. There was no gasping, sucking, wheezing rush of air into his lungs, no fluids and no sobbing, only a body lying still and cold upon the marble slab. The flesh remained unmarked by death, but all life was extinct. Permanently.

And that is how Amsuhiran har Ta-zii met his untimely end. There are worse ways to die, although not many. The Garridan are working on that, be assured.

And what of Sleet? Some say that he took his own poison and followed Amsuhiran into the underworld, and that their bodies lie together on the marble slab, cold and uncorrupt, beautiful still in death. Some say that he waits still for Amsuhiran to return, holding his hand, never faltering in his vigilant watch, never straying from his self-appointed task.

And others yet, who probably have more cause to know what they're talking about, say that he continues to work in his laboratory, day and night, consumed by a mission to isolate the poison which can kill a har's soul. For Sleet har Garridan felt his soul die when Amsuhiran did not return from the underworld. Logic tells him that the substance which produced this effect is contained within

Amsuhiran's body – on his skin, or in his blood, or other essences – and so he takes samples of Amsuhiran's golden, peach-fuzzed skin, homogenises it and subjects it to chemical analysis. He drains his blood and other bodily fluids into the channel cut around the edge of the marble slab for that purpose, and he extracts other essences of the dead har's body by means which you are probably avoiding thinking about, quite rightly.

Of course, there is no way of knowing if this is actually true or not. Perhaps none of this is true. Perhaps the whole tale is simply one big lie. There is only one way to find out and that would be to travel east of Almagabra, past the Sea of Shadows, to the high rocky mountains of Garridan.

And who would be foolish enough to do that?

The Shade of Q'orlenn

Storm Constantine

Shrive har Gloaming, artist and poet, appraised his most recent canvas. The light of a mellow Almagabran evening poured into his studio, highlighting the life-size painted figure before him. He sighed, took a step back. *No...* he thought. *Why do you elude me? You inhabited the pigment for an hour, but now...?*

A short tap came upon his studio door, and whoever was responsible didn't wait for a response. The door opened and Lustre har Welkin sailed in, bringing with him a humming sense of activity, along with a breath of wine and a smell of cooking sausages from the market of Sevriosta – their home town, a haven for creative hara, twenty miles up the coast from Immanion.

"Shrive, you're late," the har declared. He was a creature of brown and gold – bronze skin, gilded, coppery hair. He too was an artist, but a flighty one. By comparison, Shrive was dour, with more of the neurotic, fevered poet about him than a spirit of energetic life. He preferred clothes that hid rather than displayed, despite being the kind of dark har found very attractive by those drawn to neurotic artistic types.

Again, Shrive sighed. "I won't be coming to dinner. This... *thing...* just won't work."

Lustre came to stand beside his friend, put his head to one side. "Looks fine to me. Who is it?"

"It's *not* right," Shrive insisted. "The expression is all wrong... flat and dead... the glow of the skin... looks like a corpse."

"Then *who* is it?" Lustre bit into a pear he'd retrieved from his jacket pocket.

"Q'orlenn."

Lustre shrugged. "It's brilliant. All your work is. Now put down your brushes and your sighs and come to dinner." He paused. "Is it a

157

commission?"

"Yes," said Shrive glumly. "And it has to be right. This isn't. It's *not* brilliant, Lustre. Your flattery is insincere, inspired only by an empty stomach. I'll have to start again."

Lustre laughed. "Well, the model is appetising."

"He might be, but he's not Q'orlenn, or rather I can't *make* him Q'orlenn."

"Q'orlenn is a fiction," Lustre said, "He exists only in the minds of those who've read the novel, or seen the play... sang along to the gloomy musical... slashed their wrists to the popular songs..."

"He's an ideal, the unattainable, the doomed beauty," Shrive interrupted. "This picture has been commissioned by the Arts Veil of Immanion, as part of a grand exhibition in the city next year. I want to capture the essence of Q'orlenn..." He threw wide his arms. "...for my work to shine brighter than all the stars of Immanion."

The silence was broken only by the wet crunch of Lustre biting into the pear. He chewed thoughtfully. "What is lacking exactly... as you perceive it?"

It didn't surprise Shrive that Lustre failed to understand the imperfection in the work, since his own paintings were, in Shrive's opinion, lively but slapdash – and annoyingly very popular. "Q'orlenn represents the ideal of hara," Shrive said primly, "a distant spiritual perfection. He is aloof, lustrous, beguiling yet tragic, carrying within him the memories of our birth, inner scars that torture him but can't be seen. He is the vessel of love but cannot give it in return. Those who adore him are doomed, their hearts shriven in two as if by a poisoned blade. They can only die for love of him."

"That's quite enough," Lustre said, grimacing. "He sounds unbearably dreary to me. Why don't you break convention and paint him as a coquette, who dooms the unwary only by leading them to their deaths through seduction and soul-sundering aruna."

Shrive gave Lustre a stare. "You don't take my work seriously, so please don't tire yourself by commenting on it. You might as well leave now. I'm going to start again."

"From memory? Where's your model?"

"He'll be back tomorrow," Shrive said shortly. "In the meantime, I'll work from sketches."

"Who are you using?"

"Ozie har Mahan. He isn't right for the picture but the nearest I've found."

"What? Isn't he regarded as the most sublime, limpid model in Almagabra, if not beyond?"

"He is, and every artist of note in Almagabra and beyond has employed him. Sadly, his likeness has become... common."

"And how hard have you looked for another model?"

"I've looked everywhere," Shrive said tartly. He shook his head. "I've seen many wondrous visions, but still can't find the right har for this work. I can barely define the qualities I'm looking for. They're so... fluid."

"Mmm," murmured Lustre. "So, to simplify this *fluidity*, you're after a tragic, pallid, fey sort of har?"

"A luminous, eerie, indefinable sort of har."

"Well, luck is with you, because I know where you'll find him," declared Lustre.

"What? Where? Who?"

Lustre put a finger to his friend's lips. "Sssh, be quiet. Come and eat. Later I'll take you to him. I'm sure he'll be the one. Trust me."

Q'orlenn had been written in ai-cara 52, five years before, by Ayzel har Sythe and was regarded as his best work. Since then, after a glittering launch and every critic of literature in Almagabra claiming it was the perfect novel, it had undergone a number of adaptations – as Lustre had mentioned – into a play and a rather ponderous musical. It was also the subject of or inspiration for numerous songs as well as being fair game for comedians to parody.

Q'orlenn the character was, at his core, the idealised and unattainable icon of perfection that every har secretly believed existed somewhere for them to find and adore. If they couldn't discover their Q'orlenn, they could adore him in their imaginations. The plot of the novel wasn't original by any means – the tale of Shoal, an early phyle leader of a fictional tribe called the Writhen. Shoal finds Q'orlenn among a huddle of captives of war, daubed with the blood of his slaughtered comrades. Shoal is struck by an indefinable quality in the har and is touched deep within. He releases Q'orlenn but thereafter is drawn to follow him on a surreal pilgrimage, through a landscape of fundamental archetypes, as if lured by a sacred relic. Whenever Q'orlenn catches sight of Shoal he gazes upon the har with what seems to be great sadness and pity. Shoal is barbaric, undoubtedly based upon Uigenna leaders like Wraxilan or Manticker. He has no pity within his heart, no compassion, but still something within him is drawn to Q'orlenn, who is the symbol of the pain of the world. Eventually, after a number of encounters with colourful characters who symbolise aspects of the harish condition, experiences that test Shoal's belief in himself and reveal his spiritual deficiencies, he eventually finds redemption, the capacity for love and magic within himself, along with the realisation that the har he has adored for so long does not exist – except as a pleading ghost within himself. But, beyond this revelation, Q'orlenn appears to Shoal again, a shining light in the distance: another mountain of experience to climb, more lessons to be learned. Shoal might never, in this life, attain the glittering, sacred love he yearns for, but will continue to pursue it, refining himself as the alchemists once to sought to make gold of themselves from base lead.

The nuances of the tale were what enraptured critics the most. Everyhar could see a part of themselves in Shoal. Everyhar longed for a Q'orlenn to guide and evolve them. Har Sythe had a gift for playing the music of words, and his prose was like a drug to the senses.

Shrive was seeking the equivalent in paint. He wanted his image of Q'orlenn to inspire and captivate. He wanted hara to gaze upon it and weep, to fall desperately and painfully in love, knowing it would be a love never fulfilled. The face that looked down upon them from the painting must be as lovely as the most distant, brightest star of the galaxy, hanging in the cold reaches of space, murmuring of eternity.

"Where are we going?" Shrive demanded. After leaving his studio, he and Lustre had eaten at an acclaimed restaurant and were now walking the streets of Sevriosta, in the half-light of a summer evening, before the dark drew down.

"To see a friend of mine," Lustre said. "I've already contacted him and he's waiting for us."

They turned a corner into a shadowed street, where the dusk had already taken root and the tall lamps had not yet been lit.

"The only establishment here, apart from closed shops, is the Otherlanes Way Station," Shrive said. "Are we going there?"

"Yes," Lustre answered.

Shrive laughed. "Really? You have a friend there?"

"Yes, we're going on a short otherlanes journey."

Shrive shook his head. "The *sedim* liveried there are for official journeys only. You can't just *borrow* one."

"Two actually, and I don't intend to borrow. There are four in that station, and rarely used in this town, as we have few officials who need to travel anywhere urgently. My friend hires the beasts out with a pilot, and I can afford it."

Lustre, of course, was far richer than Shrive because his work was more accessible and therefore sold to excess. Shrive's dark pictures sought to capture the bittersweet trials of life through allegory and myth. Walking through a gallery displaying his work was like travelling a narrow trail through a lightless, threatening forest, where strange, twisted creatures lurked, and predatory beings of unbearable beauty crouched in the branches of trees. Emerging from this forest, a har might feel dazed, breathless, even bewitched by what they'd witnessed. By contrast, Lustre painted town scenes in glaring colours, light-hearted portraits that bordered on the pornographic, (much sought after by the influential to hang upon their walls with wry humour), or – his most formal work – very flattering portraits in bright colours of celebrities and their families. Of the two, Shrive was the more skilled and dedicated artist, and his work had greater depth, but often Shrive wished he could be more like Lustre, who had many friends in salient positions throughout the community, most of them willing to act in a dubious fashion if required. Such as now...

Only half an hour later, (and over fifteen of those minutes had been spent waiting to see Lustre's friend), the Way Station pilot dropped them off at a lockhouse beside a wide, dark canal. The land here was flat and rather bleak: cultivated land from the Human Era gone wild. Lustre gave the har a generous tip and asked him to meet them at the same spot at 2 a.m. It appeared he had allotted several hours to track down the potential model.

The air was chillier here and the light lower. The sun sulked as it collapsed into the western horizon, a bloated red globe that appeared diseased.

"Where are we?" Shrive asked, still shaken by the journey. He'd never traversed the otherlanes before, and after the bone-shattering experience, wasn't inclined to do so again, even though the journey home was inevitable.

Lustre gestured widely to the north and announced with relish, "Welcome, my friend, to Fallsend, the dung pit of Wraeththudom."

Shrive rubbed his arms, which were chill in his flimsy summer coat. "We're... in Thaine."

"We are," said Lustre. "We'll now take a boat to town. We can't arrive in Fallsend in a showy display of *sedim*. The results could be... well... it's safer this way. We won't be noticed as much."

Shrive eyed with misgiving the cluster of shabby vessels rubbing together near the lower lock gates. "You've been here before – clearly. Who is this har you promised to show me? The venue is hardly auspicious."

Lustre laughed. "I come here often. The hara of Fallsend are amazingly colourful creatures and several have appeared in my erotic fantasy works. I've seen your Q'orlenn out and about. He's always interested me, but..." He shook his head. "I'm sure he'll be what *you* need." Grinning, he approached a lean, rather grubby har who sat upon the edge of the lock, his legs dangling over the damp stone.

The rest of the journey was unforgettable to Shrive, and more inspiring than he'd expected. The lock boathar rowed up the canal passing between the long, silent, weirdly oppressive barges, with their surprisingly high sides, which were piled with lumber, furs, nuts and minerals from the northern forest territories. Barge hara crouched like beautiful, lithe gargoyles on the peaked canvases that covered the goods, smoking pipes or swigging from clay jugs. Gems glittered on their fingers and in their teeth. As the boat drew nearer to Fallsend, the walls to either side grew higher. Misshapen tall buildings leaned over the water, and the noise of the town soared up like an approaching storm. Laughter, shouting voices, musical instruments, the chanting calls of traders, handbells of hara seeking business of dubious kinds, the mournful horns of the barges, the shriek of seabirds come inland to forage. And over all an invisible smog – the breath of Fallsend.

Here perhaps lived the template of Shoal, a har who had fled east from Megalithica in the early days, a harish predator, a killer. And here, among the tall, dark, dilapidated buildings, run through by the dull serpent of the canal, he had found his captive, his Q'orlenn.

Shrive could visualise these scenes easily in this fetid hive. It was wonderful.

Eventually, the boathar – who'd not spoken a word during the trip – brought his vessel to a halt beside worn stone steps that led up to the street. Here, Lustre pressed coins into the outstretched hand and helped Shrive disembark.

The Almagabrans were caught up immediately in the atmosphere of the town, which was at once rowdy and condensed, bleak yet vital.

"This is like an allegorical painting come to life," Shrive said, as they pushed their way through crowds of the baroque along the busy, narrow streets.

"You sound almost inspired," Lustre said, clearly surprised.

"It's so extreme, I couldn't fail to be," Shrive responded, "but perhaps not in the same way you are. I don't simply see colour and depravity here but the great legacy of our history, the spectral fog of it."

Lustre laughed. "I should've guessed."

The lamps in Fallsend were living flames, voraciously chewing the air. There were stinks of refuse, but also the perfume of flowers, of incense, of cooking, savoury meat. There was an aroma of burning sugar, of coffee, of vanilla, of harish sweat, the musk of desire, with an undernote of fresh blood and gutted fish. The hara revealed in the living light could have stepped from illustrations of fairy-tales – weird costumes and adornments, bizarre tattoos and piercings, hairstyles of every extreme, whether that was a har whose fair plait dragged along the ground behind him like a train, or a har sporting such a complicated sculpture of lacquered locks it resembled a surreal organic building. There were so many different kinds of faces and shapes, it seemed Fallsend was populated by hara who'd been outcast from every tribe that existed. Then there were the occasional quieter hara, dressed in dark clothes, who clearly had business of a deadlier nature. They leaned against walls, alone or in pairs, eyeing the passers-by, their horrific trade imprinted into their long, ascetic faces. Shrive knew their look: Garridan, hara renowned for concocting poisons that could kill. Substances that could once have slain a human in a moment might bring only a sneeze to a har. It took a special kind of alchemy to create a har-killer.

To work with death, Shrive mused. *What is the inner life of a Garridan like?* He yearned to paint one of these hara.

Lustre eventually led them to the open doors of an inn. Within, all seemed a murk of dim light and smoke and the clash of discordant instruments. Lustre clawed a way for them through the packed bodies. "The canal dock workers have just finished the day shift," he shouted in Shrive's ear. "Always busy here at this time."

They eventually drew close to the bar.

"And here," Lustre said, laying a hand on Shrive's shoulder "is your Q'orlenn." He indicated discreetly a group of hara a few feet ahead of them.

At first Shrive was puzzled. All he saw was a noisy, cawing group, all smoking pipes and swigging down the raw, noxious spirits and ales of the establishment. "Where?" he asked.

Shrive said, "Leaning against the bar. Look closer. The pale one."

It was then that the har in question came into focus for Shrive. He was indeed pale, and very thin, with large brown eyes, deep set with dark skin around them. Perhaps this hue was merely makeup. His hands were narrow, one gripping a mug, the other a clay pipe. His hair was abundant, golden brown and piled up – mostly – on his head, with rags of it trailing down. His skin was... yes... luminous, but as if from the ravages of sickness rather than natural pallor. He was like a throwback to the Human Era. Morbidly fascinated by the concept of wasting illnesses in humankind, Shrive had researched the subject. As far as he knew, no har suffered from sickness of that type. If it was portrayed in literature and art, it was only as an affliction of the soul, the drive for self-destruction that might lurk within a harish heart. The har at the bar was, in a strange way, beautiful; willowy, somehow weary, a dull glow burning in those eyes, while the face grinned and chattered. He was at once repulsive yet sublime.

As they drew nearer, Shrive heard snatches of conversation from the hara at the bar. The pale har's voice was coarse. He spoke in an almost brutish manner, cursing with old human words, never now heard beyond the boundaries of wild, outlaw settlements like Fallsend. For just a moment, the har's gaze flicked towards Shrive, acknowledged his interest, then slid away. He expelled a caw of laughter, gulped his drink.

"You see," said Lustre.

"Dear Aru, he's an abomination," Shrive said, "but… yes… I see the potential for a model. If he can keep his mouth shut."

"For money, he will no doubt do anything."

Shrive drew in a breath.

"And before you say anything," Lustre interrupted, "let me pay for this. I hate to see you artistically constipated."

"Well…" Shrive considered his finances, and the fact a har of Fallsend would inevitably seek to swindle a har of Almagabra. "All right. Thank you. But he might say no."

Lustre raised an eyebrow. "You think so? But don't approach just yet. Let us observe, pique his interest."

Lustre purchased two tankards of rough red wine and stood with Shrive at the bar, some feet away from the object of their attention. Shrive could tell the pale har was aware of their scrutiny and played up to it, although he never glanced again in their direction.

"You say he interested you," Shrive said. "He doesn't seem your type."

"Oh, not in that way," Lustre said. "I'm not quite sure what to call my interest. An urge to gaze upon, perhaps to paint, although he's not what I'd usually seek to illustrate. My patrons wouldn't want to hang him on their walls – they prefer lissom and supple to emaciated." He grinned at Shrive. "Yours would, however."

Shrive bristled. "Are you aware of how insulting that sounds?"

Lustre shrugged. "You know what I mean. That har is compelling in a weird kind of way. Your customers go for the romantically strange, mine prefer the cheerfully mundane."

Shrive could not turn his gaze from the hara at the bar. He counted seven of them. They were dressed flamboyantly yet shabbily in faded, ripped silks and velvets. Elaborate jewellery of coloured glass, nestling among the folds of fabric, and around necks and arms, winked in lamplight. The group's appearance was perhaps a deliberate costume – could they be actors or musicians? As with the hara on the street, they appeared to have come to this place from all corners of the world – no single tribal 'look' could be discerned. Each of them was a different colour, a different type. A motley bunch of theatrical demons.

The pale har reached up to scratch his head, his long sleeve falling back to reveal a perfect arm, as if sculpted in marble. Brass bangles clattered down to his elbow, revealing the tattoo of a serpent, wound around his wrist three times. For a few seconds, he became still, as if a sorrowful thought had come to him. This detached him from the group somehow. His gaudy mask dropped. Shrive saw despair in the naked face beneath - and the effort required to hide it.

Q'orlenn, Shrive thought, and from that moment the pale har became this fantasy.

The har put on his mask again, slapped his friends, shrieked with crass laughter. But the image of melancholy remained, like a ghost standing behind him.

Shrive was stunned, as if he'd been slapped himself.

Lustre summoned one of the pothara behind the bar, subtly indicated Shrive's potential model. "Tiahaar, do you know that har?" he asked.

The pothar was silent, his expression full of suspicion.

"We seek to hire him," Lustre said, pushing with one finger a coin of considerable worth across the wet counter.

The pothar snatched up the coin in a svelte movement. "Maybe," he said.

"Would you tell me his name?"

"Madcat," said the pothar. "Works out of Glass Star House in the Glitter quarter." He placed the coin in a pocket on the front of his tunic.

Shrive immediately wished he could delete this information from his memory. It jarred. The har was *Q'orlenn*. He could not be a kanene working out of a disgusting musenda in Fallsend, selling himself for whatever perversions of aruna could be imagined by sick minds. The musendas of Fallsend were legendary. It was said that even murder could be bought within them if the price was met. Therefore, it was essential this enigmatic, contradictory har was transported back to Sevriosta as soon as possible, so he could pose for Shrive in the light-filled studio, where the air was fragrant and the only sounds to break the holy silence of art in creation was the song of birds, the distant murmurs of life from the harbour. In such a setting, the fantasy could not only be maintained but enlarged, glorified.

Shrive's pastel dream was shattered by the cacophony of Q'orlenn and his cronies crying farewell to those around them. They bowed elaborately and, blowing kisses in a swirl of ribbons and feathers and scarves, eliciting raucous responses, they sailed in a hectic crowd out onto the street.

"Come on!" Shrive urged, pulling on Lustre's arm.

"Wait," said Lustre. "Don't be too eager. Given the opportunity, that crew would slit your throat and steal every thread and jewel on your body, perhaps even your hair and teeth. We must match guile with guile. They know we're watching them."

"If they're all kanene, there's only one thing they'll want – our patronage."

"Don't be a harling," Lustre admonished. "By Aru, you'd last less than a day in this place without me!"

Throughout the evening, Lustre and Shrive followed Q'orlenn and his friends from one inn to another. The group drank voraciously, yet never seemed to become intoxicated; their behaviour remained raucous and high-spirited, but also keen and alert. Shrive felt he inhabited a different reality to them, as if observing from the otherlanes, or another realm entirely, gazing through a hazy window onto an alien world. For these were not the kind of hara he knew. They belonged in stories of the past, the hot, bloody history of Wraeththukind, when hara had still been struggling to *become*, and had not always been successful. From this sour cauldron, harakind as they were today had evolved. It seemed impossible that such proto-hara as the inhabitants of Fallsend still thrived.

Shrive saw hara approach Q'orlenn on several occasions, lean in to whisper a request, but the har rebuffed them sharply, shoving them away with a jeer. "My night off!" he brayed. "Fuck you!"

He wore a kind of gown, a tangle of rags of different fabrics, yet his feet were clad in heavy boots. His shoulders were bare. Once or twice, when the wine he'd bought was too foul to swallow, he spat it onto the floor. Another time, a har who must be a friend, grabbed hold of him, kissed him roughly, thrust a hand up under the skirt of the gown. Q'orlenn laughed, punched the har violently in the chest, who backed away, also laughing.

This creature, Shrive decided, was debauched, no doubt depraved, but even so... something more: a wistful spirit clothed in tatters. His loutish manner was a disguise, a survival strategy. Had to be.

Around 1 a.m., by which time Shrive felt quite drunk, he and Lustre had come to what must surely be the end of the evening's festivities for the group they pursued. The little bar they entered, this time, was nearly empty. The group sat down at a table, and their talk was less rowdy than before. They smoked and drank and gossiped, but some were yawning now.

Q'orlenn sat on a bench against the wall, a har either side of him. The companion on his left, a dark-skinned har with a mass of thin braids, leaned against Q'orlenn's side, snuggled into the arm that was offered him. *Camaraderie among the damned*, Shrive thought.

Lustre excused himself to visit the bathroom, if the primitive facilities offered by these establishments could be termed as such.

Shrive turned his back on the group: it appeared impenetrable. The idea of asking Q'orlenn to sit for him was preposterous. He and his gang would only laugh.

After some moments, a husky voice behind him said, "Har, put your money where your eyes are. A cousin needs a drink, for all his coins are gone."

Shrive jumped and turned, almost knocking over his tankard on the bar, which he steadied with both hands. Q'orlenn stood behind him, a little shorter than he was.

"C...Cousin?" Shrive stuttered. His mouth was dry.

Q'orlenn sighed, glanced aside in disdain. "Get a round in, Gelly. Your type never lacks a fat wallet. You've feasted your eyes all night for free. Small price."

Shrive dared not ask what the har and his friends were drinking. He gabbled a request at the pothar: "Drinks for that table over there, please. Would you take them over?" The bar tender gazed at him expressionlessly but began to see to the order.

Q'orlenn guffawed. "Please!" he mimicked scornfully. He smacked Shrive on the shoulder, which hurt. "This your first time here?"

"Yes…" What point was there in denying it? He rubbed his shoulder and put a handful of coins on the bar. The pothar took the lot, gave no change.

"Seen your cuz around before," Q'orlenn drawled. "You've followed us all round the fucking town. Too shy to ask? Not that you'd get anything. Night off."

"There is something I want to ask you, yes," Shrive said, finding courage.

"I've heard it all. What is it?"

"I'm an… artist. I'm looking for a model for a very important painting. Would you sit for me?"

Q'orlenn cackled. "Sit for you? Fuck! That could mean anything."

"Please… you'll be paid extremely well. Come back to Almagabra with me… us. All your expenses will be covered – a place to stay, all your meals, whatever else you might need. It's very important."

Q'orlenn narrowed his eyes. "You're fucking mad. But OK, whatever you want. Doesn't sound like hard work. Come back to Glitter. You can *paint* me there." He winked, leered.

"No, no…" Shrive blustered, feeling his face redden. "I mean, I really *do* want to paint you. The picture will be on display in Immanion one day."

Q'orlenn sniffed, stared at Shrive. "I ain't moving. Everyhar knows, if the fucking Gelaming get hold of you, you don't come back. Nah, you want to *paint* me, you do it here, in Fallsend. Take it or leave it."

"But you don't understand, it could take weeks…"

Q'orlenn shrugged. "Ain't my problem."

"Absolutely not," said a silky voice behind Shrive. Lustre had returned. "But you're not an idiot, and you know this could earn you a treasure cave." He came forward and offered Q'orlenn a coin. "Here you are. Gesture of good will. There's a good har."

Q'orlenn stared at the coin, glittering clean and gold in his somewhat grubby palm. "I won"t move," he said. "If the har wants it that bad, he can fucking well do it here."

Shrive expelled a sound of exasperation. "This is pointless," he said to Lustre. "Let's go."

Lustre smiled. "Really? Think now, Shrive." He gestured languidly at the har before them. "Is this your Q'orlenn or is it not? Might it not be part of the adventure – the act of creation even – to paint him in this environment? It's like a set of the play, don't you think?"

"Well…"

"Tiahaar," Lustre said to Q'orlenn. "Your terms are acceptable. We need only to find temporary accommodation for my friend here and come to mutual agreement concerning your compensation."

"What?" said Q'orlenn.

"I'll need somewhere to stay," Shrive said uncertainly.

"Attic's empty where I live. Ain't fancy, though."

"Convenient, however," Lustre said. He paused to examine his watch. "Time's pressing. We will have to return tomorrow. Would you give us your address and tell us when we can call on you?"

Q'orlenn grimaced. "I'm working till five."

"Fine, we'll see you at six. The address?"

"8, Smoke Alley, east end of Glitter."

"Thank you. We'll look forward to it."

"OK. Till tomorrow, *Tiahaara.*" Q'orlenn grinned, bowed flamboyantly, then returned to his friends. Shrive saw him showing them the coin.

Lustre guided Shrive from the bar.

Outside, Shrive felt lightheaded. "You said," he muttered, "you said I wouldn't last a day here without you."

Lustre laughed. "Then you'd better learn quickly how to survive."

"I'm not sure I want to."

"Yes, you do. This will be your finest work. Now, let's get you home."

All night, Shrive dreamed of the hellish town with its gibbering denizens. In the morning, feeling weak and uncertain, he hoped that Lustre would change his mind about it all. Yet at the same time he felt strangely carried along with his friend's mad whim. He was aware that despite his doubts, a part of him desired strongly to return to Fallsend. He accepted that Lustre's idea was a good one – to paint Q'orlenn in the infernal realm could only help vitalise the work.

When Lustre arrived in the afternoon, Shrive had been ready for hours and had already, almost unconsciously, packed up his paints, brushes and easel. Just in case.

Q'orlenn lived on the second floor of the leaning, crumbling house in which he rented a room – a primitive den of a building, seemingly comprised of endless dark narrow corridors and treacherous twisting stairways. The proprietor of the establishment conveyed Lustre and Shrive to Q'orlenn's room, and when knocking on the door conjured no response, used a master key on his belt to let them in. And there *he* was, sprawled on the bed, his torn flounces around him, a single leg displayed, hanging over the side of the bed, his arms outspread. His boots lay on the floor, so that his slender flawless feet were revealed. He was already drunk – more so than he'd seemed on the previous evening. He must have set to work on this task the minute he'd left Glass Star House an hour or so earlier. Shrive eventually learned he'd spent a large part of the coin Lustre had given him on a particularly poisonous brew that bestowed marvellous visions. In the dim light that fought its way through the tiny window, Q'orlenn seemed to glow, long lashes against a poreless cheek, the abundant hair undulating around him, a sense of fragility, vulnerability, innocence. An illusion, but still…

He had attempted to improve his bleak abode with a couple of colourful rugs and a faded, embroidered coverlet on the bed. There was a small fireplace, large enough to boil the kettle that swung over it on a black trivet. These embellishments tugged at Shrive's sense of compassion. He sensed the loneliness deep within Q'orlenn's life, the narrowness of it.

While Lustre haggled with the householder – an extremely thin har named Mayra who was in appearance an unsettling hybrid of some rich har's pampered harling and a violent criminal – over the cost of hiring an attic room for a few weeks, Q'orlenn slept on. Shrive sat at the small table beneath the window and began drawing in a pocket sketch book he always kept on him. He had to capture what he saw, even though he had no plans to represent Q'orlenn asleep.

Once business was taken care of, Mayra shook Q'orlenn awake. "Mad, there's hara to see you."

Q'orlenn eventually woke and struggled to sit, clawing his hair from his face. He glared at his visitors. "So, you came," he said.

"Yes," Lustre replied airily. "Let's not waste time. Here are our terms. You will be paid weekly, the equivalent of two hundred spinners. Are you agreeable to that?"

Q'orlenn's face revealed nothing, even though that sum must be far more than he'd earn in a month as a kanene. "I suppose so."

"Good. We'll let you know when the work begins. My friend's accommodation needs to be settled first."

Q'orlenn shrugged, glanced almost furtively at Shrive. "Whatever."

Lustre grinned fiercely at the householder. "Please lead us to the palatial room that no doubt awaits us above."

Mayra did not smile in return. "Follow me."

They arrived at an attic door, which the householder unlocked. Beyond lay a large, desolate chamber that spanned the width of the house. As Shrive had expected, the room was abysmal, the pinnacle of this foul lair full of leering villains, sirens and scoundrels, several of whom they'd had to squeeze past on the stairs to the top of the house. *I won't be safe here,* Shrive thought. *I can't stay.*

As if reading his friend's mind, Lustre said to the householder, "Tiahaar, there is a generous fee for you if you ensure my companion's security while he stays here. Perhaps there is a har you can trust to act as bodyguard?"

Mayra nodded, uttered a soft grunt.

"At least the light's good," Lustre said.

This fact couldn't make Shrive feel better about the place.

In the northern end of the room, a portion of the roof comprised a wide skylight. The other end of the attic was dark, but for a tiny window opaque with ancient grime. The ceiling was badly plastered; there would be drafts. In winter, this room must be uninhabitable. The inadequate fireplace was full of dusty rubbish, including a long-dead bird. The sagging narrow bed, tucked into a corner, looked as if hara had died in it; the stains didn't bear inspection. There was no other furniture but for a broken chair, lying on its side.

Lustre showed Mayra some coins of large denomination in an outstretched hand. It was clear to Shrive his friend enjoyed the power that affluence gave him. "The room won't do in this state, my friend. Please purchase a new bed, along with bed linen, quilt and pillows. Acquire also a table, a chest of drawers, rugs and curtains." He waved a hand at the bed. "That noxious object must be removed and – I suggest – burned. Have the chimney cleared, the grate scoured. Have the holes in the ceiling and around the window repaired. In fact, have the whole place cleaned thoroughly." He closed his fingers over the money, withdrew his hand. "This cash will be yours once everything is fixed to our satisfaction."

Mayra grimaced. "You pay for that up front. I can't afford all that stuff."

Lustre handed over some of the coins. "This will have to do. It's generous. It's enough."

The har stared at the money for a moment, then regarded Lustre thoughtfully. He wasn't stupid. Shrive could hear the echo of his thoughts, which were carelessly unguarded, of how the changes Lustre suggested would make this neglected corner of the house a potential source of income once Shrive had left it. But there was also another thought – albeit fleeting – about whether it was feasible to slaughter these preening fools and take the money anyway. However, the har then remembered the old tale of the golden goose and that to kill it ended the flow of gold. He decided Lustre and Shrive could be satisfyingly tapped for cash for as long as Shrive resided in the house. And maybe their friends would come after, equally eager to spend their money. "As you wish, Tiahaar," he said coldly.

Lustre turned to Shrive. "As this work will take a while to finish, let's take a room at an inn tonight rather than go home. I'll have a word with our *sedim* pilot and stay with you until you're settled in properly." He smiled at the householder. "Where do you recommend, Tiahaar?"

"*The Stone Inn*," came the reply. "Best this town has to offer."

After Lustre had delivered instructions to the otherlanes guide, who'd return the following day, he and Shrive walked to *The Stone Inn*. They stepped across its threshold directly into the main bar, which was large and high-ceilinged and surging with a restless tide of customers.

"You don't have to do all this," Shrive said weakly. Despite Fallsend's intriguing aspects, he couldn't imagine himself working here — *living* here.

"It's because I'm sure the experience of this place will do you good," Lustre said. "Just look around you. It's all an illusion, of course, maintained like this to satisfy the hara who come here seeking forbidden pleasures. I imagine Fallsend is quite prosperous nowadays, but to clean it up would ruin the fantasy. It's a mirror of the murk in the deepest well of a har's mind. They can't satisfy their secret lusts in a place of light and air, only in stinks and dirt."

Shrive eyed the surroundings. He wasn't convinced Lustre was correct. Surely, the native hara of Fallsend simply didn't care about appearances.

A mezzanine gallery ran around the room where flamboyantly-dressed hara observed the clientele below. *Kanene*, Shrive thought. *Every house must have at least a few in this pit of a town.* Ideas for paintings skittered through his mind like cackling, shadowy imps. Perhaps Fallsend would be good for his creativity in more than one way.

He wondered whether Q'orlenn would pass through this place during the evening, but of course *The Stone Inn* was not frequented by natives unless they worked there.

After breakfast the following day, Shrive and Lustre returned to the house to ensure that restoration was progressing on the attic room. To their surprise, much of it had already been completed. Mayra must have set hara to work the previous evening. The furniture had not yet arrived, but the room was clean and a sultry-eyed, dark-skinned har on a step-ladder was attending to structural repairs. Only the floor still needed scrubbing. The bed had been removed, apparently through the northern window, since Shrive and Lustre had passed its shattered remains on the path outside.

"I could start work this evening," Shrive said, "if he's... available."

"Go and see if he's in," Lustre said.

Shrive went down the stairs. He felt nervous, unable to dispel the notion that behind Q'orlenn's door – if he was at home – lurked a dangerous and powerful force. *Don't be stupid,* he told himself. *Q'orlenn doesn't exist. The har in that room is an actor, trained to fulfil fantasies. If he can bring that sensibility to the work, the painting will be what I long to achieve. This is what I'm here for.*

He knocked upon the door.

It opened almost at once. Q'orlenn stood beyond, wearing an antique dressing-robe of threadbare, mauve matte silk. He said without pause or greeting, "You want to start now?"

Shrive took a tentative step into the room. "No... the attic isn't... well... I could make sketches. Down here, of course."

"I have an hour," Q'orlenn said, "and you'll pay me for it."

"My friend... he'll give you wages at the end of..."

"No, I need the fucking money today!" Q'orlenn softened, adopted a wheedling expression. "Just a little, Tiahaar. You were so kind before."

"Well... all right... I suppose. I'd better ask."

Shrive fled upstairs.

Lustre, still inspecting improvements to the attic, glanced at his friend shrewdly. "He was in, I take it."

"He wants some money. I can begin sketching then... now... for an hour."

Lustre rolled his eyes, withdrew his inexhaustible purse from an inner pocket of his coat. "Give him only what he'd earn for an hour in *Glass Star House.*"

"I've no idea what that is."

Lustre sighed and addressed the har on the step-ladder, who had virtually stopped working in order to listen to the conversation of the Gelaming. "How much for an hour in a musenda, Tiahaar?"

"Thirty spinners, I'd say."

"The house must take a big cut," Lustre said dryly, counting out the coins.

The har on the ladder uttered a scornful laugh. "What else?"

Three ten-spinner coins in hand, Shrive went back downstairs.

Q'orlenn sat on the bed. "Here?" he said, adopting a couple of unsuitable, suggestive poses.

"By the window," Shrive answered. "Sit there." This room too faced north, although the light had to fight its way through the filthy glass.

As there was only one chair, Shrive was forced to stand against the wall. For some moments he stared at the har before him, who stared back. "Well?" Q'orlenn said at length.

"In your... profession, you are much like an actor, I expect," Shrive said. "I want you to act for me, and I'll tell you your role."

Q'orlenn, naturally, was used to this. "Fine. Tell me."

"Look out of the window, down upon Fallsend. Imagine there is pity and grief in your heart for all the depravity you know hides in those leaning buildings. Hara have come here in fear, perhaps to escape persecution, or they've come here to avoid some other terrible fate. Others have done unspeakable things and are hiding from justice. Yet their crimes haunt them. The hurt of the outcasts rises as filthy fog above the canal. It seeps into your room, into the pores of your skin. You can't do a thing about any of what you witness, even though you are the embodiment of light and hope for the future. Only... you're invisible, up here, in this dark room. Nohar can see you. Nohar can drink of the restorative light of your being. You are powerless."

Q'orlenn uttered a sound between a cough and a laugh. "Well, that's new."

"Can you do it?"

"Yes. Wait."

Q'orlenn turned his head to the window, although his body faced Shrive. His hands were at first clasped in his lap. He drew in a long, shuddering breath. He closed his eyes. For nearly a minute, he held this posture. Then his hands fell open. Then – *it happened.*

To Shrive, it was as if a spirit took possession of Q'orlenn's body. His face seemed physically to change. Shrive saw the whole character he'd asked for blossom before him, merely through body posture and expression. It was exceptional.

Q'orlenn opened his eyes and looked down upon the town. His expression revealed he knew intimately every alley, every dank chamber, because it was his doom to know them. He felt the agony of every lost soul, of every damaged mind. He saw the hiding places of those who fled the past, who drank to forget it and poisoned their bodies with any substance that could numb their hearts and make the memories go away. In the musendas, they worked in hatred, abusing and warping the most essential, meaningful act that hara were privileged to experience. They made a death of life. They trampled love underfoot, murdered it, then laughed at and spat upon the mangled, bloody corpse. Yet the pain and despair at the cores of their being hung in the miasma across the town, in the stinking mist over the canal, and in the mournful lament of the barge-horns. Q'orlenn's heart bled for it.

This was no act: it was real.

Shrive could barely breathe, his pencil flying across a dozen pages of his sketch book. He must capture this – now – before it inevitably faded. He was unaware of time passing, until suddenly the spirit fled before his eyes: Madcat the kanene took repossession of the body and said, "Time's up. I want my money."

Lustre returned to Almagabra that evening, just after Shrive had been introduced to Slay, the har who had been hired ostensibly as his 'assistant' but was there merely to make sure Shrive wasn't robbed or murdered. Slay was a graceful, deceivingly sweet-looking individual, whose hands were strangely scarred. He spoke in a soft voice with an attractive slight lisp. In his direct grey gaze, however, was the assurance he could rip out a har's throat in less time than it took to draw breath. He told Shrive he was employed solely to protect hara visiting the town.

"Blinds my brain," he said conversationally, "why anyhar would come to this dump for the dregs when they can have far better anywhere else. You lot are fucked up."

"Believe me, I'm not here to sample Fallsend's traditional amusements," Shrive said stiffly. "I wouldn't be here at all if I could have found a suitable model anywhere else."

Slay didn't comment on these words, but his scornful expression conveyed his disbelief in Shrive's explanation. No doubt he'd heard every possible excuse over the years.

Lustre had arranged for Shrive's equipment to be conveyed to Fallsend and Shrive began to position it in the attic. Now the place was clean and furnished, it wasn't too bad at all. A small island of civilisation within a flood of depravity. A bed, in the form of a mattress on the floor, had been procured for Slay. Shrive wasn't pleased this har would have to be his constant companion, but no doubt he'd get used to the arrangement.

"You must be quiet while I'm working," he said.

Slay shrugged.

Around 9 o'clock Q'orlenn came into the room without knocking, uttering the greeting, "In blood, Slay," to the bodyguard.

Shrive hadn't expected this appearance, having planned to start work the next day. "What is it?" he asked abruptly.

"Here to work," Q'orlenn said, prowling about the room. "Done this up good, haven't you?"

"I can't work yet," Shrive said. "I want to begin in the light."

"Why?"

"The north light. I want to see you in it."

"Why north? What difference does it make?"

"Northern light is not direct. It's reflected off... everything and casts no shadow. It provides a cool, even quality. Light from the south, directly from the sun, changes throughout the day, becoming brighter and dimmer, and it casts shadows that move around. The clear north light, which changes less, is preferable to artists. And also..."

"Sounds like shit to me," Q'orlenn said, ending Shrive's flow. "Light is light."

"Come up here tomorrow," Shrive said.

Shrive realised he wouldn't have to deal often with Madcat, because the har was happy to remain in character as Q'orlenn whenever in Shrive's company. Shrive explained this would assist the work, although in reality he simply couldn't bear the abrasive presence of

Madcat. The first sitting went well. Slay went out into town for some hours, leaving the artist alone with his model. Shrive sketched Q'orlenn in various poses, particularly liking the one in which the har stood at the window, staring down in profile, one hand above his head resting against the glass. But while this would make a good picture, Shrive wanted Q'orlenn to confront the viewer, to stare into them. Perhaps other pictures could be painted later, simply for sale. So eventually he stood Q'orlenn upon a crate before him.

"Stare at me," he said. "You can see into my soul. What you see grieves you."

Q'orlenn smirked for a moment, then smoothed himself, and took on the persona. "What a small thing you are," he said, in a low, clear voice. He sighed. "I am all that you murdered within yourself and I will haunt you to the end."

Shrive paused. The Q'orlenn of the novel never spoke, but this felt real. He wondered if somehar had asked for this particular act before. Without responding, he began to draw and the Q'orlenn of his imagination took form upon the page.

The process of creation did not proceed without obstruction. Q'orlenn was an unpredictable creature. Sometimes, he was almost what Shrive could call normal, other times was sullen and uncooperative. His working hours were erratic and of apparently random length. Sometimes he disappeared for a couple of days and when he returned, he was almost senseless. He boasted of taking poison bought from Garridan dealers. One drop might take a har to unimaginable countries of the mind, two drops could kill. On one occasion, he would not put on the costume Shrive and Lustre had devised between them. This was simple – trousers and tunic of soft linen, artfully ripped as if to suggest their wearer had survived harsh conflict and painted to look bloody. These shredded garments revealed a lot of Q'orlenn, however, and when – that day – Shrive finally nagged him into complying, he saw the har's body was covered in deep, spreading bruises, as if he'd been beaten with hammers for hours. There were cuts upon his arms, one of them stitched. Q'orlenn glared at him defiantly. Shrive stared at this sight, speechless, then turned away. "Not today," he said. "Visit a healer."

Q'orlenn narrowed his eyes. "These are the wounds of Q'orlenn. Do they offend you, Tiahaar?"

"Yes," Shrive snapped. "They do. Q'orlenn never took such wounds. If you'd read the book, you'd know."

"You're wrong," Q'orlenn said. "What you see before you is the rot within the heart of our kind."

"Your choice to condone it," Shrive said.

"You fuck," Q'orlenn said softly. "Look at you, with your safe, rich life, playing at being *the artist*. How did you get that, eh? Who did you leave behind? Who did you trample on? You're more of a performer than I am. Or maybe it was your parents who did that. Maybe you're the spoiled brat of those who walked away, who drew a curtain around Almagabra they couldn't see through."

"Get out," Shrive said. "See a healer. I can't paint you looking like that."

Q'orlenn ripped off the costume and stalked out of the room naked. It was only once he'd gone that Shrive realised the har had delivered his speech entirely in character. It had not been Madcat's voice.

Q'orlenn returned the following afternoon, and neither he nor Shrive mentioned the previous incident. His bruises had faded or were cosmetically covered. He put on the costume and took up the pose, gazing over Shrive's head. Shrive, that day, could not bear to look Q'orlenn in the eye, so that suited both of them.

But the brush in Shrive's hand felt as uncooperative as his model sometimes was. For the first time since he'd begun to work in Fallsend, Shrive thought, *Am I capable of bringing this spirit to life?* Perhaps it was the reality of Madcat that interfered. He wanted Q'orlenn to exist, to paint from life, yet the evidence of Madcat's occupation compromised that vision. *Q'orlenn, ultimately, existed only within Shoal,* Shrive thought. *This har before you is simply a piece of equipment like this brush in your hand, the easel upon which the canvas rests. Get hold of yourself! You are not painting him, he is merely the physical framework for a creature of your imagination, a trap for the light. Nothing more.*

Shrive put down his brush. He stared at the painting, which was taking shape relatively quickly. There was much he could do without the model there before him. He should take a break, concentrate on the background for a while.

"That's all for today," he said.

Q'orlenn said nothing, stepped down from the crate, pulled around him the old dressing-robe he'd cast on the floor. Quietly, he left the room.

Slay was sitting in the dark half of the attic, oiling and sharpening a set of knives. There was silence for a moment, then Slay said, "Tiahaar, close your heart. There's nothing you can do."

It was easy to forget this har was often there, sitting in the shadows of the room, witness to much of what happened. It would also be easy to adopt a posture of outrage for this inappropriate piece of advice. Instead, Shrive said, "It was... hard... to see that yesterday."

"Not part of your picture, I know," Slay remarked. "Perhaps you should just invent your character rather than seek him in the real world. I don't think you belong here. Madcat is on a long road heading to the bottom. He can't be pulled back up."

"The philosopher assassin might also be the subject of a painting," Shrive said, somewhat shakily.

Slay laughed. "I see what I see. This town suits me perfectly."

While Shrive had no intention on giving up on the Q'orlenn of Fallsend, he did take some of Slay's advice and dealt with his feelings. Any pity or compassion he consigned to a cellar of his heart and nailed shut the door. There could be no empathy. For most of the time, Q'orlenn performed his role faultlessly, and on the days when he went missing, or was too intoxicated to stand, Shrive worked on the background to the painting. He'd intended this to be a stylised impression of a shattered community, little detail to be seen other than grotesque shadows, but he found himself painting the silhouettes of looming, leaning buildings, half in ruins, with the broad, oily eel of the canal slinking through them. The sun in the distant sky behind the blackened walls was a deep, sullen crimson. And in the forefront hung Q'orlenn: shining, haughty, despairing, remote and ravishing. His long glowing hands were held out as a lure to his spider heart. Any who followed him would be drawn into the bleak ruins, into the heart of the devouring sun, to be burned away to black ash. Q'orlenn's mocking laughter would linger as well as the unbearable sorrow of his weeping. *I am the rot within your heart.*

This was the Q'orlenn of Fallsend, not the Q'orlenn of Ayzel har Sythe.

A month passed. The lease on the attic was renewed.

Lustre came occasionally to visit. He admired Shrive's work and encouraged him to continue, even on the days when Shrive had doubts. Lustre struck up a friendship with Slay and took him to *The Stone Inn* quite often, keeping him away overnight. Shrive was not entirely pleased about this, since any rough creature who became aware of the situation might take advantage of it, while his minder no doubt enjoyed all the pleasures of Lustre's purse and body. Later, once Shrive's masterpiece was on display in Immanion, portraits of Slay by Lustre appeared in galleries and sold well – provocative depictions of a beautiful slim har with scarred hands, naked or barely clad. Shrive never got to paint his philosopher assassin.

As his own painting progressed, his model seemed to become more luminous, more transparent, taking on entirely the persona he adopted for the work. Yet while transforming in this way, Q'orlenn also became harsher – whenever he was not posing, he derided and scorned Shrive's words and actions, under the guise of humour, usually by making remarks to Slay about Shrive, or preening Gelaming in general. It was clear he despised his employer, thought him a posturing fool. He would not comment on the painting, simply looked at it with disdain, scratching his body uncouthly, wiping his nose on his hand.

This behaviour was exasperating to Shrive. Could Q'orlenn not see how Shrive was doing all in his power to capture the evanescent spirit within, that pure creature crushed and beaten, hardly more than the faint voice of a harling locked in a deep, forgotten crypt, starving slowly to death, going blind in the darkness? As equally as Q'orlenn despised Shrive, so Shrive despised him. To be given such assets as the bone-deep beauty he possessed and the clear flashes of intelligence, only to bully and poison them into hiding. This was obscene, more so than his chosen profession. It was wanton neglect of his being, a state in which Q'orlenn appeared to revel.

During the few hours when he wasn't working or sleeping, Shrive wandered the streets of Fallsend. He didn't make friends exactly but came to be tolerated by the inhabitants. Those he knew locally had realised he wasn't rich but seemed to consider him an entertaining eccentric, a minion of Lustre, who they regarded with fond amusement. Shrive was convinced they'd decided that by being pleasant to him, they'd earn some of what Lustre had to give.

He dined in small cafes, and sometimes the food was good. He immersed himself in the town's atmosphere and found a weird natural beauty within it. He realised Fallsend was no different from the dangerous, haunted forests he painted. Its inhabitants were of endless variety. He saw travellers and traders from all parts of the world, even a few of his own tribe, although he hurried away whenever he saw one of them. Sometimes, he sought out Q'orlenn, keeping himself hidden, hoping to recapture the moment he'd first glimpsed the har within. This didn't happen, although he did notice that Q'orlenn drank or drugged himself to excess more often, having to be carried home by friends, who themselves were comparatively sober.

On one of Q'orlenn's amiable days, Shrive asked him, "Where did you come from? Why did you end up here?"

"I stepped out of a story," Q'orlenn replied in a hollow tone. "I had no choice about the character given to me."

"You did," Shrive said. "All of us have choices. You're real, not a fictional character."

Q'orlenn put his head to one side, breaking the pose. "I hang above the world. Its pain devours me."

Shrive blinked at him.

Q'orlenn uttered a small, choked laugh. "Do you see?" he asked.

For just a moment, they looked at one another, and *something* passed between them.

Countless possibilities opened up...

Shrive looked away, continued to paint. "Back in position, please. Do what you do best. Act."

The next day, Q'orlenn went missing, returning in the evening with a friend. They both came to the attic and – incoherent with drink or some Garridan toxin – Q'orlenn pointed at Shrive and slurred, "Look at him, he's a fucking idiot! Dried up and dead!"

Slay ushered the pair outside.

Shrive said nothing, continued to work. He would not allow his hand to shake.

The painting neared completion as the summer began to fade. So many contradictory feelings were caught within it and Shrive knew that – as Lustre had predicted – this was the best work he'd ever done. On the last night, when there were only finishing touches to put to the picture, Shrive sent Q'orlenn away.

"It's done," he said. "Thank you for your time."

"Done?" murmured Q'orlenn hoarsely. "Have you sucked out all the juice of me now? Am I in your painting?"

Shrive directed a sharp glance at him. "It isn't *you*," he said. "It's a fiction, a character from a novel who never existed. He can't exist."

"So now you know," Q'orlenn said softly. He stood before Shrive, took the har's face in his long cool hands and kissed him briefly on the lips. "Goodbye, Tiahaar."

Then he had glided past, like a shimmering ghost. Behind Shrive, the door creaked open but did not shut.

Shrive was frozen to his seat. He couldn't interpret what he felt or thought about what had just happened. Now Q'orlenn had left the attic, the room seemed strangely cold and abandoned, even though a fire was burning in the grate. Slay was out and even though Shrive now felt more at home in Fallsend, he wished the har was there.

Left alone, he focused entirely on his painting long into the night, adding small details and flourishes, absorbed in his work. Now the picture was finished, Shrive was once more capable of feeling. Perhaps, when *Q'orlenn* was put on display, Slay and Madcat could be brought to Immanion for the opening night. Perhaps Madcat could even forge a new living for himself as a model, for no doubt many other artists would be intrigued by him. There was a thrilling story to tell of the origin of this new, reinvented Q'orlenn, who hara would see was far more authentic than har Sythe's somewhat arid original. Madcat's Q'orlenn was truly, spectacularly tragic. The har deserved more than life had served him, Shrive thought. Perhaps in Almagabra he could change, fulfil his potential, lose the aspect of the kanene, become... cleansed. When he delivered Q'orlenn's last payment, he would speak of these ideas, hoping that the money grabber in Madcat would comply.

Around 1 a.m., Shrive became aware of a faint commotion lower in the building but paid it no attention. The occupants were always making a noise.

Perhaps half an hour later, Slay came into the room.

Shrive turned to greet him but was silenced by the expression on the har's face. "What is it?" he asked.

"Don't you know?" Slay replied.

Shrive shrugged. "I have no idea what you mean."

"He's gone. Madcat is gone."

Shrive frowned. "What do you...?"

"He's dead, Tiahaar. Faded but a few minutes ago. They've been working on him for a while. Did no good."

Shrive tried to absorb this information. The words seemed to mean nothing. He couldn't think of anything to say.

Slay came over to look at the painting. "While you finished him off here, so he finished himself below. Two drops of Garridan sweetbane might kill a har. There is no return from three."

"He... he *killed* himself? But...?"

"Some might say he was already dead," Slay said. "Poison was merely a matter of punctuation at the end of the story."

Slowly, Shrive put down his brush, stood up. "Why didn't they come for me?" he asked.

Slay laughed coldly. "You?"

Shrive went downstairs, his whole body numb. The door to Q'orlenn's room was open and there were around half a dozen hara within, clustered about the bed.

They he lay, perfect, as if asleep, as Shrive had first seen him in this room. Two of Q'orlenn's friends – no, Madcat's friends –

crouched on the floor at the side of the bed. They did not weep but stared, their faces blank. Mayra stood with a har who must be a healer, since there was an open bag at his feet, full of glass vials; a few also lying empty on the floor. They'd tried to save Q'orlenn but had been too late. He had left the attic, walked downstairs and taken the poison. Lustre's money had paid for it. He had lain down on the bed, comforted in the arms of sweetbane, which eliminated all sorrows. Somehar had come, found him, but perhaps not the har Q'orlenn had expected – dreaded, hoped? – would come.

One of Madcat's friends glanced up, caught sight of Shrive by the door. "Pelker!" he yelled. "Get out, you fucking asshole! You did this!"

Mayra kicked this har, but not too hard. "Shut it!" he said.

Shrive went out, closed the door. He stood in the dim corridor for a while, unable to move.

Then he went upstairs. He had no idea how to contact Lustre immediately. There were no Listeners' stations in Fallsend to transmit messages through the ethers. He was stuck here until Lustre came of his own accord. How would he survive? He was a pelker, who had raped a har's soul. They all knew.

Slay had left the attic, perhaps would not return. The place was as it had been before: a terrible, desolate room that had become a chamber of torture.

Shrive stood before the painting, gazed into the depthless eyes. The har in the picture was perfect. To look upon him was to fall in love, entirely and painfully, yet that love would not – and now could not – ever be returned. Q'orlenn was within the canvas now, forever.

Shrive put his hands against his face, fell into the devouring sun

The Swan and the Scorpion

Maria J. Leel

I set the heavy goblets before me, each the perfect twin of the other.

Although ancient, there is not a single flaw, blemish or irregularity to distinguish between them.

The thick, green glass bowls still hold their lustre and are set in place above golden feet by intricate stems of burnished, twisting silver.

Upright these goblets put me in mind of one of Ravansanella's old divination cards – the Two of Cups – meaning "a happy union, reciprocity, harmony".

A bitter laugh escapes me and, on a whim, I turn the glasses over grimacing as I recall *that* meaning – the Two of Cups reversed...

Disunity. Inequality. Unrequited love.

This, I muse, sums up my situation perfectly.

The rambling villa I know as home is located on a peninsula jutting down into the same sparkling sea that caresses the shores of Almagabra and the famed Immanion, magnificent capital city of the Gelaming. From my kitchen window I look down onto the sweeping bays and rocky beaches of Lake Bilancino. Here, at the height of summer, people flock to cool off when temperatures rise too high on the coast. By autumn they are gone, and the acres of bronzed, indolent flesh are replaced by a barricade of pink feathers as flamingos fly in temporarily on their journey south. I envy these birds. They can leave. I cannot.

Surrounding this lake is Toscana, a golden sleepy land of rolling hills, where dark cypress trees stand like sentinels over groves of ancient olive trees and vineyards. Sharp scents assail the nose from the countless lemon groves, whilst avocados hang heavy among the glossy leaves, and the many streams are full of fish. The people are, for the most part, sleepy and content. It's a perfect little paradise if you will, except there is a snake in this particular garden of Eden and I am shackled to him by unbreakable bonds.

I am not of this place. I do not share the chocolate-brown eyes, curled auburn hair and the warm mocha skins of the native Toscans. My face... and I rarely show my true face these days, hiding behind glamours and making myself as plain and unnoticeable as possible, is quite different.

My true eyes are dark... black... almost cold-looking, whilst my skin, my true skin, is pure white, with the luminosity of a glacier in sunlight. My hair, strangest of all, again is white but it hangs, not in single strands, but bifurcates and splits like feathers down my back.

I am har but I've never seen another har like me.

It was Ravansanella who told me what I am.

I was very young when I had gone to her in tears, having been teased for my unusual looks yet again.

"Why am I different?" I had wept to her in her kitchen.

Bones creaking, she sat me down on a stool and fetched me a sweetmeat.

"Dear one," she said, "You were a gift to this household, an Olori child, to bring luck and great fortune."

Then she snorted and rolled her eyes upwards to the family occupying the rooms overhead.

"If these fools would but recognise that."

"What's Olori?" I asked, with my mouth full.

She hunkered down carefully and regarded with intensity. "You really don't know? The Olori, the Swan People, are nomads from the north. Like swans they are white skinned and white haired but never tan or burn in the sun. Olori people always mate for life and usually raise their own..."

She ran a hand over my hair, and I remember the look of sadness that passed across her face.

"Theirs is a difficult life... Usually Olori raise their own... but sometimes..." She shrugged. "Sometimes... when their numbers become too great, they leave their new born on the doorsteps of promising households."

She smiled fiercely, her voice impassioned, "Like a benign cuckoo, an Olori child is usually regarded as a gift or a sign of good fortune."

I pondered on this for a long time. Perhaps my people had been desperate, or perhaps they were in a hurry? Looks can be deceptive, can't they? And no-one truly knows what goes on behind closed doors.

For me the Olori chose badly.

The house I was gifted to belonged to Tovel and Cecita Lamone, a lackadaisical pair of socialites with a harling of their own just a year or so older than me. Tovel was tall with classic Toscan colouring and he exhibited his clothes rather than wore them. Cecita was smaller and no less lovely to look at but he possessed a mouth twisted with discontentment and his face wore a permanent look of cunning; these spoiled his otherwise flawless features. From the outset they saw me as a burden and foisted my care onto Ravansanella our human housekeeper. It was she who gave me my name, Chiusi, ensured that I was fed and clean and gave me what little education she could.

"I named you for the town where I was born," she told me as we sat munching apples whilst she taught me my letters.

"Is it beautiful?" I asked, pointing to the letter 'C', which began my name.

"Well, I think so," she answered and guided me through the rest of the sentence.

"Will you take me there sometime?" I asked, keen to distract her.

"One day, perhaps," she replied with a quirk of her eyebrow, "when you can read and write to my satisfaction."

But she never did. And when I was old enough to visit the pretty town by myself, I couldn't find her there.

The other member of the household was Nazioni, the only son and heir to the Lamone fortune and precisely the spoiled darling and bully that I guarantee you are imagining. Older than me, taller than me and heavier than me he delighted in sending me flying at every opportunity.

"Fly birdy, fly," he'd yell, his dark eyes flashing, "You're meant to be a swan, aren't you?"

It's a miracle I didn't break any bones the number of tumbles I took at his hands. But it was his mental and emotional cruelties that hurt far worse than any of the bumps and bruises he inflicted.

Despite my initial reluctance I had learned to read and write quite quickly, in fact I was streets ahead of Nazioni, who was bored by the whole process. One of my favourite things to do was to explore the attic, which held all sorts of bric-a-brac from the days when the house had belonged to humans. No-one usually came to the attic and here I found a book of old fables. Old stories that I adored. I made myself a nest of dusty cushions by the circular skylight and spent hours reading up there.

One day, inevitably, Nazioni found my hiding place. He ripped open the cushions, drowning the attic in feathers, kicked me down the stairs, tearing the book to shreds as he went. As I landed in a crumpled heap in the hallway, Tovel and Cecita came rushing out of the drawing room to see what the commotion was all about.

"Chiusi's made a total mess of the attic," Nazioni announced in affronted tones. "And he's destroyed this old book too. It was probably quite valuable," he finished, smugly.

Tovel hauled me to my feet and slapped me. "Ungrateful wretch," he snarled.

"After all we've done for you." Cecita added with another slap. "Go to the kitchen and keep out of sight if you know what's best for you."

It took some little time for Ravansanella to calm me down. It wasn't the bumps from the staircase for I'd long ago learned how to fall and not hurt myself, nor the slaps from my adopted parents to which I now was inured, nor even the injustice of it all; it was the destruction of the beautiful book that distressed me. I knew all the stories by heart and would never forget them. But it upset me that no-one else would ever discover the lovely book or be able to read the stories for the first time or fall in love with the fables as I had.

From then on, I spent as much time with Ravansanella as I could. In her warm kitchen during the evenings when our day's work was done, we'd sit and drink her special chocolate drink. Then each evening I would tell her a different story from that lovely, now destroyed, book.

Ravansanella's favourite was the story of the frog and the scorpion.

It goes like this...

Once upon a time there was a frog. One day, Frog was sitting by a riverbank when along came a Scorpion.

"Hello brother Frog," said Scorpion. "I wonder if you might be so kind as to give me a ride across the river on your back."

Frog knew that Scorpion could not swim.

"I don't think that's a good idea," said Frog. "You have a deadly sting. You might kill me."

"But why would I do that?" replied Scorpion. "If I stung you, we would both die."

"Mmm," thought Frog. "That makes sense."

"Alright Scorpion, jump onto my back and I will give you a ride across the river," he said.

So Scorpion jumped onto Frog's back and Frog began to swim across the river. But halfway across, Scorpion took his deadly sting and stuck it into Frog's back. And as the poison filled Frog's body his arms began to stiffen and they both began to sink.

"Why?" gasped Frog in despair.

"Sorry Frog, I could not help myself," said Scorpion. "It's my nature."

And both Frog and Scorpion died. [1]

"But why do you like this one so much?" I asked, perplexed. "It's has such a sad ending."

"You'll understand one day," she answered, stoking up the fire and wrapping me in a blanket.

Thinking back, I see now... The frog could so easily have been a swan.

I learned a very great deal from Ravansanella, the names of all the wild plants and which were edible, how to make omelettes and stews and pastries, how to grow a garden of vegetables and herbs, how to preserve fruit, how to run a household and how to find joy in even the bleakest moments. Strong as an ox, although her russet hair was threaded through with silver, Ravansanella undertook any task that needed to be done, only calling in the help of the local, thick-set, pot har by the name of Arno, as a last resort. Arno would take no payment other than a bottle of Ravansanella's thick lemon liqueur and a handful of her sugared pasties. He'd grin and ruffle my hair on his way back to the inn, his mouth full of almond sweetened pastry.

Ravansanella and I worked side by side through the seasons as the days shortened and the air became crisper. Winters in Toscana were usually mild and, although I could see the beauty and appeal of this gentle land, Toscana did not fill my heart.

On wintry days, my eyes were drawn north to the mountains on the far horizon, each with their cap of iridescent snow. A restlessness would settle upon me along with an almost overwhelming pull to those lands far away.

Ravansanella followed my gaze. "Interesting..." she said.

Our happiest times were when Tovel and Cecita were away from home which, mercifully, was often. They toured the Toscan party circuit, being seen with everyone who they should be seen with, while secretly regarding themselves as rather a cut above. They preferred to travel further afield, spending significant time in Cittaeterna, the capital of our verdant peninsula, but their locale of choice was Almagabra where, whilst finances lasted, they spent their days schmoozing with the glorious and the good of Immanion. The best times were when they took Nazioni with them... which wasn't nearly often enough.

Tovel and Cecita threw lavish parties of their own when they were home. On such nights, the doors of the villa were flung wide and the music within seeped into the fragrant night air as guests languished on the terraces or inside the many parlours. The Lamones wafted about draped in expensive silks, sipping exquisite wines, and ensuring guests knew the full extent of their opulence. Meanwhile, Ravansanella and I were run ragged with preparations for the festivities, then spent the actual evening replenishing glasses, carrying heavy trays bearing every kind of delicacy and mopping up the inevitable spillages. We would tumble into our beds in the early hours hoping that another trip to Immanion was soon on the cards. Then we would idle among the marjoram and sweet tomatoes, tilling our gardens, or listening to the shrill calls of the little birds in the morning as we threw open all the windows to air the villa as we took our time sweeping out each room.

The most lavish party ever held at Villa Lamone was the occasion of Nazioni's feybraiha. Nazioni had spent weeks in feverish discomfort as the changes leading to adulthood burned through his body. Cecita flew about with lotions and potions to soothe the Lamone heir but nothing seemed to mollify his son. Negotiations had taken place with an array of potential suitors from all over Toscana for the privilege of guiding Nazioni's first experiences of aruna. Eventually a har by the name of Rotaldo, the son of a wealthy wine merchant, was selected from the nearest city, Lorenzia. Rotaldo was tallish, seemingly sweet natured and appeared overly fascinated with me.

"Such and unusual child," he'd murmur, his eyes following me around the room, as Nazioni and Tovel sat simpering by his side. Cecita scowled and waved me away.

The day of the feybraiha arrived, a clear bright day in early summer. The rooms were festooned with huge vases of gardenia, wisteria and white roses. Garlands of variegated leaves hung on the walls and the pungent scents of lavender and sandalwood, purported aids to ardour, lay heavy throughout the villa. Ravansanella had solicited the help of Arno, the pot har, and his staff for this occasion. They spent long hours in the kitchen making plans.

"The finest wines, mind you...." Ravansanella insisted. "Remember, who Rotaldo's father is..."

Arno nodded his agreement and scribbled a few notes. "Don't you worry, my lovely, we'll show them we're quite their equal if not finer in that department."

For days the kitchen was a feverish cauldron of cuttlefish and squid, pastries and truffles, melons and hams and olives and pungent parmesan. The festivities went on above us and at the allotted time, the seven of us burst through the invited guests, each of us dressed in white, bearing trays and platters containing every delight Ravansanella could muster. Excited mutterings and gasps of pleasure came from the guests who, already mellowed by Arno's excellent selection of wines, had sharpened appetites. At the top table sat Nazioni and Rotaldo, both dressed in pale green, flanked by their parents.

Rotaldo, looking slightly flushed, spied me among the crush. "Ah! The pretty one!" he crowed. "Bring me some of that," he waved vaguely at my tray.

Beside me Ravansanella hissed, "Go and serve in the other room," and she advanced on the top table.

Relieved, I made my escape but not before I saw the sour expression on Nazioni's face and received another scowl from Cecita.

I made sure to stay well out of the way for the rest of the evening. I hid at the back as the couple were serenaded on their way up the sweeping staircase to their chamber above. Dressed in white my pale hair and skin seemed to stand out more than ever and I could see Rotaldo's eyes searching the room keenly as I ducked swiftly behind a gaggle of drunken guests. I hastened to the kitchen and busied myself with the washing up. It seemed the safest thing to do. A while later Ravansanella and Arno joined me.

"Not a good match," she muttered.

"Indeed not," he agreed.

A few days later Rotaldo and his family departed; the deed done but no lasting partnership had been forged. From the kitchen I heard the polite goodbyes and well wishes as the carriage drove away. A heavy mood of dissatisfaction descended upon the house which lifted only when the family headed, once more, to Immanion.

For the next year life was relatively peaceful. A succession of suitors came and went whilst the family were at home and, as I understood it, a similar search continued when the family visited Cittaeterna and Immanion. My own burgeoning adulthood was the trigger that shattered this tentative stability. Life, as I had known it, was about to end.

Her arm protectively around my shoulder, Ravansanella approached Tovel and Cecita on my behalf.

"Chiusi is coming of age," she began. "It is important that a suitable har is found to guide him to adulthood."

Glass in hand, Cecita lounged on a chaise longue in the southern parlour. Early evening sunlight crept in through the open glass doors. From the gardens I could hear the shrill cry of a jay.

Tovel sat with a book in a high back chair, a deep frown creasing his brow.

"Surely you're not suggesting an affair similar to that we held for Naz? We're still bearing the cost of that."

Cecita uttered a cross between a snort and a laugh. "Hardly."

Ravansanella threw him a glance. "Of course not. A small gathering would be far more appropriate. But it's not the scale of any party that is of consequence here but finding a worthy suitor."

Cecita raised his eyebrows and hissed. "Worthy... *Worthy?* We have enough of a challenge on our hands finding an appropriate suitor for Naz... And you wish us to find someone *worthy* for *him?*"

I felt Ravansanella tighten with anger. "As I have told you many times..." she said coldly, "With Olori it is *different...*"

Tovel held up a dismissive hand and thought for a moment.

"Naz can do it. He's been through it recently enough... Who would be more appropriate than family?"

Cecita nodded enthusiastically. "Indeed. An honour, in fact, for a servant that a member of the family would consent to this."

I shrank back.

Ravansanella threw me a look of utter horror. "This would be a terrible choice!" she cried. "Naz has no kindly feelings towards Chiusi. It cannot be a union of any duration. No!"

Cecita stood up. "It is this or nothing."

Arguments continued until the small hours. I had fled to the kitchen and stopped my ears but could hear raised voices even from there.

The next day Ravansanella was turned out of the house.

I could do nothing to help. Semi-delirious, a fever upon me, I had been locked in the cellar.

I heard the continuing argument raging above me.

Cecita's harsh words. Nazioni's laughter. Tovel taking the moral high ground.

We weren't even allowed to say goodbye.

The last words I heard Ravansanella utter were, "You will regret this. An Olori child is a blessing upon a household if you treat them well..." Her voice rose in anguish. "Ill-use an Olori child and you will be cursed."

I put my head down into my arms and wept.

I was left in the cellar for three days with only a flagon of water and minimum rations. In truth I had no appetite. I was sick at heart, sick in my stomach, and my flesh crawled with the changes that were raging through my body. I had a hunger like I had never known. Not a hunger for food but a hunger for coupling, a union, release.

Mid-afternoon on that third day Nazioni sauntered into the cellar. I lay, feverish, upon a mat, sweat-soaked hair heavy across my face.

He pulled the sticky strands away and gazed upon me. "Well, Birdy... Look at the state of you."

My tongue was thick and over large in my mouth. "Make it stop." I begged.

One side of his mouth curled up. "Very well," he said.

There on the lonely floor of a miserable cellar he did what was necessary. There was no affection, no kindness, no love. He didn't even undress.

When he was done, he stood up and rearranged his clothing. "Get cleaned up," he ordered. "We need you back at work."

Later, much later, when I had bathed, found clean clothes and managed to force down some food, I sat alone in garden. Familiar scents tumbled together, figs and peaches festooned the orchard and somewhere a nightingale's call bubbled and sobbed in the darkness. I sobbed with it.

You adapt, don't you? You find a 'new normal'.
I can feel your frustration. I can hear you scream...
Screaming the inevitable question...
Why didn't you just leave?
But you just don't understand.
Like a swan, the Olori mate for life. Although my spirit shrank from him and despised him, my flesh yearned for him, craved his touch...
Like an addiction...
Whether I chose it or not... Like the swan that mates for life... I was bonded to Nazioni...
For life.

I put my swan-self away. Hid my distinctness behind spells and glamours.
I gave myself dull hair, lacklustre skin, unremarkable eyes.
An appearance designed to more than just fit in... I wanted to be as invisible as possible.
The first time Nazioni saw the new me he just stared at me for a full minute before bending double with scornful laughter.
"An improvement?" he sneered as I left the room.
Tovel and Cecita didn't turn a hair.

Busyness was my salvation. Busyness kept me sane.
Now that it was just me running the household, I barely had time to think or feel.
My days were filled with bed making, dusting, sweeping, gardening, the preparation of meals, ordering and the management of household accounts.
My heart and soul hungered for decency and wholeness, but my flesh hungered for Nazioni.
He came to me rarely.
Only when he was bored.
Only when his latest conquest had proved unsatisfactory.

Whilst going about my daily tasks I'd come upon them sprawled in a state of undress on cushions in one of the parlours, pawing each other, lips locked and my insides would churn, the bile would rise in my throat and I'd struggle to bite back my rage.

Nazioni's eyes would follow me around the room.

"Don't mind him," he'd say, coming up for air. "Just a servant."

In Toscana Nazioni acquired a reputation for irreverence, impermanence, irrelevance.

In Immanion... his reputation was worse.

Several months after Ravansanella's departure, Tovel and Cecita set out, once again, for Immanion. They chose, on this occasion, not to take Nazioni with them. Nazioni had, apparently, caused a scene with some subaltern of the lower echelons during a recent visit to Almagabra and his parents deemed it currently unsuitable to include their son in the party.

In the aftermath of what happened... Ravansanella's words loomed large... "Ill-use an Olori child and you will be cursed." The ship carrying Tovel and Cecita foundered and all on board were lost.

The news reached us by messenger one dusty afternoon in early summer.

Within hours the news had spread throughout the entire neighbourhood and hara came from far and wide to offer their condolences and assistance. Nazioni, seemingly prostrate with grief, lapped it up.

I carried pots of coffee, bottles of the lemon liqueur I continued to make, trays of biscuits and cake up to the room where the mourners gathered.

I had just returned to the kitchen to make fresh coffee when there was a tentative knock at the door.

Arno, the Pot Har, hovered on the threshold. His face bore a look of confusion as he saw me, and his eyes swept hurriedly around the room.

"Excuse me, I'm sorry... I know Ravansanella went away but... I wondered if Chiusi of the Olori was still here?"

Miserably I shook my head.

"Did he leave with Ravansanella?"

I shrugged. "I don't know…"

Arno held out his hand. "Forgive me, you're new, aren't you? I'm Arno, pot har from Bilancino. Family friend of sorts."

I shook his hand. "I'm Gelt," I replied. Which was the first name that came into my head.

You're going to ask me why I didn't confide in Arno, aren't you?

The truth is, the shame just ran too deep. I was paralysed with it.

There was no confiding in anyone.

Visitors offering food, wine, support and assistance continued for weeks, months after the overblown memorial services for Tovel and Cecita but then the parties started and the visitors… stopped.

Parties, not the dignified soirées of the sort held when I was younger, were debauched revelries that went on for days and attracted every lowlife that Toscana could provide.

I couldn't bear to remain in the house at these times.

The drunkenness, Nazioni's succession of lovers, the intoxicants…

Or he'd corner me. Torment me. Stroke my hair, my skin, ignite me to a blazing cauldron of need and then walk away laughing.

"You're mine," he'd hiss. "You are bound to me and I own you."

I sometimes wondered who was the more cursed, the house of Lamone or the Olori who dwelt within its walls. By my very nature, my birth right, my lineage I was bound to the har who tortured me. Like swans who mate for life… Until death do we part.

One day I spied an actual scorpion in the corner of the kitchen while I was baking. It sat there, black and squat, its tail arched menacingly over its back, the barbed sting held ready. I watched it for a moment and pondered on creatures that sting. Bees are universally loved and wasps, whilst generally disliked, also offer their services as great pollinators. What, I wondered, was the point of a scorpion? All I could see was cruelty and menace. Hurriedly, I shooed the little beast out of the house.

Keeping out of Nazioni's way became my major occupation. It was easier when he was blind drunk, because then he bothered no-one.

But on days when he prowled like a scorpion through the corridors or hunted me for me in the parlours seeking to sting and sting again, I'd take a horse and visit nearby villages, or go walking in the valleys. These forays were always short lived, and I'd find myself inexorably drawn back to the house within a few hours.

I tried, and failed, to find Ravansanella.

There was a small, stone outhouse on the edge of the Lamone estate, which housed gardening equipment on the ground floor but had an upper level of solid timber where apples were once stored. Here, overlooking rolling fields of bright sunflowers, their dark faces tracking the sun, I made myself a nest; cocooned in the lingering sweetness, the hints of fruit, I slept or read until Nazioni's guests crawled back to wherever they came from.

Then I'd return to clear up the mess.

That was ten years ago.

Things are very different now.

Nazioni burned through the Lamone fortune within a few years. He then started to sell anything he could find of value. He didn't find everything, small things I was able to secrete away kept us going through the leanest times. Fortunately, the land here is generous and the gardens, orchards and streams were able to provide an abundance of food.

Arno, the pot har, never calls now, one too many unpaid bills, and the rest of the neighbourhood shuns us.

The house has become shabby and rundown. Shingles slip from the roofs, plaster sags and bulges on the walls. I effect what repairs I can. Only the kitchen and my little bedroom off it are warm and comforting. The other rooms, save Nazioni's lair, are devoid of furnishings and stand pitifully empty. My footsteps echo as I pass through them.

Nazioni took up residence in a parlour furthest from the kitchen. Here he relocated his parent's bed and surrounded it with couches, thick rugs, silken cushions, a drinks cabinet and a table where he used to conduct his business.

His room smelled permanently foetid, no matter how often it was aired, and I visited him as little as possible.

Each winter, as the days cooled in the few hours of fragile light, my eyes would be drawn to the northern mountains and I'd feel the pull of desire to find my people... But that pull was permanently eclipsed by the trauma bond that kept me in Toscana and at the House of Lamone.

And so, today, I sit contemplating the goblets, silver and green, ancient and indistinguishable.

Today, everything will change. I can no longer live this life.

Today, I put my plan into action.

I began two days ago. Leaving the Scorpion sleeping off another indulgence, I took our only horse and journeyed out on my own. I had set my usual glamours aside, dressed in Nazioni's clothing and, that day, wore his face. I was confident I could also give a good approximation of his voice.

It was an early autumnal morning after a night of heavy rain. Low level mists hugged the courses of streams and rivers and the meadows were bejewelled with dew. The chilly air smelt damp and musty and I was glad of the jacket I wore.

I took the winding road to Lorenzia. Beside me, the sunflower fields had lost their summer vibrancy, petals shed, the heads hung low, each weighed down with a complex mosaic of tight packed seed. Further on, as the mists began to rise, I passed hilltop towns, the slopes below them covered in the neat stripes of vines. Below bluffs stood villages of square houses, their pantiled roofs glowing in shades of ochre and umber. On any other day I would have enjoyed this journey, but that day my muscles were knotted with tension, my body taught with apprehension and I was sick with nerves.

My entire future depended on this.

Close to midday I entered the city of Lorenzia. I found a place to tie the horse and continued on foot. Clearly the rain had not reached the city as beneath my feet the cobbles and flagstones were dry and dusty. My eyes rose to the skyline dominated as it is by a forest of campanile and the great central dome. Lorenzia is split in two by a wide river and then stitched back together again by many bridges. I crossed one of these and entered an area frequented by artists and the cultured who sit and sip coffee or wine in the many piazzas or wander the serpentine streets breathing in the atmosphere of this ancient city. I had plenty of time and could easily have indulged in the fragrant coffee or sweet pastries at one of the street side cafes, but I had no appetite and my visit here had a much darker purpose.

I followed alleyways watched over by statues of marble and alabaster. In one of these alleys, close to a trio of bronze figures spattered with verdigris, I entered a rather questionable antique shop. Nazioni is well known here and under his guise I sold the last few trinkets I had hidden from him. No-one doubted my disguise and, feeling a slight release of tension, I hurried on with my pockets considerably heavier with coin.

Lorenzia and its surrounds is the territory of a Garridan merchant by the name of Mius who specialises in recreational drugs and other toxins. It's all highly illegal of course and so Mius constantly moves his premises. If you know the signs and sigils to follow, Mius is easy enough to find. Unsurprisingly, I found him in a dingy shop in a poky little backstreet. He was writing in a ledger and looked up as I came through the door.

"Ah! Tiahaar Lamone. It is a long time since I saw you last." Mius closed the ledger and set it to one side. His dark eyes swept over me as he pushed back a length of obsidian hair.

I gave a half smile and gestured helplessly with my hands. "Alas. Funds."

He nodded, half rising. "I understand. Please, sit. Tell me how I can help you today."

I took the battered wooden chair he offered.

"I take it you enjoyed your last... ah... flight of discovery?" he asked.

I settled myself back, attempting an appearance of ease that I in no way felt. "I did... I certainly did."

"Yes, Snakeroot is an excellent choice of narcotic. Quite the queen of chemicals. You are... here for more?"

I paused for a moment as if considering.

Mius continued to watch me closely, his head on one side.

I sat forward, as if eager. "I wondered... I had heard... You see, I'm in the mood to try something new and, well... There is talk of something called Snowberry?"

He looked at me sharply. "An unusual choice... Expensive."

I wavered for a moment. Did he suspect? What would Nazioni do in this situation.

I gave the half smile again and sat back in the chair. "My tastes are, as you know... eclectic?"

Mius gave a low laugh. "Indeed."

Immediately he grew serious again. "You are aware of the issues with Snowberry and alcohol, aren't you?"

"Oh yes, quite aware."

He watched me for a long moment then nodded and stood up. "I believe I have some in stock."

Gliding to the back of the shop Mius disappeared through the door. He was gone for some considerable time.

I sat patiently for a while and then began to drum my fingers on my leg. Sweat broke out between my shoulder blades, and it was all I could do to sit still. Had he seen through Nazioni's face to my true self beneath?

Garridan are shrewd.

Ravansanella once told me an old saying, if you want to find a fool in Garridan, *take one with you...* Had Mius discerned my plan? Was he, even now, informing on me? I was just about set to make a run for it when he returned through the door carrying a small jar containing large, waxy, white berries.

Mius set the jar on the counter. "They took some finding." He opened the jar releasing a slightly sour odour.

I smiled, attempting once again to let the tension go.

"A single dose?" he enquired.

I nodded.

Mius packaged the berries up and continued with a little small talk as we negotiated the price.

With considerable relief, I left the shop carrying the small parcel, my pockets considerably lighter. The berries cost more than I would have liked but I had no desire to linger.

"Call again," Mius said as the door swung closed behind me. "Let me know how you enjoy this ah... pleasure."

I left the dingy backstreet as quickly as I could, the packet secreted safely in my jacket. I made my way back to the broad piazzas and the far friendlier crowds that mingled there. Despite my success, my nerves jangled like rusting chains and I wished to be quit of the city as soon as possible. With some surprise, I realised I was hungry, so I stopped briefly in a small grocery store to purchase a fragrant wine and some bread and cheese. Then I hurried to retrieve my horse and headed back swiftly to Villa Lamone where, unaware of my absence, Nazioni remained sprawled, snoring in his bed.

He has only just surfaced and has called for some refreshment.

Have you guessed my plan?

I am ready.

As I've told you, Olori mate for life. It is 'until death do us part' in the truest sense.

So there you have it.

Death.

Death is my only way out.

There are few toxins and poisons that are permanently harmful to the harish frame.

Snowberry is one of them. But Snowberry is peculiar. Taken on its own it is a powerful intoxicant, rumoured to give the taker visions of other realms and a long lasting heady sense of euphoria.

Mixed with alcohol it is swiftly and spectacularly lethal.

And so, you see my plan? You do. I know you do.

Except...

I have a problem.

For two days now I have debated with myself.

The simple truth is, no matter how dreadful my life is, no matter how appallingly awful Nazioni is... I cannot be a murderer.

And so I have hatched another plan.

The two goblets sit before me on a tray.

One has been smeared inside with the juice of Snowberry and, having spun them on a rotating table, I no longer know which goblet is which.

There is no odour or residue to give me a clue or give me away.

Nazioni's bellow for refreshment reaches me once again and I fetch the bottle of fragrant wine I purchased in Lorenzia. Picking up the tray, I head out of the kitchen and up the stairs into the hallway. I pause briefly at an old mirror that still hangs on the wall. A face that is not mine peers back at me. This simply will not do. I will be myself again.

I let all the glamours go. My swan-self reappears. My dark eyes, iridescent white skin and the feathered hair. I am struck by the beauty I see there and by the pride in the gaze. Once more I continue through the house.

I shall let fate decide.

If I am successful. I shall be free.

If I am unsuccessful. I shall be free.

If the Fates choose me I will leave this place today. I will take the horse and what little coin remains and head north to those mountains far, far away where I shall look for and find my people. With every step I find myself more certain of my path.

I offer up a little prayer to the Fates. *I am Chiusi, choose me…*

Finally, I reach Nazioni's chamber. He has made it out of the bed and is sprawled at the desk. His eyes track me blearily as I enter the room and I see confusion and then a dawning recognition as he realises I am me again.

"It's a long time since I saw that face."

Despite his dishevelled appearance and bloodshot eyes his voice is steady. His mind appears clear.

I give no answer as I set the tray down before him and draw up my own chair.

He raises an eyebrow. "You're joining me? I didn't give you permission."

I shrug, lift the bottle and pour two measures.

He gives a half laugh and holds up his hands. "Oh well, why not, I suppose. You are my oldest friend."

Still I do not respond. He picks up a glass. I take the other.

He leers at me slightly. "We should have a toast, I think... To what should we drink?"

I pause a moment before answering as I lift my glass, "To freedom."

A slight frown, a slight shrug as he lifts his own glass, "To freedom, then."

We drink.

1 – The story of *The Frog and The Scorpion* is often attributed to Aesop but does not appear in any of his collections prior to the 20th Century. It would appear that the story has a much earlier origin, possibly from a collection of fables from Persia.

River Crossing

Nerine Dorman

"Oh, come on, Rai. You can't possibly be scared of a little water?" Korhaan swam into the great Aranye River and allowed the silty, cobalt-hued waters to carry him twenty, maybe thirty feet downstream before he cut back to our side of the bank. His limbs slashed the current with minimal splashes, with as much purpose as a crocodile.

Speaking of crocodiles... I glanced left and right. My heart beat faster, and I swallowed against a dry throat.

I remained where I was, my toes squelching into the fine mud while the reeds cut into my fingers. The little water that licked and lapped at my skin was hungry and cold, and the entire river was vast. A great orange setting sun had already mostly bled into the west, and even if I was brave to try and swim to the settlement, we'd come out the other side bedraggled and frozen as the first pinpricks of stars ashed the sky.

And the other side was so desirable, yet those forty or so feet across the wide swathe of water might as well have been as many miles. Date palms swayed in the balmy evening breeze. Harlings shrieking and playing on the wide green lawns. Little palm-frond roofed, wattle-and-daub chalets beckoned with canvas tent verandas that billowed like sails.

Beyond the settlement, with its orderly vineyards that chequered the fertile flanks of the river, was the sloping red-rock ridge, afire in the last of the sunlight, where several score mausoleums stood in orderly rows. White-washed and regimented with neat columns at their façades, they were apart from the dwellings of the quick.

How curious. Korhaan had mentioned something of a funerary cult here at Norlyn, but I'd not imagined we'd make the detour to see it. Yet the bridge was out a few miles up, washed away in an early flood, and he was hoping we'd get somehar to bring us across with a pontoon – and the only ferry for miles being here at Norlyn. Yet we were tired, and so far nohar had paid us any mind, despite our hollering across the water for assistance.

Whether it was a trick of the evening air or the slow, relentless wash of the Aranye in its course, there was no telling why we were being ignored. Korhaan still reckoned we could swim across. Of course he did. He often managed brave and foolhardy feats while I huddled where it was safe. And now he wanted to challenge the current, which appeared far too strong for my liking. Then again, any water that reached beyond my knees filled me with a clutching dread and caused my lungs to close up.

Soaked through, his nipples pebbled from the frigid water, Korhaan came and threw his arms around me, buried his chilled face against my neck. I squirmed, allowing myself to mock struggle in his embrace.

"You're cold as death!" I cried, but I was laughing, and was able to put aside the horror of the great water and our predicament while we shared breath. Korhaan was earth and sky, lightning on a dusky horizon.

We broke apart just as somehar hailed us from across the Aranye.

Grinning like fools, we yelled our greetings in return, and watched as two hara guided the pontoon out. The cable spanning the waterway creaked, the watercraft's progress was slow, and it took them the better part of ten minutes to reach us. By the time the taller of the two held out a strong brown hand to help us across the gap, the first stars were bleeding into the charcoal sky.

"Where're you from?" our host asked.

"We've been travelling," Korhaan answered. "Up the West Coast, trading this and that. Mostly jewellery." He patted his backpack.

"And repairs," I added as I frowned at him. I hated sometimes that he was so upfront about our business. Not all hara we met on the road were honest. Or kind.

"Oh? The Norlyn will be glad to hear that. He may have some work for you." The two shared glances.

"But this place *is* Norlyn?" I asked.

Korhaan tutted, as though I were slow, and a warm flush stole up my cheeks.

"He *is* Norlyn, or the Norlyn, depending on how you speak," the har said, as if that were a profound statement, which to him I suppose it was. "But we are being rude." He heaved at the cable and the water lapped at pontoon hull. The Aranye was tugging hard at our craft. I shivered and swallowed hard.

"I am Hama, and our strong silent friend is Djobba."

A brilliant smile lit up Djobba's face, yet he still did not speak.

As a courtesy, we shared our names, and while Korhaan kept up the chatter, I seated myself in the centre of the craft as much as possible. I had to remind myself Korhaan had intended for us to swim across, and if I could endure less than a quarter of an hour in the relative comfort, despite my fear, then that was a small sacrifice I was willing to make.

By the time we reached the other side, a small welcoming party awaited us. Harlings took our hands and guided us to one of the wattle-and-daub huts, where bowls of steaming water were brought for us to wash the dust from our hands and faces.

Though our accommodation was simple, it was neatly furnished – a quilt lay upon a reed mat in the corner, and there was a *kist* for us to stow our things. A gemsbok hide covered a dung floor inlaid with peach pips, and there was even a shelf that held books from the far south. Hand-printed things, carefully stitched and bound in worn leather. At a glance, mostly travel journals and memoirs. The kind of reading that did not tax.

Korhaan grinned and dropped his pack, then sprawled on the bed. "Now this is what I call a welcome!"

I hovered by the door, where I peeked past the reed covering, but nohar lingered outside. "I don't trust them."

"Just because the hara at Ganarra tried to steal our things doesn't mean these will too." He smirked at me.

"You trust too easily," I shot back.

"I can read hara well, and these ones won't do us in. You can see they're set up for guests. Besides, it's their trade. Hara come from all over to visit the tombs and ask the blessings of those who have passed."

"You know a lot about this place."

"I visited here when I was a harling. My hostling came to ask that he may be blessed with another pearl, and it came to be."

"And where is your brother now?" I asked. We rarely spoke of our families.

He gave a small shrug. "Walking with the dehara. Who knows?"

I wrung my hands, paced a bit.

"Oh, for the love of the stars, Rai, relax. We have some time to unwind. They will call us for the evening meal, and we can meet this Norlyn har that has you so puzzled."

"That's exactly what I'm afraid of."

A harling came for us within the hour, a gangly youngster on the cusp of feybraiha. He brought us to a great *boma*. The walls of the open-aired, circular enclosure were painted with a river motif in red ochre on pale grey, and featured a veritable bestiary of elephant, dancing therianthropomorphs with antelope heads, and harish figures with fish tails instead of legs, along with stylised papyrus and lotus motifs. I was particularly fascinated by the depictions of giant catfish, that seemed more dragon than fish.

But we had no time to linger, for we were brought to the reed mat at the head of the *boma*, nearest the fire pit, where a har reclined upon stuffed hide pillows. He was tall and fine boned, his shaven head a well-formed dome. His appearance spoke of a mixed heritage that gifted him with tawny skin and bright green eyes outlined heavily with kohl that missed nothing. His three companions – chesna? – were arranged about him, and all were garbed in linens so sheer I was able to see their limbs and more. How did they keep their clothing so clean?

Our own appearance was decidedly grubby in comparison – both Korhaan and I wore much-patched leather britches with tunics so old their combined colours ranged from muddy browns to dull olive. Beggars, if I were entirely honest.

We offered the universally accepted bow of respect, and waited for the Norlyn to speak, for that was the polite thing to do.

"Korhaan of the West Coast and Rai of the Hoerikwaggo," he acknowledged us. "You are most welcome."

"We thank you, most esteemed one," Korhaan said, and I was

happy to let him speak, for he was far more eloquent than I.

Clay tankards of beer were offered, as well as a sweet wine, and we dined at the community leader's circle, which was a great honour. Roast sweet potatoes and various greens, as well as fish and venison were served, and afterwards, we enjoyed small carob cakes, sweetened with honey and crunchy with roasted seeds.

I couldn't remember when last we had eaten so well, though I couldn't quite shake my suspicions. Why would we be shown such honour? Yet this did not appear to bother Korhaan one bit, for he was in top form, regaling all present with tales of the many happenings in the land, be it the completion of the transcontinental railway to the discovery of a new gemstone in the Great Sand Face, that had even hara from the northern hemisphere scramble to the newly formed town.

All this these hara should know, for they were situated not far from a prominent northerly route, and the great Aranye's banks themselves were an important agricultural area. But who was I to complain if we were such honoured guests?

Throughout our meal the Norlyn's chesna remained quiet and demure by his side. I wasn't sure what to make of this, whether it was his presence – being near him was rather like sitting beneath the noon-day sun – or a local custom where hara of lesser social standing measured their words. But being quiet did not equate to being unaware – and both Korhaan and I were observed, no doubt to be later discussed.

One of the hara, I noticed, stared at me fixedly, hardly drinking nor eating throughout the evening. Unlike me, with my mixed heritage, he tended more towards the finer-boned, ochre-skinned locals with dark embers for eyes. Intricate patterns had been shaved at the sides of his head, but he wore longer locks at the top, which had been decorated with carved bone and glass beads that clinked musically every time he tilted his head. Which, mind you, was not often, but I kept returning his gaze.

Nohar else seemed to notice, and I thought nothing more of the matter by the time harlings came in to dance for us. Korhaan clapped his hands in delight, and yet again the notion that we were undeserving of being such esteemed guests struck me. However, the wine and beer were intoxicating, and I allowed myself to be lulled into comfort. With promises that on the morrow, Korhaan would show the Norlyn his wares – and I have to admit, they are fine; there was absolutely nothing to be ashamed of – we retired for the night replete and warm, instead of having to shelter in the lee of stone outcroppings beneath naked stars.

I kept my peace all the way until we reached our hut, and to my horror, I found that somehar had been here before us to light a lamp and prepare the bed for us. They had even gone so far as to bring a tray with fresh water in an ornate glass jug, complete with matching glasses.

"This is nice," Korhaan said.

"This is weird. Check your bag. Somehar may have taken our things."

"And turned down the bed?" He arched a brow at me. "And even left small sweets on the pillows? Here, have one."

I shook my head at his offering. "This is not some upmarket hotel in Table Bay with Gelaming pretensions," I sniped.

"And you need to calm yourself down. Not everyhar is looking to take advantage of weary travellers. Norlyn is renowned for its hospitality. Their entire livelihood is based on how well they treat their guests. Word would spread if they were rude and inhospitable."

"Nothing is without cost."

"And I expect that on the morrow the Norlyn and I will fall to bartering. So why don't you relax, maybe visit the cemetery and pay respects to Sweetness. Put a silver mark before his bier. Perhaps a wish will be granted."

"Who is Sweetness?"

He raised a brow, his smile indulgent. "You don't know the story of Sweetness?"

"What sort of a name is that for a har anyway?" I asked, irked and perplexed by equal measure.

"Oh, it's an old story. A century or so ago, if not more, Sweetness, the son of the Norlyn at the time, fell in love with an unsuitable har – a travelling storyteller, said by some. According to others he was an emissary of some lord of the north come to prospect for diamonds. Whoever the har was, it matters not. The Norlyn forbade the union, but the son was headstrong. He would seek his fortune with this rootless wanderer, this vagabond who'd stolen his heart along with his apparent good sense. And one moonless night the pair decided to abscond without the father's blessings.

"Yet they chose the wrong time of the year to make the crossing – for they were not prepared to meet resistance and sought to cross the Aranye directly without the aid of the pontoon or by travelling up road to the bridge where they may be dissuaded from continuing."

I shivered, for I already felt the disaster spidering its ragged fingers up my spine.

As if sensing my growing horror, Korhaan raised a brow, his teeth flashing white in the lamplight as he grinned. "It had been raining well that summer, far, far to the north, and the Aranye carried the season's bounty so that she nudged past her flanks, her waters thick with silt and unseen currents.

"Sweetness saw the strength of the waters and had second thoughts, said to his chesna that perhaps they should reconsider, choose another night, perhaps make a better plan. As it was, the horse they shared snorted and stamped, and would not set hoof into the waters, despite much coaxing.

"But at that point, somehar in the homestead must've noticed Sweetness missing from his rooms and set up the alarm. Lamps were lit. Hara were calling out to one another. Dogs began to bark. This was all the encouragement Sweetness's chesna needed to set his heels into his mount's flanks. Its eyes rolling in fear, the beast nonetheless obeyed his master and began the crossing.

"Yet the dehara can be cruel, for although the storm had happened hours before upriver, a sudden and immense downpour such as the land had not seen for many moons, the floodwaters chose that hour to arrive at Norlyn. Even as the valiant stallion struggled with his burden, the Aranye's current grew stronger and turbid, and by the time they were just past the halfway mark they were already swept into a part where the river entered a series of cataracts.

"The Norlyn of the time sent out a search party, and after a day, they eventually encountered Sweetness's body in the reeds about ten kilometres downriver."

"Dead?" I asked somewhat unnecessarily.

Korhaan grimaced at me as if I were a halfwit. "You know, I'm not going to take that seriously. Of course he was bloody dead. They took up his body and brought him back to the settlement. So full of grief was the Norlyn, that he sent for embalmers, who bathed the body, removed all the internal organs. Even the brain." Korhaan smacked his lips, because he could see my growing discomfort. "With a hook. They stick it up your nasal passages, break the bone and swish it around until your grey stuff is goop that runs out of your nose. They washed out the abdominal cavity with the finest brandy and then packed Sweetness's remains in special salts for seventy days and nights, all the while reciting hymns to the dehara over his remains so that his soul might fly free. And then they painted him in resins, garbed him in fine linens and placed him in one of those pretty mausoleums you saw up there on the slopes.

"No expense was spared when the Norlyn built that mausoleum, and when you go up tomorrow – for I do believe you should go – you will see how Sweetness's body remains as beautiful as the day he died – preserved so that he is a perfect likeness."

I pulled a face at that. "I've heard stories about what the bodies of the drowned look like."

"Hush now, you ruin the story. And, besides, the embalmers were masters of their craft. If they weren't, do you think that Sweetness would reside in his glass coffin for all to come see?"

"That's just gross," I said. "Who wants to see a har's dead body?" And then I squinted at Korhaan, for he was filled with silent mirth. "But that's not the end of it, is it?"

"Ah, you know me well. Go fetch me a glass of water then come join me on the bed."

I did as he asked and snuggled up next to him. Korhaan trailed lazy fingers down my nape so that I shivered at his touch.

"And there the story of Sweetness would have ended if it were not for the miracles – a pretty dead har preserved as a memorial for his father's grief. It began with the next Norlyn's chesna, whose pearls blighted before being delivered. What prompted him to visit the mausoleum the dehara alone knew. It's said he had set a small shrine nearby Sweetness's for each pearl that had failed. And perhaps his tears had fallen on a moonshadow while he prayed and made libations, or perhaps in his sorrow, he'd somehow parted the veil between life and death to reach beyond.

"Afterwards, he told all that Sweetness appeared to him, or perhaps a spirit that claimed his likeness, and placed a hand upon his belly. He said, 'Do not sorrow, for the dehara have taken note of your tears, and you will be blessed among hara.' And soon after, not one but two harlings emerged from his next pearl, and both grew up to be fair of face and good of nature."

"That sounds like a made-up story," I said, nudging Korhaan in the ribs.

"Oh, it's not, for after other hara discovered that if they brought libations and set their troubles before Sweetness, while they perhaps did not receive a visitation, per se, they would often inexplicably find the missing item they'd been searching for, or a long-lost chesna would return, or a problem that seemed unresolvable would be fixed in an unexpected way. And so it has been for years. And hence each Norlyn tends to Sweetness's mausoleum, and he has a bevy of attendants to ensure that his mortal remains do not suffer beetle, damp or rot."

I frowned. "That sounds…"

"Rather grim, I know. My tribe returns ours to the earth. There are some who send their dead into the ocean, and others still who practise sky burial. Who is to say what the right way of caring of our dead is, if it's done with the respect that it deserves?"

I wasn't so sure. My own hara burnt their dead upon great pyres and sent their ashes into an ebbing tide, washed into the ocean from which all life comes. This notion of preserving a corpse, venerating it even, so that it became an artefact, a relic, unsettled me. I shuddered.

"You don't like this story?" Korhaan asked as he nuzzled my hair.

"It's weird. To be so attached to one's past."

"Who are we to judge how hara practise their being?"

"True, but…"

"Well, I can think of something to practise with you."

We shared breath, and soon had more to occupy ourselves than old, unsettling stories. Later, if I dreamt, I did not recall. For once it was a blessing to be out of the sharp wind, and to not continuously have half an ear listening out for prowlers in the dark.

The following morning, we rose with the sun, when a harling brought us a covered tray of food so that we might break our fast on sticky-sweet dates, boiled eggs seasoned with spices, and black, bitter coffee that made all the small hairs on my arms prickle.

"Now I'm awake," I said to Korhaan.

He slugged back the last from the tiny earthenware cup and offered up such a comical grimace that we couldn't help but laugh. We sat upon the small veranda that gifted us with an unobstructed view, to the cobalt water rushing past and the orderly vines greening the south bank.

"I should have returned much sooner," Korhaan said as he gazed out, now pensive. "I forget how hospitable these hara are."

"But you have itchy feet," I said.

"True. And I wouldn't have found you under that *bitou* bush."

"And we wouldn't have discovered the many wondrous things we've seen since."

"And yet" – he chewed his lip – "I can't imagine what it must be like to set roots."

"You having thoughts? What happened to our plan to walk all the way to the top of the continent?"

"We have forever. There's nothing stopping us from lingering awhile."

And I grew silent, because I couldn't help but think of Sweetness, who no doubt also thought he had forever, until those waters swept him away.

Korhaan went to attend business with the Norlyn, which left me at odd ends, for bargaining had never been my strong point and I found such talk dull. I was content, as always, to go with Korhaan's wish for me to explore. Not that I didn't have a will of my own – at present I simply didn't feel strongly about anything in particular. Ever obedient to Korhaan's will, I headed towards the mortuary shrines while he spoke business with the Norlyn.

Korhaan liked to say I was a sprite that lived from heartbeat to heartbeat, and to a degree I supposed he was correct. I was a wild thing when he'd found me wandering the territories beyond my tribe's settlement. Some might say I was rudderless, a scrap of down dancing on the wind, but truly, is that such a terrible existence? To be in the moment, *each* moment? Korhaan was the first who understood, and I'd been happy enough to be caught up in his wake all these years. I was his reflecting pool, he told me. I reminded him of those moments of wonder so easy to forget when a har grew careworn. I was the one who noticed the otter's pawprints in the mud of an estuary or picked up the one piece of quartz crystal that lay among random pebbles.

A neat causeway had been laid on the other side of the wagon track that followed the route of the river. It must have taken hara years to find all the pieces of slate, shape them and fit them so that they lay almost seamlessly, like an arrow straight up to the ridges. Every five paces, on either side of this causeway, which was wide enough for two to walk abreast, were reclining lions. These had been carved from the same red stone as the ridges above, though I did not see a quarry nearby. Upon closer inspection, I saw that their eyes had been inlaid with tiger's eye gemstones, chosen carefully so that a vertical slit was suggested for each pupil. How cunning. How exquisite.

On either side of the causeway was an avenue of cedar trees, which, as far as I knew, were not native to the area. Somehar must've been looking after them well, for they stood proud regardless of the blasted appearance of the surrounding desert scrub. Despite it still being early, the day's heat was already rising, and a cicada chorus shimmered out a wall of sound.

If only I'd brought a hat…

So, I hurried onward, towards the entrance, which was made up of two tapering, rectangular, white-washed towers about two storeys tall. Each was topped with a cornice, and when I passed through, a sense calm washed over me.

Dozens of mausoleums were set in orderly rows, finished in shining white or earthy ochre. Some were no larger than a bread oven while others were more like small, rectangular cottages, yet Sweetness's final resting place was unmistakeable, for all others stood in subservience to its glory.

Two sentinel cypresses stood on either side of the doorway, which could be reached by ascending nine steps, upon which paired lanterns shaped like lotus blossoms had been positioned. I supposed at night these lamps would be lit; a faint smell of resinous incense rose from the heated stone. A discreet sign requested that all hara should remove their footwear and leave them outside. Not that I was wearing shoes, but I nonetheless took care to wipe my feet on the mat outside. No other pairs were waiting, so I assumed I was the only har present

It took a few heartbeats for my eyes to adjust to the dim interior, but what I saw had me pause. Somehar had carved tesserae and created a mosaic for the floor, in such fine detail so as to depict a flowing river picked out in various shades of blue, grey and maroon that drew visitors from the doorway up to a glass-covered bier. Ornate brass censers on either side of the bier released slow twirls of blue smoke into the already hazy air, and small, rectangular windows running along the top of the walls let in azure light, for the hara had somehow contrived to find blue glass so that the interior was bathed in coolness.

Paintings adorned the walls in such profusion that I didn't know where to look first. Highly stylised, they nevertheless possessed an aching beauty, depicting dancing hara, a multitude of birds, such as ibises, flamingos and storks, as well as greenery such as a har might only rarely encounter in the dusty hinterlands.

My mouth had gone dry, and my feet were reluctant to carry me forward, but simultaneously, I felt the strong attraction, an inevitability, as if my entire life lived so far had conspired to bring me to this point. Step by step, I moved, and it was as if a great rushing of water flowed with me, and distant voices threaded together into a song that was just beyond my hearing.

Coming face to face with Sweetness himself was almost an anti-climax. I felt as if I gazed upon the har himself rather than a mere effigy of him. In death, and no doubt thanks to the mummification process, he was shrunken, his features flattened, and his skin dark with the oils and resins used to preserve him.

White teeth peeked past lips pulled taut, so that he appeared in pain. Eyes were sunken in the sockets, but I could still discern each lash. High cheekbones had been dusted with glittering flakes. Sweetness was garbed in sheer linen and a necklace of many lapis lazuli beads that rested on his chest. Delicate hands, the skin almost translucent and paper thin, were clasped on his chest and a ring set with a cabochon ruby the size of a quail's egg adorned his left middle finger. But it was his lustrous hair, spread about him, that was the true wealth of this vision. Never before had I seen so much auburn, rich like a rare wood polished to a high sheen that framed the face of the dead har.

All that separated us was the glass box that enclosed his final resting place, and so perfect was he that all I could do was stare in silent wonder. The aroma of fragrant incense grew stronger, filled my senses until this vision before me wavered, and the interior of the tomb grew lighter. It appeared as if I were viewing this scene not only in the present but also the past, for Sweetness's image shifted and shimmered. A blush of life stole across his resin-coated skin, lips plumped up, eyes filled out the empty sockets so that the lashes fluttered.

Then he opened his eyes and sat up with a cry, turned and stared at me with wide, light green eyes like the rarest topaz.

I knew nothing after that.

I awoke with my head cradled on the lap of a strange har. Not strange. I knew him – he was one of the Norlyn's chesnari, the one who had studied me so intently the night before.

Unaccountably I started crying, great wracking sobs, and I had no understanding of why it was that a heavy sorrow overwhelmed me, close on the heels of a terrible, choking fear. The air was too thick, like water pressing itself down my nose, into my throat.

I thrashed about, as a har would when drowning, and the Norlyn's chesnari spoke to me with quiet words in a language I did not understand He helped me to my feet and brought me out of the funerary chapel.

Immediately the sun's brightness beat down upon us, but the har drew me staggering around the back of the building, where a small mud hut stood that was clearly used for storage, for its shelves were filled with boxes, flasks, pots, and assorted tools. Here he bade me sit on a rickety bamboo stool.

"Hush, hush," the har said as he rubbed my neck and shoulders with strong, assured hands.

"What's happening?" Gradually my breathing was subsiding, and the tremors that wracked my body became less pronounced.

"He came to you," the har said.

"Who?"

"Sweetness, of course. In all these years..." Wonder laced his words.

I craned my neck so I could look behind me. "What do you mean?"

"We tend this shrine, and often Sweetness will bless supplicants, but he has never come to a querent the way he has to you today. Not in a long, long time."

I frowned. "This was some sort of...visitation?"

"You are blessed. Sweetness obviously favours you above all others."

"All... right." My thoughts were treacle thick. "What does this mean?"

"It means he has chosen you to serve."

At this I laughed. "I'm nohar. I'm a traveller. What could Sweetness want with me?"

"We are all called, though some hear the calling more clearly than others." His face was beatific, as if my lapse in sanity was a cause for celebration.

What would Korhaan say? After he stopped laughing at my mystical experience, that is. He was not a har given to excesses of devotion to the dehara. And by default, neither was I. What could this Sweetness possibly want with me, a rootless wanderer?

As it turned out, my benefactor's name was Muna, and as soon as my legs no longer gave beneath me, he had me up on my feet and hurried us down to see the Norlyn. The sun already approached its zenith, which scrambled my sense of time. How long had I been insensible?

Yet I was in no position to argue as Muna linked his arm with mine in a way that made his possessiveness over me all too apparent. All I could do was keep my eyes slitted against the glare, at the way that the ground gave the appearance of bulging and rolling beneath my feet as we made our way back to the *boma*, where the Norlyn held court.

I had hoped that Korhaan would still be there, in his meeting with the Norlyn, but when Muna dragged me in, the har was busy with two rangers – I knew them by the matching olive-green uniforms. The pair gave me shifty-eyed looks while we hovered in the shade nearby.

By now the heat was stifling, and not even the slightest wisp of a breeze could stir the thick white ash in the central fire pit. Muna's excitement rolled off him, yet the Norlyn pointedly did not look our way.

"You're making a mistake," I told Muna. "This is not something to bother your Norlyn with. He is evidently an important har."

"Hush," Muna said, and placed a finger on my lips for emphasis.

I sighed, rolled my eyes, and settled down to wait. As it was, I couldn't bear standing. The ground still gave the uncomfortable sensation of rolling beneath my feet.

Muna sensed my discomfort and beckoned over two harlings who were playing in the dirt not far from us – some game involving knucklebones.

In a rapid-fire dialect with many clicks, Muna told the pair to run off and do something for him. I couldn't quite follow what he was saying, but it sounded as if he meant that we be brought something cool to drink.

"Where's Korhaan?" I asked.

"I'm sure he's around," Muna said.

"I need him."

"All in good time. Hush now. Close your eyes. You can lean your head against my shoulder if you're feeling unwell."

He was right. My head did hurt, and I felt immediately better when I closed my eyes. I must've slipped in and out of wakefulness, because the next I knew, the harlings were back with a tray. Upon it was a cup of pomegranate juice and a bunch of big red globe grapes such as I'd never eaten before. Fit for royalty.

"You must drink," Muna urged when I hesitated.

"But this is too good for me."

He dismissed my refusal as if he was shooing flies. "It's juice and fruit."

Perhaps he wouldn't take such bounty for granted if he walked the wide-open spaces between settlements. Ours was a land of unforgiving blue sky and parched earth.

Careful-like, I reached out and took the glass. It was handcrafted, cut with crystal facets that threw ruby stains of colour on the ground, on my skin. Everywhere the light danced through the contents.

The pomegranate on my tongue was icy and tart, and before I knew it, I'd emptied the glass. Muna watched avidly as I popped first one and then another red globe into my mouth. Sweetness almost unbearable filled me, and delicately I spat out the seeds and placed them on the rim of the plate.

"They're good," Muna said, "aren't they?"

I nodded. "Very. But why...?"

Muna's hand on my wrist silenced me, and I followed his gaze to the Norlyn. The har now stared in our direction in a way that suggested he was ready to speak to us. The hara with whom he'd been in discussion were already making their way across the *boma* to the entrance.

"Come, we speak with him now," Muna said, and helped me up.

Unaccountably, I found myself shaking, for I did not desire such scrutiny from such an important har, and yet I was powerless to prevent this meeting from taking place. Where was Korhaan? I cast about for him, but that was a futile gesture.

The Norlyn observed me with the faintest traces of amusement quirking his lips. He was as splendid during the day as he was during the night, the warm tones of his skin glowing with health – indeed the very essence of this har shone. Why I was so attuned to it now, the dehara alone knew, for I had not noticed this the night before.

"You have seen the funerary chapel, I am told," he said. Those eyes never left mine.

I nodded, and for some reason I bowed my head too, as if this were some holy har.

"Please, take a seat, let us speak." He gestured to the cushions before him, as though I were an honoured guest.

I hesitated, wet my lips. "Please, Norlyn, I am nohar important. I don't under—"

"Sit." The authority in that one word was unmistakeable, and the hawk-like glare he focused on me made me feel like the prey of an animal that was about to pounce upon me.

I sat and focused my attention on the beaded pectoral collar the har wore. It was an intricate thing, made up of oblong carnelian and malachite beads – the creation of so many similar components must've taken a har months. I knew all too well, since I was often the very har to do work like that under Korhaan's direction.

"Muna tells me that you met Sweetness."

It felt as if all the blood rushed from my head, and a faint whining started in my ears. "I – I am sorry if I did something wrong."

The Norlyn's laughter was a merry bell. "Oh, your face, dear har. You look like you are about to faint on the spot." He clapped his hands and shouted over my shoulder, "Neldi, bring this young har something a little stronger than fruit juice."

I shrank from the suddenness of the sound and motion, as he placed a large hand on my shoulder, and those bright green eyes were directed right at me. I could feel his power rippling beneath his skin – vast, like the great Aranye. He would draw me away from the safety of the banks and drag me into the unknown.

"You must learn to breathe, Rai. You are like the *intukwane* in the underbrush, with wide, white eyes always flitting here, there, and darting when you get a fright."

I tried to speak, but to my eternal shame an almost inaudible whine escaped me.

To be the Norlyn's sole focus was like standing in a furnace, and I wilted before him. Thankfully the har whose name was Neldi brought the beverage – icy beer in a bottle slick with condensation. It felt awfully good to have something to hold, hopsy liquid in my mouth that washed the fear from my throat. I took three long gulps until half the bottle was gone, and then was able to settle my shaking hand and meet the Norlyn's gaze.

"Yes, I went to the funerary chapel, and it was… It was like a dream. It is a beautiful resting place. I saw… It was like I saw the har who was and that which remains, and the two became one, and he rose as if to speak to me, and then… Then nothing more until…" I looked sidelong to where Muna was sitting next to his Norlyn. "It was then that Muna found me."

"You remember nothing?"

I shook my head.

The Norlyn turned his regard to Muna. "How certain are you that this is not some sun-dazzled young har making up stories?"

I wanted to bury myself far, far beneath the ground. This was all a colossal waste of time. Yet I knew what I'd seen, what I'd experienced, and I still felt as if I'd taken a queer turn.

Muna cocked his head, his smile inscrutable. "Sweetness's left hand has moved to his heart."

The Norlyn offered a mollified, muted, "Oh." Then he rubbed at his chin and returned his gaze to me.

I squirmed, feeling as if I were about to spontaneously combust on the spot. I desperately wanted Korhaan to be here. He'd know what to say. He'd tell these hara that it was all a terrible mistake, that I'd never meant to cause a stir. And then he'd berate me in private, tell me how careless I was, and that would be the end of it. We'd leave, and most likely not return.

Yet Korhaan wasn't here now. I was alone. Among strangers.

I straightened my spine and returned the Norlyn's gaze as evenly as possible. "With all due respect, tiahaar, I know what I saw. I am not a har who's given much for matters of magic and the spirit, so I am not prone to making up stories. You can ask Korhaan. I am but a simple har." I cringed at that last sentence. I'd been accused of being simple-minded often enough.

For a few heartbeats, the Norlyn's face remained a mask, but then mischief twitched the corners of his lips. "I like you, Rai. Very well." He turned to Muna. "What do you suppose we do about this. He is not one of ours."

"Neither was your father," Muna said. "And yet Sweetness spoke to him."

"Indeed." Those green eyes focused on me again, and I stared back, helpless.

My breath came short then, and the light grew dim at the edges of my vision, but I remembered Korhaan's lessons about inhaling and exhaling slowly through my nose until the little tingling bites at my extremities went away.

"We'll have to conduct a Mystery tonight, then," the Norlyn said.

"And see what shall be seen."

"Does that mean I can go?" I asked, ever hopeful to escape their scrutiny.

Muna patted my arm. "My dear har, we are only getting started." His smile was anything but reassuring.

They took me to a residence near the cemetery, which I supposed was some sort of preparation place or nayati. I had not much experience with this. Muna and a cohort of younger hara stripped me of my drab rags and bathed me with fragrant water.

When I was cleansed to Muna's exacting standards, I was perfumed with rare scents I could not fully describe, which carried hints of jasmine and myrrh, and something else mysterious, that spoke to me of moonlight shining on ancient stones.

Thereafter, they garbed me in a fine linen robe, much like the one Muna and the Norlyn's other chosen wore.

Muna expressed horror at the state of my locks, at the apparent sun damage (according to him) of my skin and the condition of my fingernails.

"This will simply not do," he said while he filed and buffed, and a dextrous har worked at my hair with scented oils.

Somehar came with a small pot of kohl and a brush, and his breath tickled on my cheek as he carefully outlined my eyes. Obedient, I opened and shut my lids as he commanded.

"I want to see Korhaan," I said, once I had a small measure of space about my person.

"In good time," said Muna. "Now stand and turn, so that we may see what work still needs to be done.

One of the serving-hara brought an ancient mirror, a relic from the age of humans, and I started at the vision that looked back at me. Who was this har with the high cheekbones and dusky skin, whose locks gleamed earthy brown now that the dust of months had been washed out of them? A stranger's kohl-rimmed eyes stared back at me.

All this while, my anxiety had been growing and gnawing while flexing its limbs, and not just because these hara had plucked me out of all that was familiar and safe. I worried what Korhaan would say.

I hadn't discussed any of this with him, and I had a feeling he would have quite a lot to say about the matter, if he were given a chance.

Yet he did not have that opportunity, nor did what followed make any sense to me, a har who'd grown up strange in a small settlement, unused to religious ceremonies more complex than a shaman smudging a circle with smouldering *impepho* and calling down the dehara. Whatever caste work I'd done had been desultory at best. Enough to get by, and ever since I'd taken up with Korhaan, I'd not had to worry about anything further.

Whatever plans he'd had for us here in Norlyn, I was certain they didn't involve any of *this*, with me stealing the attention of our hosts from him.

Muna and his serving-hara were busy with me all afternoon and all the way into the early evening. By then I was nearly faint with hunger. Yet no meal was forthcoming. Instead I was given a too-sweet spiced wine to drink, and my world grew peculiar at its edges. The colours became soft and split into scintillating rubies, emeralds and sapphires, and the voices around me speeded up or slowed down in uncomfortable ways so that it became all but impossible for me to follow what others were saying.

At times my skin was too hot or too cold. The ground beneath my feet pulsated in time to hidden drums, and the rafters above became a ribcage alive with hairy, shivering filaments. Dimly, the small, rational part of my mind whispered that they'd drugged me, that a narcotic substance was swimming in the wine, yet I was helpless to stop any of this.

Too-bright eyes gleamed in the low light of the room in which we'd been preparing, and smoke curled up from small cones of incense that had been placed on saucers at strategic spots, so that soon we were inhaling a blue haze that tasted of roses and something else wilder, more bitter.

Hara helped each other with their hair, shared goblets that wet their lips and brought a flush to their cheeks. Then somehar found a drum and started up a rhythm that shuddered right through me, shivering through my bones and dancing on my heart so that I found it impossible to keep still.

Chanting started up, first with one har, then another, and a deeper-voiced har bringing in a counterpoint of dissonance that made all the small hairs on my body prickle. Somehar nudged me, and soon I was swaying, singing along, despite not knowing the words. Deeply, I understood that my anxiety had a source, but whatever that was slipped through my fingers, and soon no longer mattered.

A kaleidoscope of stars burst before my eyes, and I was adrift in this current that poured out of the door and into the crisp air. The heavens pulsated and stuttered with a scattering of fire bursts, and inexorably I was dragged along this stream that wended its way along the pathways.

Somehar had brought the drum, and our breath smoked before our faces as we traced the steps of a dance so ancient it was encoded in my blood, my bones. Dimly, I was aware that we were watched, but most of the hara who spectated joined in with the chanting and followed in our wake, clapping, ululating, as we wended our way towards our inevitable destination: the cemetery.

For the briefest moment, I thought I saw a scowling Korhaan, standing aloof from the others, leaning against the trunk of an acacia, but then I was swept past, as hara twirled me away.

Sweetness was whispering, his voice as honeyed as his name, as he drew me ever closer. A multitude of coloured lanterns lit our way, in dizzying jewel-like hues, as our bare feet slapped onto the still-warm causeway. I had no knowledge of what was expected of me, yet it mattered not. It felt right to give myself over to this wash of magic that breathed against my skin, calling me with the inevitability of water tumbling over falls to release a silvery spray to the sky.

The funerary shrine's door yawned open, two harlings standing sentinel at either side, each holding a lantern that cast soft, sapphire glow. And then I was inside, and the door shut behind me with a finality that should have terrified me. Whatever drugs had been racing through my blood dissipated instantly, and I was suddenly, awfully *present*.

Did they mean to entomb me? I shuddered, clutching at my arms as I turned to face the shut door. Outside, their singing was soft, almost a lullaby. The door was not bolted, but I gained the impression that I had to remain inside the shrine a while.

But why? I was not some damned priest.

My breath rattling in my lungs, I raised a fist, ready to pound at the barrier, to demand egress.

But that would make everyone unhappy, wouldn't it? They'd gone to all this trouble, and here I was about to upset their elaborate ceremony? It would have helped if they'd explained my circumstances to me. The way they'd prepared me meticulously; it was like I was some sort of offering.

"*You are. Of a sort.*" The voice was soft, resonant. As though I heard it from another room.

"Who's there?" I spun around towards the bier.

Apart from the softly dancing candles set in small glass bowls every two paces, it was only me and the bier in there. My shadow wobbled like the flames as I turned on the spot, unsure of where to go.

Soft laughter washed over me, bringing with it the smell of the slow, vegetative decay of reeds and river water.

"*We are here. You. Me. I.*"

I didn't want to approach the bier, but the path laid in tesserae on the floor led me there in a way that I could not disobey. I did not wish to look upon Sweetness's well-preserved remains with his little teeth and tightly shut eyes. Yet I was powerless to stop my feet from moving.

"*You don't need to be afraid.*"

"I'm not afraid."

"*You can't lie to yourself.*"

I fetched up against the bier, but the light was so deceptive I saw only my reflection in the glass box, and the contents were obscured, for which I was relieved.

"What do you mean?" I asked.

If I'd expected movement from within, I was disappointed. Except I was not truly disappointed, because I honestly had no taste for the macabre remnants.

"*You are so blind, my sweet har.*"

"No one is telling me what they want from me," I said. "How am I supposed to know what to say or do?"

"*But have you ever asked what* you *want?*"

"I..." My words dried up, and I stared at my silhouette on the glass.

"*Take my hand.*" As before, a likeness of Sweetness sat up, all loveliness and grace, and not that dried husk in repose. It was as if the glass was not there, for his fingers snagged mine and his skin was soft, warm, like early morning sun playing through the boughs of a fever tree.

"The river's too high already," Sweetness told Loras. He swallowed back the alarm that was clawing its way up his throat and clutched even tighter to his chesnari's back.

"Don't be ridiculous, Sweet," Loras replied, though his voice was not as certain as his words. "I've forded worse." Yet he reined in their mount, that stood less than two feet from the water's edge. Where the hooves pressed down, the sand crumbled and dissolved away like sugar stirred into coffee.

"But not with two of us..." Sweetness said.

The horse snorted, jerked its head then jigged sideways, further from the onrush of the river dark beneath a moonless night sky. This was a terrible idea. And an even worse time to travel. They should have waited, figured out a different plan to work around the Norlyn's refusal of their match. Yet Loras had been insulted. Loras had been the one to trade angry words with Sweetness's father, and now this. He couldn't bear to be parted from the har yet the thought of leaving behind all he had ever known for this... "rootless existence", as Sweetness's father put it. That hurt just as bad.

Pride. Both Loras and Sweetness's father possessed a surfeit of it, and Sweetness was trapped betwixt the two.

The great Aranye was a living, hungry thing, its waters rain-swollen and silt-laden, having tumbled many miles over distant falls, churning along its bed for weeks. Higher, and higher, faster and stretching out its spine, carrying with it entire trees and the occasional dead thing, all moon bellies and stick-legs.

Not a river to cross.

"We can ride to the bridge, I don't mind," Sweetness said.

Loras gave a cough of laughter. "What, and in a few hours that's exactly where they'll find us. I wouldn't put it past him to send a message to the bridge warden."

"We can go north, then."

"That's not where I want to go," Loras returned.

But what about what I want? Sweetness pressed his lips together in a firm line. It didn't do to argue with Loras when he was like this.

"I'm not going to wait for you to make up your mind," he'd told Sweetness earlier that day.

Dogs began barking behind them, in the settlement. Voices calling out. Somehar started ringing the assembly bell. That could only mean...

Loras cussed and dug his heels into his mount's flank. The stallion shook its head but then, obedient to its master's will, made the leap into the water. Immediately the current had them, and the shock of icy water was so sudden, so much, that Sweetness's chest closed up, and he rasped after air. For a few paces, the stallion's powerful limbs still found purchase on the riverbed, but the next they were scrabbling against loose debris, which was torn away.

Sweetness squeezed his eyes shut and clung to his chesnari as they were dragged along. Everything was darkness and cold and so much water. The horse bravely swam, but even as they were making headway, Sweetness could feel how the beast was growing weaker, sinking lower and lower, so that eventually, with each dip and surge, Sweetness was sunk up to his shoulders.

"Hold tight!" Loras cried. Or at least that was what Sweetness thought he'd cried.

All was lost in the roar of water.

They needed to cross soon, for around the bend the river entered a series of cataracts. Not quite falls, but the rapids when the Aranye was threatening to burst its banks would be lethal.

They should never have even tried this.

A heavy object thudded into them with stunning impact. A lost canoe, a tree trunk. It didn't matter. All Sweetness felt was the strike of a hard surface against his shoulder. His already numb fingers lost their grip on Loras's cloak and he was swept away.

All became blacker than night as he tumbled end over end beneath the surface. No air in his lungs but liquid, and his chest burned with the effort not to cough, not to draw in water. Not even a har could survive drowning. He struck what felt like a wall, and it all went—

My vision blurred in the soft lamplight as Sweetness gazed sadly at me. He still held my hand, and he felt so real, so solid. Warm.

"What?" I croaked then sniffed, as my nose was clogged up from tears.

"*Do you remember now?*"

I gazed deep into his eyes, and *I knew*.

Our lives were one. Our thread had been imperfectly cut. Like frayed strings placed next to each other, unfinished. *Un*-whole.

"How?" My vision tunnelled, growing brighter where I focused on Sweetness's lips.

He gave a small shrug of one shoulder. "*We have come together. But all this...*" Sweetness gestured around us. "*Neither of us will be able to truly reunite unless...*"

"Unless what?"

"*Burn it so that the ash scatters to the four quarters. Then we'll be free.*"

I scoffed. "I *am* free."

Sweetness arched a perfect brow. "*Are you so sure about that? You might not see the chains, but they are there. Just as I am locked away in an exquisite display case for my adoring supplicants.*" His lips pulled back from his pretty little teeth as if he tasted something sour.

All this talk was making my head hurt. How could he be me and I be him? It was the stupidest thing I'd ever considered, yet here, now, holding this ghostly har's hand that felt so solid in mine, I knew it for an inescapable truth.

"*We are broken. We will remain broken unless you act.*"

A rushing as of great wings filled my head, and a sharp chemical smell cut through my sinuses and the next—

A warm, damp cloth pressed to my forehead, smelling faintly of mint and *buchu* brought me to my senses. I was lying on a comfortable pallet, and my entire body ached. Dim lamplight cast my surroundings in a soft, golden glow, and the face of the har tending me was unfamiliar.

"Where...?" I tried to sit up, but his hands were strong, and he pressed me back down.

"Quiet, rest, dear heart."

Who was he to call me 'dear heart'? I opened my mouth to protest further, but he placed a finger on my lips.

"Hush."

Muna. His name was Muna.

Inexplicably, hot tears blurred my vision, and an unbearable sadness had me in its grips – I'd lost something, *somehar*, very dear to me, yet even as I stretched the fingers of my memories back, the recent past blurred and stretched, like a cat arching away from being stroked.

"Where am I?"

From what I could see, we were in small bedchamber, its adobe walls painted in pale red ochre, its floor gleaming with small river pebbles. Rounded, arched windows were finished with a wealth of azure glass, so that the light within was cool.

"We are in my chamber. Breathe. Lie back. You have experienced much."

Still I struggled, this time managing to shove aside the light sheet that had covered me. I was naked, my skin scented with rose.

"Where are my clothes? I must go to Korhaan."

How much time had passed?

Muna pulled his lips into a moue of disappointment. "Oh, you are a stubborn har."

I glared at him. "I did not ask for any of this."

His hand was firm on my shoulder, keeping me from rising. "What did *he* say to you?"

Somehow, I knew the 'he' Muna spoke of was not Korhaan, and my skittish memories nibbled, made shadows I could almost grasp.

The funerary shrine. The cloying incense. And Sweetness.

Our lungs full of water, the cold river dragging us under...

A shudder wracked me, and for a heartbeat Muna's fine bedchamber greyed out. His strong warm hands gripped my shoulders.

"Stay with me, Rai." Genuine concern underpinned Muna's words.

The ghost of a chemical stench touched my sinuses, but I remained present. "What have you done to me? *All* of you?"

"You have been touched by the dehara, Rai. You are chosen by our beloved Sweetness to be his mouthpiece here among the quick."

"For the last time, I do not want this!" I jerked away from him and staggered to my feet. "Now, where is something that I can wear? I cannot go about naked like the day I emerged from my pearl."

My fury must've reached Muna, for he brought me a tunic and hose. I all but snatched the garments from him, and although they were nothing I'd ever choose to wear for myself I pulled them on as quick as I could. My urgency to go to Korhaan trumped my fear of being seen in motley.

I padded out, my pulse a wild drum as I blinked in the late afternoon sun. A wall of heat struck me with such ferocity, I nearly fell. Whatever charms kept the interior of Muna's home cool had left me ill prepared for the natural world.

Hara glanced at me curiously as I stumbled past like a drunkard, my feet leading me unerringly to the hut where we'd stayed. But I knew. Oh, in my heart of hearts and with my very being, I knew that Korhaan had gone. The pallet was neatly made, everything folded away in readiness for the next guest. Not so much as a note or a trinket.

Where were my things?

Fresh panic welled up in my belly as I spun around, the seared air short in my lungs as I turned on the spot. Here I was, abandoned among strangers. That Korhaan would just desert me without so much as a word.... No, he'd never do that. Or would he? Or had they driven him away, sensing that he had a hold on me?

My treacherous memories dredged up flashes from that mad night, where my life had curled and twisted like a centipede dropped on a hot stone. Korhaan, standing alone, disapproval written on his features as I danced past him. How had that felt to him? Perhaps he was the one who thought I had abandoned *him*.

Bitter dismay bloomed on my tongue and at the back of my throat, and I had to sit down on the hut's small porch, because my head was spinning.

"I'm not going to wait for you to make up your mind."

No, Korhaan had never said that. *Loras* had. Then darkness rushed over me, and I didn't know which way was up or down, and it took me many deep breaths before my world stopped dipping and weaving.

Why, oh why, could I not go back to the har breathing in the sun and the sky beneath the *bitou* bushes? The slow hum of the bees and the flitting birds that came to steal the ripening berries. So what if other hara thought me simple or addled? There'd been a simplicity in that life, unencumbered with harish words and conflicts.

The hours I could spend watching a stream dance over its steppingstones, the pollywogs wiggling in the stiller pools, and if I were lucky, the emerald-and-white cuckoo would offer his slurred whistle to me, so close I could nearly touch him.

Korhaan gave me form, had the words for things when I didn't, and now he'd abandoned me to these strangers, and I was many, many months north of the shadow of my beloved fold mountains, where the cold grey ocean washes their sandstone faces.

Yet if Sweetness had it right, my destiny had brought me here, to put a great wrong to right so that both of us could move on. Though it was passing strange to try and imagine how I could be two people at the same time. If only I'd paid attention more to what our elders had tried to teach me when I was younger. Soulcraft was way beyond my ken, and I didn't trust any of the Norlyn's hara on the matter.

The mere thought of Muna's long fingers made me shudder.

Lost, alone. So far, far away from all that was familiar.

A small ember of defiance glowed within me. What was wrong with being alone, really? It meant I was not reliant on anyhar but myself. I didn't have to go along with what others wanted. If Sweetness had listened to his heart of hearts that fateful night, he'd never have been dragged down into the rapids where the river narrows into the first of the cataracts.

He'd have stood up to his father instead of finding the path that resulted in the least conflict. He'd been nothing but a trinket, a trophy. Perhaps spoilt, yes, but not a bad sort of har. And me? I had been indulged ever since I'd crept out of my pearl. And where had that brought me?

Apart from almost a thousand miles north from familiar territory.

The question remained: what was I going to do about it? I couldn't huddle here, in an abject bundle of misery till the ravens came to roost. I sure as all the dehara couldn't stay. And Korhaan had proven himself to be faithless right when I needed him most. The only har who was going to dig me out of this mess was me. And Sweetness.

I could walk now. Follow the river road north to the bridge that was hopefully repaired by now. Leave all behind.

And something told me that Sweetness would visit me in my dreams, that he would not leave me alone now that our bond had been formed, and so much was unresolved. My deep-rooted fear of water made sense to me now. In theory, at least.

Sweetness would never have felt the need to elope with Loras all those years ago, if it weren't for the fact that his father had sought to bind him. And in that, my own rootlessness had its origin. I would not be tied down, and that was no good either.

This I could admit to myself with no small amount of wryness.

My father and hostling would laugh out loud if they could see me now, finally with some sense in my head. All it took was an ecstasis. Yes. That was the word. I'd heard it somewhere before. Perhaps from the priest who'd tried to train me. How easily these thoughts flowed now, one to another. More so than I'd ever been able to grasp before. Perhaps this was Sweetness's doing.

And I would give Sweetness what he wanted. Now.

Why wait?

At that very moment, a wind gusted up, carrying with it the baked heat and dust of the desert. The acacias that shaded my hut shook, and a feathering of small leaves rained down. Small dust devils whirled, and I had to blink rapidly to get the grit out of my eyes. Somehar's hat came wafting past, followed by the luckless har chasing and laughing after his headgear.

I was not much of a one for omens, but this, if ever there was, came as a sign to me that my decision was the right one. Winds scoured clean, if allowed to do so. Even as I began the hike up to the mortuary shrine the sky took on a brassy quality. Black scraps of birds were torn from their perches, cawing miserably at the unexpected windstorm that had driven up dark clouds from the north-east – a sudden thunderstorm brewing where only moments before the sky had been washed aquamarine.

I thought I heard a har call my name down in the settlement, but

I pressed on, the heated stone of the causeway singeing my bare feet. I welcomed the pain as it sizzled up, through my blood, reminded me that I was here, now. Alive.

There behind the mortuary shrine was the mud hut where Muna had brought me after the first spell I'd had. After casting about, I found a flask containing a fragrant oil I could only assume was intended for lamps. Votive candles always burnt inside the shrine, so I had no worries about how I was going to set it alight.

My mouth had gone dry, my heart beating so fast I was close to fainting. I was going through with this. Destroying the very soul of this settlement. What if I was wrong? What if I was the one who was deluded? Given to fancies.

Yet it was as if I could hear Sweetness breathing my name, drawing me the way the lilac-bloomed *ilotana* shrub attracts butterflies. A heady, drunken fragrance that had me hurrying back around the shrine. In the time that I'd been in the hut, the sky's brassiness had turned bruised. An actinic flash had me shudder to a stop, then a low, rumbling growl shuddered through the air.

I couldn't recall when I'd last been in the midst of a storm, and the potential of the elemental violence enlivened me, made all the tiny hairs on my body prickle. The contrast as I entered the shrine itself was immediate, as if I'd pierced a bubble and fallen into silence. Even the next flash of lightning hardly pierced the gloom, and the ensuing thunder-rumble was muted.

Only a pair of votive candles flickered at the head and foot of the bier, and the censers had been allowed to die. Despite the stillness, an air of expectation lingered.

I set down the ceramic flask. Snakes of doubt wound themselves around my feet, curled around my spine so that I was tempted to turn around and leave right away. Vanish into the desert so that the wind erased my tracks, and I would simply stop exiting to these hara. They sought to possess me but did not realise that they were the ones who pressed an adder to their breasts.

All this beauty they had wrought would be destroyed or marred by soot and smoke.

Yet as I gazed upon the pitiful remains of my past self, the horror of this fixation that possessed the hara of this community struck me afresh. And Sweetness too, was trapped, as was I. I could accept this burden and live out my natural years as a living embodiment of this idolatry. And what would happen once this mortal shell passed? Would it too be enthroned? Would Sweetness and I reunite beyond the veil? Both cursed and bound?

"*Or you could free us both. Nothing worth possessing is gained without some form of sacrifice.*"

And if I allowed the Norlyn and his hara to have their way with me, I'd be no better than Sweetness: fine fabrics my manacles made pleasing to the eye with rouged cheeks and a scented brow. I was nohar's living doll. Nor would I again be anyhar's tail following in their footsteps, hither and thither.

"No, no, no, no," I muttered as I uncapped the flask and stepped towards the bier. I couldn't make myself break the glass, but I found the fastenings for the top of the glass cabinet, and I lifted the lid.

Of the Sweetness from my visions there was no sign, but I understood then that the mortal remains, while not containing his essence, most certainly created a link that bound him to this place, and that was more than I could bear.

Without further hesitation, though my hands shook, I upended the flask on his remains. It was a sweet-smelling oil that sang to me of tall cedars stark against a blue-blue sky. Then, before I could give in to a last pang of self-doubt, I grabbed one of the candles and kissed the flame to the linen covering. Thick smoke curled up as a lazy tongue licked from the wick to fabric, and I watched and waited until I was certain the fire would spread.

The heat as the remains and its decorations began to burn, smacked into me with such physical force, I staggered back. Black smoke thickened the air and the scented oils barely masked the acrid stench of burning hair. Tears blurred my vision, the air seared my throat, and I inched ever backwards, towards the door.

If I had expected a spectacular release, a display of fireworks or exultation, I was disappointed. Only bright orange flame and a crackling as bones were devoured – I had done my job well. Yet there was a rightness to my actions. I didn't have to wait for anyhar to tell me that, least of all Sweetness.

I stepped out into a downpour. Fat drop after fat drop drummed into the ground, and I turned my face up into the sky and smiled as the water washed me clean. Even as the first shouts rang from the settlement below, I was already walking along the west way.

If the rain continued, the river would flood, and I had a bridge to cross. The south was calling me to the shadow of the Hoerikwaggo, to the land of my bones.

The Hidden One

Martina Bellovičová

In the beginning there was chaos.

In a world torn apart, the last vestiges of humanity fought a losing battle for the reign over the realm of madness, famine and plagues that used to be the planet they called home. Yet, like a phoenix born from the ashes of its ancestors, a new race arose from the ruins of civilisation, and with it, new heroes. It was the dawn of a new era: A new history was being carved both by blades and by magic, the latter budding cautiously like wildflowers sprouting in the spring sun. This raw mix of opportunity and risk provided many ways in which to mould one's name into legend.

After five years of fighting to survive, even thrive, in the hinterland of Alba Sulh, inhabited mostly by hostile humans struggling to come to terms with the new world order, Leith considered himself a true leader with all the makings of a revered hero. With his ever-growing pack of war thirsty followers, he had cleaved his way through the whole Midlands, taking all there was to steal from the scattered human communities; and incepting boys who appeared to be willing or worthy, not necessarily both at the same time. The City of Caves was their biggest challenge yet: One of the last functional human enclaves on Alba Sulh, a sanctuary of concrete and bricks, perched atop ancient underground systems and surrounded by lush wilderness that would not cease its attempts to reclaim the town.

Why the obsolete human civilisation clung to life so fiercely here, of all places, was anyhar's guess. In the old world, the area used to be one of the poorest in the country, but as other enclaves fell one by one, those with any money, skills, weaponry or other highly prized equipment began to flock to the area, and they grew stronger together. Luck played no small part in their survival, for the enclave remained untouched by the plagues that had ravaged most of Alba Sulh. Despite the losing combination of short lifespans and fragile bodies easily claimed by disease, the locals knew that the enclave gave them a chance of survival far greater than those outside; and it was a chance they were willing to die defending or kill to defend.

Screaming echoed through the forest, carried downwind by the leaves of ancient oak trees rustling in disagreement. Leith and three hara from his tribe dashed along the stream, backpacks heavy with loot. The phylarch was in the front of the pack, picking the path through the overgrown wilderness for the others, his elaborately braided, maple brown hair whipping his back and collecting twigs and leaves along the way. He was in his element; a wild thing racing the wind, jumping across tree roots, balancing on slippery stones in the forest creek and easily avoiding the thickest bushes.

"Fuck, fuck, fuck!" Keevan chanted behind him before diving headfirst into a thick thorny bush that ripped at his clothes, bare hands and face. "You didn't say they'd have guns! How do they still have guns?!"

The group of humans pursuing them were no match for their agile, battle trained bodies, which could move with panther-like speed and accuracy But bullets carried far, and they tended to do more damage than even a magically gifted individual could readily heal. The other two were less vocal about their shock, careful not to reveal their exact position to the enemy, but Leith could hear their rapid breathing.

"We need to split up!" he commanded without turning around. "Don't lead them to base camp! Meet up after sundown!"

On most occasions, splitting the party was a bad idea, for there was safety in numbers; but in the middle of a chase, four hara were easier to target than one. As a bonus, the pursuers were likely to waste precious time on deciding who to follow. Leith hoped it was going to be him. He was confident enough to believe he would emerge the winner, no matter how many automatic weapons were involved. Perhaps he could give fate a nudge – show himself just for a moment to draw them?

Laughing, Leith zigzagged among a group of ancient oaks, unconcerned about the projectile that whizzed past his shoulder, chipping off a chunk of bark from a tree mere inches away. Instead of making him fear for his life, danger invigorated him, sharpened his senses and made him feel giddy with primeval joy. There was no better feeling than outsmarting a group of angry half-sexes. And sure enough, the stomping of feet so much heavier than his clung to his trail. Whichever direction his friends had taken, they were safe for now.

He led them deeper into the forest, where a couple of small, rocky hills rose out of the treetops. Close to the foothills, the ground was slippery, covered by mossy grass. The shots were sporadic, as Leith made sure to keep out of sight and his pursuers were merely playing a guessing game. Ammunition must have been rare; it had already been hard to come by back in his time among humans. Gradually, their voices began to fade. He'd probably put enough distance between himself and the group to hide now and let them traipse around aimlessly until they acknowledged it was time to give up the pursuit.

The har went down on all fours and crawled through a small thicket, intending to curl up squeezed between its densest point and the rock. That was when he spotted it: an opening in the sandstone, nearly overgrown by ferns, all but hidden in the foliage, yet undeniably large enough for a grown har to slither in. It didn't bother him at all that some animal might have taken refuge in the hole; he'd much rather take on a badger than those filthy humans. Besides, if skinned and soaked in a fast-flowing river for two days, a badger could make a delicious dinner. He dived in, pushing himself forward on his elbows.

Interestingly, the tight tunnel was fairly short, opening into a rather spacious cave a few metres in. Before his transformation, Leith wouldn't have been able to proceed any further, because darkness had grown thicker around him. With the eyes of a har, he could just barely make out the vaguely circular wall ridden with irregular oval holes like some kind of cheese. In the middle of the space, there was a structure whose shape very much resembled a stone table with benches around it, except the 'furniture' was all part of the rock.

Intrigued, Leith slowly crossed the mysterious hall. From the central cave, many corridors sprouted deeper into the mountain, some of them shaped by nature, others created or widened by human hands. It was impossible for Leith to tell whether they had been formed decades, centuries or millennia ago. Even with simple tools, a patient enough man could have made sandstone yield. Perhaps, he hoped, one of the dark openings he could sense rather than see would give him what he had been looking for: A secret passage through which he could lead his people into the heart of the city.

One hand on the wall, he lingered on the threshold of the closest tunnel, peeking in. Even with his superior eyesight, he could see nothing but pitch-black, all-encompassing darkness. The young har made a hesitant step inside, then another... and stopped mid-motion. The darkness swelled around him, stirred and spoke in a voice older than age.

"Harbinger of future."

Leith could feel the hairs on the back of his neck stand up as something cold blew past his nape, but he knew even without looking that there would be nothing there.

Nightfall found the tribe in high spirits, distributing loot and cheering whenever something particularly unique was revealed. Aside from weapons and jewellery, food of their ancestors was in particularly high demand among some members of the pack. Not the tasteless chemical goo people used to eat in the last years of the apocalypse, but canned delicacies from generations past, that were still good decades after their expiration date. The tribe prided themselves in being warriors and conquerors of the new era, not househara. Mundane tasks like cooking, they would often joke, were something the Sulh might be inclined to do.

"They'd probably call it magic," Keevan grinned, popping a slightly rusting can open and sniffing at its contents with a dubious expression.

Branwyn lazily picked up another container and schooled his elfin face into a mask of dignified regality. Easily the most soume-looking of the group, he could imitate the tribe that considered themselves the nobility of the island marvellously. "I have channelled the energy of the universe to create this highly elaborate meal of...", he lifted the can to the level of his eyes, squinting at the aged label, "...minced beef in tomatoes with red wine and oregano."

As the tribe roared in laughter, Keevan's eyes flickered to their leader, who seemed way too silent this evening. He shifted closer, holding the opened can out in front of Leith enticingly. "Want some?"

Leith shook his head. "I'm good." He was biting his lip absentmindedly, twirling a blade of grass in his fingers.

"Is something the matter?" the other har inquired, a touch of concern in his voice. Leith was never quiet when others were rejoicing, and he rarely rejected a morsel.

"Oh, I was just thinking of the best way to take this enclave. It's a good place, and well equipped. Cleanse it of humans and we could settle here for a while, until it's time for the next challenge."

Keevan nodded, satisfied with that answer. Leith was feral, hungry for life with all the adventures and discoveries it offered, and no matter what goals he might have managed to achieve, it was never enough for him. The force driving him forward never relented, but it wasn't a blind, misguided desire to harness power, nor to pillage and kill any surviving humans or hostile hara. There was always a plan behind his actions, that was why so many followed him. Most warring tribes in the country eventually succumbed to one of three ends: an internal death wrought of infighting; being reduced to a vulture-like existence on the fringes of society; or joining the ever so self-aware Sulh. Yet the Kernetei thrived; and many knew it was their leader they had to thank for this.

"I trust you have a plan in which we don't get shot in the head when we storm the enclave."

"Not yet. But I will," Leith promised, his piercing blue eyes glowing unnaturally as darkness crept in over the campsite. "These things cannot be rushed."

They sat in silence by the fire, enjoying a stolen moment of tranquillity in the turmoil of the changing world, filled with music of the night. The crackling of the bonfire in the middle of the camp, the crunch of the leaves on the ground, the parting songs of the birds finding shelter in the warmer airs of the world, and the voice of the wind that danced and played through it all.

Hara added to the song with some music of their own, a melody both joyful and haunting with lyrics that were born from the night and would die with it. Calder, a har younger than most, with a velveteen voice, struck the strings of his guitar, setting the rhythm and tune. He had found the tribe of his own volition after a raid on a seaside colony his family lived in, carrying nothing but the instrument – his most beloved possession – and a kitchen knife, with which he'd hoped to be incepted. He didn't bring many combat skills to the table, but he had ideas and dreams to spare. Leith had bought into it and Calder had never given him a reason to regret taking him in.

The song rose and rose, both a question and an answer. And though the hara had joked about how much importance was given to magic among the Sulh, they felt its presence strongly in those late hours. Many of them rose along with the music, swaying, spinning and leaping in tune with the universe. Any thought formulated into a wish then and there could come true, any promise given in the privacy of one's thought binding. As Leith lay down to sleep, the music was still resonating in his mind. He could see the future he believed he deserved, the one he wished to give his tribe, more clearly than ever before; so close he could touch it if only he reached out for the stars.

In his dreams, he found himself deep in the now familiar forest, struggling through the undergrowth on all fours. The air was musty and the earth under his feet slippery. Each movement brought down a shower of raindrops from the bushes and trees surrounding him. And instead of soothing cold, the droplets felt like sizzling embers on his skin. In an attempt to prevent his face from being burnt, he wanted to shield it with his arm, but found himself unable to force his limbs to perform that simple movement. It wasn't because his muscles were too weak, but because they simply weren't built for that. Confused, Leith looked down to where he expected to see his fingers and was shocked to find two pairs of split hooves on long, elegant legs covered in chestnut pelt instead. As he puzzled over his changed form, a vague feeling of danger began to well up inside har. Har scanned the thick undergrowth all around, sensing invisible fingers reaching out from every shadow. Leith didn't know why he was in the forest, nor what was pursuing him, but his subconscious was telling him that he couldn't allow it to catch him, and so he tore through the branches, his antlers painfully tangled, legs unsteady. He spent what seemed like the longest moment trying to figure out how to control this new form and which muscles were in charge of what kind of movement. His steps were tentative at first, but soon he picked up the pace, feeling almost cheerful as he dashed through the forest, jumping over tangled roots and fallen tree trunks. Yet no matter how rapidly he moved, he could not outrun the sense of looming danger.

Suddenly, a breath of wind licked the top of his head as something passed above him on silent wings. Under his hooves, a small creature stomped through the fallen leaves, making too much noise for an animal of its size. A hedgehog, he thought; and there on his right – a rabbit dashing through the undergrowth. The forest was alive with its restless inhabitants, and wherever he looked, something was hopping, running, shuffling, flying, crawling, galloping in the same direction Leith himself was instinctively heading. In the heart of the forest, there was a sanctuary as old as time itself, forgotten by the human race. All it would take was to find the right way, say the right words, and it would pull the forest creatures into its healing embrace. There, he sensed he would always be safe.

The plan that had formed in Leith's brain overnight wasn't exactly new. He had hoped to utilise the cave systems scattered under the entire town and the surrounding area as a way to get into the heart of the human enclave since before the tribe even arrived there. Their existence had never been a secret; Leith had briefly read about them in a travel guide about the Midlands way back in his past life, when reading constituted ninety percent of his free time. Books that spoke of distant and not so distant places he would never get to see, preferably with photos and lots of detailed descriptions, had been his absolute favourite. These were closely followed by adventure books, where a hero who'd been dealt abysmal cards overcame all obstacles to rise in glory. They hadn't quite satisfied his need to explore and live, but they'd been a welcome refuge from his then daunting reality. Now, they were old friends and advisers whispering in his ear.

When the Kernetei began to roam the outskirts of the town and the surrounding woodland, they discovered a rather large and easily accessible complex of caves and set up camp in its halls. The tunnel that shot off to one side had been a dead end, though. A massive cave-in that must have occurred as a result of the turmoil in the society or changes in nature that had come with the apocalypse completely blocked whatever path there may have been beneath. The idea to infiltrate the enclave like rats climbing out of the sewers at night had been put to rest, until the chance discovery the previous evening.

Leith took five of his hara down the rabbit hole he hadn't had the chance to explore properly. And this time, he came equipped. The warm torchlight flickered, casting odd and unnatural shadows on the walls as they gathered in the entrance hall, about to explore the tunnels Leith had only peeked in. It didn't escape him that the others, especially Calder, moved in a cautious way, as though unknown dangers could loom behind every corner. The phylarch didn't share the sentiment. On the contrary, excitement was beginning to bud inside him as he breathed in the atmosphere of the place.

"Do you have the paint?"

"Here you go." Aiden presented a bowl of the white cream they used to paint their faces when going into battle. "What is it good for?"

"I feel there might be an entire labyrinth in front of us," Leith explained, dipping a finger in the paint and testing it on the closest wall. It was going to work just fine. "We mark each tunnel we choose to enter. Whenever we turn a corner, we mark it. That way we'll be able to find the way back easily, and we'll always know where we've already been."

They formed groups of three to make the exploration faster; should one of them encounter difficulties or get lost, they were to signal by blowing a whistle in regular intervals and stay put until the other party located them.

"I bet if you were here alone, you'd piss your pants like a little brat," Leith heard Calder say to Aiden as they progressed deeper into the enclosed space of the leftmost passage. The other answered by giving him a light kick, which elicited a yelp. Their teasing, Leith knew, was meant to dispel the uneasiness that came over them down here. And, miraculously, he felt his own excitement grow in sharp opposition to their anxiety.

"Have you ever wondered who might have found and shaped these caves first, or what they were using them for?" Aiden's voice rang oddly sharp in the darkness.

"One folk might have been hiding here from another at one time," Leith explained, drawing on snippets of ancient knowledge. "Some parts of the cave systems served as a tannery, I think. Poor families took shelter in them, too. During the wars, they'd meet here and plot against the enemy. And at one point, people even had the idea to turn a couple of caves into prison cells."

"We could hide an army here," Calder mused, peeking into a small side corridor they were about to turn down. "Creep into the enclave at night. Just imagine the news! *Dozens of members of this new Wraeththu gang magically appeared in the streets and seized the enclave, leaving no man, woman or child alive!*"

Aiden and Leith both laughed, one of them dutifully, the other with the glee of a hyena looking forward to digging its teeth in fresh entrails. There was nothing more satisfying than hearing his own idea verified from somehar else's mouth.

Aiden tilted his head with a dubious expression. "Pray tell, who's gonna spread that news if no man, woman or child is left alive?"

"Actually, there has long been a common belief that there are tunnels branching off the caves under the town which extend long distances and connect to the castle," Leith interjected. "One passage, I believe, was supposed to start at the gates, another should have led from the forest."

"And you're hoping that this is it?" said Aiden.

"So... we're actually doing it?" Calder visibly perked up.

"This, or one of the other tunnels, yes. It's definitely worth a try."

Yet the goal to take the city wasn't the only motivation driving him forward. They were onto something and it was getting nearer by the second, Leith could sense it in his gut. He needed a validation that the words he'd heard in his mind weren't just a figment of imagination, created by a subconscious that had always longed for greatness. The previous evening, he had been chosen, and he wouldn't leave here without proof of that.

They progressed through the labyrinth for what might have been half an hour – time liked to play tricks in the darkness – the tunnels becoming progressively steeper and more cramped. Eventually, they encountered places where they could no longer walk upright, or else had to turn sideways and shuffle through a narrow opening. After a particularly unpleasant crawl, the passage in front of them forked like a snake's tongue.

"Where to?" Calder whispered. They hadn't talked for a long time and it suddenly didn't seem appropriate to disturb the silence.

Leith was about to answer that it didn't make a difference, when a strong gust of wind blowing out of a passage caught his interest. It brought along a mixture of scents; autumn leaves, grass sprinkled with dew, the first flowers in the snow, but also wet pelt with the undertone of fungi and flesh in a late state of decomposition. It filled his lungs with such intensity that he had to stifle a cough. The peculiar thing, though, was that the flame of his torch hadn't moved at all.

"It's taking too long. You two go left," he heard himself say, contrary to his original order never to split the groups. "I'll go right. We'll meet here when we're done."

Aiden rewarded that idea with a dubious glance. "You sure about that?"

"Yeah. You know, it wasn't me pissing my pants," Leith attempted to feign impatience. It was essential that he went alone, and it was almost equally important for them not to realise that. "Just go. Hurry up! I'll be fine. If anything happens, I have a whistle on me."

They disappeared from his view with a shrug, allowing Leith to enter the passage that both enticed and appalled him. He began to descend into the heart of the hill. Apart from having a very low and irregular ceiling, this tunnel was rather steep, making movement with a lit torch a challenge. On the plus side, it was fairly short and in what must have been mere minutes, the opening spat him out in a fairly large, round cavern. Not only could he straighten his back again, but he would have also fit inside even if he were twice his size. Just like the entrance hall, this space looked like an underground room and he could see a large piece of sandstone furniture on the other side of the cavern. Intriguing writings and shapes populated the far wall, but it was impossible to make out any details from where he stood.

Leith's nostrils flared. The scent was almost maddening here, though there appeared to be no source of it in the barren cavern. He raised the torch, hoping to illuminate as large a space as possible while crossing the distance that separated him from what he had wrongly considered a table. From up close, the object rather resembled an altar, but not the kind the vestiges of humanity who still believed in something used to put in their churches. The slab, shaped out of sandstone, was covered with intricate twirls and knots that seemed to be of ancient origin, much like the art on the wall. Curiously, he traced the carvings with his finger.

This whole place could be a sanctuary, a temple dedicated to an ancient, primal deity. A monstrous god, who would not shy away from a blood sacrifice, and the blood would make the flowers grow. A creature who would lure wanderers into its underground home to bless them with magic, strength and fertility; or perhaps peel their skin off and feast on their bones. If there was any hideout where a forgotten spirit of nature might make a home, he thought, it would be someplace like this. Mysterious, hidden, difficult to navigate. Perhaps if he spent enough time down here, the entity would visit him and whisper in his mind all the secrets of the universe that would otherwise have been lost forever.

Wryly chiding himself, he recalled that the Wraeththu had discarded gods along with other human-made concepts. Half-sex deities, so similar to humans in their petty desires, were of no use to this race that had newly inherited the Earth. Why hold on to such idols, when a simple sharing of breath was a greater miracle than anything humans used to pray for? Why ask an invisible power to bend the world to your will, if you could do it yourself? Why care about ancient concepts of life after death, when they were obviously false, and ageing was no longer an issue? For the teenage boy Leith had once been, the har he was now would have been the equivalent of a god. *I could be worshipped here.* A fleeting thought that he entertained briefly, wallowing in the grand illusion such thoughts invoked.

With a cold smile, he picked up something that looked like an ancient ceramic bowl, probably intended to be filled with small offerings. Its inside was discoloured, covered in rusty stains that might or might not have been blood. At the very bottom, Leith found a single marking, similar to those on the walls. He put it back in its place and returned his attention to the writings. Light revealed elaborate patterns in green and brown paint, interrupted by what must have been runes of a language he had no way of interpreting. Their placement was interesting, though. They were always shaped into a concentric circle, with the largest, probably most important sign in the middle.

And then, finally, Leith illuminated a painting that answered some of his questions and posed some more. It depicted the creature who must have resided in this labyrinth. He was a tall, proud yet spindly deity with long, twig-like fingers on his hands and hoofed legs, hair of autumn leaves, decorated by a set of magnificent antlers. An impersonation of nature and perhaps its protector, for he held a spear in one hand. The figure looked like something one never wished to see emerging from the bushes and shadows, yet Leith was oddly drawn to it. The horned god, forgotten, lying in wait.

If it wasn't a false, laughable idol of a dying race, what then? Could it be that this energy, this concept had always existed, and men had only claimed it, unaware of what they were toying with? If that were the case, it could be reclaimed. Awoken. Slowly, as if not wanting to startle anyone who might be watching, Leith placed the bowl back on the altar. Driven by a sudden urge, he removed a pin from his jacket and drove it deep into his forearm, not even blinking at such an insignificant amount of pain. As he held his arm over the bowl and fresh crimson droplets slowly added another layer to the ancient stains, Leith felt no wish to reconsider, although the implications were clear: He could be feeding something he did not quite understand.

Time seemed to stand still, but an attentive person could perceive subtle changes in the atmosphere. The air was colder, thick with humidity, and the ever-present scent also changed, its stale quality morphing into the freshness of first summer days. The cavern took a deep breath. And as Leith looked up to the writings on the wall, he found them moving, dancing, shifting as though they had come alive solely for him. Their form was unknown to him, and so was the culture that had left them behind, yet he felt uniquely attuned to the meaning each of them carried.

"Stag of the woods. Master of the wild hunt."

What creatures composed the wild hunt Leith could not be certain about, but he was fully aware that no soul touched by the Wild Hunt could be saved. The knowledge no longer scared him. In his past life, he wouldn't have been able to outrun the tortoise his teacher had brought to class one day, but now he was a wolf. He would howl with the pack and run at the lead of the race. And when the beasts began to feed, he would be there to challenge them for the best pieces of flesh.

The runes were still now, but appeared aglow, as though a fire was burning behind the sandstone wall and one could see it flicker through cracks in the stone. Leith's eyes stopped at his shadow, dancing in the light of his own torch: the outline of his slender form, and behind him… A second one, an ominous figure, tall enough for its head to be obscured from view due to limited reach of the torchlight. Despite that, the har was certain he could just barely make out the shape of majestic deer horns. At the very same moment, the sharp sound of a whistle cut through the air, travelling through the tunnels with shrill urgency.

Without thinking, Leith dashed through the cavern and darted into the tunnel, crawling up the sloping surface as fast as he possibly could. Whoever was using the whistle had completely foregone the intervals they had agreed upon and was blowing it non-stop, effectively making it impossible for the others to identify the source of the sound. It might have been just behind the corner, or very far away, Leith simply couldn't tell. When he arrived at the fork where they should have met, Calder and Aiden were nowhere to be seen. This in itself was not surprising. After all, he had no idea how long he'd stood mesmerised by the dancing runes in the chamber. But someone was clearly in trouble and the thought it could be one of his closest friends made every decision more critical.

Seconds dragged as he hastily traced their footsteps, occasionally hitting his head on the low ceiling and slipping on uneven ground, until he caught up with his companions deeper in the tunnel. The whistle was still screaming out its call for help, but the har in charge of it must have run out of breath and finally began to make pauses. Leith used his own to signal that they were coming and took a moment to inspect his friends with keen eyes; aside of the obvious fear written in their youthful faces, nothing seemed amiss.

"What happened?"

"Are you two alright?"

Calder and Leith both spoke at once, eliciting a little chuckle from Aiden despite there being nothing laughable about the situation.

"Nothing that I know of."

Whatever did happen couldn't have possibly been caused by his bloodletting, or could it? "I hit a dead end."

"We're fine. Our tunnel has plenty of tiny caverns further on, but there's nothing in them aside from a rodent skeleton here and there. But the air did feel a little stiff, you know?"

"It felt oppressive," Calder interjected. "As if we were being watched, and the feeling intensified. But I thought it was just the atmosphere playing tricks on my mind."

Leith didn't do anything to validate or dismiss their concerns. He didn't have to; they had no time to waste. Together, they returned to the entrance hall and followed in the other group's footsteps, urged to haste by occasional sounds of the whistle. Fortunately, the paint had done its job and it wasn't difficult to find their way according to the signs they'd left , but the party had made good progress and everyhar felt it was taking entirely too long. Had immediate assistance been needed, the time window in which they could have offered it had closed long ago.

The passage where they finally met was wide enough for two grown hara to sit next to each other, and that was how they found Tyrone and Keevan. Branwyn was lying on the ground, his head resting in Tyrone's lap, and Keevan was dabbing at his forehead with a wet cloth. When he noticed Leith, Branwyn leaned on his palms and tried to sit up, struggling a little.

"Hey, take it easy," Tyrone warned, supporting his back from behind. "Here, let me help you up."

"Is he injured?" Calder rushed to their side, looking for blood or signs of trauma that weren't there. He wasn't a fully-trained healer but had begun to manifest some skills recently that could possibly be of help. The Kernetei were well-versed in the art of war, but less in that of caste training so popular with the Sulh. Ironically, it was Branwyn who could manipulate energy and facilitate healing best of the whole tribe; few ever stopped to wonder what would happen if the har himself required help.

"I don't think so," Keevan shook his head, his fawn-like eyes flickering between Calder and Leith. "He just... collapsed out of the blue. We were walking, when he suddenly began to mumble, like he was having some kind of seizure, and then he dropped like a fly and was out cold until a moment ago."

"What was he saying?"

"Something like... *he's coming, or it's coming.* One of those, on repeat, until he passed out."

Transfixed, Leith lowered himself to his knees and grabbed Branwyn's shoulders, squeezing them just a little too hard, but resisting the urge to shake the poor har. He hated to admit it to himself, but this could no longer be a coincidence. "Who was coming? What did you see?"

It took Branwyn a moment to focus, as if he were recovering from a shock, but the phylarch's firm grip brought his mind from wherever it was wandering back to reality. "I... don't know. I couldn't tell. It was... Can I have some water?"

Keevan handed him the bottle; he drank ravenously, gulping water like a har who'd spent a week in the desert. Then he wet his lips with his tongue and looked back at Leith. "It felt like an unknown presence had suddenly filled the entire space around us and there was no air left for me to breathe, no agmara to draw from. Like something powerful was sucking out all the life energy, not perhaps with evil intent, but because it needed it more."

His ominous words were followed by a long silence, more profound in the underground darkness than any sound could ever hope to be. They helped Branwyn to his feet, offering him a shoulder to lean on, pushing and pulling one another whenever the terrain allowed as they beat a hasty exit from the caves. Few words were spoken during their flight, and nohar dared to ask the question that was at the forefront of their minds: *Is it still here?*

No immediate disaster followed the incident in the caves. The sun set and rose again over the treetops; Branwyn recovered from his experience; the building and fortification of the camp was in full swing. Spirits were high and further plans were slowly being set into motion. While Leith had decided further exploration of the caves would have to wait a couple of days, there were certainly other ways to make life a little harder for the enclave and benefit from its resources.

It only took a couple of strategically placed spies to find out that the town wasn't completely self-sufficient. Twice a week, on Monday and Wednesday morning, an armed vehicle would leave the town and head out North, only to return much heavier in the evening. They had to be visiting one of the fenced-in farms Leith vaguely recalled from early childhood, or a still functioning factory operated by humans that spewed out disgusting synthetic meal replacements. It was hard to tell which option was more likely, or how far away this place could be, but the vehicle, while large and impressive to someone who'd never had the chance to sit behind the wheel, didn't move very fast. It couldn't, because gas had been difficult to come by for decades, and it was anyone's guess what they were feeding the coughing and sputtering engine. Probably moonshine.

What it lacked in its unimpressive speed, the vehicle made up for in intimidating design. At one point in history, a van and a tractor must have engaged in passionate coupling and this was their lovechild. One with some serious mutations, including a cage-like superstructure on its back that was always populated with two gun-wielders. Together with the driver and his back-up, this made a total of four enemies, at least two of which were heavily armed. But the tribe had numbers, agility and the element of surprise on their side. They'd succeeded in much larger scaled raids before.

The key was to map the route carefully and find the perfect spot for the ambush, and then... A couple of strategically placed and masterfully hidden spikes, a few halfway cut trees, skilled archers, oil, fire and the monstrosity on wheels would be largely immobilised and ablaze.

Two days later, as plan became action, one of the armed guards dropped dead immediately, a fist balled around the arrow protruding from his eye, the other tried to crawl away into the trees, but the forest was alive with hara. They attacked like a pack of wild animals; incredibly fast, fierce, and able to communicate without words as though they shared a hive mind. Having reached the perceived safety of the trees, the soldier struck a defensive posture and scrambled to ready his weapon. Before he could shoot, they descended upon him from treetops and bushes, and it was impossible to tell whose blow sent him across the bridge.

Leith was the first to reach the vehicle's cabin, out of which they pulled two struggling males, armed only with knives to defend themselves. Their fighting skills were those of enclave men, lulled into a false sense of security by the armour of the beast they drove. One of them tried to bite him; he failed to cause any real harm, but the display of adaptable aggression intrigued the phylarch. Neither human was a teenager, but perhaps they could be salvaged. Inception wasn't easy on adults, but there was one among the Kernetei who had made the leap of faith at twenty-four. It was hard to tell if those two were younger or older than that, as the ability to guess a human's age faded fast once one was no longer a member of that species.

They'd have to try and see.

The bastard van was fully stacked with beans. Sacks upon sacks of dried beans that probably tasted like dust and small rocks, but could provide a lot of nutrition and had an incredibly long shelf life – sought after qualities for a tribe that couldn't care less about growing their own food. But the most useful loot was definitely the two guns with some extra ammunition. Leith decided not to give them to anyhar until he was sure they knew how to use firearms, because ammunition was far too scarce to be wasted on training warriors how to shoot.

Once in the distant past, some sections of the underground had been used as prison cells. History is known to repeat itself, and indeed there was no better place where the two young humans could be held pending inception than an isolated cavern. For three days, they would receive nothing but water. During this time, the entire process as well as its ultimate result would be explained to them in detail. Until they emerged from the imperfect, distasteful human shell like a butterfly forcing its way out of a cocoon, the tribe had no interest in them. But Leith couldn't help but wonder if someone else might...

Each Wraeththu tribe had their own cultural standard, and as such each approached inception differently. For the Kernetei, it was a small feast. To set themselves apart from the unsightly remnants of humanity, they often expressed themselves by wearing bold make-up, styling their hair into impressive mohawks or braiding it elaborately, and clothing their lithe bodies in whatever would have been considered rebellious or inappropriate in the now non-existent society of their childhood. But a feast day was different. This was an opportunity to display their most extravagant pieces without concerns about the practical side of things.

Leith and Branwyn, transformed from the battle-hardened hara of the ambush some days earlier, swept into the cave. To the two humans lying strapped to cold stone slabs, they appeared terrifying and beautiful in equal measure. Tight leather, spikes and chains combined with natural elements such as fur, colourful feathers and delicate skulls that once belonged to rodents and small birds, marked them as shamans bridging the old and the new world order. Branwyn's sculpted face, with distinctive cheekbones and eyes framed in black, appeared elfin in the half-light; Leith's eyes shone dangerously from the shadows. Pre-inception, they'd had a rare light blue colour, the change had turned them almost turquoise. *Unholy eyes*: So had pronounced an old woman whose life had expired under his hands during a raid in another town. He'd laughed about it, but actually took a liking to that description.

Each approached one of the captives, holding precisely sharpened knives in their hands. Trial and error had proven that if one har tried to incept several candidates at once, chances of survival diminished, and, in rare cases, imperfections such as diminished hearing or sight could occur. Leith chose the fierce one, who seemed much more docile now after three days of starvation, but defiance still sparkled in his eyes. When the har slashed the blade across his wrist, he only hissed, while his companion cried out in shock as the same was done to him.

"We will now give you our blood, and when - or if - we next see each other, you'll be one of us," the Phylarch stated ceremonially before slicing his own wrist open. As he pressed the wounds together and allowed their blood to mingle, his eyes locked with the hazel hues of the prospective har. He appeared to be struggling to speak, and so Leith leaned closer to give him the opportunity, curiously tilting his head.

"Fuck. You."

Leith began to laugh, an ugly sound like hailstones raining down on a metal roof, and slowly pulled away. "I might just let you later. If you're lucky."

Outside, the feast was in full swing, with a selection of venison and wild game with a bowl of their best alcohol sweetened with forest berries as the star attraction. Calder was putting on an impromptu performance, accompanied by two hara: One pounding a set of small drums, the other torturing a home-made flute. Branwyn grabbed Leith by his good wrist and began dragging him towards the small crowd joyfully spinning and jumping in the rhythm of the song. His efforts were met with polite resistance and pleading eyes.

"No, Bran. I don't dance, you know that. I never do."

"That's exactly why you need to try!" the healer insisted but stopped with the pushing.

"I think it's better not to. But you have fun, I'll go mingle, okay?"

Eight years of being har, almost nine, and he hadn't danced a single time. Everything else had been so easy to learn once he received the blood and life flowed like magical tidal wave into his previously useless legs! A couple of days to discover the simple joy of walking, a week of wonder about the careless ease with which other people performed trivial tasks, a fortnight until he was able to run with the wind. From there, it was just a step to swimming, climbing, horse riding, sparring, or sliding on a frozen lake, and he had repeated each of those activities long past the point of exhaustion until he excelled at them. But he'd never learned to dance and somehow he knew he never could.

Luckily, there were other ways to entertain oneself; ways that were guaranteed to gloss over the bitter memories. The lush woodland that surrounded them was home to hundreds of species of bird, insect, mammal, tree, plant and fungi. Most kinds of the latter were poisonous for humans, but hara soon found out that ingesting them was the beginning of a spiritual journey, rather than death in agonising pain. There would be an abundance of those at a party like this, and although the night was still young, some of the hara lying about on the grass had most certainly partaken already.

Gradually, the psylocibins now coursing through his veins began tugging at his already heightened senses. Colours became brighter, the whirling bodies and dancing fires each producing an aura that surrounded them and lingered slightly behind each movement. Scents and sounds, too, were amplified. Leith felt too lazy to slip away with somehar and take aruna, but he did initiate a spontaneous sharing of breath a couple times, exchanging euphoric feelings and chaotic images via mind touch. A most peculiar feeling, to hear somehar's laughter in his head and confuse it with his own, while grinning soundlessly. The grass whispered as he lowered himself onto it to observe the aura around each of his hara, the colours melting with a whirr whenever two of them touched.

And then everything spiralled out of control. Leith was slipping fast. He'd been on too many trips not to realise that this time, something was slightly off. It felt gradually more and more difficult to focus on anything as minutes stretched like hours and anxiety began to gnaw at every thought. He felt as if his blood had turned into liquid metal, scorching his veins from the inside, but at the same time he was completely detached from the sensation, as though it was happening to somehar else. The disembodied feeling was worrying at first, but to worry meant to be aware, which soon became impossible. The dreamy quality of the world around enveloped him like a bubble, making reality very elastic. The moving figures blurred into a shimmering abstract painting: Colours morphed and shapes reformed in an ever-changing kaleidoscope that was turned by movements in the flickering light. Every now and then, he had the feeling that somehar was bending over him with a lantern, as bright light blinded his eyes and distorted voices filled his ears. Other times, he believed himself to be back in the caves, the cold sandstone a soothing balm to his overheated skin. Occasionally, he was alert enough to notice that he was parched, but water was a tantalising elixir which he could neither locate nor bid his frozen limbs to fetch.

That was when a wave of actual panic crashed over him. Deep down, he was instinctively aware that he couldn't die of this; and no matter how long the minutes and hours seemed right then, in reality, it would soon be over. But the smothering immobility, this helplessness he found himself unable to escape: It hit too close to home. It cast him right back to that time in his life he'd fought so hard to suppress. Fighting the panic, which threatened to suffocate him, he willed himself to roll over, somehow tumbling into a sitting position. This small victory broke the vice-like grip of induced emotion, leaving him staring blankly, but calmly, into the forest beyond. During the time he had lost, darkness had descended upon the land, and mist had bloomed between the trees, pooling around the legs of a lonely figure poised at the treeline.

Leith's eyes snapped wide open, his distended pupils soaking up all the turquoise, making them look entirely black. As the world gradually sharpened into focus, at its epicentre was a vision unlike any he had previously encountered. Body: Flawless as a har's, yet undeniably male. Skin: Perfectly stretched over a lean yet muscular form, a coppery hue seeming to radiate from within. Arms: Cradling a large serpent; and more impossibly, a raven perched querulously upon his right bicep. As Leith's focus widened, he perceived a wolf, fox and stag – unlikely companions but seemingly protective of, or perhaps captivated, by the entity they surrounded. Encompassing all, a huge and ancient oak tree, branches protectively spread over the being and his entourage. A few scattered leaves had fallen, almost as if to decorate the central figure's long, dark hair. Crowning all, the creature's magnificent antlers perfectly defined the vision of power, grace and beauty that filled his vision. Although the two of them were observing each other from a considerable distance, Leith could feel a mind reaching out for his as surely as if they were sharing breath.

What are you? Leith formed a clumsy thought, like a toddler flailing his arms in shallow water. *Did I bring you here from the caves?*

What came back was an onslaught of thoughts: Raw, primal, unkempt. It hit his mind like an avalanche, leaving him buried under the intensity of the message.

I arise from your anger. Your blindness. Your progress. Your need. Your sorrow. Your bloodshed. Your wisdom. Your ignorance.

It was the scariest, most profound moment in Leith's life. A feeling similar to the experience of looking into the eyes of the first har he'd incepted. The joy of creating a flawless new being out of a lesser species; the fear that the blood of his blood would turn against him on account of the forced change. But multiplied by a thousand. This was his doing. His will, his emotions, his blood could reach into the depths of time and bring something powerful and ancient to the light of day. Yet, as with the unparalleled bond that inception created, he knew then that the weight of the alien mind battering his consciousness could, eventually, be accommodated.

What do you want? he thought, testing the tenuous mental bond between him and this creature, even as the vision began to evaporate and blend into the mist. This time, the answer was feather-soft.

To be the Hidden One no more.

In any moment of decision, Leith was inclined to choose the path most likely to lead to victory, fame and power, even if it was lined by thorny bushes, some of which might have been laced with poison. On this occasion, Branwyn's mysterious turn in the tunnels had given him pause. Compelled by his own powerful vision, there was no longer any doubt the cave exploration had to continue. Of course, that meant marking the tunnel that had led him to the altar as a dead end to assure that nohar would go traipsing around down there and unwittingly disturb the entity he'd awoken, and which he now claimed as his own.

The failure of the bastard van to return didn't go unnoticed. Keevan, who was in charge of spying on the northern gate, reported that a sizeable search party had left the enclave and headed down the road. Upon discovering the carnage, they fanned out and began to comb through the area in a widening search pattern. The tribe was happy to let them waste time and energy on that; given that their camp was located southeast of the town, there was nothing the half sexes could possibly find. They recovered the bodies of their fallen comrades and withdrew into the relative safety of their homes before sunset.

Branwyn visited the incepted twice a day and always came back disgusted, bringing ambivalent news. The process was a complete agony in and of itself, and the inceptees weren't having an easy time of it. One was almost certain not to pull through. Leith made sure not to show he was marginally interested to know which; a fifty percent success could still be considered a good outcome, but there were no certainties where inception was concerned. Only fate could decide whether they would open their eyes to a new reality or leave extremely unsightly corpses. If they didn't make it, surely there would be other adepts in an enclave of that size, populated by such capable, well-fed humans?

Unsurprisingly, one of the captives died on the third evening of his private hell. The other was found, unconscious but breathing, with one hand outstretched towards the bloated, rancid corpse covered in oozing boils that never got the chance to heal. He'd managed to free his right wrist from the cuffs, but any injury that might have caused was now healed. Keevan and Calder brought a bucket of water and washed off the worst of the grime with a sponge, revealing pale, flawless skin. They covered the body of his late friend with a sheet before Branwyn attempted to use his healing powers to wake him up; he was har now and deserved compassion.

"How are you feeling?" Leith asked softly, throwing a blanket around the har's shoulders. He was shivering, but cold might not have been the only culprit.

"Like death warmed up."

"The change isn't easy. But you'll be amazed at how fast you'll recover now!" Leith smiled, kneeling down so as to give the new addition to the tribe a chance to look into his eyes and see the sincerity of his words. "Your senses will be more accurate than you could ever have imagined. No sickness or poison will be able to harm you. Every imperfection, gone." And if that sounded a little bit like the words of a priest advertising the wonders a soul would experience in Heaven, Leith saw nothing wrong with that. Inception had turned him from a cripple, who had lived by waiting for favours from others, to a leader who could take anything he pleased, and whether or not it had been forced on him back then was completely irrelevant.

The new har's hazel eyes were speckled with gold now, adorned with lashes long enough to touch his cheek as he looked down to inspect his elegant hands. "Why are you so kind to me all of a sudden?" he asked, suspicious.

"You're one of us now. This is our way. We don't make attachments to anyhar until they can be fully accepted into the fold. But once they are, they become family. And as per tradition, they receive a new name." Gently, he cupped the har's face, making him look up again. "In honour of the forest that currently provides us both shelter and food, I have chosen for you the name Oisín. It means newborn deer in an old language people used to speak in some parts of Alba Sulh."

Oisín acknowledged that name with an almost imperceptible nod of his head. And somewhere at the back of his mind, Leith felt that the Horned One - unseen, yet vigilant - acknowledged it too. This new life was just as much his as it was the tribe's, even if, for now, the existence of the Horned One was a secret known only to him. And what a strong, resilient life it was going to be!

Like the clumsy fawn that was his namesake, Oisín rose on uncertain legs and wrapped the blanket tight around his body, lifting his chin with newfound pride.

"I will not thank you for this." His defiant stare shifted from the Phylarch to the vague outlines under the stained white sheet that used to be his colleague, perhaps even friend, and lingered there.

"I don't expect you to. But I can promise you that in time, you will feel thankful. For now, why don't you go with the others? They'll find you something to wear, you can clean up properly, eat, drink and rest as you desire. We will talk later about what is to come next."

He wanted to get Oisín away from the corpse, which would be burnt somewhere out of sight later that day. Before that, however, it could still serve a purpose. Leith waited until he could no longer hear the fading sounds of voices and footsteps, then he crouched over the unlucky hybrid and pulled the blanked down to his waist. The sight of the dead body, forever suspended halfway in the process of transition, instantly made him want to retch, but he'd seen similar failures before and was able to suppress the urge. Bracing himself against the stench that was sure to assault his nostrils, he took a deep breath and delved his hunting knife into the corpse's chest.

Inside, the organs were malformed, and some appeared to have fused together due to the unsuccessful process of mutation, but he was still able to locate the discoloured heart and pull it out of the chest cavity. The organ was considerably softer than it should have been; the tips of his fingers sunk into the mass. With utmost care, he ripped off a piece of cloth and wrapped the damaged organ with it. It simply wouldn't do if the heart turned into a mush too soon, because he knew just the place for it.

The droplets of his blood in the bowl on the altar had long gone dry, having left a fresh glaze at the bottom. The heart made a wet, squelching sound as Leith dropped it inside. He placed the bowl in the middle of the sandstone slab.

"I heard your call. I gave you my blood," he spoke deliberately, considering each word carefully. "You touched my mind, and within it there was the warmth of a candle's flame as there was the rage of a wildfire, the cool relief of a breeze and the biting chill of a winter storm, the shadow of the forest and the light of the clearing."

To worship doesn't mean to convey one's emotions, but to declare one's faith. It doesn't require a place, a ritual or carefully chosen words... only devotion. Leith didn't know that. Until recently, it hadn't occurred to him it was something he'd ever wish to find out. But here he was, calling on an entity as old as the earth upon which he trod. He called with feeling, curiosity and desire, his hands clasping the bowl that contained his gruesome offering.

"Life grows, dies, decays, and is born again. I gave you life. And now, I give you death."

He assumed words alone would not be enough. Holding the image of the Horned One firmly in his mind, he willed the god to hear him. He called until the hair on the back of his neck stood up and goosebumps ran down his arms. With his eyes shut tight, he called and called again until he smelled the earthy scent of forest in decay. A familiar presence filled the cavern the with raw, primal energy of the wild, carried in every feather, every leaf, every flower, every stone, shell, stick, and bone.

Leith had only seen the deity once before, during the visitation at the edge of the forest, and he hadn't even got a clear look at his face, yet he was able to visualise the being down to the smallest details. He was the majesty of the deer, the strength of the boar, the agility of the hawk, the cunning of the serpent, the wisdom of the owl and the elegance of the fox. Like the stag, he carried the beauty of what is, just as it is by bridging har, animal and human. Leith knew now that his limbs were well-muscled, only slightly more elongated than a har's. They had appeared spindly because of their unusual pliancy and the way he moved, as if he didn't want to disturb a single blade of grass or rustle a single leaf. Similarly, him towering over Leith had as much to do with his silent confidence and boldness as it did with his actual size. Light reflected off his skin like the sheen of a pelt, and his hair, crowned with antlers, was so dark it was impossible to tell where it ended and the shadows began.

You gave me your blood. You gave me life, and death. Now you have one last offering to make.

Slowly, as in a dream, Leith reached out to where he perceived the creature's torso to be and was almost confused when his fingers touched warm skin and fumbled up a muscular chest. It was slightly warmer than his own, and the heart under his palm was beating a little faster than he would have expected, both qualities of a wild animal. And even before allowing his eyelids to part, he knew he was going to be looking into almond shaped, mossy green eyes. It was only when he lowered his sight that he was stricken by surprise. The entity he had summoned stood before him completely unclothed, fresh from creation, and rather than being male, it was undeniably har.

"But... how is this possible?" Leith withdrew his hand, somewhat abashed at the lameness of the question. He knew with complete certainty that the deity had existed long before the first member of the Wraeththu discovered he was different from anyone else in the world. "What are you?"

The master of wild things and places. He smiled kindly, but the flash of strong, sharp teeth cast an almost feral aspect to his features. *I am the first breath and the last gasp; the craving of the hunter and fear of the hunted. I am as I have always been, yet my forms are many. This is the shape you gave me.* Another smile, mischievous this time, and a step forward. *And I think I will quite enjoy it.*

As the deity leaned closer, Leith felt breath like pines in a summer breeze brush his cheek. The blunt invitation was immediately understood and accepted. And as their lips locked in a sensual sharing of breath, so did their minds, thoughts and emotions mingling, combining, becoming one.

All that Leith was spilled out in a waterfall of memories, emotions and untold secrets. The blurred faces of his parents, always providing but never there. The thousands of tiny cruelties from his brothers. The night they almost pushed him out of the window; resources were scarce, and nobody wanted to waste them on a cripple. The feeling of complete resignation as he lay under the bed waiting for the rogue gang to kill him, abandoned by everyone who could run. Agony. And then first steps, first laugh, first aruna, first journey, first battle, first kill, first followers, first raid. A multitude of firsts and eternity or repetitions that had ultimately led to this chamber. Fate or chance, in this moment Leith neither knew, nor cared.

The exchange was not one sided. Knowledge and understanding poured into his consciousness. His was the world of the Wilds. Long forgotten, he'd lain eons in silent repose. Like a volcano dormant for generations, the creatures stumbling around the surface had no idea of the power deep beneath their feet. But it was there, and he was magnificent. He'd been born from the rituals of primitive humans, eager to demonstrate their thanks for a successful hunt; or to sacrifice in the hope of one. And while humans had long lost their capacity to perceive or understand a god such as he, members of a race that inherited the earth could accept him as their own.

Once, we had been one. The land, the creatures inhabiting it, the humans, and I, we had been one. But they have forgotten about me. Lost all respect for the earth that gave them life, my soil, my animals, my plants, my water, my air. My reign gave way to their rage, their progress, their destruction. But I have been waiting for a new wind to come blowing.

Only a har could make a pact with something so powerful, yet so powerless, and give the essence a new guise - how many had there been? A harish mind alone could shape and name it. Not really a god anymore, but not quite a har, Leith realised. And the collective unconsciousness supplied him with the correct term that somehar else had very recently coined in another cave, on a faraway continent he had only ever seen in those old travel guides he'd so loved to browse through.

And time was on my side. The cycle is endless.

"Dehar," Leith mouthed, pulling away for breath.

There is one offering you have yet to make, the dehar reminded him. He hadn't once spoken aloud, yet Leith could perceive every nuance in his tone and hear his voice as loud as if it were echoing through the caves. It was playful yet demanding.

You know where offerings are placed.

There is much that can be said about the ancient intimacy between the hunter and hunted, though a lot of the sacredness, the divinity of the animal, has been lost. On a conscious level, Leith was unaware that his role on this night was that of the prey, but in his very core, the part of him that was connected to the workings of the Universe knew. And he wanted it like he had never wanted anything before. Driving him was the desire to own a shadow of a deity, a connection to the primeval wilderness and something beyond mortal comprehension.

With that strength reflected in every motion, he reached for the dehar's hand. Walking backwards slowly, he pulled him along until his back was pressed against the altar, the cold stone like ice on his skin. Leith hoisted himself up elegantly and shifted back on the slab where offerings were placed, letting his legs open so he could pull the dehar closer. There would be no discussion regarding which role either of them was to assume; that had already been decoded in the word 'offering' thousands of years ago. It wasn't what Leith would normally have chosen, not because he couldn't find it in himself to enjoy the soume aspect of his body, but because his ambitions as a leader reflected in all aspects of his life. This time, though, it felt completely natural. Any pack leader could recognise a stronger predator.

The dehar's hand settled at the base of his neck, with his thumb resting in the hollow just below his throat. It was a position that was simultaneously harmless and yet carried the potential for him to exert more control over Leith, if he chose to tighten his grip. Leith's lips parted in surprise. He went completely still, watching the entity he had helped return to life with cautious expectation, the gems of his eyes shining turquoise in the darkness.

No, he was no fool. He was very aware that the fact that he'd been helpful to the Horned One so far in no way meant those powerful hands wouldn't snap his neck like a dry twig. Something in him desired this, though, the danger that came with submission. Perhaps he was about to discover something about himself he hadn't known before, and perhaps he simply revelled in the fact that for once, he didn't have to be in charge.

As he began to explore Leith's body with his other hand, the dehar's touch was surprisingly gentle, but the skin of his palm had a rough, leathery quality. Not unwelcome, but definitely different. Good. It needed to happen like that, everything about the act had to be raw, challenging and new. He could feel his heart beating in his throat as he ran his own hands down the dehar's torso to where he knew he would find perfection, because everything about this guise was exactly the way he had dreamed it up.

The dehar's canines were sharp like a predator's when he pressed a kiss to Leith's jaw, grazing the soft skin. That alone was enough for his body to become soume, the ocean of his passion eager to swallow the heat of his god, whose wildfire could raze entire continents. They came together like two halves of a broken sword, joined again by molten metal. And even with his eyelids shut tight, Leith could perceive the shadow of antlers falling over his face.

He felt the forest closing in around him with all its scents, sounds, wonders and dangers, but he had no fear of getting lost. That was part of the pact. No animal, plant or inanimate object would harm him, while he was lying there bare-skinned and helpless, at the mercy of the elements. Amid the throes of passion, the har understood the dreams that had been plaguing and enticing him. He understood the notion of wearing antlers on his head, moving about in the consciousness of the animal, seeing the world through the buck's eyes and assuming the weight of that blessing. The trees breathed his name, and he whispered a name in turn.

"Saor. You are Saor, dehar of the wilds."

It came out as a quiet moan, as his hips bucked up in a plea for release. The sensations were so intense that pleasure became almost unbearable. Yet at the same time, he wished for this to go on forever, because he hadn't felt so amazing in his entire life. He felt all of his sikras, his energy centres, resonating, each singing its own melody that, together, formed a perfect harmony of pleasure. Balancing on the edge of a precipice for the longest time, he finally allowed himself to take the final plunge, and as he braced himself against the altar, he was surprised to feel nothing but the softest moss under his hands.

Slowly, his ebbing waves receded further into the ocean, but they were still lapping at the shore, powerful in their silence. He waited until they stilled completely, and their roar became a whisper, before he spoke again: "Saor". His voice echoed through the caverns, returning multiplied like a rumbling storm. There was great power in naming a dehar, but an even greater power had been bestowed upon the entity through this act of initiation. The cavern was filled with a lovely scent of autumn leaves, weeping pine trees and flowers abloom, and if there was anything treacherous about it, Leith remained blissfully unaware.

In the days that followed, Leith committed himself to the wants and needs of his tribe. He would solve their petty disputes; go with them to the river or for a ride; hunt and pick berries; train with weapons; teach Oisín what it meant to be har; keep an eye on the enclave; work on securing the camp; explore the caves; or sing and share stories by the fire. Yet all the while, he felt like a sleepwalker, unconsciously executing tasks and actions whilst his mind focused on a higher goal. More than ever before, he encouraged everyhar to practice mind touch. And despite not disclosing the fact even to his most trusted tribeshara, plans to take the City of Caves in a violent assault had been put on hold.

Pacifism and patience were traits none had ever associated with the Phylarch. Whilst few had any objections to this new, relaxed pace of living, only Keevan dared state that the Phylarch was behaving like a har in love. Indignant, Leith called him ridiculous and promptly took mediocre, uneventful aruna with him the same evening just to prove a point. That put the joke to death before it had the chance to spread, but Leith was privately concerned. Inwardly, he told himself that it was not love, it was simply a fascination with what he had created. But how could he be sure? He'd had little experience of love, even less of romantic love. He'd known pleasure in abundance, but merely as a distraction on his quest for loftier goals, but how could he be sure what love was supposed to feel like? It had avoided him completely, while he filled his life with grander goals and meaningless encounters.

The nights, by contrast, were full of wonders. On clear nights, when the stars shone like a thousand fireflies and fog crept among the trees, making everything seem haunted and silent, he felt fully alive. Soon, he knew he would have to explain this to his tribe. Open their minds to a reality in which deities did exist and anyhar with a strong enough mind could not only invoke such deities, but even determine their form. Imagine the power that a tribe of likeminded hara could harness! Of course, it was crucial to get the timing right. That glorious moment when the City of Caves was finally claimed for the Kernetei would be the moment they would be most willing to accept and celebrate the dehar. For the moment, however, Saor was his own marvellous secret. Every spare moment he yearned to know more about, to explore, to learn from... to hold ...him. The dehar of the wild seemed volatile sometimes, like the forces of nature, and he wasn't always gentle, but neither was Leith.

But it was infinitely more than that. His own perception of reality was evolving, as his mind opened to things he had always considered unnecessary. The forest had more voices than he could ever have imagined, and he could now hear them all: the flow of the sap under tree bark; dozens of mice hearts beating in a burrow; a flurry of leaves moved by sudden gusts of wind; rain worms aerating the soil under his feet; the ultrasonic calls of bats gliding overhead. The beasts no longer feared him; they would let him come close enough to touch their fur or feathers. Close enough to touch their minds.

He floated on silent wings and saw the world through the binocular vision of an owl, huddled against small warm bodies in a fluff of rabbits, swam against the stream with pikes. He knew the mating ritual of dragonflies and the taste of fresh blood on a wolf's tongue as he tore into the flesh of a deer; equally the pain, fear and panic of the deer as it took its last breath. If anyhar noticed that Leith would often be found sleeping long after sunrise, half dressed, with muddy boots still on and hair full of grass, they didn't mention it. For all his newfound wonder and experience, time moved on in a world unaware of Saor.

One evening, Oisín didn't return to the camp at dinner time. Nohar was bothered by it at first, until the Moon stood so high in the sky that they had to admit he wouldn't show up anymore, as 'today' had morphed into 'tomorrow'. Branwyn was concerned that something might have happened to him, but Leith was fairly certain the har had simply run off in hopes to return to his old home. It was unfortunate that the enclave was close enough for him to do so any time, because the temptation must have been great for one so new.

"He'll be back," Leith said dismissively, and with that, the discussion about forming a search party was put to rest. He'd seen hara try and return to their human families before, and it was an abysmal idea in every single case. For their loved ones, they were strangers, freaks of nature and, what was worse, a constant reminder of their own short lives. Never aging, neither male nor female, and capable of hurling heavy objects by will alone when angered. Who wouldn't want such a child or sibling, right?! And even if the family was willing to try and accommodate a har, no matter how unwise that decision, there were always others who would drive him out, or clobber him to death.

It took a total of three days for Leith's prediction to come true. Oisín appeared in the camp without a word of explanation and seemed to wish for one thing only: To be seen as little as possible until the others forgot he'd ever been gone. One of his eyes was swollen shut and the way he carried himself spoke volumes about what other injuries lay hidden beneath his clothes. Nohar found it appropriate to admonish him, not straight away at least. Instead, they gave him a herbal drink to help with the pain and Branwyn treated his eye best as he could.

"It's not their fault, you know," he said soothingly as he worked, focusing on lowering the temperature of his palm so as to cool the injury. "It's a coping mechanism, I think. They'd rather see us dead than changed. But can you blame them? I mean, the world's rejecting them and catering to us. It is evolving in front of their eyes, but they can't be a part of that process. *You* can."

Oisín's healthy eye snapped at the healer, effectively putting a stop to his chatter. "Maybe *I'd* rather see myself dead than changed."

Branwyn, ever so calm, gave him one of his innocent smiles. "Would you, though?"

The other suppressed a sigh, suddenly taking great interest in the grass under his feet. "No."

Having watched the whole exchange, Leith peeled himself off the tree he'd been leaning against and approached the pair, crouching down beside Oisín. He wasn't comfortable with the situation. As endearing as the scene he'd been privy to had been, it was time to put sympathy aside so that important matters could be addressed, and the responsibility fell on him to do that.

"I get why you wanted to go back; I do. But it wasn't very smart." He was doing his best not to sound patronising and failing miserably. "You need to understand it is us against them, and no matter where your loyalties lie, you are on this side of the barrier and there's no crossing back. You might have put us all in danger with this stunt. Are you sure you weren't followed?"

There was little left of the defiance that had been so typical of Oisín before, perhaps because the realisation finally hit home that he truly had no other options other than to accept his fate or perish. "I don't think so, no." His hesitant tone of voice made it obvious that he really had no idea; the notion simply hadn't occurred to him.

The expression in Leith's eyes hardened as he tilted his head to the side, suspicious. "What did you tell them about us?!"

"Nothing," came the answer, after a moment of contemplative silence.

Leith couldn't believe that. Mistakes had been made, and he was ultimately responsible for them. Unfortunately, those who were incepted past their youth always had a harder time adjusting, and this particular one likely had someone he still cared about. Most of Leith's tribeshara had either been left alone in the world or came from an 'everyone fends for themselves' type of background. Leith barely remembered his parents and wished he could forget his brothers. Still, it had been wrong of him not to anticipate such an outcome, just because his own family wasn't something he'd ever miss, much less mourn.

"Oisín. You need to be honest with me now."

His tone bordered on intimidating, and Oisín didn't fail to notice. Jerking away from Branwyn, he straightened up, the familiar defiance creeping back into his eyes. "Look, I've only spoken to my sister, and she'd never do anything to endanger me. You are wrong, both of you. This…" He made an all-encompassing gesture, alluding to his bruises, "…wasn't her doing. She's been hiding me in the cellar most of the time."

Branwyn rolled his eyes, concluding his skills were no longer needed. "Whatever helps you sleep at night, fawn," he smirked, patting Oisín's shoulder. Leith didn't buy into the optimism either. It would be nice if this particular action didn't generate a reaction, but in his experience, that wasn't how life worked. From now on, somehar would stand watch day and night, securing the perimeter.

The air was like molasses: thick, hot and clammy. Even in Alba Sulh, the sun could occasionally make the grass sweat in the middle of the summer. The body of a har, strung from a pole in the middle of a disused horse racing course that lay between the town and the Kernetei, was utterly still. There wasn't the slightest breeze. A cloud of flies buzzed around the corpse in the eternal dance of death, undisturbed by the semi-circle of hara who'd assembled to sit in silent vigil. Soon, decomposition would begin to gnaw at his pale form.

"What are you waiting for?!" Leith snapped, ready to vent his frustration at having been right, yet still incapable of preventing the murder of one of his tribe on anyhar who was unwise enough to get too close. "Take him down!"

Calder took a step back, mistaken in his belief that his reluctance to comply would go unnoticed and the terrible task would fall on somehar else's shoulders. "Move it!" Leith hissed into his ear and, intent to lead by example, began to climb the pole so that he could cut the rope. Dutifully, Calder and Kiaran, a rather solitary har who'd walked into the grim scene when at the start of his watch, moved to stand beneath the pole and catch the body as it dropped down into their arms.

A few steps away, Oisín was watching them with his arms protectively crossed on his chest, somewhat shell-shocked. From his vantage point, Leith pointed his dagger at him before sliding back down. "You take a good look." Nothing more, nothing less. Was there blame to be placed? Perhaps. But in that case, he'd have to carry his own share of it. Meanwhile, Kiaran had rolled the body over, so that everyhar could take in what he had briefly glimpsed earlier: on the har's back, a spray-painted inscription in bold capital letters spelled F R E A K.

The hara were no strangers to death: The turbulent era they had been born into and their chosen way of life ensured that. But that didn't mean it wasn't keenly felt or mourned, especially when the loss was unexpected and felt so unnecessary. For several long minutes, the group stood there in silence, unable and unwilling to fill the empty void left by the departed with meaningless words. Then the phylarch made a barely perceptible gesture with his chin and Kiaran set to preparing the body for transport.

Leith finally broke the smothering silence. "There is now a war between us." His voice was quiet, but internally the fire of wrath consumed him. The truth was, there had always been a war. Ever since the first Wraeththu realised his uniqueness and superiority, the two species had been unable or unwilling to coexist in peace. Leith had allowed himself to forget about that for a short time, embarking on a journey of discovery instead, and this was the outcome. If he didn't find a way to combine the two from then on, there would be an even higher price to pay. The following day, they would all focus on exploring the rest of the tunnels, and if no passage leading to the town was found, he would devise a different, riskier plan. In either case, retribution would be delivered.

The service was held at dusk, when the reddening sky provided a matching backdrop to the flames of the funeral pyre. Cremation was the way they had all agreed on years ago, allowing their remains to be scattered across the water and earth they belonged to, rather than dug out by hungry animals or curious human scoundrels. Engulfed in flames, the body seemed to twist and change shape, as though grisly reanimated in a final macabre dance . Aside from his best clothes and flowers gifted by the mourners, no other possessions were burned with him. Some believed that harrish consciousness survived death to become omnipresent; others that the spirits of the dead would be reborn in an endless cycle. Some that this one life was brief and absolute. However, all agreed that resources were scarce and the deceased would definitely have no need of them.

It took some time for the flames to die down, and those sluggish, melancholic hours were ideal for reminiscing,hatching bold plans and finding comfort in each other. Leith fell asleep late, and it felt like he'd only closed his eyes for a minute when somehar shook him awake. Instinct and muscle memory reacted before his brain had a chance to catch up. Full on survival mode, he grabbed the intruder by the chain around his neck, which happened to be the first thing he could reach, while drawing his knife with the other hand. There was a hiss from above him, but little resistance. "Easy there! It's just me."

The voice sounded familiar enough for Leith to slowly let go of the accessory and lower his hand holding the knife. He hoisted himself to a sitting position. Fully back to his senses, he could now make out the shape of an extremely tall har towering over him like a ghost. "Darragh?" If memory served well, he should have been keeping watch over the road from the south, but not alone. In the light of recent events, everyhar guarding the camp at night was supposed to be patroling in pairs - four groups, each pair protecting one of the compass points. "What's going on? Who was the other? Aiden? If something happened to one of his closest friends…"

"We caught two riders heading to town," the har dispelled his concerns. "I reckon they had no clue about whatever happened last night."

"Did you get them both?"

"Aiden had to shoot one, but the other is like new. Want to come and see?"

Given the circumstances, there wasn't much Leith would rather see. A few minutes ago, the only thing he'd wished for was a nice long rest, but as he followed Darragh out of the cave and through the clusters of makeshift tents to where Aiden was guarding the horses, he realised he'd never felt so awake. And there was more. He could now smell fear. It wasn't an odour he could liken to anything, except perhaps the pheromones of a soume-shrew angling to get laid. Despite its sulfurous odour, Leith couldn't help being excited and invigorated by it, though rather than lust, he felt aggression building inside him.

The human exuding this potent aroma was an aging male, tied up and thrown over the saddle of his horse like a sack of potatoes. As the pair of hara approached, he tried to raise his head enough to see their faces - an unsuccessful attempt that did nothing but make his messy combover split, revealing a bald spot in the middle of his greying hair. The other horse, too, carried a body on its back, fastened to the saddle by its waist with two limbs dangling on either side of the animal. This one sported a mass of thick, wiry auburn hair. Leith grabbed it with mild disgust and lifted the body as far as the rope allowed.

"Interesting," he noted, since a quick inspection revealed a round face with soft, feminine features and a pair of breasts sitting high on the chest. One of those useless mounds was adorned with a dark crimson stain blooming like a morbid flower. Leith hadn't talked to a female in years, and apparently tonight wasn't going to change that. Instead, he walked up to the old man and unceremoniously pulled him off the horseback, letting him land on the ground with a thud.

"I've been told you went for a little ride," he purred, circling the human like a cat that had just cornered a fat rat. "Where to?"

There was no immediate answer, but the maddening scent intensified tenfold. Amused, Leith momentarily thought the old timer's bladder must have released its content, but when he grabbed him by his collar and hoisted him on his feet, he could see no evidence of that.

"So?" he tilted his head playfully.

"I'm not telling you anything, kid," came in a weak, tired voice.

Truly, the old dog deserved some credit for that. Shaken to the bone, fear evaporating from his every pore, surrounded by hostiles, and he still found it in himself to complicate things? Leith nodded appreciatively, and suddenly the knife was back in his hand. Before he could even register the har's swift movement, the man had the tip of the blade pressed against his Adam's apple.

"They were coming from the south," Aiden interjected, perhaps perhaps in nervous reaction to the rapid escalation to violence. "There's nothing there but harish teritory."

To their knowledge, the majority of surviving humans had either stuck to the Midlands or fled to the east of the country. The south, as well as the north of Alba Sulh belonged to peaceful tribes that had settled seaside towns and villages, slowly spreading inland, and engaged in mundane activities.

Leith ignored him, because he wanted answers rather than assumptions. "Now, we all know you're going to die here, which probably makes you think it doesn't matter if you cooperate or not," he growled, all softness and humour gone from his voice. "But I can tell you how you'll die, if you don't give me an answer fast." He'd quickly tired of the cat and mouse game. Failure to comply may have been cute in a new har like Oisín, but it was despicable when displayed by a half-sex with a turkey neck and squashed up nose reminiscent of a pug.

"I will have you tied to a chair, and then I will make a cut around your entire face." Without warning, the pressure of the knife increased, tentatively drawing first blood. "Like this. Then, I will peel your face off, and I will have a mirror brought so you could look at yourself. Do you know that, if done correctly, everything comes off at once? Ears, nose, lips. And then... I'll cut off your cock and stuff it down your throat, and I will watch until you bleed out or suffocate on it. So, what will it be?"

Given his age and the overall situation, the man's skin tone had been far from healthy to begin with, but as Leith continued to describe the macabre future he had planned for him, it paled to sickly grey. "We went to the Sulh!" he shouted, doing his best to pull away from the blade. "Please. After the first few times you showed up close to the gates, the Major was afraid things would escalate, so he sent us to the Sulh. One of the guys said they like to act as negotiators. We thought they could come and… ask you to leave."

Aiden snorted with contempt, thereby expressing everyhar's opinion. None of them liked the Sulh, exactly because they so enjoyed forging peace between the rogue tribes and remaining human settlements - a hobby that rarely met with success, since nobody was interested in their meddlesome presence. Their telepathic abilities were superior and so were their arunic arts, but they appeared to use those skills solely for academic purposes, rather than actually asserting power or enjoying themselves. Their tediousness was hard to beat.

"And what did they say?" he asked on everyhar's behalf. "Are they coming?"

"Yes. Yes, they agreed to it."

This time the answer came immediately, which was just as well, because Leith didn't think he could stand being so close to his clammy skin any longer. Not if he didn't get to peel it off, slice by slice. That idea seemed much more exciting than it should have, which gave the har a pause. He felt a little feverish, and that in itself was strange, since it was impossible for Wraeththu to come down with a sickness. The blade flashed in the moonlight, and as he was about to put it back in the holster, he could have sworn that he saw the reflection of a horned face on its surface, but it vanished in the blink of an eye.

"Darragh? Could you please bring him to the cell, while we take care of the horses? I want to sacrifice him tomorrow."

If Leith's voice appeared overly polite as he made that request, it was because he struggled to overcome the novel urge to lick the bloodied tip of the knife. At least the human was now gone from his sight. Hoping that a small discussion about their current predicament would bring some clarity and distract him from this strange bout of bloodlust, Leith turned to his friend. "Well, what do you think of this? The Sulh…"

"I think it was smart of them to send a woman and an old geezer to visit a Wraeththu tribe!" Aiden smirked, while working on removing the unfortunate female from the saddle. "I guess they don't know that the Sulh don't incept boys against their will."

Leith chuckled at that, letting the other horse nuzzle the top of his head. The animal had taken to him marvellously, just like all the forest creatures he now felt uniquely attuned to. "They don't need to, apparently. Rumour has it that one or two of them have spawned a... harling of some sorts."

Aiden paused, confused. "A harling? You mean like a young? But... how?!"

"Yeah, a young. Fucked if I know! Can you imagine?"

With the unadulterated horror of somehar who had still been male three years ago trying to imagine a delivery, Aiden visibly shuddered and pushed the idea out of his mind as fast as he was able. "I think I'll pass on that one. If it even works. I mean, thank you for the nightmares."

"If it even works," Leith repeated, not at all keen on the idea either. "Anyhow, we'll have to act quickly now. It will be much better if we are already sitting inside the enclave when those hara arrive."

"But how long can it take them, a couple of days? They might be on their way as we speak..."

"Right. Better to consider the possibility they could get here as soon as tomorrow and we'll have to get rid of them."

Fast and efficient, they gave the horses a good rub-down, poured them a bucket of water and tied them as close to the cave entrance as possible. They were excellent animals, well-fed and full of energy, sturdy, not too old and with a healthy sheen to their pelts. Unlike the van, they'd definitely be of use to the tribe.

All the while, Aiden kept glancing at Leith off and on, until he dared himself to ask the question that had been burning on his tongue. "The sacrifice... You were just messing with his head, right?"

"What's it to you?" Leith shrugged dismissively, because he wasn't quite ready to elaborate, nor did he want to belittle the dehar by pretending he'd only been putting up a frightening performance for the old guy. "He will die with his face still attached, as I promised."

Aiden paused, stunned by the realisation that the prospect of the sacrifice might actually be real. "I know you're not tripping." His forehead crinkled as he briefly considered the possibility. Funerals weren't typically the occasion to indulge, but on the other hand, everyhar handled mourning in their own way. "Wait, are you tripping?"

No, this wasn't how Leith had intended to start sharing his revelation with others, but what choices were there? A leader who acted in an inexplicable manner without providing a good reason for his behaviour could easily lose the respect of his tribe, although he was in no way obliged to answer nosy questions. Besides, he resented having to treat his connection with the dehar as a dirty affair to be ashamed of in front of his friends. Nights were for secrets, the best time for difficult revelations. Hastily deciding not to wait, Leith could only hope this particular secret would be well received.

"I found a place of worship down in the caves," he said in a low voice, locking his eyes with Aiden to impress upon him that nothing he was about to hear was a joke. "In the centre of the system. Dedicated to a forest deity, I believe. I don't quite understand every detail, but Aiden... it is magnificent. There are elaborate symbols and paintings everywhere, writings in runes. They felt so familiar I was almost certain the place had been waiting there for me, for hundreds, perhaps thousands of years. And the deity..." Leith paused, a feverish glow pooling in his piercing blue eyes. "He is no longer entirely forgotten."

As he tried to recapture the scene, Leith discovered he lacked the words to describe the unique atmosphere of the place, the dehar's lingering presence at the back of his mind, much like a premonition of an approaching storm on a hot summer day. And so far, he was being heard, yet not understood.

"Deities are human concepts, not actual things. Believing otherwise is the sign of a weak and gullible mind. This kind of thinking has set humanity back farther than any other in existence," Aiden readily supplied; Leith's very own words, spoken back when they'd caught a freshly incepted har still wearing his cross.

"That is what I thought," Leith admitted calmly. There was no purpose in denying it. "It's what we all thought. But we've been wrong! These concepts... they have always been there, and always will be. And we can summon them. More than that, we have the power to make them our own, and it is so absolutely amazing!" Pleading now, he reached for Aiden's shoulder. This was his first performance in the role of a missionary trying to convert a staunch nonbeliever, and he couldn't afford to fail. "Do you trust me?"

"I don't get half of what you're saying, Leith, and honestly I'm not sure I want to. But I trust you. We all do."

"Then give me the benefit of doubt on this until we take the town. After that, I promise you'll understand." A preternatural intuition told him that something tremendous would come to pass as they stormed the enclave, after which opening everyhar's eyes to the essence of Saor would be a far simpler task. But if he happened to be wrong, he would find a way, even if he had to share his experience via mind touch with every single har in the camp.

In stark contrast to the lighthearted days that preceded the murder, the tribe now had a single focus: to prepare for taking the enclave. Leith had set a clear condition: going through the previously unexplored tunnels was an absolute priority, but should a passage to the town not be discovered within two days, they would stop the fruitless search and opt for a straight on attack before dawn. As the others left to carry out their search, Leith ordered Oisín to stay behind for one last heart-to-heart.

"Your help could be invaluable," he stressed repeatedly, "you could give us useful information about the layout of the enclave, the number of inhabitants, the placement of guards, what weapons they'll have at their disposal, where to find the Mayor... This, right now, is the time when you absolutely have to decide - are you with us, or not? Because I can just leave you here until it is done." There was no hint of unspoken repercussions for electing to stay behind, which perhaps is what moved the har to respond the way he did..

"I am with you. I'll give you everything and more, under one condition. You'll leave my sister's house alone. No harm will come to her."

Although Leith didn't quite share the sentiment and fully believed that one should cut all ties with their human family upon joining the Wraeththu, he could live with that condition. What was one human life? "Very well," he smiled, " we have an agreement."

There was no reason why Oisín should be mistrusted; after all, the safety of his sister gave him the strongest possible motivation. The advantage of an insider on the mission could make all the difference.

And the late afternoon delivered another breakthrough. After ten hours in the tunnels, a group of hara led by Keevan returned from their expedition, hollering cheerfully across the meadow. "We've got it! Leith, we've got it!" Large travel bags groaning under a mysterious weight were strapped the their shoulders, but they didn't dampen the spring in their step.

"Check this out!" Keevan said proudly, dropping his bag on the ground at Leith's feet to pull out a... battleaxe. A real medieval battleaxe with a patina of time, which, back in the day, would have most certainly been a prized possession of a history museum. Not anymore. As the apocalypse progressed, valuable artifacts like this one reverted back to to their original purpose, because an axe was still an axe, and when you needed to fight for every meal, you could benefit much more from actually using one than from staring at it through thick glass.

"Where did you find it?" Leith inquired, trying to keep excitement at bay. He picked up the weapon, weighing it in his hand. It was surprisingly light and left a rusty stain on his palms.

"In the tunnel where Branwyn had his little sleep, but much further down. But wait, there's more!" Keevan grinned as the others started opening their bags, immediately fishing in them for loot, as though he was the only one who deserved to take credit for their finds. "There were some bones, too," he chattered on. "Like two full skeletons worth, but we didn't bring those, of course. What's a pile of human remains good for, right? Unless you have some extravagant fashion sense."

Leith wiped his hands on his hips, rewarding Keevan with a light chuckle. He didn't touch the armour. "So you think this is the way to the town? The castle, maybe? Did you go all the way through?"

"You bet your pants it is! It ended in some kind of cellar. The walls still looked cave-like, but there were real tiles on the floor, and some old barrels and crates. An awful lot of rubble, though, and everything stank like an old beggar's feet. We saw a door, but it looked pretty heavy and we'd have to remove some of the crap first to look out, so we thought we'd better not mess with it now in broad daylight, in case there was someone on the other side."

"I could kiss you right now," Leith exclaimed. Actually, why shouldn't he? Taking his friend's face in his hands, he placed a brotherly, noisy kiss on his forehead. They both laughed as Keevan made a mock attempt at swatting him like a pesky fly. "Do you know what this means? The City of Caves will be ours, hopefully without a single life lost!" Their excitement was contagious and soon everyhar around was cheering, patting each other's back and making bold claims about the future. It had never looked so bright.

At nightfall, they gathered in the meadow where the funeral pyre had burned bright the previous night. News of the planned sacrifice had spread like wildfire and every member of the tribe wanted to be present for it, whether from morbid curiosity or genuine need to trade death for death, so as to be able to move on. A couple of onlookers lingered around the ladder and ropes Leith had found somewhere, idly wondering how they were going to be utilised. And when the phylarch arrived with his entourage, he appeared completely changed. Gone was the friend, lover and brother in arms they usually saw in their leader. Of course, he could be ruthless when dealing with the outside world, but was never too distant from the hara in his care. In his place stood a stranger, beautiful and deadly. Calmly, he walked into the centre of the meadow, face half hidden by a black hooded cloak that revealed his bare chest, adorned with an intricate, concentric glyph in red paint.

Keevan and Aiden had dragged the old man out of his temporary cell and were poking and prodding him like an beast, so as to force him to hobble in front of them. The brief rebelliousness he'd displayed the previous night all gone, he was desperately searching the crowd for anyhar who could be persuaded to show him mercy. "Please…" he whimpered to nohar in particular. "I have children."

A couple of bystanders burst into laughter. Why was it that people always thought bringing up this particular argument would avert whatever evil was going to befall them?

"Pray tell," Calder beamed at him like the insolent brat he was, "are any of them boys?"

More laughter.

Leith let them enjoy the preface to the performance; a happy crowd was a crowd easier to please. When the amused sounds died down, he took a moment to shift his eyes from the assembled hara to the small group of his closest friends by his side. Waiting for his orders, Keevan and Aiden were holding the man firmly in their grasp, although he was no longer putting up a fight. "Stretch him on the ladder and tie him up," Leith prompted them, watching silently as they set out to perform the task. Helpful as ever, Calder held the ladder up for them, easily catching up with the phylarch's plan: to expose the prisoner so that no eye would fail to see what was about to be done to him.

"This man has children!" he turned to the crowd. "He will tell you that he is innocent. That he wasn't even around when Fenn was labelled as a freak and left hanging in the sun for the flies to feast upon! And perhaps that's true. But he's a representative of those who did that, and the only reason he couldn't participate is that he was busy licking the asses of the Sulh, trying to plot against us. He's a member of a dying race which refuses to finally leave the earth it destroyed to its rightful heirs! That's an offense not only to us, but to nature itself!"

His little speech worked like a charm, riling up those hara who might have otherwise doubted a public execution. Content with his eloquent preambl, Leith approached the human with barely hidden anticipation, much like a starving wolf circling its prey. Twisting his neck curiously to scrutinise him from head to toe, the har appeared to be looking for the juiciest piece of flesh to start feasting on. Dissatisfied with the outcome, he stepped back and drew his knife, the tip of which was still stained crimson.

"You can repay your debt towards nature now," Leith hissed, his expression cold and unforgiving. "By feeding it." The careful choice of words was part of his act to impress the audience, but pronouncing them seemed inherently right. Hadn't the humans been living on Earth as carelessly as if they had another planet to go to? Wasn't it the wrath of the very nature they'd destroyed that reduced them to unwelcome guests in the world they'd once called themselves masters of? The wrongdoings of this particular specimen hardly mattered; one molecule of a virus wasn't any less guilty or innocent than another, they all needed to be purged.

Strong in his conviction, heart filled to the brim with concentrated hate, Leith grabbed the man's shirt with both hands and ripped it apart with one swift movement. The skin underneath was sickly pale, beading with sweat and sprinkled by sparse, grey hair. The canvas was far from perfect, if Leith were to judge, but he would make sure to make the art all the more spectacular. Above his head, crows were beginning to flock, providing a macabre backdrop to the scene. Normally, those omnivorous scavengers would only appear to feast on
the carrion after the kill has been made, and their early arrival p augured acceptance of the sacrifice by the dehar.

Though he tried maintain his composure, the man was trembling now, his heart practically bursting out of his chest. His heavy-lidded eyes darted from one face in the crowd to another in the last desperate attempt to find someone with enough compassion to stop what was about to happen, until they fixed on Oisín. There was a moment of hesitation; inception had polished the har's features, taken off the rough edge, sharpened his cheekbones and erased the tiny wrinkles in the corners of his eyes. Eventually, recognition set in, igniting a flash of hope in the man's age-worn face.

"Daniel! Please, don't let him do this! Daniel..."

Though not everyhar was immediately able to connect the never-before heard name with its wearer, quite a lot of them did, and Oisín was forcefully pulled out of his role of a spectator to become one of the main attractions of the show. Would he ignore the pleas and lower his eyes, hoping the attention would soon shift from him? Would he laugh a profanity the man's way, thereby proclaiming fealty to the tribe? Would he beg Leith to be merciful, jump in front of the victim, or perhaps run like a coward? The phylarch himself expected none of those obvious, predictable reactions from the headstrong har he'd incepted, and he was not disappointed.

Unflinching, Oisín slipped through the first few rows of hara to stand right before Leith and locked his hazel eyes with the man's desperate stare. "I could not stop him if I tried," he said calmly, stating a simple truth. Whether there was a glimpse of defiance, acceptance or apology in his voice, nohar could quite tell. He disregarded them completely, refusing to look away from the sacrifice site, making it very obvious that their opinion of him was of no importance.

A cruel smile ghosted over the phylarch's lips, crushing any hopes for salvation the man might have had. "I do love to hear you beg, but it is getting late. Now all I want to see is your entrails spilled out in front of you, with the birds feasting on them," he described the gruesome scene that was about to unfold without even the slightest hint of unease. Then, he moved towards the captive with slow gliding steps and drove the knife into his upper abdomen, his ice-cold gaze drinking the pain and horror from the man's eyes.

The scream that came was as deafening as it was invigorating. It sent pure excitement shooting up his spine, the rush of it going to his head like the most potent drug he'd ever experimented with. His hand was steady as he led the knife all the way to the man's groin. The incision was deep enough for him to be able to reveal the inner organs easily, without immediately damaging them and causing premature death. Next, he made another, smaller cut, perpendicular to the first, and stepped back to watch a bloody cross forming on the writhing canvas. The agonising groans intensified, building up into a morbid symphony that was driving Leith into frenzy.

This is for you, Saor.

He thrust his left hand into the open wound, visualizing the concentric glyph in his mind, rotating in an endless spiral, as his fingers squeezed around something warm and slimy. And he pulled.

I have brought you an offering, and I am asking for your assistance in the battle to come. If you grant me this, I will make certain you will never be forgotten.

The sight that followed was enough to make quite a few of the onlookers turn away, unable to watch the unnecessarily sadistic act, regardless of how justified it might have been. Somehar gasped. The howls were nearly inhuman, torn from the man's throat with such vigour that if he were to live to see the next day, it was certain that he would be unable to talk. In the back of his mind, Leith was aware that seeing someone innards spill to the ground in front of him should fill him with disgust, but in reality it was no different from gutting a sheep.

Yet not everyhar shared the sentiment. While some watched out of some sort of morbid curiosity, others lowered their eyes. For a couple of hara, revulsion overcame their reluctance to leave, and they slunk wordlessly back into the camp.

"Can you just end it!" somehar called.

Branwyn was holding one hand over his mouth, either to hide his shock, or in attempt to stop the bile rising up his throat. Calder wasn't joking around anymore either; his eyes seemed to be scanning the crowd for some guidelines that would help him figure out what the appropriate reaction was, so that he could mirror it.

Pleased with himself, Leith stepped away from his work, disregarding the few unfavourable reactions. They didn't understand yet, but they would soon. One day in the not so distant future, they would all learn of the Horned One, he thought as the prickling at the back of his neck alerted him to the shift in the atmosphere, because there was nothing worse for a deity than to be forgotten. They would understand what it was like to feel for a powerful entity so deeply that you wouldn't hesitate to sacrifice anything, no matter how cruel, to appease it; Just as they would understand what it was like to ask everything in return. And they would understand all that through him, because the deepest connection to Saor would always be his alone.

The dehar's attention was on him now; he could feel the familiar presence in the back of his mind, hear the scurrying of paws, batting of wings and thundering of hooves repeated in an eternal echo. He breathed in deeply, the scent of pinecones and leaves in decay was stronger than it had ever been. Gazing upward, arms outstretched in invitation, Leith watched the flocks of black birds in the cloudless sky circle lower and lower above the bloody spectacle. Unafraid, they began to descend upon the still living human, some taking perch on Leith's arms and shoulders to await their turn to feast on the offering. Attracted by the exposed and easy meal, a street dog that had ventured into the Kernetei camp from the outskirts of the town lingered nearby. It didn't dare to be so bold as to enter the ritual site but moved forward stealthily whenever it felt like nohar was looking.

As the night descended upon Alba Sulh and the screams turned to moans, then gasps and finally the silence of death, the tribe began to disperse in hopes of a few hours of sleep before storming the enclave. Even the phylarch had long left the scene, satisfied that the sacrifice had been well received by the dehar. Yet a single figure remained, looming over the insatiable crows aggressively quarrelling over a bloody organ. Oisín had not moved for hours, observing the carnage with unflinching eyes and a blank expression that revealed nothing of his feelings.

There was grace in this act, which some may have attributed to either defiance or devotion. But it was, in fact, a display of respect. He'd known that there was nothing he could have done to intervene or prevent this death; but he could at least inflict upon himself the penitence of staying until the bitter end. He stood vigil, and as the hours passed, he became aware of a strengthening fragrance in the air - the scent of pine trees, mossy ground, fresh berries, the first blooms of spring and fallen leaves decaying in autumn. These and other wild scents mingled in a heady mix which he knew was not quite normal, but he was at a loss to understand the source. The dog curled up at his feet and the last crow perched upon his shoulder, neither turning against the other out if inherent respect to the single deity that could tame predator and prey so they might lie down together.

In the darkest hour before sunrise, when even the dogs aren't sure they're supposed to be awake, the tribe stalked through the underground passage Keevan had discovered and cleared a path in the cellar of what had obviously once been an alehouse. According to Oisín's estimations, they were most likely underneath Jerusalem, an ancient building resting against Castle Rock, last used as a brothel frequented by the wealthiest inhabitants of the town to briefly waylay thoughts of the apocalypse. Now all that remained was a partial ruin that nobody was interested in rebuilding. The guards were changed every morning at six, which meant that those unlucky enough to have drawn the graveyard shift would be at their drowsiest, perhaps relaxing there attention somewhat as they anticipated the end of a long night; relieved to have passed another night without danger. All these factors played into the hands of the silent invaders.

And they had nature on their side. The first raindrop had fallen when Oisín finally retreated to the caves for two hours of restless sleep, and the rumbling of thunder accompanied them the entire way through the underground, echoing ominously in the caverns and corridors. As Keevan began to fumble with the lock of the metal door, it was storming heavily outside, lightning ripping the sky, accompanied by howling wind and the crash of thunder. Leith was certain that the abysmal weather must have been the work of the dehar himself. In such a tempest, even the early-risers were sure to stay at home, and the senses of the guards would be impaired.

The enclave encompassed only a small part of the city that had stood atop the caves - the historical centre and several neighbourhoods that seemed reasonably safe and not too desolate. The housing estates, suburbs and other outlying areas behind the gates had long succumbed to the ravages of time, leaving only corpses of buildings covered in vegetation. Despite that, the enclave was still too large to proceed house by house without a plan, and the humans too many. For one last time, Leith unwrapped the makeshift map drawn on the backside of an old band poster Calder had once held on to out of sentiment. Residential areas had been marked in black; guards represented by red circles. Only slightly removed from the very centre, an X marked the location of the Mayor's estate.

"Everyhar knows their focus area. Don't draw unnecessary attention to yourselves, make this a quick job. If someone wakes up and starts screaming, shut them up fast. Do your best to avoid the guards: They're my responsibility and I'll try to take care of them before they become an issue." Some leaders were happy to devise a plan and leave the execution to their tribe, comfortable in their certainty that they would live to see the next battle. Leith believed a good leader led by example, so as soon as Keevan had finished fumbling with the ancient lock, he was first through the door, darting through another storage room and up the crumbling steps into the alehouse. Having been looted and trashed a number of times, it was largely empty, its doors and windows barred with rotting wooden planks.

Leith regarded the hara pooling into the main room of the alehouse with a mixture of pride and reservation. He knew that a mis-step here could cost the lives of many, even risk the destruction of the tribe itself. All he had worked for; all his ambitions and dreams had led to this moment. Instead of fear, he felt certain that the dehar would stack the deck in his favour, winning him not just the enclave itself but more importantly the conviction of those hara he knew still doubted this strange new devotion in their leader. Deciding further speech was unnecessary, his feverish eyes locked with Keevan's. He gave an almost imperceptible nod. It was enough. Silently and efficiently, Keevan and his trusted lieutenant, Rodrick, slipped out the front door and disappeared into the shadows. On cue, the others filed out in small groups or couples, each with their own targets and strategy.

In reality, the plan was simple: Fan out through the streets and enter one house at a time. Where possible, kill adults first: A screaming child in the night was little cause for concern, but an adult could raise the alarm and eliminate the element of surprise. It was a game of chance, and everyhar realised that sooner or later, their cover would be blown. They entered the first house on the serpentine route that would eventually take them to the Mayor's residence. Like shadows within the shadows, the pair crept to the side of the house where a network of pipes revealed the location of the bathroom on each floor. Bathrooms were the best place to enter at this time of night, providing a relatively safe place from within the home to work out the best plan of attack.

Here the superior agility and strength awarded by inception provided a huge advantage. Keevan easily scurried up the pipes and prised the already ajar window open until he could slide in, lowering himself softly to the mosaic tiled floor between the sink and the bathtub. He signalled down to Rodrick who then quickly scrambled up and through to land gracefully beside him. They knew from previous raids that the main bathroom typically sat beside or opposite the master bedroom, with children's rooms allocated to smaller areas to the side and back of the house. Eyes wide and bodies flush with adrenalin, they communicated without words and then cricked the door open as quietly as possible. It took less than a moment to determine that in this house, the master bedroom stood opposite the bathroom.

Taking the lead, Keevan padded across the narrow hall and gently turned the knob on the simple wooden door of the main chamber. Their superior sight meant that no light was needed, so the opening of the door itself was not sufficient to rouse the two sleeping humans in the double bed at the centre of the room. He gave a tiny hand signal and moved to the other side of the bed where the male half sex was snoring. In perfect synchronicity, they covered the mouth of each human with one hand, at the same time jamming a blade up through the larynx and into the brain of their victims. Beyond a wet gurgling sound, there was nothing to signal anything out of the ordinary. Satisfied, they moved on to the children's bedrooms.

The same pattern repeated itself with only minor deviations for the rest of the first, second and third streets they ventured down. It was gruesome work, to be sure, but he and Rodrick had established an efficient, deadly rapport; a silent ballet of death spiralling ever closer to the main target. They had just turned the corner into the street where the Mayor's house stood. Unlike the quieter, darker residential streets they'd murdered through so far, this street was bathed by the harsh halogen glow of streetlights, an honour reserved only for the wealthiest citizens of the enclave. As they paused in the shadows to plan their assault, a piercing scream rang out from somewhere in the distance.

The moon cast an eerie glow on the streets as Leith followed Oisín along the walls, prowling and predatory, never letting him get more than a few steps ahead. Oisín was uniquely placed to aid in the quest of eliminating the guards, for he knew their exact positions, their routes, the seemingly insignificant habits that could easily become their downfall, such as a weak bladder or taking a smoke towards the end of one's shift. He wanted to trust his progeny, but had deliberately paired himself with Oisín, reasoning that in addition to his invaluable insight, he'd be given no chance to make the wrong decision. Agreement aside, there was no telling what he might or might not do when confronted with his past life, so close yet forever out of reach.

With every step, Leith's confidence grew. His senses were that of a hunter; the darkness and heavy clouds obstructing visibility didn't bother him at all. The unfamiliar smell of old sweat and urine soaked into wet brick and concrete stood in sharp contrast with the earthy scent of the forest, which both irritated and enticed him. Through the beat of rain against cobbles and tin roofs, he could hear the heavy tramp of combat boots, two pairs, far and faint, even before Oisín gestured for him to hide under an overhanging roof in the darkest corner of the alleyway. And something else was approaching along with them: a large beast with senses just as keen as his own, already aware of him.

Their minds collided, and it was easy as a kiss to make the dog submit. He could feel the dehar's power rushing through his veins, anointing him the leader of the Wild Hunt. Animals were his subjects, and free-growing vegetation an extension of his limbs. The guards were talking in low voices, petty complaints about the weather and small rations on their plate. The Great Dane they led on a leash ambled along, never alerting its masters to the lurking danger, its small mind subjugated into a feeling of calm routine. Crouched in the darkness, Leith awaited their arrival with throwing axe in hand.

The first death came swiftly, as soon as the guards turned the corner, the swoosh of the weapon completely inaudible in the relentless rain. It lodged itself in the man's forehead, and as he went down with a muffled cry, blindly reaching for the handle, the other man spun around only to find himself knocked down and pinned to the ground by his own animal. Perplexed by the sudden attack of a companion he'd personally trained, he made the fatal mistake of not shooting to kill. Instead, he attempted to shake off the dog, barking a command to come to heel. But it had already received a different order.

Kill.

Motionless, Oisín watched the animal sink its massive teeth in its master's flesh, tearing an agonising scream from the man. He would not contribute to this massacre physically, but that didn't make him any less responsible for it. The trade he had made doomed him to be a silent witness and forever bear this shame, but it had to be worth it. If all went to plan, his sister would have a chance at a future, although what kind of future awaited her with the tribe he didn't dare to guess. The three of them had arrived in the enclave with nothing and no one but themselves to ensure their survival. His elder brother died in the very caves where Daniel had been reborn as Oisín, a bitter irony not lost on the har. If becoming a monster was the only option, it was a trade he was willing to make.

Yet, as he watched the guard being torn into pieces, wondering how many times this revolting scene would replay itself on this night, a thought bloomed in his mind that was most decidedly not his own. It didn't feel intrusive or overwhelming, as his first sharing of breath had been; rather than that it was a subtle, polite request.

Tiahaar. Please, don't be afraid, I mean you no harm. I am Amalyth har Sulh, a hienama of the Phylarchy of Assanid. Try to act as normal as you can and listen to me.

He pressed his back into the wall, wishing he dissolve into it, and scanned the shadows for whoever had contacted him in this way, but found nothing. He knew from his teachings that the hara could communicate via mind touch, and his own tentative attempts had proven as much, but he had never believed it possible with a har that wasn't close enough to see.

Your tribe has unleashed something very powerful without having the most basic understanding of it. But this ancient force, this being cannot be used as means of personal revenge against an entire species.

Leith wasn't looking at him at all; the brutal murder had enticed him completely. Suddenly, it didn't even seem to bother him that it wasn't silent. Somewhere on the other end of town, another dog began to howl.

I know. A pause, shorter than a breath. *They are not my tribe. Please, wherever you are... make it stop.*

I can't make it stop. But you can! Only two hara have a strong enough connection with the entity to do so. And I could sense one of them is you.

But I don't know anything about...

Right now, the other is drawing on the being's raging protectiveness of the Earth's condition: Its disappointment with humankind, their selfishness evident in every piece of trash, every careless wildfire, every greedy deforestation, every spoiled water source, every animal harmed without need.

But it is not a cruel deity. Just like death, it brings life to the dawning spring, the feel of breath in your lungs. You have to offer more than he does. You have to offer balance. I am here to guide you through it. Others are performing a grissecon as we speak, to give you the energy you need. We are all here for you.

A strong pair of hands grabbed him by the shoulder, squeezing painfully. "Come on. Where next?" Apparently, Leith was done watching the murder he'd orchestrated, and was ready to be led to the next guard's slaughter. His eyes were like burning ice, besotted with carnage and consumed by madness. Oisín's own appeared blank, as they had been ever since the sacrifice. "I know a shortcut. Come on."

Whilst outside of the enclave, vegetation ran rampant, consuming most of the remaining human dwellings restoring its realm, it was pitifully scarce within town. The shortcut he'd taken ran beside a long, tall stone building, obviously an administrative centre of some kind, before opening onto a small residential street lined with terraces and low cottages. He instinctively turned left, retracing a route he'd taken countless times returning home after a gruelling day's work. There ahead, no more than 50 meters away, was the central heath. A small, elliptic green space, which served as a kind of communal garden to the houses that lined the circle, as well the houses in the streets that radiated out from five points.

At this hour of the morning, he knew that the old guard that patrolled the quarter where he'd lived with his siblings for so long would be resting his old bones on a bench in centre of a small copse of trees and shrubs at the heart of the green. Oisín motioned Leith to keep close behind him, ambling sideways under the awning of a shuttered inn at the junction of the street. Leith observed his most recent inception, a growing sense of pride that he was proving to be a worthy bearer of his blood.

Crouching down, the pair scurried across the narrow, cobble stoned lane that circled the heath, taking care to move between the feeble lights, widely spaced, which were all the wealth of this area warranted. From their vantage point behind a low shrub, the old guard could be seen, sitting watching the pale light of dawn creep into the sky to the east of the city.

One had held a cigarette, which he lazily drew to his lips. The other was stroking the head of the old Alsatian who'd been his companion these many years.

Leith felt the familiar tingling sensation as the smell of the air changed, somehow more earthy than before but definitely a sign the dehar was ready to witness this next sacrifice. He lunged forward, Oisín sluggishly lurching up to follow. Without breaking stride, he viciously wrenched control of the dog's lethargic mind, evoking a savage attack so swift, the guard died with his throat ripped out, the cigarette sputtering out on the damp ground where it had fallen from his limp hand.

Rage and disgust tore through Oisín's mind. This was no way to treat another being! His instinctive urge was to attack the monster who had done this. But the words of the Sulh were pulsing in his mind. He, too, had felt a tingling sensation as the dehar's presence filled the glade. Unlike Leith, Oisín experienced it as a focussing calmness, the scent of fresh rain in the spring. Raising his arms as he'd seen Leith do at the sacrifice, he lifted his arms. He felt the strength rush into him, a raw but directed energy. Unaware of how it was possible, he nonetheless knew that the vines and roots which now raced from the trees towards Leith were both guided and built upon his connection to the dehar, whose immense spirit now coursed through him. Perhaps inspired by his unwillingness to see yet more death, he knew that the foliage would restrain, but not kill, its target.

Hearing the rustling sounds of the god-driven vines now racing towards him, Leith whirled around, his fascination with the slackening pulse of blood from the guard's rent throat sharply halted. Seeing the vines, he was momentarily dumbfounded. Scanning left and right in disbelief, his eyes locked on Oisín's. Immediately he recognised the haunted, detached gaze. With a howl of rage, he drew his dagger and darted towards Oisín, the fury and humiliation of betrayal, both by his god and by Oisín, lending him an almost supernatural speed.

Locked in a spell he could barely comprehend, let alone control, Oisín could only watch hopelessly as his creator advanced. Time slowed to a trickle, his vision tunnelling on the flashing blade and manic eyes almost upon him. He only had time for the thought *I have failed* to flash through his mind before there was a loud bang, and he sank to the ground.

A girl stood among the trees, perhaps fourteen or fifteen years old, though she appeared younger than her age, clad in nothing but rain-soaked pyjamas with a picture of a cartoon mouse digging into a bowl of cereal. In her hands, an old handgun that she couldn't seem to let go of was trembling as much as her lower lip. Her voice so tiny it could have just as well belonged to that mouse. "Danny...?"

Like in a dream, she crossed the small distance that separated her from Oisín, whose attention was split between her and Leith's motionless body on the ground. He was lying on his stomach, face buried in the grass, and Oisín couldn't be sure whether he was alive or not. He felt that the deity was calm now, appeased either by his own proposal, or this final death. The har turned away from the leader he had never asked for and slowly reached out to take his sister in his arms.

The sky turned indigo blue and the clouds began to clear, but Leith didn't see the birth of the new day. He didn't witness the gates open to let in a group in hara clad in colourful, hand-made robes, who spread through the enclave to help, heal and reconcile the survivors, whether har or human. He couldn't appreciate the restful silence that descended upon the city when the dogs stopped howling and the birds huddled in their nests under the eaves. And he couldn't hear Amalyth har Sulh speak, as he approached Oisín and placed a hand on his shoulder. "You did so well. Now why don't we go and take your sister home?"

All he saw was a temple, surrounded by a lush forest, more beautiful than he had ever seen. A trail wove through the woods, left by beasts of all sizes, a path worn into the earth by countless paws and hooves seeking a sanctuary where they would all be safe. He felt betrayal, and rage, but those feelings diminished the longer he walked the path towards where he would find Saor, as magnificent as he always had been, seated upon a throne of evergreen trees. And as he approached the dehar, there was nothing in his mind but a single question. "Then... this is not the end?"

As loving as he was cruel, the dehar smiled down upon him.

Nothing ever ends. Everything. Goes. On.

Mengk

Amanda Kear

Every time I re-read The Bewitchments of Love & Hate I am intrigued by the character of Mengk. He's a bit part-player, a spear-carrier appearing in the scenes leading up to the final fate of Terzian, war-leader of the Varr Tribe. There is obviously something intense going on there yet it does not and could not ever rival Terzian's 'true' relationships with his lifelong consort, Cobweb, or with Cal. A few such musings, and the plot bunnies began to breed!

Lord Terzian was dead.

Mengk sat on the bare, scorched earth where the pyre had been. The smell of charcoal was in the air; nothing else remained of his Lord. The fire had been encouraged to burn fiercely – hotter than any wood fire had a right to burn – and no fragments remained. No hunks of charred wood, no cremated bone, not even the metal of a ring or belt buckle. There had been ash of course; the flaking residue of flesh and bone indistinguishable from that of timber or clothing. Yet now that too was gone. Cobweb had taken the scant handfuls left from the fire's hunger, powdered them in his hands and thrown them one by one into the wind. All that was Terzian erased from existence by the breeze.

His Lord's family had ordered the huge pyre to be constructed in the farmland out beyond Galhea. Mengk had thought at first this choice of location might be to permit all the hara of the town to attend the funeral, but such was not the case. The mourners were few: Terzian's blood relatives, his consort, a few house hara and some high-ranking soldiers who had remained with the garrison at Galhea.

Of course, there was that one Gelaming there too – he might call himself Seel har Griselming, but he was of the Gelaming mould and mindset. So a Gelaming was permitted to be present, yet of the ordinary hara whom Terzian had ruled, and the rank and file of the army that he had commanded, there were none.

No, the location of the pyre had not been chosen to celebrate Terzian's life, but because the place was isolated and undistinguished. There was to be no memorial to his Lord. No gravestone, no statue, no plaque. Terzian was to be quietly forgotten. The Gelaming had no doubt insisted upon it.

That seemed to be their style; to edit the universe and the hara in it until they conformed to the Gelaming ideal of perfection. Terzian's name would undoubtedly be erased from history as smoothly as those of the myriad human rulers and warriors that Wraeththu had already forgotten.

Mengk would never forget. His grief was raw and sharp and burned as hot as the flames of the pyre. Every day he would remember Terzian's name.

"Fuck you!"

The Wraeththu dragged him spitting and snarling from the battlefield and threw him on the ground in front of the sleek, golden haired creature who was their leader. The young soldier struggled to his knees, hampered by the cord that bound his wrists behind his back. Other survivors knelt or lay around him, shell-shocked by their sudden reversal of fortunes.

His unit had been sent to relieve a town that was under siege by a Wraeththu gang. The 'gang' had turned out to be an army, and the 'siege' had turned out to be a trap. Wraeththu had need of guns, ammunition and young men to incept. His unit commander had inadvertently supplied them with all three.

"Is this the last of them?" the creature asked.

"Yes, Tiahaar Terzian. Unless Ithiel catches any of those that fled the battle."

"I don't want the ones who fled, I want the ones who stood and fought. We need more warriors. Slaves and consorts I can find anywhere."

"These ones barely count as warriors, Tiahaar. They're all new conscripts, with only the most meagre training."

"Hmm." The golden haired creature stepped closer and jerked the young soldier to his feet to inspect him, as if he was livestock for sale.

Shame and rage filled the soldier at the Wraeththu's touch. "Go fuck yourself, freak!"

He spat at the creature and received a backhand that laid him out on the ground, senses reeling from the blow. Other Wraeththu stepped forward to continue the retaliation, but this Terzian waved them back, seemingly amused by his display of defiant rage.

"Oh, this one will do. This one will definitely do."

Within days the soldier found himself with a new name and a new body. He never looked back.

Warriors were ouana. Warriors espoused the masculine virtues of virility, strength and valour. Warriors trained in all forms of combat, from the direct confrontation of a knife fight or cavalry charge, to the guile and strength of a sniper in the hills or an assassin in the enemy's camp. Warrior and ouana was the benchmark by which all else was measured. Those who failed to meet expectations were relegated to the lower status of soume-aspected hara: to be consorts or kanene; to labour in the fields or to work in the houses of the great and the good. To serve the warriors in every way.

Terzian's soldiers had all been born male. It was easy for Mengk and the others to slide back into male aspects, male expectations. Female warriors had been few and far between in the cultural context of their previous lives. Now, as they constructed a new culture, it took little persuasion from Terzian, Ponclast and the other leaders that warriors should be ouana in look, word and deed.

For those who didn't want to kill – who didn't glory in battle or accept the discipline and hardship of a soldier's life – then the alternative was to become feminine. The protected, not the protectors; the soft, the beautiful, the pampered. Human concepts were adapted to Varrish needs: the faithful army wife who waited at home while her husband went off to war; the diligent housekeeper; the tart with a heart of gold.

Lord Terzian did not permit camp-followers on campaign. Ouana-warriors all, from the loftiest general to the lowliest supply clerk. Terzian wanted neither the tactical inconvenience of a rabble of untrained civilians over which he only had tenuous command, nor the ill-discipline of soldiers whose comradeship might be split by squabbles over some kanene.

Of course – soldiers being soldiers and hara being hara – aruna was not far from anyhar's mind. On the campaign trail, hara did what came naturally and took aruna with each other. It was acknowledged, even expected.

Yet warriors must be ouana. Warriors should resist submitting to the soume aspect of their nature, lest they be relegated to the status of consort or kanene. Unspoken rules emerged. Lesser ranks were supposed to submit to those greater in rank – become soume to their ouana – but not too swiftly. Shifting too readily into a soume role would be undignified for a warrior. You had to bare your teeth and snarl – a lioness submitting to a lion – not succumb with kittenish softness.

Where two warriors were equal in rank or status, aruna could become a battle, each striving to force the other to become soume. Mengk had revelled in aruna where both remained ouana; he and a partner poised on a knife-edge of willpower that prevented one or the other slipping into soume.

In Gebaddon…

In Gebaddon there was no respite from the need to be ouana. No home coming. No consorts awaiting them, no kanene to soothe their needs away, no conquered hara to submit to their new overlords.

The first time Terzian had taken him, Mengk was selected almost at random. He was one of a dozen scouts, sent out to try and make sense of the twisting, haunted forest that the Varr army had stumbled into. The forest laughed at their attempts. Scouts walked south and found themselves emerging from the trees to the east or north of the army. They battled for days through impenetrable vegetation yet returned to find that only minutes or hours had passed for their companions. Some were found near catatonic with fear or raving about the horrors they had seen. Most never returned at all.

Mengk had gasped out his report to Terzian and the generals, telling of how he had fallen asleep in a frosty pine forest and awoken in a humid jungle. Of using the stars to navigate when his compass crumbled to dust in his hands, but somehow passing the same clearing filled with bones again and again and again. He did not speak of how the skulls turned to watch him as he passed by, nor of the carrion birds calling out the names of all the hara whom he had killed in his time as a warrior.

The other scouts gave similar reports, and they were dismissed. Mengk was filing out of the tent with the others when Terzian seized him by the shoulder and curtly ordered him to remain. He stood patiently while his Lord debated with his generals what he had heard. When they too had left, Lord Terzian all but threw Mengk to the floor, his steely eyes filled with rage and lust.

Mengk fought back, as a Varr warrior was supposed to, but nevertheless ready to submit to his leader after a token effort. However, Terzian's growl of frustration as Mengk's ouana-lim began to withdraw made him pause. He hurriedly summoned the willpower required to shift back to ouana, thinking Terzian wished them both to hover together on that precipice of masculine desire.

It soon became clear Terzian wanted not an ouana partner, but a prolonged battle; a battle Terzian could win. The enemy was denied him, all his tactics and strategy in war useless in this cursed forest. What his Lord needed from Mengk was a victory – a hard won, bitterly fought engagement in which he could be triumphant in defiance of all that the Gelaming forest threw at them.

It was not exactly pleasure, this aruna-as-warfare. Nevertheless it was what his Lord required, and Mengk saw it as his duty to provide. Every day – if time could be measured in days in that accursed place – Terzian demanded his presence. He would dutifully obey the summons, and then transform into the fierce opponent his Lord needed to conquer.

The forest knew what they were doing and threw it back at them. Mengk would find himself in a waking dream, reliving the moment when Terzian first grasped his shoulder and ordered him to stay. Only it would not be Terzian, but a demonic parody of him, with claws and fangs. Or he would turn to find his shoulder seized not by fingers, but torn by the razor-sharp thorns of some shrub, or lacerated by shards of broken glass from a ruined building. If Terzian wondered at the scars that now marred Mengk's flesh, he never mentioned them.

The army dwindled around them. With every passing hour hara would become separated from the main force and vanish. Sometimes you could hear their screams, yet when warriors ran to the place from which the sounds emanated, there was never anyhar there.

"Curse you Gelaming cowards! Fight us!" Mengk slashed at a curtain of hanging moss that clutched and tangled in their hair, as he and Terzian tried to push through it.

"Save your breath," his Lord snapped. "Do not give them the satisfaction of…"

Mengk turned to see what caused Terzian to halt his words.

His Lord was nowhere in sight. He was alone, no sign Terzian or any other had ever been there.

"Lord Terzian?" The words were soft, disbelieving. Mengk whipped his head from side to side, turning on the spot, frantically searching for his leader.

"Lord Terzian!" He screamed out the name, running in panic through the trees, searching, searching.

He found himself once more in the clearing of bones. The skulls looked at him with pity in their empty sockets. Mengk sank to his knees and wailed his grief and despair.

Thiede plucked them out of the forest as easily as he had lured them into it. Mengk awoke to find himself on the other side of the world, in a place filled with bright sunshine and the scent of the sea. At first, he could not recall who he was or how to communicate beyond wordless cries of distress. He was surrounded by Gelaming warriors who looked at him with pity and disdain.

There were many other Varrs there, gaunt and hollow-eyed creatures who stared vacantly at nothing or flinched from shadows. He was given a hunk of bread, but for a long while could not comprehend what it was – that something as mundane and harmless as this bread actually existed. It did not occur to him to eat it until one of the Gelaming reminded him such was bread's purpose.

On the fourth day he went in search of his Lord, wandering to and fro amongst the shattered remains of the Varr army, pausing to stare at anyhar with bright blond hair in the hope it might be Terzian. On the seventh day he found his voice and began to ask anyhar who would listen where their leader might be.

"Thiede has him." It came as a whisper, passed from har to har, as if uttering the words might draw Thiede's attention to those who spoke them.

It took several days of shivering through nightmares for Mengk to gather his wits enough to speak to one of the Gelaming guards. "My Lord Terzian... I serve him... he will want... will need..." He could not explain what Terzian might need him for, since giving support and succour to his Lord was likely forbidden, and could only repeat "I serve him" over and over again.

Each time he asked, the Gelaming gave him pitying smiles and gently pushed him back to where the other Varrs sat, listless in the sun. One must have reported his words, however, since eventually a Gelaming officer came to look him over. From the questions this har asked, he realised the Gelaming had mistaken him for an aide-de-camp, rather than an aruna partner. Mengk did not correct them.

His mumbled replies to the questions must have been the correct ones, for the officer came back some days later and escorted him to Terzian's side. He wept when he saw what they had done to his Lord: skeletally thin, the steely eyes dull, his vitality and purpose leached from him. He knew without being told that his beloved Lord was dying.

Mengk's own function in life became to care for Terzian. The Gelaming treated his leader like an invalid, like a helpless harling. Mengk threw himself into the role of servant rather than nursemaid. If Terzian uttered a word, he sprang to obey. He performed no task without his Lord's permission; giving his Terzian back command, even if it was of just one har. A tiny defiance in the face of what Thiede and the Gelaming had done.

They crossed the ocean in the blink of an eye, travelling on magical rafts – another way for the Gelaming to flaunt their power and the Varrs' helplessness. Galhea emerged from the mists and they drifted towards Terzian's house.

Towards Terzian's family.

Terzian's firstborn and the house hara did not want Mengk there; denied his right to be at his Lord's side. They viewed him as an interloper or a distasteful reminder of Terzian's defeat. Though he struggled and threatened and cursed, Mengk was too weak to fight any of them except the human woman who ran the kitchens. He was a warrior with no strength.

"What's going on?" The har who interrupted his struggle was a dark beauty who caused Mengk to freeze like a deer at the scent of a predator. Cobweb the Sulh. Cobweb the witch. His Lord's consort. Elegance and splendour that only served to highlight Mengk's own weakness and wretched state.

"What is it you want exactly?" Cobweb asked. Words froze in Mengk's throat. This beauty could banish him from his Lord's side with a mere gesture.

"Well?" Cobweb looked at Terzian's firstborn, but that har was silent too. Mengk dared to hope it meant they knew that he was in the right – that his Lord *needed* him.

The human woman spoke up. She still gripped his arm, trying to pull him back into the servants' areas of the house. "This har travelled back to Galhea with Terzian. Now he is concerned for Terzian's welfare. Swift was trying to explain that Terzian is comfortable... and..."

Mengk freed himself from the human's grasp, self-consciously straightening his posture under Cobweb gaze.

"I must see my Lord," he said, fighting to keep the desperation out of his tone. "I have cared for him a long time. Only I know what he needs at this time." He held back from explaining more, not wanting to shame his Lord in front of a servant or his Heir.

Cobweb raised his eyebrows at his statement. Mengk dared to meet his gaze, hoping all he had heard of Sulh perceptiveness was true.

"You are probably right."

Relief flashed through him at Cobweb's words, so overwhelming that he missed the instructions which were passed to Terzian's firstborn.

Mengk was under no illusion Cobweb truly wanted him there,

but there had been in that instant of shared gazes an unspoken pact: Terzian's needs took precedence over their own. They both knew with icy certainty that Cobweb would not have to tolerate Mengk's presence for long.

Mengk had been neither invited to nor excluded from the funeral.

He drifted out to the fields in the wake of the house-hara, then stood on his own, separate and distant from the servants and family alike. He watched numbly as Cobweb scattered the ashes and realisation struck that glorious, golden Lord Terzian was to be erased from memory.

When the party headed back towards *Forever* he began to follow, then fell further and further behind. The death of his Lord had left him without purpose or function. What point returning to Terzian's house when his leader was no longer there to command him? Mengk drifted back to the site of the pyre.

There was a portion of the blackened earth where the heat had fused the soil into glass. Mengk clawed at it, prising up a fragment. It sliced his fingers, red beads welling up and spilling onto the charred ground. He touched his lips to the smoky glass, tasting ash and soil and blood.

He had been Mengk har Varr. He would not – could not – be Mengk har Parasiel.

He turned his back on the scorched and blackened ground and began to walk. Blood continued to drip from his hand where he clutched the small piece of glass that was all that remained of Lord Terzian.

The Self Second

Ben Fouracre

He keeps them in a box by the riverside
Takes them out when he gets lonely
These are my precious things
No one can take then away from me

Take them out when it all gets dark
Hooked on the lights

Imagine me in a crowd
What would I say to turn your head around?
I'm still learning how
Faking it so good

Take it out when it all goes quiet
Hooked on the lights

First they tie your legs
Then they pull you under
Deep blue water

If I could hold on
I could drag you under
Deep blue water

Glossary of Terms

Aghama – the first of all Wraeththu, regarded as a dehar.

Almagabra – lands corresponding roughly to what was once Mediterranean Europe.

Althaia – a time after inception during which a human transforms into a har.

Aruna – sexual union between hara that is both spiritual and physical.

Arunic – pertaining to aruna.

Chesna – (chez-nah) a close physical, emotional and spiritual relationship.

Chesnari – a partner in a chesna-bond.

Dehar – a Wraeththu deity (pl. Dehara).

Fallsend – a city in northern Thaine known for musendas and Garridan

Ferelithia – a tourist town near Immanion. (*Ferelith*: the tribe that occupies it.)

Ferike – a tribe of Jaddayoth.

Feybraiha – a period of time equating to puberty in humans when a har matures sexually. The term also refers to a day of celebration for this. At the end of his feybraiha, when he is physically ready, a har will take aruna with another for the first time. This is regarded as an important rite of passage.

First Generation – hara who became Wraeththu by being incepted as humans.

Fulminir – a fortress of the Varrs in Megalithica, often held in dread.

Garridan – a tribe of Jaddayoth, renowned for their expertise with poisons.

Gebaddon – a forest of unnatural growths transformed into a prison by the Gelaming, where the remains of the Varrs were imprisoned after the Fall of Fulminir.

Gelaming – the most influential tribe of Wraeththu, whose tribal home is Almagabra.

Girdle of Tiamat – what was formerly the Atlantic Ocean.

Grissecon – a sex magic ritual.

Har – a Wraeththu individual (pl. hara).

Harling – a young har not yet at feybraiha.

Hienama – equivalent of a priest/teacher/healer.

Hostling – the harish equivalent of a mother, a har who hosts and carries the egg, or pearl, in which harlings grow.

Immanion – principle city of Almagabra, founded by the Gelaming tribe, regarded as a centre of culture and learning.

Inception – the process by which a human becomes har, involving a transfusion of blood.

Jaddayoth – a country corresponding roughly to what was formerly northeast Europe and parts of Asia.

Kalamah – a tribe of Jaddayoth.

Kanene – hara more than usually adept in the arts of aruna, especially of a darker nature, who sell their services to other hara. Kanene are regarded with contempt by the majority of hara, since aruna is viewed as a sacred act, and the practices of kanene as profane or sacrilegious.

Lachrymide a- presiding dehar of the Shadetide festival.

Majhahn – a magical ritual.

Megalithica – the landmass once known as North America.

Mind touch – a method of psychic communication between hara.

Musenda – an establishment where hara can buy unusual forms of aruna.

Natalia – harish festival of the Winter Solstice.

Nayati – a temple or sacred space for spiritual work

Otherlanes – the etheric pathways between realities that can be travelled using *sedim*.

Ouana – the masculine aspect of Wraeththu

Pearl – the egg or sac within which a harling forms. Hara carry pearls within their bodies, which are expelled or 'born' some weeks before the harling reaches to state to emerge. *Pearl* is also a term of affection used by harish parents for their offspring. (*With pearl* – a har who is carrying a pearl.)

Pelki – Wraeththu term for rape, or else aruna taken with a har without their permission.

Phylarch – leader of a phyle

Phyle – a distinct community within a tribe, a subtribe

Ponclast – former leader of the Varrs, which gave to the derogatory term 'ponclastic', denoting an overbearing, tyrannical personality.

Prosperiel – presiding dehar of the Smoketide festival.

Pureborn – a har who has been born to harish parents rather than inception from human. A second-generation har and beyond.

Nahir Nuri – a har of high spiritual rank, who has undergone all caste training.

Samuntala – Thiede's personal etheric realm.

Sedu – an otherworldly creature used as transport by Wraeththu in the Otherlanes, plural *sedim*.

Shadetide – a harish festival celebrated at the former Halloween.

Share Breath – similar to a kiss, this is a deeper mark of affection that allows the transfer of information between hara in a quick, deep and easy manner.

Smoketide – a harish festival celebrated at the Autumn equinox.

Soume – the feminine aspect of Wraeththu

Thiede – influential har who founded the Gelaming tribe.

Tiahaar – a polite form of address (as in Sir, Madam)

Uigenna -the proto-tribe of Wraeththu.

Unneah – a Wraeththu tribe of Megalithica.

Varrs – a Wraeththu tribe of Megalithica that controlled a large portion of the country – oppressively – until they were vanquished by the Gelaming.

Wraeththu – (ray-thoo) androgynous race that came to replace humanity.

About the Contributors

Storm Constantine has written stories since she was a small child and first went to school. Before that, she made them up in her head. Her first novel – the initial Wraeththu book, *The Enchantments of Flesh and Spirit* – was published in 1987, and has been followed by over 30 other books, both fiction and non-fiction, as well as nearly a 100 short stories. In 2003, she founded Immanion Press, in order to bring her back-catalogue novels (and those of writing friends) back into print, but it has since grown and thrived to publish new works, and – enjoying the freedom of publishing her work through her own company – Storm now releases her work exclusively through Immanion Press, although the first two Wraeththu trilogies, and her epic fantasy *The Magravandias Chronicles* remain in print through TOR in the United States. She's currently working on a new novel and more non-fiction titles in an esoteric vein. Storm lives in the Midlands of England with her husband and four cats.

Wendy Darling is based in Atlanta, Georgia, USA, and is co-author of *Breeding Discontent*, published by Immanion Press in 2003 as the first Wraeththu Mythos novel. She has been involved with Wraeththu in many different capacities, including editing various Wraeththu novels, maintaining the Inception and Forever Wraeththu fan web sites, and staffing several Wraeththu conventions. With Storm she also co-edits the Wraeththu Mythos story collections. Her full-time job is as a digital projects manager at Emory  University, but she engages in many side projects and hobbies, including photography, historic preservation, and fan fiction. She has also forged relationships with Wraeththu fans around the world and has been fortunate to meet several authors whose work is included in this collection. At home she is ruled by three cats, cats she did not have in her life until she met and visited with Storm, who as usual had a strong influence on her. Wendy enjoys international travel and tries to visit Storm and her husband Jim as often as she can. Connect with Wendy online at about.me/wdarling.

Martina Bellovičová is a professional translator, copywriter and language teacher, who resides in Brno, Czech Republic. Her first published short story, "A Piece of Meat", appeared in the fantasy collection "Rytiny". Since then, she published several fantasy/science-fiction stories in both Czech and English, one of which has been adapted for a comic, and is currently working on a steampunk novel. Next to fiction, she enjoys writing lyrics for a variety of bands. Prior to focusing more on writing, Martina devoted years of her life to theatre, music and dance, and some of these passions remained with her. A jack of all trades, she is the lead singer of the steampunk band Clockwork Animals, spins CDs at subculture parties under the pseudonym DJ Zlyhad and dances Irish and tribal styles. She considers herself a lifestyle goth/steampunk and does her best to revive the dying community in her country by organising a number of alternative events, most notably the regular goth party Clubbers Die Younger and the gothic belly dance festival Danse Macabre. Refusing to become a crazy cat lady, she decided to get a small collection of snakes instead.

Nerine Dorman is a South African author and editor of science fiction and fantasy currently living in Cape Town. Her novel *Sing Down the Stars* won Gold for the Sanlam Prize for Youth Literature in 2019, and her YA fantasy novel *Dragon Forged* was a finalist in 2017. Her short story "On the Other Side of the Sea" (Omenana, 2017) was shortlisted for a 2018 Nommo award, and her novella *The Firebird* won a Nommo for "Best Novella" during 2019. She is the curator of the South African Horrorfest Bloody Parchment event and short story competition and is a founding member of the SFF authors' co-operative Skolion, that  has assisted authors such as Masha du Toit, Suzanne van Rooyen, Cristy Zinn and Cat Hellisen, among others, in their publishing endeavours. Do follow Nerine on Twitter at nerinedorman

Ben Fouracre is a British lyricist and poet who started writing from a young age but found direction within the alternative music scene of the 1990s. Initially heavily influenced by Gothic rock culture, Ben experiments with words and musical styles, having been the singer, songwriter and guitarist in a number of bands, with styles ranging from Goth, Punk and Hardcore, to being founder and songwriter for post-rock group, Gauge. It was during this period he began to use language as an

instrument to convey feelings of disconnection and isolation, chaos and loss, often spoken in whispers or shouted in pain against a dynamic background of intricate and delicate guitars and heavy distortion. Gauge's main body of work was realised in *The Gatehouse* which was issued in 2002. With a deep affinity for Japan and Japanese culture Ben then moved to Tokyo and has been based there since. Still fascinated by the complexity of language he continues to write and produce work exploring themes of nostalgia, memory, beauty and violence.

Amanda Kear hails from a small town in the north-east of Scotland, where the bookshops all shut down long before the internet was even a twinkle in the universe's eye. Fortunately there were fellow small-town geeks to help preserve sanity by introducing them to the concepts of fanfic, fanzines and tabletop roleplaying games. They fled to Aberdeen University to study Zoology, then to Bristol University to spend three years watching deceased sea creatures rot, or — when the experiments went right — turn into fossils. Strangely, this expertise with decaying squid and rotting ragworms turned out not to have long term career prospects! Instead they worked for 23 years at the BBC Natural History Unit on series such as *The Natural History of an Alien*, *Predators, Fossil Detectives, Deadly 360, Andy's Dinosaur Adventures* (time travel for the under 5s) and *Nature's Weirdest Events*, and was part of a website project which won a BAFTA. Finally they ran away from telly to join the circus, but the jobcentre must have misheard, as they are now a civil servant. Their first published fiction was a short story in the *Para Animalia: Creatures of Wraeththu* anthology. Usually to be found messing about with fanfic, running RPGs, self-publishing RPG scenarios or hanging around with fellow geeks at science fiction conventions and gaming conventions.

Fiona Lane was born and brought up near Glasgow during the Time of The Flared Trouser and Unfeasibly High Platform Shoes. By the time we all came to our senses, she had relocated to Aberdeen, and spent several years waiting for a number six bus, in a horrible collision involving the nature of time and the Aberdeen weather. During the eighties, while she was waiting for the Internet to be invented, she acquired a husband and a couple of replacement units, and they all now live in a field full of sheep in Aberdeenshire, along with the odd cat or two and Fiona's posse of obsolete computers, many of which she has single-handedly restored to a completely non-functioning condition. She once kept chickens, but they were messy, and she couldn't use them to buy vintage shoes from eBay. The eggs were good though. She likes gin and hats and dislikes the oppression of the proletariat. Her hobbies include cooking, gardening, and staring into the abyss.

Maria J. Leel is now enjoying early retirement after a varied career, which included everything from Urban Ecologist, Braille Transcriber, First Aid Trainer and Reflexologist. She lives in Shropshire with her husband, Malcolm, three cats and a varying number of chickens. They are turning their large garden into a permaculture paradise, complete with veggie beds and a food forest. Maria has travelled widely volunteering on many projects such as the California Condor Recovery Program, the Australian railway Puffing Billy and the Fiji Pine reforestation scheme. For a time she lived on a Kibbutz near Jerusalem, and as a result has an abiding interest in alternative living styles and communal living. She has been writing plays and stories almost all her life and has contributed to several Wraeththu Mythos projects including her first novel 'Song of the Sulh'. She is now working on her second entitled *Last Ride to Lyonis*.

Daniela Ritter

Daniela was born in the little German town of
Salzgitter on a Leap Year February 29th. People once
wondered if she had a face at all because since she
had learned how to read, it was always covered by a
book. When the internet became wide-spread, she
started writing fan-fiction. She was fascinated by
the idea to re-enter her favourite fantasy worlds in
that way, being more than a spectator. Her
contribution to the Wraeththu Mythos short story
collection *Para Genesis* was her first published story
ever. Daniela plays the violin and loves singing and
karaoke. Her very vivid (and sometimes weird)
fantasy roams freely in pen & paper roleplaying

sessions and online in World of Warcraft. Daniela took her first steps on the
spiritual path as a Reiki practitioner, and has since found a home in Dehara
Magic, about which she is passionate. Supported by a loving husband, she now
lives in Hamburg, where they are building their private paradise for their son
and daughter.

Ruby is the official artist for the Wraeththu Mythos,
who creates all the covers for the Immanion Press
editions. She started drawing from her imagination long
before she could or indeed would talk. Still heavily
influenced by the fairy tales and myths absorbed from
her childhood, Ruby has grown into a multimedia
illustrator interested in exploring the darkly sensual,
symbolic and surreal undercurrents of life. Ruby's
illustrations blend perfectly the mythological, the
classical and the future fantastic and are also evocative of
Beardsley and Mucha. She is now a much sought-after
cover artist and interior illustrator for books across
many genres, and is the creator of the ongoing
Wraeththu Tarot project. Ruby is up for designing
anything as long as it fits in with her bohemian
aesthetic and animal-loving ethos (her dream is to run a combined cat sanctuary
and art gallery by the sea). On any one day she might be fleshing out a tattoo
design and then the next sketching concept art for a theatre set or perhaps
sourcing unusual props for a photo-shoot.

E. S. Wynn is the author of over seventy books in print and is the chief editor of Thunderune Publishing. In his spare time, he spins stories, builds board games, stitches together battle jackets, runs a pair of magazines and encourages people to create new art constantly. He's openly transgender and does what he can to pursue acceptance and love for and within the trans community. During the last decade, he's worked with hundreds of authors and edited thousands of manuscripts for nearly a dozen different magazines. His stories and articles have been published in dozens of journals, e-zines and anthologies. He's taught classes in literature, marketing, math, spirituality, energetic healing and guided meditation. He's also worked as a voice-over artist for several different horror and sci-fi podcasts, albums and eBooks. E.S. Wynn has written a Wraeththu Mythos trilogy, entitled *The Gold Country Series*, available through Immanion Press.

Books by Storm Constantine

The Wraeththu Chronicles
The Enchantments of Flesh and Spirit
The Bewitchments of Love and Hate
The Fulfilments of Fate and Desire
The Wraeththu Chronicles (omnibus of trilogy)

The Wraeththu Histories
The Wraiths of Will and Pleasure
The Shades of Time and Memory
The Ghosts of Blood and Innocence

The Alba Sulh Sequence (Wraeththu Mythos)
The Hienama
Student of Kyme
The Moonshawl

Other Wraeththu Books
Blood, The Phoenix and a Rose (triptych of novellas)
A Raven Bound with Lilies (short stories)

The Artemis Cycle
The Monstrous Regiment
Aleph

The Grigori Books
Stalking Tender Prey
Scenting Hallowed Blood
Stealing Sacred Fire

The Magravandias Chronicles:
Sea Dragon Heir
Crown of Silence
The Way of Light

Hermetech
Burying the Shadow
Sign for the Sacred
*Calenture
Thin Air
*Silverheart (with Michael Moorcock)

Short Story Collections:
The Thorn Boy and Other Dreams of Dark Desire
Mythangelus
Mythophidia
Mytholumina
Mythanimus
Mythumbra (forthcoming 2018)
*Splinters of Truth (NewCon Press)

Wraeththu Mythos Collections
(co-edited with Wendy Darling, including stories by the editors and other writers)
Paragenesis
Para Imminence
Para Kindred
Para Animalia
Para Spectral

Songs to Earth and Sky
(Stories of the Seasons, including a novella, a novelette and a short story by Storm Constantine, and six other stories by Mythos writers)

Non-Fiction
Sekhem Heka
Grimoire Dehara: Kaimana
Grimoire Dehara: Ulani (with Taylor Ellwood)
Grimoire Dehara: Nahir Nuri (with Taylor Ellwood)
*The Inward Revolution (with Deborah Benstead)
*Egyptian Birth Signs (with Graham Phillips)
*Bast and Sekhmet: Eyes of Ra (with Eloise Coquio)
Whatnots and Curios (essays and reviews)

(All titles available through Immanion Press, except for those marked with *)

IMMANION PRESS

Purveyors of Speculative Fiction

A Wolf at the Door by Tanith Lee

Includes 13 tales, most of which appeared only in magazines or rare anthologies. 'A wolf at the door' implies hidden threat – until the door is open, we don't really know what's out there. And now the beast is upon you, scratching at the wood, its hot breath steaming on the step. Will you survive the encounter? Perhaps, once the door is opened, what you might have thought to be a threat turns out to be something else entirely. But of course, it can also be a werewolf...
ISBN 978-1-912815-04-3, £11.99, $15.99 pbk

Breathe, My Shadow by Storm Constantine

A standalone Wraeththu Mythos novel. Seladris believes he carries a curse making him a danger to any who know him. Now a new job brings him to Ferelithia, the town known as the Pearl of Almagabra. But Ferelithia conceals a dark past, which is leaking into the present. In the strange old house, Inglefey, Seladris tries to deal with hauntings of his own and his new environment, until fate leads him to the cottage on the shore where the shaman Meladriel works his magic. Has Seladris been drawn to Ferelithia to help Meladriel repel a malevolent present or is he simply part of the evil that now threatens the town?
ISBN: 978-1-912815-06-7 £13.99, $17.99 pbk

The Lord of the Looking Glass by Fiona McGavin

The author has an extraordinary talent for taking genre tropes and turning them around into something completely new, playing deftly with topsy-turvy relationships between supernatural creatures and people of the real world. 'Post Garden Centre Blues' reveals an unusual relationship between taker and taken in a twist of the changeling myth. 'A Tale from the End of the World' takes the reader into her developing mythos of a post-apocalyptic world, which is bizarre, Gothic and steampunk all at once. Following in the tradition of exemplary short story writers like Tanith Lee and Liz Williams, Fiona has a vivid style of writing that brings intriguing new visions to fantasy, horror and science fiction. ISBN: 978-1-907737-99-2, £11.99, $17.50 pbk

All these and more on our web site
Immanion Press
www.immanion-press.com
info@immanion-press.com

Wraeththu Mythos Novels

Breeding Discontent by Wendy Darling & Bridgette Parker
Terzah's Sons by Victoria Copus
Song of the Sulh by Maria J. Leel
Scatterstones: A Tale of the Gimrah Tribe by Fiona Lane
Whispers of the World That Was by E. S. Wynn
Echoes of Light and Static by E. S. Wynn
Voices of the Silicon Beyond by E. S. Wynn

Further details of Wraeththu Mythos and other fiction
can be found on our web site

Immanion Press
www.immanion-press.com
info@immanion-press.com